Lorna Hill wrote her first stories in an exercise book after watching Pavlova dance in Newcastle. Her daughter Vicki, aged ten, discovered one of these stories and was so delighted by it that Lorna Hill wrote several more and soon they were published. Vicki trained as a ballet dancer at Sadler's Wells and from her letters Mrs Hill was able to glean the knowledge which forms the background for the 'Wells' stories.

A Dream of Sadler's Wells tells of Veronica, whose great ambition is to dance in The Sleeping Beauty at Covent Garden. After numerous setbacks she finally gains admission to the Sadler's Wells School of Ballet.

Veronica at the Wells, the second title in the series, takes Veronica back to London to the Sadler's Wells Ballet School where she eventually becomes successful and appears in her first star roles at Covent Garden.

Lorna Hill

A Dream of Sadler's Wells

Illustrated by
Kathleen Whapham

PIPER
PAN MACMILLAN
CHILDREN'S BOOKS

A Dream of Sadler's Wells first published 1950 by Evans Brothers Ltd
Copyright © Lorna Hill 1950

Veronica at the Wells first published 1951 by Evans Brothers Ltd
Copyright © Lorna Hill 1951

This Piper edition published 1994 by Pan Macmillan Children's Books
a division of Pan Macmillan Publishers Limited
Cavaye Place London SW10 9PG
and Basingstoke
Associated companies throughout the world

ISBN 0–330–33870–6

This Piper edition collection copyright © 1994

9 8 7 6 5 4 3 2 1

A CIP catalogue record for this book is available from
the British Library.

Printed and bound in Great Britain by
Cox & Wyman Ltd, Reading, Berkshire

For my daughter Vicki,
who was once a pupil at the
Sadler's Wells School of Ballet

AUTHOR'S NOTE

I should like to express my thanks to
Dame Ninette de Valois for reading
the manuscript of this book, which is so
closely concerned with Sadler's Wells.

Contents

Part One

The Dream

Chapter 1

The Flying Scotsman

ONE of the blackest days of my life was on a certain Tuesday at the end of July. Not that you could call the day itself black. In fact the sky was so blue, the sun streaming through the carriage windows so hot, the fields so green where they were not gilded all over with buttercups, that all these bright things only seemed to make my gloom all the deeper.

The very train, hurling itself into tunnels with a triumphant shriek, snorting over bridges, snaking round corners, its back end curling after it like an outsize in caterpillars, racketing through unimportant stations with a disdainful hiss, and finally grinding on its brakes at Darlington – the very train seemed to say: 'Well, here you are, you Sassenachs! Not much of a place, is it? Take it or leave it – all the same to me! I'm a Scot myself, of course. Haven't any time for these English towns. Take your seats, please! ...'

'Oh, dear!' I said under my breath. It was awful having to leave dear old London at a moment's notice; to say goodbye for ever to the warm and noisy Underground with its escalators crowded with chattering, laughing people, all being carried up or down as if on a magic carpet; the bus drivers with their friendly Cockney voices; the well-known statues and monuments – Nelson on his column, Eros in Piccadilly Circus, Peter Pan in Kensington Gardens. Then there was the Zoo. My heart ached to think of the Zoo with my own favourite little monkey, Jacko, in it. For one thing I was pretty sure nobody would think of taking him liquorice all-sorts – the little round ones covered with comfits that he loved so much. It was sweet to watch him lick off the coloured sweets and stick the liquorice on the bars of his cage like chewing gum! All this was bad enough, but added to the sum total of my misery was the awful thought of the Unknown Relations waiting to pounce on me at the other end of my long journey.

The relations lived in the cold and unfriendly North of England, where people spoke practically a foreign language. At least Mrs Crapper, who'd looked after me since Daddy died, said so, and *she* ought to know because her sister is married to a man who lives in Newcastle. Mrs Crapper said that people called you 'hinny' – even in the shops – instead of 'modom' like they do in London. 'Hinny' was a word I'd never heard before, and I didn't like the sound of it very much. Mrs Crapper also said that if you were a man, everyone called you 'Geordie', even if your name wasn't George at all, but Harry or Archibald.

The relations were rich, and they lived in a large, grey unfriendly house. I'd never seen the house, as a matter of fact, but I felt quite sure that it *was* grey and unfriendly. The relations had three cars – a shooting-brake for Uncle John, the little Morris for Aunt June to go shopping in, and the Rolls. The latter was driven by a chauffeur because it had to be treated with care, being terribly valuable. Fiona, one of the Unknown Cousins, had told me this when she'd spent a week in London with Aunt June ages ago. They'd come to see Daddy and me, and I remembered vaguely that Fiona was fair, very pretty, and beautifully dressed. I rather wished now

12

that I'd taken more notice of her, but at the time she hadn't seemed terribly important.

I sighed again. The carriage was a non-smoker, but the occupants – two men and three women – were all now smoking like chimneys. They had politely asked each other's permission to do so, but they hadn't asked mine. I expect they thought that I was only a child – not old enough to matter, or to have any feelings. I wondered what would happen if I were to be sick in their dignified midst! I decided that it would jolly well serve them right for being so thoughtless and selfish. On the other hand it's not a very nice feeling being sick, so I hastily got up and dashed out into the corridor, nearly colliding with a fellow traveller coming in the opposite direction.

'S-sorry!' I gasped. 'But I just *had* to get out of there quickly. In another minute I'd have been sick. All that smoke! ...'

'Golly! ...' The voice was a boy's voice. It sounded a bit anxious, due I expect to my explanation about the hurry.

'Oh, it's all right,' I assured him, gulping down breaths of fresh air from the open corridor window beside me, 'I don't feel a bit sick now. It was just the smoke. They were *all* smoking,' I added reproachfully, 'even the women.'

'Women do smoke nowadays, you know,' said the boy pleasantly.

I glanced at him suspiciously, but he didn't look as though he were being sarcastic.

'It was a *non-smoker*,' I told him severely.

He looked at me with raised eyebrows.

'I'm afraid you're what you might call a bit temperamental, my child.'

'Temperamental? How dare you! I'm not the least bit temperamental! The carriage was absolutely *full* of smoke. And I'm not your child!'

13

'Naughty, naughty!' said the boy, with more than a hint of laughter in his voice.

'Do you mean them – or me?' I demanded stiffly.

'Take your choice,' said the boy easily. 'In other words – if the cap fits, wear it! Personally I like a bit of a fug.'

'Well, I *don't*,' I said emphatically. 'Not in a small space like a railway carriage, anyway. And if you like it, why are you out here? Isn't there a seat for you? I'm sure you can have mine?'

'Now don't go getting your rag out, or I shan't give you a sandwich,' said the boy. 'I've got some lemonade, too! When I travel I always carry my own canteen with me. You can't trust the meals on these trains. Too expensive, anyway.'

I hesitated, torn between pride and loneliness. Finally loneliness won.

'Have you come far?' I asked him as he led the way to the end of the corridor.

'No – got in at Darlington. I've been staying there with an aunt on my way home from school. We broke up nearly a week ago.'

'I've come from London,' I said importantly. 'I'm going to Newcastle to live with my cousins. You see, my aunt and uncle promised Daddy they'd look after me.'

'London?' said my companion with interest. 'All the way from London! You must find things very different here, poor child – savage and so on?'

I glanced out of the window at the neat little fields flying past.

'No – not very. In fact it's really just the same, only a bit cleaner and colder looking. But I don't believe you meant that seriously. You were having me on.'

'*Me* have you on?' echoed the boy. 'Oh, never, dear lady! Noel Coward, by the way,' he added. 'I mean the "dear lady" touch. Great favourite of mine, Coward.'

'Oh, is he?' I said eagerly. 'I like him awfully too – as an actor, I mean. I like his plays and films as well. The film of *Brief Encounter* was grand.'

'Yes, wasn't it?' agreed the boy. 'Especially the music. I went three times just to hear the Rachmaninoff Concerto. It was Eileen Joyce playing, you know, with the London Symphony Orchestra.'

'Was it?' I said. 'I didn't know that, but I loved it all the same. You like music?'

The boy stared out of the window.

'As I won't be seeing you again, I'll make a confession. Yes, I do like music. I like it so much I'm going to make it my career. Nobody knows that yet, of course. At the present moment my father thinks I'm going to be – well, something quite different.'

I drew a deep breath.

'I'll make a confession too then,' I said. 'I'm going to be a dancer. How I don't quite know, but I intend to do it somehow.'

'You'll have to get going, won't you?' observed my companion. 'You have to begin young, haven't you – in the cradle practically.'

'I've already begun,' I told him. 'I began when I was ten which is the right age. I'm fourteen now. The question is how I'm to go on learning, now I've got to live in this place.' I stared disconsolately out of the window at the cathedral towers of a city we were passing.

'Durham,' said the boy, following my gaze. 'I see – well, I expect you'll manage it somehow, if you've made up your mind.'

'I expect I shall,' I said, 'or die in the attempt! One couldn't have four years under Madame, and then give it up – just like that.' I snapped my fingers.

'Madame who?' queried the boy.

'Oh, we just call her "Madame". Her real name's a bit weird, you see. It's Madame Violetta Wakulski-Viret. She's part Italian, part French, and part goodness knows what! Added to that she married a Russian – hence the "Wakulski". She speaks every language under the sun. If she's pleased with you, which isn't very often, she coos at you in French or broken English. If she's frightfully annoyed, she shouts at you in Russian or Italian, and if she's talking business, she does it in German. It's useful because you know what sort of a mood she's in by the language she uses!'

The boy whistled.

'She sounds an odd customer!'

'Oh, yes,' I said. 'All the best teachers seem to be odd. I once gatecrashed into the Wells School at Colet Gardens—'

'The Wells?—'

'Sadler's Wells,' I explained. 'Everyone who goes there just calls it the Wells, you know. Well, as I say, a girl who's a student there – she lived on the floor above us – smuggled me in. I wore her grey tunic and pink tights and my hair screwed up as if I were going to have a bath – just like all the other students. It was at the beginning of term so I expect they thought I was a new girl. Anyway, I crept up into the balcony above the Baylis Hall and watched one of the classes, and no one knew I was there.' I shuddered. 'Gosh! I'd hate to think what would have happened to me if I'd been found out – they hate you to watch their classes! The master who was taking the class was frightfully temperamental. He shouted, and stormed, and banged with his stick on the *barre* – I'd have been scared to death – but it was obvious that they all thought the world of him. Oh, he was grand!'

'U-m,' said the boy dubiously. 'Sounds a rum go to me! And you really want to study there?'

'At the Wells? I should just say I do! I shouldn't care how they shouted at me. Of course, I want to get into the Sadler's

I'd work and work and watch the principals

Wells Ballet – everyone does – everyone who dances, I mean. But you've got to be terribly good, even to get into the school; I'd be in the very back row of the bottom class. Then, if I got into the Company, of course I'd be in the very back row of the *corps de ballet*; everyone is when they begin. But I'd work and work and watch the principals, and then one day I'd be the Lilac Fairy in *The Sleeping Beauty*. I know *exactly* how I should do it. Not brilliant at all – just dreamily, like lilac on a cool summer evening in the moonlight with the dew falling.'

'Wouldn't you like to dance the Finger Variation – the Breadcrumb Fairy?' said the boy quite seriously, so seriously that I stared at him in astonishment. 'They call her the Fairy of the Golden Vine now, I believe – a great mistake in my opinion. I liked the old name much better.'

'Look here,' I said. 'You seem to know an awful lot about ballet?'

'Matter of fact I'm dead keen on it,' said the boy. 'Another confession!' Then his face changed as if he thought he'd been serious too long. 'I once went to see Helpmann in *Hamlet*. Grand!' He went down on one knee on the floor and gave a vigorous imitation of Hamlet in his death agony. I couldn't help laughing.

'I thought you said something about sandwiches?'

He got up hastily.

'Oh, yes – here they are. Ham and tongue. Aunt Alice's best! And you can have a drop of my lemonade as well if you like. I'll let you have a pull at the bottle first. Always the little gentleman!'

I accepted the bottle and took a long refreshing drink. Really, he was the strangest boy I'd ever seen. As he munched his sandwich I stared at him curiously.

He looked about fifteen, and he was very thin, with what you would call an 'interesting' face, rather than good-looking. His eyes were blue – not light blue, but dark, and sparkling, and slightly on the slant. His hands fascinated me. They were strong, and slender, and very sensitive, and he moved them about continually as he talked. I'd never seen anyone with hands like that. In fact I'd never seen anyone like him at all. I wondered what his name was.

'Go on,' he said, between bites. 'I see it coming. Spit it out!'

'I don't know what you mean.'

'Oh yes, you do. You were going to ask my name.'

I blushed.

'Well, what if I was?'

'Nothing – only I'm not telling you, that's all! I've told you quite enough without unfolding the folly of my name.'

'Oh, then it's an odd name?' I teased.

'Well, it's not the sort of name a fellow likes to take to school with him. Otherwise it's original and it'll be a great asset to me in my musical career. By the way, you said you were going to live with relations up north. Father in the Army?'

'No,' I said stonily. 'A clergyman.'

'Oh—' There was a note of mock solemnity in my companion's voice. He took a pair of compasses out of his pocket, clipped them on his nose, folded his hands, and gazed at me parsonically over the top of them. 'Oh – parson's daughter?'

'I *was* a parson's daughter,' I said, stifling a sob, and I suppose I still am – in a way. You see – Daddy died not so long ago.'

The teasing look faded from the boy's face as if it had been wiped away with a sponge. He took off the mock spectacles, dropped them into his pocket, and put his arm round me.

'Oh, bad luck! Sorry and all that. I had no idea.'

'Of course you hadn't,' I said, struggling with my tears. 'But it's so *awful*. If only I could have stayed in London, Mrs Crapper would have looked after me and I could have gone on dancing. But of course it was impossible – at least Uncle John said it was when he came to settle things a few weeks ago. He was horrified at the very idea of Mrs Crapper, though I can't think why. Uncle John isn't what you might call very understanding. Anyway, I couldn't get him to see that ballet is a perfectly serious career, and not just showing off. Then there was the question of school. You see, when Daddy was alive he taught me himself.'

'Have another sandwich,' my companion said, looking the other way while I dried my eyes. 'I'm most awfully sorry. I wouldn't have joked if I'd known.'

'Of course you wouldn't,' I said. In spite of his weirdness I liked him awfully. He seemed my only friend in a strange and alien world. 'And thank you for the lemonade and the sandwiches. I think I'd better go back to my compartment now. We're just coming to Newcastle, aren't we? Mrs Crapper said it was after Durham.'

'Good Lord, yes!' exclaimed the boy. 'I'd better be getting back to mine, too. It's right at the other end of the train and all my traps are in it. S'long! I hope you manage the dancing lessons all right. By the way, are the relations meeting you?'

'Oh, yes,' I answered. 'I'll manage somehow – the dancing, I mean. And thank you again.'

I dashed back along the swaying corridor to my compartment and collected my things at lightning speed. Then, after I had straightened my beret, I put on my gloves and braved myself to face my dismal future.

Chapter 2

The Unknown Relations

They were all there – all of them, that is, except Uncle John, and I expect he was still at his office in Nun Street. Uncle John is what Fiona calls a 'shipping magnate'. I'm not quite sure what the 'magnate' means but when I asked Mrs Crapper she said it was a thing you picked up pins with when you were dressmaking. I can't imagine Uncle John picking up pins, even with a magnate, so I expect it's something different when you use it with ships. As we rolled out from under the dark station portico in the large shining car, I stared at them curiously, and I must say that if it was rude of me to stare, they were rude too – even Aunt June. I think she stared even harder than Fiona and Caroline.

'Well, Veronica,' she said at length, holding on to the tassel that hung down beside the window, as if she were strap-hanging in a bus instead of reclining in a palatial car. 'You've changed a great deal since I saw you last. You're not at all like your mother.'

I knew at once that this wasn't a compliment because I'd been told so many times that my mother was beautiful. A pang shot through me. When you get to be as old as fourteen, you like to be thought pretty, especially when the people you're with are pretty, and there was no doubt about it – Fiona and Caroline were both lovely. At least Fiona was beautiful now, and you could see that Caroline would be too when she was older and had slimmed down a bit.

'I think I'd rather be like Daddy,' I said stoutly, crushing

21

down the pang. I felt it was hard luck that no one should want to be like him. 'You see I can't remember Mummy, but Daddy—' Tears came into my eyes.

'No, of course not,' Aunt June said in a matter-of-fact tone of voice, adding as an afterthought: 'Poor child!'

'Are you older than me, or younger?' Fiona asked as the car purred up Westgate Hill which leads out of Newcastle.

'I'm fourteen. I was fourteen last May.'

'I'm fourteen and a half,' Fiona informed me in a superior tone of voice.

'Fourteen last April,' corrected Caroline. 'That's not fourteen and a half. It isn't even fourteen and a quarter. You're only a month older than Veronica.'

Fiona didn't look very pleased at this interruption.

'I'm eleven,' Caroline went on, quite unperturbed, 'but I'm so big that everyone thinks I'm as old as Fiona.'

'No, they don't,' Fiona said flatly. 'You aren't nearly as big as me, Caroline, so don't tell stories – unless it's big *round*.'

This silenced Caroline for a bit.

'What I can't understand,' went on Aunt June, 'is the fact of your Mrs Cripps—'

'Crapper,' I corrected firmly.

'Crapper, then. I simply can't understand the woman allowing you to travel all that way by yourself – and not even in a first-class compartment. Most reprehensible!'

I didn't know what 'reprehensible' meant, but I gathered that it wasn't anything nice, and I wasn't going to have poor Mrs Crapper blamed.

'Oh, but Mrs Crapper would never even *think* of first class,' I said. 'And anyway, I go about everywhere at home by myself. On the tops of the buses – in the Tube—'

'The *what* did you say?' interrupted Caroline.

'The Tube – underground train, you know,' I repeated. 'Don't they have a Tube in Newcastle?'

Fiona gave a peal of laughter.

'Gosh, no! Wait till you've *seen* Newcastle. It's just like a village compared with London. Caroline's never been to London. *I* have – several times.'

'Twice,' Caroline stated flatly. 'And once was only a weekend on the way to somewhere else.'

'Well, anyway, I've been there,' Fiona argued. 'And I've been on top of a bus, *and* in the Tube, and on the escalators, and I've seen the Houses of Parliament, and the Tower, and Marble Arch, and when I came back here everything looked terribly queer – as if it had shrunk, and all in slow motion.' She glared at me in anything but friendly fashion as if it were my fault that her sister persisted in taking her down a peg.

I glanced at Aunt June, wondering what she thought about all these heated arguments going on over her dead body, so to speak. But she didn't seem at all perturbed. As a matter of fact I don't think she was listening. Later on I discovered that whatever Fiona and Caroline said and did when their mother was there, they were ten times worse when she wasn't!

We had left the suburbs by this time, and the car was speeding along white roads, bordered at first by neat little hedges and railings, then by taller hedges and less neat railings. Finally the hedges and railings were replaced by low stone walls or sunk ditches filled with bracken and meadowsweet. Sometimes the road wound through shadowy plantations of fir and larch, the overhanging branches of the trees brushing the car roof as we passed. Rabbits ran out, stared at us, then disappeared with a flicker of their white tails. Pheasants and partridges – Caroline told me their names – rose out of the green depths of the woods with a metallic whirring sound, as if they were made of clockwork. It was all very cool, and peaceful, and North Country.

I sighed. It was so unlike my beloved London.

Presently we turned sharply to the right, and the car

stopped outside tall wrought-iron gates, beside which stood a cottage with glittering, diamond-paned windows under the eaves, and queer twisted chimneys. I expected the little green door to open and a rosy-cheeked gardener's wife to swing open the gates for us as in *Little Lord Fauntleroy*, but the door remained shut, and Perkins, Aunt June's chauffeur, began to get out of the car to open the gates himself.

I sprang up.

'I'll do it, shall I? ... It's all right, Perkins!' I yelled through the glass partition, nearly tripping over the luxurious fur rug that covered the floor. But to my surprise he didn't stop getting out. Instead Fiona stared at me, and Aunt June gripped me firmly by the arm.

'Sit down, dear. Perkins will see to it.'

'Oh, but poor man!' I exclaimed. 'It's awful when you're driving a car and have to open things yourself; it takes three times as long, and wastes ever so much petrol. Mr Salmon – he's a friend of Daddy's, and he has a frightfully old car – well, if he stopped to open gates, he'd simply never get the car to start again. So he always takes me with him. I mean, he always *took* me with him,' I corrected hastily, remembering that all these things were now in the past. 'So you see I'm frightfully good at gates, I know all their little tricks, the ones you have to lift, and the ones—'

'How amusing!' Aunt June said, cutting me short, and I had a feeling that she wasn't a bit amused really. 'Perkins opens the gates for us here.'

By now we had come to the front door, and this time I didn't try to jump out first and give them a helping hand. I waited for Perkins to walk round and open the car door, which he did in a very dignified manner.

'You'd better take Veronica upstairs,' Aunt June said when we were in the hall. By the way, the latter was large and square and panelled like a room, and there was a fireplace at

24

each end. There were great blue jars, filled with pink and blue lupins, standing at each side of the shallow oak staircase leading to a gallery above. There were soft carpets which went right up to the panelling, and covered all the passages that led off from the hall – quite unlike the vestibule of Mrs Crapper's house which had a cement floor and smelt of disinfectant.

'She's to sleep in your room, you know, Fiona,' Aunt June was saying.

'Oh, all right, Mummy,' Fiona said obediently, but I saw her screw up her face behind Aunt June's back in a way that made me feel she didn't like the arrangement any too well. 'Come on, Veronica.'

'By the way, Veronica,' Caroline said when we had reached Fiona's bedroom and had taken off our coats and brushed our hair, 'you mustn't try to open gates and things for Perkins when Mummy's there. She'll be frightfully annoyed. I hope you don't mind my telling you.'

'All right,' I said slowly. 'Thanks for the hint. It did seem awful though – three of us, all with arms and legs and things, and poor Perkins—'

'Yes, I know, and when we're in the car with him by ourselves we always do it. But Mummy thinks it's *infra dig*.'

'So it is,' snapped Fiona. 'I think Perkins ought to do it. After all, he's a chauffeur, isn't he? It's what he's paid for.'

'Sebastian doesn't think like that,' Caroline retorted. 'Sebastian says when you can do a thing for yourself, you jolly well ought to do it. He says he's never going to have a chauffeur; he says people who have chauffeurs lose the use of their legs.'

'He's having you on!' Fiona said scornfully. 'You know what Sebastian is; you can never believe a word he says. Anyway, he isn't the least bit likely ever to have a chauffeur. Uncle Adrian's frightfully hard up.'

'You remember the other day when we were waiting for Mummy at the Women's Institute meeting?' Caroline said, stealing a sidelong look at Fiona from under her eyelashes. 'Well, I heard Mrs Musgrave say we were *nouveau riche*. What do you suppose she meant?'

'How do I know!' snapped Fiona. 'I don't care, either – revolting old hag! Who's Mrs Musgrave, anyway?'

'Well, she's frightfully ancient and historic, isn't she?' persisted Caroline. 'I mean, her family is. They come in *Young Lochinvar* ... "Fosters, Fenwicks, and Musgraves; they rode and they ran".'

'She can come in "The boy stood on the burning deck" and ride as hard as John Gilpin for all I care!' declared Fiona. 'She's an interfering old hag all the same.' Then she turned to me: 'I'm sure I don't know where you're going to put your clothes – mine take up all the room in the wardrobe.'

'Trixie said she was going to bring in more hangers,' put in Caroline promptly. I gathered that Trixie had been Caroline and Fiona's 'nannie' when they were children. 'You'd better move your things along, Fiona – there's loads of room.'

'There isn't loads of room,' Fiona grumbled. 'I hate having my things all squashed together.' She moved a couple of dresses along the rail and grudgingly showed me the space. 'You can have that bit if you like. I hope you haven't got masses of clothes.'

I'd have laughed if I hadn't felt so near crying.

'Masses of clothes? Why, I've hardly got any. I can get all my things in there – easily.'

'Oh, well, that's a good thing anyway. I don't see why it's always me who has to have someone stuffed into their room.'

'Mine isn't big enough for two beds,' Caroline said; 'You know that, Fiona. If it was, Veronica could share mine. I'd like her to.'

A glow went through me at her friendly words.

'I don't mind about a bed,' I said emphatically. 'I'd *like* to sleep in your room, Caroline. I'll sleep on the floor. I've often

26

done it at home when Daddy had a guest. We hadn't a spare room.'

'Don't be stupid!' exclaimed Fiona impatiently. 'Mummy would have a fit.' Then she added: 'I should have thought you'd have had loads of room in the vicarage. Our vicar's always saying that vicarages are miles and miles too big for any modern person to live in.'

'Our house wasn't a real vicarage, you see,' I explained. 'The real vicarage was quite a nice house, but it was bombed in the blitz on London, and the new one hasn't been built yet. So the vicarage was just an orinary flat – a bit of a big house. It belonged to Mrs Crapper and she lived on the ground floor, and let off the rest to all sorts of people. That's how she made a living. You see, Mrs Crapper's husband was what Daddy called a waster; he just walked out and left her high and dry, and she didn't know where he was, so the apartment house was a good idea. The basement was the parish hall.'

'How ghastly!' commented Fiona.

'It wasn't ghastly at all,' I flashed, an awful pang of home-sickness shooting through me. 'I loved every minute of it. Two girls who were going to be dancers had rooms over ours. One was going in for musical comedy – tap dancing and things – and the other was a ballet student. She was at the Wells – Sadler's Wells School I mean. I used to watch them practising and sometimes I practised with them. Then on the very top floor – as a matter of fact it was really one huge attic with a perfectly enormous skylight – there was Jonathan. I should say Mr Rosenbaum, but everybody called him Jonathan. He was an artist, and he used to let me paint on the backs of his canvases – the ones he said he couldn't stand at any price. As a matter of fact he painted me last year . . .'

'Painted you?' Fiona broke in scornfully. 'Whatever for? Were you supposed to be a gipsy, or a child of the gutter, or what?'

There was an awful silence. I turned scarlet.

'It isn't only people with golden hair and pink faces who get painted,' I burst out hotly. As a matter of fact artists prefer the other kind. Jonathan said I had a very striking face . . .'

I was speaking to the empty air. Fiona had fled.

'I'm frightfully sorry,' Caroline muttered, staring after her sister with puckered brow. 'That was awful – what she said. You mustn't take any notice of her, Veronica. She didn't mean it – really she didn't. She's jealous, that's all.'

'Jealous?' I echoed. 'What on earth of?'

'Of you.'

'Of me? Oh, but . . .' Words failed me. The bare idea of Fiona, with her golden hair and beautiful face, being jealous of me sounded just ridiculous.

'She's jealous because you lived in London,' explained Caroline. 'Fiona thinks it's marvellous to live in London.'

'Oh well – if that's all that's the matter with her, I expect she'll get over it,' I said slowly.

'Sebastian says she's spoilt,' went on Caroline. 'Sebastian spends most of his time squashing Fiona.'

'Look here, who *is* Sebastian?' I demanded. 'You're always talking about him. Is he a gardener or someone?'

'The gardener?' laughed Caroline. 'Gracious, no! He's our cousin. His father is Daddy's brother, only Uncle Adrian, Sebastian's father, is Sir Adrian Scott. He's the eldest son, so he came into the estate; that's why they're as poor as church mice. Estates do seem to eat away fortunes, don't they? Daddy was the youngest son, and a plain "mister", so he went into trade. We were very poor at first, though Fiona won't admit it, but now Daddy's got oodles of money. That's what Mrs Musgrave meant when she called us New Rich. I looked it up in the French dictionary. I expect she'd call Uncle Adrian and Sebastian New Poor!'

'How old is Sebastian?' I asked, getting back to the point.

'He's fifteen – just a year older than Fiona,' Caroline said. 'That's what annoys her. She can't put on airs with him.'

'Do you like him?' I asked.

'Frightfully,' confessed Caroline. 'Everything's exciting where Sebastian is. He's a marvellous rider and he swims like a fish.'

'You mean he's clever?'

Caroline looked blank.

'Clever? You mean at lessons? Haven't an earthly. I expect he is, though – he's going to be a lawyer. I can't imagine Sebastian *not* being able to do anything – even Latin irregulars or algebra ... Oh, there's the gong! That means tea's ready; we have it in the schoolroom now. Fiona gets frightfully annoyed if you call it the nursery.'

Chapter 3

The Fate of a Frock

It's queer how, when you stay at a strange place, an hour can seem as long as a week – even when it's the holidays which usually go like a flash, however hard you try to spin them out. By half past seven I felt as if I had been at Bracken Hall for at least a year. Not a very pleasant year, either!

'We don't go down for dinner,' Caroline explained. 'We have supper up here in the nursery – I mean the schoolroom,' she added hastily, seeing Fiona's disapproving eyes upon her.

I sighed. To tell you the truth, I was getting heartily sick of the schoolroom. To my mind it was a terribly uninteresting place. There were two bookcases: one was full of school text-books, like *Longman's Geography, Elementary Algebra,* and *Caesar's Gallic Wars.* The latter made me shudder even to look at them! The other was crammed with school stories: *Winifred Wins Through, The Head Girl of Saint Anthony's, Fenella of the Fifth,* and so on. Nothing decent like a book about ballet, or even *The Children's Encyclopedia.* There were no decent pictures on the walls, either – just colour-prints of animals and fairies; not an original among them.

'What time do we have to go to bed?' I asked as we began on the tomato soup and chocolate blancmange that was set out on the nursery table. I knew quite well by now that there would be a set time for going to bed, and that it would be early. Not a bit like home, where I went to bed any time I liked.

'You and Miss Caroline go at eight,' Trixie said. 'Miss Fiona goes at half past. The mistress thinks you need a lot of sleep and good wholesome food, Miss Veronica, you being so pale and thin. We must make you a big bonny girl like Miss Caroline, mustn't we? Now eat up every scrap of that nice blancmange, and I've got a big glass of fresh milk for you before you go to bed.'

'Sounds like fattening up a pig for market!' Fiona put in scoffingly.

'Now none of your rude remarks, Miss Fiona,' Trixie said severely, looking at Fiona with disapproval. 'You must be kind to your little cousin and make her feel at home.'

I'm afraid I wasn't nearly as grateful to Trixie as I ought to have been. For one thing, I didn't want to be big and fat – not for dancing. Whoever heard of a big, fat, bouncing *ballerina*! Still, she meant to be kind, so I smiled at her when she brought the milk and said 'thank you' in what I hoped was a grateful-sounding voice. As I said before, Trixie had been the Scotts' 'nannie' when they were little. Now she was – well, it was really hard to say exactly what she was. Even Fiona found it difficult to explain.

'She looks after us in the hols, and sees to our clothes and things,' she said vaguely when Trixie was out of the room. 'When we're at school she helps Mummy with the house. Really I think Mummy just keeps her out of charity. She does hardly anything.'

'Oh, I don't know,' put in Caroline. 'Trixie's always busy, and I've heard Mummy say she's as good as a housekeeper any day.'

'You'd better have your bath first tonight, Miss Veronica,' Trixie said when she returned. 'You'll be tired after your long journey. And don't be too long over it. Remember there's Miss Caroline after you.'

'Oh, yes – I'm to use Mummy's bathroom, Trixie,' Fiona

31

said loftily. 'I shall use loads of bath salts and talcum powder.'

'Not Mummy's, I hope?' Caroline put in.

'No, it's my own. Aunt Millicent gave it me at Christmas, and it seemed a waste to use it in the mouldy nurs— schoolroom bathroom.'

After we'd finished our supper, which was a lot nicer than it looked I'm bound to admit, and I'd collected up my dressing-gown and slippers, I trekked off to the bathroom, Caroline close on my heels.

'You can't lock the door,' she explained. 'Fiona used to go in there for her bath and stay in simply *ages* – just to annoy Trixie. So the key was taken away.'

'Well, I don't mind,' I assured her. 'If people like to barge in when I'm having my bath, it's OK with me!'

As a matter of fact Fiona did barge in, without even troubling to knock. She had on a lovely, pale blue, quilted silk dressing-gown, that exactly matched her eyes, and blue satin slippers with swansdown round the tops of them.

'I'm just finished,' I said, tying my belt and spreading out the towels to dry on the airer. I was about to pull the bathplug so that I could wipe out the bath when Fiona stopped me.

'You needn't bother to do all that,' she declared. 'Trixie will do it. That's what she's there for. By the way, you won't need *that* tomorrow' – she poked with her finger at the frock I'd been wearing, and which I now held in my arms on top of my other things. 'I'll lend you some shorts and a blouse until your trunk comes from the station.'

I stared at the dress in my arms.

'What's the matter with my frock?' I demanded.

'Well, it's on the dirty side, you must admit,' Fiona stated. 'Quite frankly, it looks like something the cat's brought in.'

Another awful flood of homesickness swept over me. The frock meant a bit of home to me, though Fiona was quite right

– it was certainly crushed and not very clean.

'Mrs Crapper gave it to me,' I explained. 'She got the material at a sale, and it was a terrific bargain – only ninety-nine pence a yard. She made it for my birthday, and she took no end of trouble over it. So, if you don't mind, Fiona, I'll just go on wearing it until my own things come. Then I can wash and iron it. Thank you for offering to lend me your shorts all the same.'

'That's all very well, but what about *us*?' demanded Fiona. 'What about Caroline and me having to go about with you looking like the dog's dinner, and everyone *knowing* we're cousins.'

I stared down at the dress and thought of dear Mrs Crapper making it all by hand because she hadn't got a sewing-machine, and, if the stitches *were* rather big and uneven, it was only because her eyes weren't what they had been. I felt I simply couldn't bear Fiona making fun of it.

'I *will* wear it!' I shouted. 'And I'll go on wearing it all the time I'm here if I like. I wouldn't wear your beastly shorts for – for anything!'

'Oh – that's all right,' drawled Fiona off-handedly. Then, without the slightest warning, she snatched the frock from me, and dropped it into the bath.

I leapt forward to rescue it, but her arms were round me. In spite of her fragile and fairylike appearance, she was a lot taller than me, and much stronger than she looked.

'There!' she exclaimed. 'How about wearing it now?' Then she began to laugh. 'Golly – the colour's running!'

It was only too true. The dye of the ninety-nine pence bargain print was evidently not 'fast'. The bath water was rapidly taking on a lurid hue. It turned pink, then brown, and finally a reddish-purple.

We stared at it, fascinated. An exclamation from the door made us turn. Trixie and Caroline stood there with their mouths open, and the most horrified expressions on their faces.

'It's all right,' Fiona said with a giggle. 'There hasn't been a murder or anything! It's only Veronica's frock. It fell in. It needed a wash, anyway; it was frightfully dirty.'

'Tch! Tch! How careless!' Trixie exclaimed, bustling forward with a great fuss and flurry. 'It needed washing certainly, but *not* in the bath water. Whoever heard of such a thing! Why, the colours aren't "fast"—'

'They aren't, are they?' Fiona said, her giggles increasing.

'It should have been put in salt and water first,' Trixie went on. 'Dear, dear! I'm afraid it's ruined!'

She fished the revolting red and purple mass out of the water, and wrung it out, whereupon streams of red dye covered her hands and flowed into the bath. Finally she draped it over the hot-water cistern to dry.

'Tch! Tch!' she said again. 'I do hope you aren't one of those careless, untidy little girls, Miss Veronica. Such a lot of trouble untidy people make.' She went on reading me a lecture on tidiness while Fiona stood by with a mocking, triumphant expression on her face.

I said nothing, waiting for her to own up, but she didn't. After a few minutes she turned her back upon us, and we heard her singing as she turned on the taps in her mother's bathroom at the other end of the corridor.

'I say,' whispered Caroline when Trixie had finished airing her views on tidiness and had left the room, 'Fiona threw it in there, didn't she? I think it was hateful of her not to tell Trixie, but I couldn't give her away. You do understand, don't you, Veronica?'

'Of course,' I whispered back. 'I wish I were sharing your room, though.'

'I wish you were, too. But cheer up – Fiona will come round. She isn't always such a pig as this. Anyway, Sebastian will be here tomorrow, and he'll keep her in order!'

Sebastian! Sebastian! I was getting quite tired of hearing about him. Probably he'd be horrible like Fiona. Probably his coming would make things worse than they already were.

Chapter 4

Running Away

When Fiona came to bed, I pretended to be asleep. I think she was rather disappointed because she made enough row to wake ten ordinary sleepers. When she found that nothing she did made me so much as wink an eyelid, she got into her own bed near the window and after a while there was silence, so I guessed she had fallen asleep.

I tried to sleep myself, but however hard I tried, I couldn't. Thoughts kept going round and round in my head – thoughts of darling Daddy, gone where I could never see or speak to him any more; of kind Mrs Crapper who'd been a mother to me. It was on Mrs Crapper's shoulder that I had sobbed when someone had sat on my first pair of 'blocked' ballet shoes and squashed them flat; Mrs Crapper who had fastened my ballet dress, and helped pull up my tights when I had entered for my Elementary exam at the Royal Academy of Dancing; she who had consoled me when I'd failed by one mark. Then I thought of Madame kissing me and saying how queer it was that the pupils who would never make dancers, not if they stayed with her for a hundred years, should be left to her, whilst the one she thought might one day succeed should be taken away. She'd offered to let me stay with her for a nominal sum – just enough to pay for my food – so that I could go on with my dancing. Dear Madame – so kind and generous; it had nearly broken my heart to refuse – to tell her that Uncle John had called the idea 'ridiculous nonsense', and forbidden me even to think of it. Finally I thought of Mrs Crapper again and the bargain frock, and the awful mess it had looked when Trixie had fished it out of the bath ... Fiona and her beastly shorts ... Caroline ... tomato soup ... Sebastian ... Sebastian.

I heard the clocks all over the house chiming in different keys – eleven, twelve. After this they seemed to get a bit mixed, so I expect I dropped off to sleep. Anyway, the next thing I remember was the grandfather-clock in the hall striking six.

Suddenly I felt that I could stand it no longer. My mind was made up. I would run away. I had enough money left to get me back to London – by bus, anyhow. I knew it was a great deal cheaper that way than by train because I had heard Mrs Crapper discussing it with a friend. Once I got back to dear old London, I'd be safe. Never, never would I come back here. Anyway, they wouldn't want me if I ran away. I had an uneasy feeling at the back of my mind that there was something disgraceful and cowardly about running away, but I crushed it down firmly. I told myself that Mrs Crapper would understand; that Madame would be overjoyed to have me back; that Jonathan would approve, and that Miriam and Stella, the dancing students in the rooms above ours, would be frightfully pleased to see me. I stole into the bathroom and dressed there for fear of waking Fiona. I picked my dress off the hot-water cistern, and put it on. It looked frightful, but there was nothing else for it. Then, hunching on my blazer, I tiptoed back into the bedroom, shoes in hand, and collected together a few things that I considered necessities – nightie, brush and comb, toothbrush, and a clean hankie. I put them all in my small attaché-case, and on the very top I placed a little parcel wrapped in layers of tissue paper. I couldn't resist the temptation to unfold it and gaze lovingly at what was inside. To any ordinary person the small objects I held so carefully in my hand might have looked like a pair of dirty old pink satin ballet shoes, but to me they were the most romantic shoes in the world. They had belonged to Madame, and she had danced *Lac des Cygnes* and *Les Sylphides* in them. They had danced on Covent Garden stage, and that was enough to make them precious to me. Madame had given them to me with all her love, and I had never been parted from them since. I was certainly not going to leave them behind at Bracken Hall to the tender mercies of Fiona and Aunt June. I wrapped them up tenderly and put them in the case with a sigh.

Swan Lake seemed a thousand miles away from me up here in the savage north of England. And as for *Les Sylphides* – I felt it was indeed a fairy glade which I would never enter!

I took my purse out of the right-hand dressing-table drawer that Fiona had grudgingly said I could use, dropped it into my pocket and gently shut the bedroom door behind me.

Everything was silent in the big house. It was a lovely summer morning, and the early sunlight streamed through the windows with their leaded panes, and flickered through the virginia creeper that framed them, falling upon the floor in pools of warm light. The grandfather-clock in the hall ticked aggressively as I crept softly over the thick carpet towards the front door. The man-in-the-moon on the dial stared at me with a crooked smile, seeing he was just between the quarter and the full, and so was a bit lopsided.

The front door was quite easy to open, and in a very short time I was walking briskly down the drive towards the gate. On my left was a high wall, evidently built to keep out the cold north wind and also curious strangers. It was much too high to look over, let alone climb. Beyond it you could see the tops of the fir woods, and beyond them, rising in misty folds, the high moors of the Border country. Over to the right was a thick shrubbery, with here and there a gap through which you could see gardens and lawns, and, in the distance, parkland with sheep grazing on it.

Presently I came to the gates. They were shut – I had ex-

Swan Lake seemed a thousand miles away from me

pected that – but I certainly hadn't expected them to be locked as they evidently were. I found this out, much to my dismay, when I tried to open them. The question was what to do now. I supposed you had to ask at the little gardener's lodge for the key. I couldn't help wondering what you did if you were on the outside, since the cottage was on the inside. Perhaps you were meant to throw stones at their bedroom window and wake them up that way, but this proceeding seemed a trifle undignified for so stately a place as Bracken Hall!

Of course it was quite easy for me – I was on the inside; all I had to do was to walk up the little garden path, bordered by geranium and blue lobelia, and ring the bell by the side of the green door. But somehow I just couldn't screw up my courage to do it. For one thing it seemed awful to go ringing people's bells – even the gardener's – at half past six in the morning. For another, he might ask awkward questions. Indeed I felt pretty sure he would, seeing me and my attaché-case!

I decided to by-pass the gates. The left side was obviously hopeless because of the wall. I tried turning to the right, only to be met by the wall again. It looked as if it went on and on, right round the estate, even shutting in the sheep!

I came back to the gates. There was nothing for it but to climb them, and I set about doing it. First of all I hooked my case on to a spike at the top of the gate by its handle so that I could reach it afterwards from the other side; then I swung myself up.

All went well until I was just rounding the top. Then my frock hooked itself round a spiky bit of wrought-iron work in that maddening way frocks have when you climb things, and I was caught with one leg over the top of the gate, and the other foot precariously wedged between a wrought-iron waterlily and an outsize in iron spider-webs.

I tried to unhook myself, but couldn't. It was ghastly. I was just thinking that I should have to tear myself free – an awful

40

decision, considering the fact that I hadn't another dress to wear – when a drawling voice below me said:

'I say – if you don't mind my asking – are you breaking in, or breaking out?'

It was so near the truth that I blushed hotly. Screwing round a bit, I looked down, and if it hadn't been for the fact of my dress being so firmly hooked, I'm sure I'd have fallen off that gate with shock, for the owner of the drawling voice – the boy standing outside the door of the little cottage – was none other than my acquaintance of the train. I must say that he looked quite as surprised as I did.

'Gosh!' we said both together in awestruck voices. Then the boy laughed. 'Well, fancy coming across you again! Of all the queer things! So these are the relations you talked about – the Scotts of Bracken Hall. Well, I'm dashed!'

By now I had recovered a little. I said rather crossly: 'I do think you might come and help me, instead of just talking. It's awful being stuck up here.'

'Of course,' said the boy, his mouth taking on its funny one-sided smile. 'I'm only too willing to lend a hand – always ready to oblige a friend, you know. At first I thought you were just taking the air, or admiring the view, or something.'

'Don't be silly!' I said indignantly. 'As if anyone would admire the view on top of a gate as full of spikes as this one is! ... Ouch! ... They stick into you every time you move.'

'Well, people usually go out *through* the gate, not over the top,' teased the boy. 'Still, as I say, I'm only too ready to lend a hand.'

He approached the gate, swung himself up beside me, put an arm round my waist, and heaved me up a few inches. My frock came off the spike and I was free. I began to descend in as dignified a manner as possible, but my rescuer, having jumped down himself, swung me on to the ground beside him. He was really amazingly strong for anyone so slim.

'By the way – as I said before – are you breaking in, or breaking out? I mean, which side of the gate do you want to be on?'

'I want to be on the other side, of course,' I said. 'And I must say I think it's a terribly stupid idea having your gates locked. No one locks *gates* – only doors. A gate would be no use to keep out burglars, even if it *was* locked.'

'No,' agreed the boy. 'But it's quite a good idea for keeping out cows.' Then, seeing the puzzled expression on my face, he added: 'You see, Arkwright – he's the blacksmith in the village – well, he has one or two cows, and he drives them up here every morning into that field over there' – he motioned towards the far side of the road. 'Well, his blessed cows have an annoying little habit of making a beeline for our drive. They scoff all the young wallflowers and so on. Mind you, I don't suppose Arkwright would bother his head about a little thing like that, but a short time ago one of his beasts took a fancy to a yew tree and poisoned itself. Now *that* was quite another matter. There was the dickens of a fuss, and we decided to shut the gates just before going to bed.'

'I can see that,' I said. 'But why go *locking* them? Surely cows can't open gates, and it must be frightfully awkward for visitors—'

'There aren't many visitors after eleven o'clock at night,' answered the boy with a smile. 'And if any do come, there's a bell on the other side that rings into our cottage. As for the cows – no, they can't open gates, though you'd be surprised at some of the things they *can* do – like chewing up your bicycle tyres, and licking the wet paint off the fences. But as a matter of fact, we lock the gates on account of the postman. He has a habit of taking a short cut through the park, and nine times out of ten he leaves the gates open.'

'Oh – I see. Well, how do I get out?' I asked.

The boy put his hand into his pocket, produced a key,

inserted it in the lock, and the gates swung wide.

'We each have one – my father and I,' he told me. 'By the way, I suppose you'll have gathered that I live there?' He nodded towards the pretty cottage. 'Mind if I come along with you for a bit? I'm at a loose end.'

'I'm going pretty fast,' I warned him. 'I mean, I'm not just out for a walk, I'm running away.'

The moment I had said the words I regretted them. After all, if I *was* running away, it was no one's business but my own – least of all the gardener's son, if that was what he was.

'I had a sort of suspicion you were,' the boy remarked. 'If people run away, they usually do it at darkest midnight or crack of dawn. You're a bit late, you know; it's nearly seven o'clock.'

"What about you?' I demanded. 'What are you doing out here so early? You surely can't be digging the garden at this time in the morning?'

'Digging the garden?' echoed the boy. 'Why should I be digging the garden?'

'Helping your father, of course,' I said. 'I expect he's a bit rheumaticky, isn't he? Most gardeners are, Daddy says.' I sighed, remembering the occasion when Daddy had said these words. It had been on one glorious spring day, when we had gone out into the country and had bought some nasturtium plants for Mrs Crapper's window-box at a nursery garden. 'I suppose he finds you a great help – weeding, planting things out, and so on.'

'Oh – er, yes,' said the boy rather doubtfully, I thought.

Then I remembered about his music.

'Oh, but of course – I forgot about your hands. I suppose you won't want to spoil them, messing about with soil,' I said. 'I wonder what your father will say when he finds out you want to be a musician instead of following in his footsteps?'

'Y-es – I wonder,' said my companion still thoughtfully.

43

Then the queer expression I had come to know so well came back to his face and he added: 'Oh, I expect the old boy will soon get used to the idea of his One-and-Only wielding a conductor's baton instead of a Dutch hoe! More dramatic, what? – if less useful!'

All this time we were walking along the country road.

'As a matter of fact,' said the boy, 'I was just off for a swim in the lake when you hove-to on the horizon. The lake, by the way, is in the park – away behind those trees.' He nodded over his shoulder in the direction of the house. 'And after my swim I was going for a ride. I keep my pony in a field behind the Hall. Well, now I've told you all my business, how about telling me yours? Let's hear for a start why you're running away.'

In spite of myself I told him the bits he didn't know already, trying my hardest to explain about my cousins without telling tales.

'Honestly – I don't think they like me,' I said soberly. 'At least, I'm quite sure Fiona doesn't. Of course it's an awful nuisance for her having me barge in. I take up lots of her wardrobe, and half her dressing-table. I can quite see her point of view, and really I think I'd be much better at home.'

The boy said nothing for quite a long time. Then he remarked: 'I'll tell you what – I'll bet you're just a bit homesick. You'll be OK tomorrow. Why not try it and see?'

I shook my head. 'No. I've quite made up my mind. I couldn't – I simply *couldn't* stay here another minute … what are you looking like that for?'

'I suppose you realize, my innocent Cockney brat, that there isn't a station in this place?' he said. 'No, not even the Tube round the corner!'

I stood stockstill in the middle of the road. I certainly hadn't reckoned on that. Still—

'Not even a bus, my child,' said the boy, reading my thoughts. 'Not today. Buses only on market days. Market day,

Tuesday – this is Wednesday.'

'Well, I shall walk,' I said. 'I shall walk to somewhere where there *is* a bus. After all, it can't be so very far.'

'Can't it?' said the boy. 'My poor child, you don't yet know your Northumberland. Nearest village, Burneyhough – nine miles.'

Dismay surged over me, but I wouldn't admit it.

'I'll walk there if it's a hundred and nine!' I flashed. 'I'll hitch-hike.'

'Quite a good idea,' said the boy, 'if there was anything to hitch to. Distinct lack of traffic on this road, at seven in the morning—'

'*Will* you stop butting in!' I shouted, completely losing my temper. 'I wish you'd go home and hoe your beastly onions, and mind your own business!'

A change came over my companion's face. The bantering look left it, and suddenly his eyes were serious.

'Look here, you can't go through with this, you know. I can't let you – honestly I can't.'

'Can't let me indeed!' I yelled. 'I'd jolly well like to see you try to stop me!'

'Please,' begged the boy. 'Of course I could stop you. You know I could, so do be sensible.'

'And if I won't be sensible?'

'Well, then I suppose we shall have an all-in wrestling match in the middle of the road,' he answered, the fun coming back into his eyes. 'And you'll lose! You'll end up just where you started – on the inside of the gate. You see, boys are always stronger than girls when it comes to a free fight so, lady, have a care!'

'I've told you I won't go back!' I shouted, stamping my foot. 'I can't go back. I can't! I can't! I'd die if I went back!' Tears began to stream down my cheeks.

'Now! Now! Stop this temperamental stuff!' ordered the

boy. 'It won't work with me. I know that temperament is just plain temper more often than not, so cut out the dramatics, please!'

'I think you're a h-horrible boy!' I gulped.

'I expect I am,' he agreed. 'But you'll stay – please. I want you to stay – really I do.'

A ray of warmth stole through me at the mere thought of anyone wanting me.

'I suppose I shall have to,' I said slowly. 'I haven't much choice, have I? But I shall still run away later on.'

'OK. We'll discuss that afterwards. It's a dashed good thing you started early on your evil deed! No one need suspect anything. How about coming with me to the lake? Then you can say you went swimming if they ask why you got up so early.'

I hesitated. For one thing I hadn't got a bathing costume or a towel; for another, I felt pretty sure that Aunt June would disapprove frightfully of my going swimming with the gardener's son. Evidently my companion read my thoughts.

'There are loads of swimsuits and things in the boathouse,' he assured me. 'We keep 'em down there.'

I wondered who he meant by 'we', but I didn't like to ask him for fear of seeming inquisitive.

'I – Aunt June—' I began hesitatingly.

'Oh, Aunt June won't mind,' the boy said quickly. 'She knows me. I often swim with Caroline and Fiona in the hols – er – when I'm not hoeing the onions, that is.'

My doubts vanished. After all, if Aunt June didn't mind Caroline and Fiona bathing with the gardener's son, she certainly wouldn't mind *me* doing it. And, after all, he seemed a very superior sort of boy. It occurred to me suddenly that he wasn't a bit like a gardener's son – he didn't speak like one for one thing, and he didn't look like one for another. Although his clothes were old, they were exceedingly well cut, and he wore them with an air.

'I'd love to come,' I said quickly. 'And thank you for asking me.'

'Look here,' said the boy suddenly, as we retraced our steps and walked back through the gates, 'about all those confidences we exchanged yesterday, thinking we were never going to see each other again – all that about our careers and so forth. Let's keep it under our hats, shall we – keep it dark, I mean?'

'Oh, *yes*,' I said emphatically. I certainly wasn't too keen upon Aunt June and Uncle John knowing about my determination to go dancing. 'Yes – let's not say anything to anyone.'

Another glow of warmth stole over me. When you share a secret with someone it gives you a sort of fellow feeling with them. Suddenly everything became much more cheerful. As we strolled across the park, I saw what a perfectly gorgeous place it was. In London the trees had lost their early summer freshness and were becoming tired and dusty. Here they were still so green and glossy that they looked as if they had just been varnished. Not that I loved London any the less; it would always hold first place in my heart, being my home, but I saw how lovely and unspoilt this bit of Northumberland was.

The lake was the most thrilling place I had ever seen. It was fringed by willows on three sides, and on the fourth, where the boathouse was, it had its own little beach of fine silvery sand and pebbles. There was even a tiny island in the middle of the blue water, where, my companion told me, two swans had built their nest in the spring. Now the eggs had been hatched, and the cygnets were quite big.

'Now, about swimming costumes,' the boy said when we reached the boathouse. 'Take your choice, lady. We have them in a variety of styles by well-known fashion designers. Here we have Rhapsody in Stripes by Molyneux.' He held up an ancient black and yellow garment. 'Or would you rather have Spotted Peril by Maggy Rouff? Or perhaps a little creation called Darkest Night by Norman Hartnell? As you will perceive it is exquisite in line and material – but of a simplicity *tout à fait ravissante. Mais oui, madame!*'

'You are silly!' I giggled. 'No I don't think I'll have that one,' I added, pushing aside the Spotted Peril. 'It's got mildew. And I *think* the moths have been having a feast on Darkest Night.'

'Moths?' My companion bent closer to examine the costume. '*Mais pardon, madame!* A thousand thousand apologies! Monsieur Hartnell will be *absolument* prostrated to perceive his so beautiful creation *tout à fait* ruined! *Quelle horreur!* It is indeed a tragedy of the first water! *Quel dommage!* ... That's all the French I know!'

'I think I'll have this one,' I said firmly, picking up the striped garment from the side of the boat where he had flung it. 'It'll make me look like a wasp, but who cares!'

'You're a jolly decent swimmer – for a girl,' said my companion, as we finished a race round the island. 'I believe you're better than either Fiona or Caroline.'

'Am I, do you think?' I said eagerly. Suddenly it seemed terribly important to me to be able to do something really well.

He nodded.

'Yes – but as a matter of fact they're not very good, though Fiona thinks she is! How about landing on the island, and I'll show you where the swans nested. There are moorhens in the reeds as well, though you don't often catch sight of them – they're very shy.'

We spent quite a long time on the island, which was bigger than it looked from the shore. The ground was covered with wild strawberries, and when we were tired of exploring, we sat down in an old duck-punt that was moored among the reeds, and ate masses of them. They had a curious tang – not a bit like garden strawberries; they were the first I'd ever tasted and I loved them.

Suddenly the boy stopped eating, a handful of the tiny scarlet berries halfway to his mouth.

'Gosh! The stable clock!' he exclaimed as a faint, silvery chime reached us from over the water. 'It's a quarter past eight, and breakfast is at half past. I think we'd better be getting back if you don't mind. It won't do to be late; they're dead nuts on punctuality up there' – he nodded in the direction of the house.

'Don't I know it!' I exclaimed, pulling a wry face. 'I expect breakfast will be in the *nursery* – Fiona and Caroline seem to spend all their time in the nursery – I beg its pardon, schoolroom! I don't believe they *ever* go out!'

'Oh, yes they do – when I'm here, anyway,' the boy told me. 'We have no end of good times, so cheer up! There'll be four of us, now you've come. The more the merrier!'

'You forget – I'm running away, as soon as I've got rid of you,' I told him solemnly.

'If you do, I shall come after you and spank you,' he said, equally solemnly. 'So don't say you haven't been warned!'

But somehow we both knew that I had given up the idea of running away. I didn't even want to now, though how I should put up with Fiona I still didn't know.

For the second time that morning the boy read my thoughts – he seemed rather clever at doing that.

'You needn't worry about Fiona,' he assured me, 'I can manage her all right. She's OK if you keep her down!'

'You said something about a ride?' I said, casting a regretful glance at the rest of the wild strawberries.

'I shall have to put it off till after breakfast. Too late now.' He stood up. 'Race you to the boathouse.'

'By the way,' he said, when we were once more on the mainland, 'hadn't you better dry your hair a bit before you appear at breakfast? It's making a waterfall down your back.'

Suddenly I became acutely conscious, not only of my dripping hair, but of the awful crushed mess that had once been the bargain frock.

'Look here,' I said, looking down at myself ruefully, 'I'm not always in such a mess as this – I mean the frock – but you see, it – it fell into the bath last night, and there was no time to iron it this morning. Besides, the colour ran.'

The boy's blue eyes narrowed.

'I suppose you mean Fiona threw it in?' he said calmly.

I was silent, the colour rushing to my face.

'It's all right – don't look so guilty; you haven't given anything away. You've got an awfully expressive face, but I don't need that to tell me what happened. I know Fiona and her little ways only too well! She's always doing that.'

'What? You mean she *often* throws people's clothes into the bath?'

He laughed.

'Oh, not always in the bath, though she often used to throw her own clothes in when she was a kid – to make poor old Trixie wash them. Once she threw my tennis shoes into the rainwater butt. I'd just whitened them too, and that water barrel was anything but clean, I may tell you. It was full of frog-spawn, soot, slime, not to mention dead woodlice!'

'Gosh!' I exclaimed. The mere thought of anyone daring to take such liberties with the possessions of the boy who stood before me, appalled me. 'What did you do?'

'Fished 'em out,' he said with a short laugh.

'And then?'

'Then ... well, never mind! I thought I'd taught her not to go chucking other people's things about, but evidently I hadn't.'

'Oh, I expect it was just because I was a stranger,' I said.

Somehow Fiona and her queer, unfriendly ways no longer seemed so very important. 'Perhaps she'll stop doing things like that, now she knows I'm here for good.'

'Perhaps,' echoed the boy, but he didn't sound too sure about it.

'Well, goodbye,' I said, as we reached the terrace that stretched all along the south side of the house. Incidentally I noticed that Bracken Hall wasn't the cold, grey house I'd imagined, but low, gracious and mellow with its covering of warm virginia creeper. 'And thank you for being so decent.'

'Don't mention it!' he said, with a mock bow. 'Honoured, I'm sure! Well, so long! I expect I shall see you again today sometime.'

'Oh, I don't suppose so,' I said gloomily. 'As I told you before we seem to spend all our time in the nursery. Besides, there's a horrible boy, called Sebastian, coming – a cousin or something – and I expect we shall have to be polite to him.'

'If you haven't met him, how do you know he's horrible?' demanded my companion.

'He *sounds* horrible,' I declared firmly. 'You don't have to meet some people to know they're horrible. Fiona says she hates Sebastian.'

'Oh – she does, does she?' said the boy. 'And do you always go by what Fiona says?'

'N-no,' I faltered.

'Well, then why not wait and judge Sebastian for yourself. You never know – he might be quite a decent chap.'

'He *might*,' I said, not very hopefully. 'But somehow I don't think so – he's Fiona's cousin. Well, goodbye again. There's the gong! I'll be late for breakfast after all. I must dash!'

Chapter 5

Sebastian

I ran headlong into Fiona who was flying across the hall towards the door I'd just closed.

'Where's Sebastian? Has he gone? Why didn't you tell him to come in and have breakfast with us? I wanted to see him *most* particularly about something, and now – gosh! You are in a mess!'

But I was past being annoyed by anything so trivial as a remark on my appearance. I was trying to take in her first words.

'Who – *who* did you say?' I demanded.

'I said Sebastian, of course,' Fiona repeated. 'And by the way, I didn't know you knew him. Have you met him before in London or somewhere?'

'I don't know what on earth you're talking about,' I declared. 'I've never seen your silly Sebastian in my life.'

'Then why did you go swimming with him?' demanded Fiona, staring at my dripping hair.

'I didn't go swimming with him,' I exclaimed. 'I think you must have gone quite batty. I went swimming with the boy from the gardener's lodge.'

'But that *is* Sebastian, you idiot!'

I said nothing. My thoughts began to whirl. Frantically I tried to remember what I had said to Sebastian – if indeed it was he – and the more I thought, the more awful it became. When I remembered my last words, I grew cold with horror.

'You mean – you really mean that *that* was Sebastian?'

'If by "that" you mean the boy I saw you with out of the landing window just now, of course it was Sebastian. Who else could it be?'

'I – I thought he was the gardener's son,' I stammered. 'He told me distinctly he lived at the lodge at the bottom of the drive.'

'So he does,' put in Caroline, who had appeared by this time, and had somehow gathered what we were talking about. 'You see, as we said last night, Uncle Adrian, Sebastian's father, is frightfully poor, so we live here in the ancestral home and they live in the gardener's lodge. Sebastian says he likes it no end, and Uncle Adrian says it's a lot better to live there and keep it decent than to hang on here and let the old place go to rack and ruin.'

'Veronica thought Sebastian was the gardener's son!' Fiona said with a giggle. 'Gosh! Imagine Sebastian hoeing the cabbages! I must tell him that one!'

'Well, I shouldn't if I were you,' Caroline said quietly. 'If you do, it'll be a *faux* – whatever its name is – I mean the wrong thing to say, because Sebastian spent loads of time last hols weeding out the strawberry-bed. He's often told me that if he wasn't going to be a lawyer he'd very much like to be a gardener. He says it's a grand life watching things grow, and being out in the sun and wind all day long – loads better than working in a stuffy office in town.'

Fiona didn't know what to say to this so she turned her attention to my frock.

'Golly! I wonder what Sebastian thought of *that*?' she said, staring at it. 'It's like Joseph's coat of many colours in a thunderstorm!'

'I'll bet he wasn't rude enough to make personal remarks about it, anyway,' Caroline said pointedly.

Fiona grew red, but she couldn't think of anything more original to retort than: 'Mind your own business!'

'Do you two realize that the breakfast gong went ages ago,' Caroline went on calmly. 'Trixie's already called us twice. If you want any breakfast, you'd better stop discussing Sebastian and get a move on.'

'You were discussing him as much as anybody,' Fiona said sulkily.

I was so quiet at breakfast that Trixie got quite worried, and asked me whether the train had made me feel sick or if I was always as quiet as that. She also said that something would have to be done about my frock – I couldn't go about looking like that.

I glanced down at Mrs Crapper's bargain print sadly and in my heart I agreed with Fiona and Trixie – it *did* look rather as if it had been out in a thunderstorm, though it wasn't its fault, poor thing. After all, you can't expect a ninety-nine pence-a-yard bargain print to be in 'fast' colours, can you?

'After breakfast we'll look out something for you to wear,' Trixie said from behind the teapot. 'Some shorts of Miss Fiona's, and a blouse, I think. You'd look nice in shorts, Miss Veronica, as you're so slim.'

Fiona didn't seem to approve of this remark.

'Veronica isn't any slimmer that I am,' she said indignantly. 'Anyway it isn't nice to be skinny, and I haven't any spare shorts.'

'You said last night you had,' Caroline said accusingly, taking a large bite of toast. 'In fact, it was you who mentioned them.'

'Well, I made a mistake,' Fiona declared, spreading marmalade on a piece of bread and butter with great deliberation. 'I thought I had then, but now I find I haven't.'

'What about those khaki ones you said were too tight for you?' Caroline demanded. 'Only the other day you told Trixie—'

'Oh, shut up!' exclaimed Fiona. 'I wish you'd leave my clothes alone! If Veronica wants something to wear she can have my brown check dress.'

I was just about to observe that it wasn't *me* who wanted something to wear when Trixie settled the matter by getting really annoyed.

'I shall go through your clothes myself and decide what Miss Veronica is to wear, and that's flat,' she said with decision. 'Really, I never knew such children for arguments, and at breakfast-time too! ...'

After breakfast Trixie was as good as her word, and I was presented with a pair of khaki shorts and a buttercup-yellow linen blouse to go with them. I brushed my dark hair till it shone, and then looked at myself in the long mirror of Fiona's wardrobe. I was no beauty, of course. My small face looked even thinner and paler than usual in contrast to Fiona's pink and white one. I was very slim – rude people might call me skinny, as Fiona had already done – and I wasn't even as tall as Caroline. My dark hair and eyes were my only consolation. All dancers like to have dark hair and eyes, though really I don't know why. Perhaps it's because it's the traditional style of a classical ballet dancer or perhaps it's because they show up well on the stage.

After Trixie had seen me and said I looked a great deal more like a young lady now, we went down to the kitchen to see Sheba, the Persian cat, who'd just had a family of gorgeous blue Persian kittens. While we were arguing about names for them, and had decided upon Cleopatra, Pharaoh and Tutan-kamen, Aunt June appeared at the kitchen door talking to Trixie about the lunch. She kissed us, and I thought she looked at me critically. As she went out, still talking to Trixie, I heard her say something that sounded like: 'What an amazing difference clothes make – the child looks almost pretty!'

My cheeks glowed. To anyone like Fiona who'd been considered beautiful all her life, a remark like this would have meant nothing. But to me, who'd always been thought a Plain Jane, it was like a bouquet.

'Almost pretty' – the words rang in my ears all the way to the kitchen garden, and lasted until we reached the gate that led out into the North Meadow where the ponies were grazing.

'Now for it!' Fiona exclaimed, propping open the gate with a handy log, which had obviously been used for the purpose many times. 'I only hope Melly won't be as hard to catch as she was yesterday. Thank goodness, Sebastian's already caught Warrior! He always makes her extra skittish.'

'Do you bring them into the stable every day?' I asked. 'I should have thought it would have been much nicer for them out here during the summer.'

Fiona stared at me coldly, and shrugged her shoulders, but Caroline attempted to explain:

'You see,' she said, 'they're hill ponies, so a lot of rich grass isn't good for them. They'd get far too fat for one thing, and they might even go lame. So in the spring and summer we bring them in here during the day. That's why we keep them in this field, too. The grass isn't nearly as rich as it is in the fields facing south. It's so near the moor, you see.'

'Oh, ' I said vaguely. 'I never thought of that.'

The field the ponies were in was certainly a great contrast to the lush meadows I'd caught glimpses of that morning when I'd made my sad attempt at running away. There the grass was long and rippling; here it was short, and there were patches of turf and marshy ground, where lovely moorland flowers were growing. There were several outcrops of rock too, with heather on them. The field was bounded on three sides by a rough drystone wall. I didn't know about drystone walls then, but Caroline explained to me later that all the walls in Northumberland used to be built without any plaster to hold

56

the stones together, but, as the art is slowly dying out, more and more fences are being used. On the fourth side was a sombre little fir wood. Beyond the wall was open moorland, rising steeply in folds of purple and russet to a considerable height.

'That's Horsley Fell,' Caroline said, following my eyes. 'When you climb to the top you can see Three Tree Moor, and beyond that Corbie's Nob. There's a cairn on the top of the Nob to mark the highest point of the fell.'

We caught the ponies easily enough. At least we caught Caroline's Gilly – which was short for Gillyflower – and drove Fiona's Melisande through the gate and round into the stable yard. Finally we got her inside the building.

I tried not to get too friendly with the ponies, because it's no use hankering after something that isn't yours, and that you can never own. Still, I couldn't help gazing at Melisande's beautiful chestnut neck which Fiona was grooming till it shone like satin, and wishing that I was lucky enough to possess a pony all my own. Any sort of a pony would do for me; it wouldn't have to be an aristocratic chestnut like Melisande, or even a common or garden bay-like Gillyflower. I felt that even a little broken-down pony would do for me. In some ways it would suit me better, because everyone knows that mongrel dogs have more affectionate natures than thoroughbreds and I expected it was the same with ponies. I was wrong, but I didn't know that then.

My thoughts were interrupted by a shout from Caroline.

'Here's Sebastian ... Coo-ee! We're here in the ponies' box!'

When I saw Sebastian's slim figure coming towards us, I felt awful. I shrank into the shadow of the stables, and wished that the floor would open and swallow me up. But of course it didn't, and I heard Sebastian say: 'Hullo, you two! Who's that hiding behind the corn bin?'

'It's Veronica,' Fiona said. 'You remember – she's our cousin. We told you about her.'

'Of course,' said Sebastian. Then he made me a mock bow. 'Methinks we have met before, lady!'

'We certainly have,' I said coldly. 'And I do think it was frightfully mean of you to take me in like that.'

'What? Oh, you mean the onions and things? Really, I felt it no end of a pity to curb your horticultural instincts!' said Sebastian with a grin. 'More than human nature could stand, in fact! You asked for it, you know, and when people ask me for anything I consider it discourteous not to give it to them. Besides, I was tickled to death at your character reading; it's not often a person hears exactly what another person thinks of them.'

'Well, you didn't hear what I thought of you,' I retorted, 'because I didn't know it *was* you. But you're hearing it now. I think you're perfectly beastly!'

'May you be forgiven!' said Sebastian devoutly, looking down his nose. 'You thought I was the perfect little gentleman – at the time, anyway. And if you didn't, you jolly well ought to have.' Then he changed the subject and said abruptly: 'You look jolly decent in those shorts, if you don't mind my saying so. In fact, I hardly recognized you ... shorts by Woolworth's – beg pardon, I mean Worth – without the Wool!'

'They're *my* shorts,' put in Fiona, sounding anything but pleased. 'I lent them to her.'

'No, you didn't,' Caroline said flatly. 'Trixie did. You said you hadn't any spare shorts. You wanted to lend her that mouldy old brown print frock that you knew she'd look ghastly in. *Anyone* would look the world's worst in that.'

'Pussy cat, pussy cat, where have you been?' sang Sebastian softly, openly enjoying the puzzled looks on both his cousins' faces, since neither of them knew which he meant. 'How about a ride,' he added, 'now that we've all been so painfully polite to each other?'

'We can't,' Fiona said with an angry glare at me, as though it were my fault that I was ponyless. '*She* hasn't got a mount.'

There was a short silence after this remark.

'Golly! I never thought of that,' Sebastian said at length. 'Suppose we go round to the farm and borrow old Mr What's-his-name's donkey. He goes OK, I've seen him. I'm pretty sure Mr What-do-you-call-him would let us have him for a bit.'

'You mean Septimus Keenliside of Pasture House?' queried Caroline.

Sebastian nodded.

'Yes – then we'd all have *something* to sit on, at any rate. We could teach Veronica to ride on our ponies, turn and turn about.'

'You aren't suggesting that I'm to ride Sep Keenliside's filthy little donkey, are you?' Fiona demanded.

Sebastian cocked an eyebrow in Fiona's direction.

'My good girl, I'm not suggesting anything. Far from it! You needn't join in the scheme if you don't want to. If you like to go riding your own pony all by yourself, I shouldn't dream of stopping you—'

'I should jolly well think not!' exploded Fiona. 'I'd like to see you try!'

'Bait me not, fair lady!' Sebastian said in mock heroic fashion. 'If you throw down the gauntlet, you'd look mighty queer if I picked it up! But as I was saying when you so rudely interrupted it's only if you come with *us* that you have to share. If you go off on your own, of course the question wouldn't arise. You couldn't share your pony then; there'd be no one to share it with, would there?'

Fiona looked as if she didn't quite know what to say to this statement, and before she had time to make up her mind,

Sebastian went on calmly: 'That's settled then – we ask Sep Keenliside for the loan of his donkey. All we want now is a saddle and bridle for the animal.'

'There are several snaffles that no one ever uses in the harness-room,' Caroline put in. 'And there's a saddle in the potting-shed. Goodness knows what it's doing there, but I saw it with my own eyes only yesterday.'

'I'll make a guess,' Sebastian drawled. 'It's there because Fiona dumped it down on the bench when she came in from a ride, and then forgot about it. Naughty! Naughty!'

'How dare you! I didn't!'

'Yes you did, Fiona. Sebastian's quite right, I remember now,' Caroline said. 'It was after the Pony Club meeting, ages ago – last autumn, in fact. It hasn't improved the look of it either, I can tell you! It's sprouting mould inches thick!'

'Well, let's go and salvage it!' Sebastian exclaimed. ' "Ship ahoy!" "Scots who hae wi Wallace bled", and all the usual oaths! We can clean it up.'

Suddenly Fiona leaped out of the hayloft where she'd been perched during the argument. She sprang in front of us and stood right in the doorway.

'That's *my* saddle!' she yelled. 'Veronica can't have my saddle!'

'*Your* saddle?' queried Sebastian, with raised eyebrows. 'If it's the one you had at the Pony Club, I have a vague idea it was in the harness-room long before your people took over Bracken Hall, my child. So by rights it belongs to my father.'

'*We're* living in the house now,' flashed Fiona, 'so everything that's in it is ours.'

'Oh, ho! So that's what you think, is it?' Sebastian retorted. 'Chummy view of life, what! Let's not pursue the argument any further, it offendeth my sense of – of – well, in short, it isn't – you know what I mean.'

'I *don't* know what you mean, you horrible boy, and I don't

60

'believe you do yourself, either,' Fiona yelled, aware that Sebastian was laughing at her.

'Granted,' Sebastian said calmly. 'Blame it on to my Irish grandmother.'

I stared at him thoughtfully. He was quite a different person from the serious boy I had talked to in the train about ballet, and argued with about running away in the early morning. I suspected – and later knew quite definitely – that not many people saw the serious side of Sebastian. In fact, only a handful of his closest friends knew that it was there at all.

'*Have* you got an Irish grandmother?' I asked curiously.

Sebastian nodded.

'Yes, rather! Old girl pegged out twenty years ago. She's in Heaven now – if she isn't in the other place! I rather suspect the latter. Everyone says I take after her. I hope so! Jolly old girl – if you can go by the family records. Used to traipse about dear old Ireland in one of those jaunting-cars. Turned up at all the race meetings – even when she was eighty – and woe betide anyone who impeded her line of vision! She landed him one with her umbrella!'

'I believe you're making all that up,' Caroline said accusingly. 'Everything I've heard about old Granny O'Rourke was perfectly respectable, and anyway she lived in Devonshire.'

'She retired there when she was old,' Sebastian said, not a bit taken aback. 'On her ninety-fifth birthday. I remember it as if it were yesterday.'

Then seeing Caroline's mouth open to make a crushing reply to this statement, he added quickly: 'Well, let's get back to the point, shall we? We were talking about a saddle, if you remember. You hardly ever use it Fiona; in fact you've never used it since the day we mentioned, and that's eight months ago. You'd never even have thought about it if I hadn't said we'd lend it to Veronica.'

'You're *not* going to lend it to Veronica!'

'Oh, yes I am, you selfish little beast!'

'You're not! I forbid it! Just because Veronica's new, you try to curry favour—'

Fiona stopped with a gasp. Sebastian's blue eyes had narrowed, and his face had gone quite white with fury.

'Be quiet! You say another word and you'll be sorry for it!'

Fiona didn't say another word. I think that for once in her life she was scared.

'Get out of my way!' ordered Sebastian in a furious voice. Then he got hold of himself and dropped back into his usual bantering tone: 'Roll up! Roll up, ladies and gents! World-famous wrestling champion, Bumpemoffski, about to perform one of his prodigious feats of strength! Watch him throw lady over his left shoulder clean into horse's manger ...' he advanced upon Fiona purposefully.

But Fiona didn't wait for any more. She turned and fled away up the garden path, dashed into the little potting-shed that stood by the wicket-gate leading into the kitchen garden, and banged the door behind her.

'Open this door!' yelled Sebastian when we reached the place a moment or two later.

There was no answer.

'She's bolted it,' Caroline said, as we rattled the sneck.

'Open the door!' Sebastian ordered in a tone of voice that showed quite plainly he hadn't yet got over the insult that Fiona had flung at him before she'd fled. 'If you don't open it, I shall break it in.'

Still there was silence.

'Right-ho! Then here goes!' he put his shoulder to the door, the rusty bolt gave way and the door flew wide.

We all crowded in. Fiona was standing underneath the tiny window with a queer expression on her face – triumphant I think I'd call it – and there was a strong smell of disinfectant that stifled even the smell of mould, damp and dust. The saddle lay, as Caroline had said, on the little bench that stretched along one side of the shed. Sebastian picked it up; then dropped it again very quickly.

'What's up? Is it as bad as all that?' Caroline said anxiously, as Sebastian rubbed his hands on a heap of dry leaves. 'Oh, golly! it's all – all – what on earth is it?'

'Creosote,' Sebastian said shortly. 'The little tick's emptied the whole tin over it!'

It was only too true! The saddle was mouldy no longer. It was a disgusting wet mess of creosote; impossible for anyone to touch, much less ride upon. A large empty creosote tin stood in the corner – silent witness of Fiona's crime.

Sebastian's mouth curled.

'Crude!' he drawled. 'Very crude, my dear cousin! Well, now as you haven't got a saddle—'

'You mean Veronica hasn't got one,' Fiona corrected sweetly.

'As I was saying,' Sebastian continued, 'when you so rudely interrupted, Veronica will have to use *your* saddle now. So, as you haven't got another one for yourself, there's not much point in you coming with us, is there?' He waved us out of the shed, shut the door again, and lashed it firmly with an end of rope that was lying near, seemingly oblivious to Fiona's scream of fury from within.

'How dare you! I'll get out somehow!' she yelled.

'Well, I advise you not to try the window,' drawled Sebastian. 'If you do, you'll be in a jam – literally! And by the way,' he added softly through a crack in the door, 'you'd better not try any more fancy work on that saddle. If you do, I'll go one better with yours – with white paint! It'll look like a blinking wedding cake when I've done with it!'

He retreated from the hut and its furious occupant singing cheerfully:

> '*Here comes the bride,*
> *Fifty inches wide! ...*'

We all yelled together:

> '*Here comes the groom,*
> *Although there's hardly room!*'

Chapter 6

Bacon and Shakespeare

I don't know whether you've had any experience of donkeys. If you haven't, then you're lucky! If you have, you'll know what was in store for us when we trooped into Sep Keenliside's field, having first asked his permission, of course. We had also got permission to borrow his donkey – if we could catch him.

'Of course we'll catch him,' I said rather scornfully, I'm afraid. In those days I didn't know much about animals; I'm wiser now! 'A donkey isn't like a racehorse. He may be a bit slow and obstinate, but he won't be hard to catch—'

'U – um,' Sebastian said doubtfully, being country bred.

We began our task. Round and round that field we walked and Sep Keenliside's donkey walked round in front of us. It was like a procession! Then we tried running, and the donkey trotted. We trotted. We tried heading him off, but he dodged us; we tried cornering him, but go near a corner he wouldn't. Finally the others said that they'd go and get the ponies, and see if they were more successful when mounted.

'All right,' I panted. 'I'll wait for you here.' I sank down on the grass at the edge of the field, exhausted.

It wasn't long before they were back again, Caroline riding Gilly, and Sebastian his chestnut gelding, Warrior.

'By the way, Fiona's got out of that place,' Caroline told me. 'She must have yelled and someone's let her out.'

'She was lucky!' said Sebastian. 'Not many people go into there as a general rule. Well, if she goes riding, she'll have to do it bareback because we've got the one and only saddle' – he motioned to Fiona's saddle that lay beside me on the grass, waiting until we had caught the donkey. 'Anyone got any bright ideas about nabbing him?'

'Perhaps if we walk up to him softly and call him by his name he might let us catch him,' I said. 'By the way, what *is* his name?'

'It's Shakespeare,' Sebastian told me. Then, seeing my astonished face, he added: 'You see, there's usually a pig in this field, and that pig is a bosom pal of old Shakespeare's; so we call 'em Bacon and Shakespeare! Get the idea?'

'Sort of,' I said jumping up. 'Well anyway, let's try it.'

The others dismounted, tethered their ponies to the railings and the operation began.

But Shakespeare didn't respond to the coaxing any more than he had to the chasing. Sometimes he let us get within a few yards of his tail, but never near enough to grab him.

After this we tried with the ponies but this was even worse. The animals seemed to excite Shakespeare and he grew terribly frisky, galloping about like mad and kicking up his heels. I began to feel quite nervous! It wasn't that I was afraid of falling off, but I was terribly scared I'd break or sprain something, for this would mean the end of my dancing career.

'I – I'm wondering—' I said to Sebastian, as we retired for a breather underneath the one tree the field possessed, 'I'm wondering whether after all I *ought* to ride, because of – well, you know what I told you yesterday?'

'Oh, the dancing!' Sebastian said seriously, his eyes on Caroline, who was still trying vainly to trap Shakespeare in a far corner of the field. 'Well, I shouldn't let it stop you riding, if I were you – not at this stage, anyway. It's not as if you were a *prima ballerina*, and I should think it would improve you – slim your thighs and calves, and make you nice and strong, being out in the fresh air, I mean.'

'But supposing I fell off?' I said anxiously. 'It's not that I'm *afraid*, you know, but—'

'Of course I know that,' said Sebastian. 'You wouldn't have far to fall, though – not on old Sep Keenliside's donkey, would you? He's only about nine hands—'

'Nine hands?' I echoed.

'Oh, don't you know – that's the way you measure horses. A hand is four inches. So you see he's not very big.'

'No, I suppose not,' I admitted with a smile. 'I expect you're right.'

By this time Caroline had returned crestfallen, and we all decided to call it a day – for the time being, at any rate.

'We'll come back after lunch with a rope, and lasso the little blighter, if all else fails!' declared Sebastian with determination. 'Can't be beaten by a donkey!'

We took Fiona's saddle into the house with us, and Sebastian sat on it all through lunch, much to Trixie's disgust. Fortunately, though, the meal was in the schoolroom, so there were no other grown-ups there, and Sebastian, I had already found, could twist Trixie round his little finger when he wanted to. She grumbled and said she didn't know what modern children were coming to, that in her young days people sat on Christian chairs, and not on nasty heathen saddles, but that she supposed if Sebastian couldn't eat his dinner in any other way, she'd have to put up with the contraption, but it wasn't her idea of how a young gentleman ought to behave at table.

Sebastian solemnly assured her that he couldn't possibly eat as much as a spoonful of blancmange, sitting on a chair: 'And anyway,' he added, giving me a sidelong look, 'I'm not a young gentleman, am I, Veronica?'

'Whatever do you mean, Master Sebastian?' demanded Trixie indignantly.

'Veronica knows!' Sebastian said, winking at me behind Trixie's back.

After the meal was over we returned to the attack. Fiona hadn't come with us; she'd gone off on Melisande without a saddle, and I must say it was peaceful without her.

'If we could only get the little beggar through the gate into the lane,' Sebastian said as we reached Sep Keenliside's field once more, 'he'd be in a trap. We could nab him easily in that narrow space.'

But alas! Shakespeare saw the trap as well or better than we did. He just wouldn't go through that gate. Every time we got him up to it, he swerved, and was away over the field with a kick of his heels, leaving us standing looking silly.

Suddenly Sebastian gave a shout.

'Gosh! I've got it! ...' He dashed away before Caroline and I'd had time to ask what it was he'd got, and disappeared into the lane. Presently there came the sound of grunts and squeals from the other side of the gate.

For a moment we were completely taken in.

'It's the farm pig we told you about – the one Shakespeare loves like a brother!' yelled Caroline. 'It's jolly old Bacon! No, it's not; it's *Sebastian*!'

Somebody else was taken in as well as we were, and that was Shakespeare. His ears waggled, he gave a delighted bray, then trotted off through the gate as meek as a mouse!

'Got him!' yelled Sebastian, jumping up and slamming the gate shut. 'What a blessing I'm so good at imitating animals.'

We couldn't say anything to this modest remark, because for the moment we'd been taken in ourselves, and there was no denying the fact that he *was* good.

We found it very easy to catch Shakespeare after this. In fact, when he found himself cornered, he gave himself up. We saddled and bridled him, and then began the business of teaching me to ride him.

'It's terribly queer teaching anyone to ride a donkey,' Sebastian said in a rather worried manner when I had at last succeeded in scrambling upon Shakespeare's back. 'You've just *got* to tell them to do all the wrong things, such as kicking him like mad, or walloping him, because he won't go at all if you don't.'

It was only too true. In fact even walloping wouldn't make Shakespeare move much faster than a snail, which was strange because in the field he'd charged around as if he were winning the Derby! The only way to make him trot was for someone to ride behind and keep sloshing him on the hindquarters with a riding-crop. And even this had its drawbacks, because Shakespeare resented the sloshing and showed it by buck-jumping, and turfing me off into the nearest clump of nettles. Not dangerous, but most undignified and distinctly painful!

After a bit, Sebastian suggested that it was time we began our turn-and-turn-about scheme, and said he'd take on Shakespeare.

Anyway,' he added, 'I think Veronica had better learn to ride on one of our ponies. It takes a really experienced horseman to manage a donkey! Perhaps you'd better let her have Gilly, Caroline, and ride Warrior yourself. Might be safer!'

I must say I was thankful I hadn't to mount Warrior. For one thing I felt I was nearer the ground on Gillyflower, and for another she didn't dance and show the whites of her eyes quite as much as Sebastian's pony did.

Well, by four o'clock we'd had a good afternoon's sport though, as Sebastian had said before, you could hardly call it a riding lesson.

'In fact, though I hate to admit it, I feel that Sep Keenliside's donkey isn't such a very good idea after all,' he confessed. 'We'll have to think of something else.' We reined in our mounts and stood still where we were, thinking deeply, Caroline and I on the ponies and Sebastian, his legs trailing in the grass, astride the Immortal Bard – by that I mean old Shakespeare. Incidentally, Shakespeare passed the time away by scratching his tummy with his hind leg and yawning.

Suddenly Caroline gave a yell:

'*I've* got it!'

'Fetch a butterfly-net quick somebody,' drawled Sebastian. 'Caroline's got it – rare, almost unknown specimen. Looks to me very much like a daddy-long-legs . . .'

'Do shut up!' Caroline said, cutting him short. 'I wish you'd try to be serious for just two seconds. How about *hiring* a mount for Veronica?'

'Hiring?' echoed Sebastian. 'Excellent scheme. Only snag as far as I can see is the financial question. Cash – or rather the lack of it.'

'Cash?' echoed Caroline in her turn, as if she'd never heard of it.

'Cash I said, and cash I meant,' went on Sebastian. 'In other words tin, brass, filthy lucre. Call it what you will. Personally I haven't a bean.'

'Neither have I,' I said, feeling a trifle guilty. 'Not enough to hire a pony, that is.' I must explain here that the guilty feeling was due to the fact that I wasn't absolutely penniless. I did possess a small amount of money of my own – but it was earmarked for more important things than hiring ponies; things that I didn't think Caroline, at any rate, would understand: such as ballet shoes, perhaps even ballet lessons. I was quite determined to keep the small amount of capital I had intact for the golden opportunity if ever it came.

'I suppose Caroline's got oodles of the stuff,' Sebastian went on. 'Else she wouldn't have trotted out her brainwave?'

Caroline grew red.

'No, as a matter of fact, I haven't a bean either,' she confessed. 'We'll have to make money somehow. How *do* people make money, Sebastian?'

'Well, the quickest way would be to burgle the bank,' Sebastian suggested helpfully. 'Or a rather safer way, though less exciting, would be to embezzle the fortune of some rich old aunt who trusts you with her last shilling. Or then again, one might break the bank at Monte Carlo.'

'You are beastly,' Caroline said. 'I do wish you'd come out with something sensible.'

'Well, how about a Bring and Buy Sale?' I put in. 'When we wanted funds for anything in our parish we always had a Bring and Buy.'

'Jolly good idea,' Caroline declared. 'But what happens if people just *don't* – bring and buy, I mean. Or if they don't turn up at all? I have an idea they wouldn't if we asked them. You see, we aren't like the Women's Institute—'

'I should just think not!' Sebastian said in such a horrified voice that we couldn't help laughing. 'There's nothing I should hate more than being like the Women's Institute.'

'I didn't mean that at all, idiot!' exclaimed Caroline. 'I meant – goodness, what *did* I mean?'

'Take it as said,' drawled Sebastian. 'Only don't ask me, that's all. I felt it was a trifle mixed at the time. Well, let's wash out the Bring and Buy, and make it a Wayside Stall like the cricket club had last summer. We could nab all the cars coming past—'

'Or we could have it in the village hall,' Caroline said.

Sebastian shrugged his shoulders.

'Now I ask you – how could a Wayside Stall be in the village hall? Sounds like a popular song!'

'The cricket club had one there last Whit-Monday,' declared Caroline triumphantly. 'So what?'

For once Sebastian was silent.

'OK,' he said at length. 'Have it your own way. We'll have a Wayside Stall in the village hall.'

'As a matter of fact I think it *would* be better here, outside the gates,' admitted Caroline rather sheepishly. 'I like your idea of nabbing the cars; besides we'd be able to crash into your house, Sebastian, and make lemonade for the people in the cars. Five pence a glass!'

'Well, I'm dashed!' exclaimed Sebastian. 'After all that arguing! How like a girl!'

'What sort of things would we sell?' I broke in, seeing that Caroline was beginning to get really annoyed. 'At home we used to collect up "white elephants" – things people didn't want.'

'I know !' yelled Caroline. 'There's Mummy's tea-service – the one in the cabinet in the drawing-room.'

'Oh, but we couldn't go selling tea-services,' I objected. 'Most especially not Aunt June's.'

'I wasn't exactly thinking of selling it,' explained Caroline. 'I thought we'd put it on the stall marked SOLD, like they do at the Women's Institute garden fêtes when anyone wants anything special. It would make the stall *look* good.'

'Sounds a batty idea,' Sebastian declared, 'but if it's the done thing at these shows, it's OK with me. We mustn't scandalize Veronica, though. I'm sure they didn't do such lawless things in London.'

I laughed.

'We did worse than that!' Then I was silent. It had suddenly occurred to me that I had never once thought of London since before breakfast!

Chapter 7

The Wayside Stall

We chose Saturday for our Wayside Stall as we thought more
cars were likely to pass on that day than on any other except
Sunday, and of course we couldn't have a Wayside Stall on a
Sunday – the whole village would be scandalized. Fortunately, Aunt June was away that afternoon, and Trixie had gone
into Newcastle to see about school clothes for Fiona and Caroline, so we were left with a clear field. I found that Sebastian
had been right about Bracken Hall and that, apart from meals,
we didn't spend much of our time indoors. In fact, the grown-
ups seemed quite glad to get rid of us, and as long as Sebastian
was with us nobody seemed to mind where we went or what we
did.

I wish you could have seen the things we collected for our
stall. Sebastian went round the village with a handcart – bor-
rowed from the Boy Scouts who used it to collect jumble in –
and came back with a dozen tennis balls that the moths had
got at and didn't bounce, an ancient kitchen fender that had
once been someone's pride and joy but had since been parked
in an outhouse and had turned green; a pair of Wellington
boots that leaked; two ladies' handbags with broken catches;
and a doll with no legs.

Caroline and I went round the big houses in the district and
our haul was a stuffed owl in a case; a silver-plated soup
tureen with all the silver plate worn off; a tin bath with a hole
in the bottom; three pairs of Venetian blinds; and a bathchair.
Fiona refused to collect anything; she said she drew the line at

73

begging, but that she'd help with the refreshments if we liked.

'OK. But if you do, you'll have to wash up the glasses, as well, I warn you,' Sebastian said.

'Oh, all right,' Fiona said rather sulkily. I think she thought the whole affair somewhat beneath her dignity, but she didn't want to be left out of it, all the same.

We set out our stall on the wide grass verge near the lodge gates, and waited for our customers, Aunt June's tea-service having the place of honour in the middle. But alas! There were shoals of cars with masses of people in them passing all the time, but not one of them stopped. After a bit, we got desperate, and Sebastian wrote a large notice which said:

DANGER!
YOU DON'T KNOW WHAT YOU ARE
MISSING!

But even this didn't do the trick. I think some of the people actually thought it was a joke; anyway they grinned at us and waved as they shot past. Terribly aggravating!

When an hour had gone by, we changed our tactics. Caroline stood bang in the middle of the road brandishing the tureen lid in one hand and the legless doll in the other just as an especially big and palatial-looking car came rushing round the corner.

'Hey! Wouldn't you like to buy something at our Wayside Stall?' she yelled.

The car swung to a standstill with a jerk – it jolly well had to, or commit a murder! – and the occupants swept super-cilious eyes over our collection of white elephants.

'How quaint!' said one of them, getting out of the car and poking one of the Wellington boots. 'You haven't any home-made cakes, or fruit, little girl, have you? No fresh eggs, or poultry? . . .'

'Our stall is a white elephant stall,' Sebastian said firmly. 'Cakes and fruit aren't what you might call white elephants; neither is poultry.'

'No, they aren't, are they?' tinkled the lady with an odious smile at her companion who was still sitting in the car. Incidentally Sebastian called that smile a leer when we talked the matter over afterwards. 'Have you got any refreshments?'

'Oh yes – we've got lemonade. Fizzy-Fountain,' Caroline said eagerly. 'Five pence a glass.'

'It's not terribly nice,' put in Fiona. 'I didn't want them to have it, but they would. The bottle's been in the schoolroom cupboard for simply ages and it's frightfully flat – even with the bicarbonate of soda that Sebastian put in to make it fizz.'

We glared at Fiona, while the supercilious lady exchanged another meaning glance with her companion.

'You can give me a glass,' she said at length. 'John! Would you like a glass of Fizzy-Fountain lemonade, with a dash of bicarbonate in to freshen it up? These quaint children are selling it for something or other.'

'Good Lord, no!' said John. 'I can think of nothing I should hate more! ... Fizzy-Fountain lemonade! ... Bicarbonate of soda! ... Good Lord!'

He hastily ran up the car window as if we were going to produce a hose with lemonade and drown him with it – which I must say I'd have dearly loved to do.

'I feel much the same way myself,' said the lady, 'but one feels one must humour children. Thank you, dear' – this to Caroline who had appeared with the glass. Then, to our horror, she took the glass, poured the contents into the hedge, and laid down five pence on our stall. After which she got back into the car and the two of them drove away.

'Well . . .' we said. 'If only she'd let one of *us* drink it, it wouldn't have been so bad. But a whole glass of that gorgeous stuff wasted.' We gazed sadly at the patch of damp grass that lay flattened, silent witness of the wasteful sin that had been committed by the car-owning lady.

'Or if she'd only drunk it herself,' Sebastian said, 'it wouldn't have made us feel so cheap. After all,' he added gloomily, 'it wouldn't have poisoned her.'

'It *might*!' put in Fiona with a superior smile.

'What on earth did you go saying that for about bicarbonate of soda?' exploded Caroline. 'You know very well that the stuff wasn't flat – we only put the bicarbonate in to make it fizz still more. If you hadn't given the show away she'd just have thought how nice it was.'

'It was only fair to warn her,' Fiona insisted.

Sebastian stared at his cousin thoughtfully for a few seconds.

'I've wondered more than once why you wanted to be in this show at all, Fiona,' he said. 'But if you have ideas of sabotaging it, you can give them up here and now, or get out.'

Fiona stared back at him; then she laughed and said scornfully: 'Well, I hope trade keeps good, and that you don't all collapse with exhaustion in the rush-hour!' After which she turned her back on us and walked away towards the house.

We sat down with our backs to the Wayside Stall, lost in our gloomy thoughts. Half the afternoon gone, and all we had made was five pence.

By teatime we were desperate. Half the village seemed to have heard of our stall and had trekked along to inspect it. But although we had begged them to think of the usefulness of a tin bath, even if it *had* a hole in the bottom, and Sebastian had offered the bathchair practically with tears in his eyes, they hadn't bought a thing – not even a glass of lemonade. Lots of the village kids came along too and jeered at us. They stood in a crowd on the opposite side of the road and said rude things about our white elephants. Two prominent members of the Women's Institute pounced on Aunt June's tea-service and wanted to know how much it was, but when we explained firmly that it was sold, and pointed to the notice propped up against one of the dark blue and gold cups, they just looked at each other significantly in that maddening way grown-ups have, and went away muttering that they were sure our parents didn't know what was going on and that somebody ought to tell them.

'Old cats!' Caroline said to their retreating backs. 'Fiona always said Mrs Musgrave was a cat.'

'Fiona was right for once,' Sebastian declared, and began to sing:

> *'Pussy cat, pussy cat, what do you mean*
> *By being so terribly awfully mean? . . .'*

'You can't say that,' I broke in. 'It doesn't rhyme. I mean, it's two words the same.'

'I don't consider Mrs Musgrave deserves a rhyme that rhymes,' declared Sebastian. 'Anyway, the next bit's smashing! It goes:

> *'You could at least have bought a tureen*
> *To set before the king, not to mention the queen.'*

'It doesn't scan,' I objected.

'You're too pernickety,' pronounced Sebastian. 'Look out! Here's another car. Golly, it's actually stopping!'

A gentleman and a lady got out. The man had a little black beard and wore a black, large-brimmed hat made of something that looked like velvet, and his coat was made of velvet too. His trousers were blue, and wide, and flapped as he walked, and his flowing tie and socks were orange, with little scarlet fishes on them. The lady wore wine-coloured corduroy slacks, flat-heeled shoes of red stuff like cork, and huge blue sunglasses. We blinked as we looked at the two of them.

'Oh, Claude!' exclaimed the lady, picking up a cup and turning it this way and that, so that the gold on it caught the light. 'Surely a real Crown Derby tea-service!'

Hastily we explained for the umpteenth time that afternoon that Aunt June's tea-set wasn't for sale. Really, it's amazing how many grown-up people don't seem able to read!

'Oh...' said the lady in a very disappointed-sounding voice. 'I thought it was too good to be true.'

'We've some Fizzy-F ...' I was beginning, when the man gave an excited sort of yelp.

'Look here, Yvonne. This is interesting ...' He had picked up one of the paintings that I'd done in Jonathan's studio. Trixie had found them in the bottom of my trunk, and I'd only just been in time to stop her burning them. We'd had the happy idea of putting them on the stall. Not that we thought anyone would buy them but, as Sebastian said, they would brighten it up a bit. One was a still-life – tomatoes, a cucumber, and a lustre bowl that Jonathan loved as a brother; the other consisted of a red Paisley shawl draped over a pale duck-egg blue figure made of something that looked like soap.

'Who painted these?' demanded the man, looking at us in turn.

'I did,' I answered. Then I saw that he had turned the canvases over and was looking at the proper sides. 'Oh – *those*? Jonathan did those,' I added.

'Jonathan who, dear?' said the lady with the glasses.

'Jonathan Rosenbaum. He lived on the floor higher up than us in London.'

'You mean *the* Jonathan Rosenbaum?' persisted the lady.

'All I know is that Jonathan painted those pictures and that his name is Rosenbaum. He said those canvases made him feel sick, and that I was doing him a favour when I daubed on the back side of them.'

'Well – can you beat that, Claude?' said the lady. 'To find a Rosenbaum on a village Wayside Stall! Can you beat it?'

'No,' said the bearded man. 'But there you are – life is full of surprises!' Then he turned to us again: 'Look here, kids. Are these things your own? I mean, can you sell them?'

'Of *course* we can sell them!' I exclaimed, stopping myself just in time from adding: 'What do you think a Wayside Stall is for?' Really, grown-up people are exasperating sometimes!

'Well, I'll give you five pounds apiece for them,' went on the bearded gentleman, clasping the canvases to his breast as if he feared we might snatch them away again. 'Is that enough?'

'Five pounds – apiece?' we gasped, almost too astonished to answer. 'Golly!' Then Sebastian managed to stammer: 'I should just say it is enough! Thank you most awfully, sir.'

'Thank *you*,' said the man with the beard, and he laid two five-pound notes on the Wayside Stall. 'Come along, Yvonne.' Then he made us a little bow and said again even more fervently: 'Thank *you*.'

'You'd really think we'd done him a favour,' Sebastian said thoughtfully, looking after the pair as they hopped back into the tourer and drove away. 'By the way, Veronica, who *is* your Mr Rosenbaum? They seemed to think an awful lot of him.'

'I haven't the least idea who Jonathan is,' I answered. 'At least I don't know who his father was, or what public school he went to, if that's what you mean. I shouldn't think Jonathan ever went to school at all. He's – well, somehow I can't imagine Jonathan going to school. He just wouldn't fit in.'

'But what sort of an artist is he?' persisted Sebastian. 'Has he had any pictures in the Royal Academy, for instance?'

'The Royal Academy?' I repeated. 'Oh, yes – I think so. But Jonathan doesn't think much of the Royal Academy. He says the Royal Academy is the dullest, stuffiest institution ever set up by a group of stuffy Englishmen – and that's saying something! He's exhibited there, but he despises it, really.'

'Um – he sounds an odd sort of cove!' said Sebastian. 'Does he ever sell any of his pictures?'

'Oh, yes – a few,' I answered. 'He's very well known, really. But of course he doesn't make an awful lot of money – Jonathan says no real artists do – not until they're dead. He says only fashionable portrait painters make money, and they only do it by imperilling their immortal souls and flattering a lot of horse-faced society women.'

'Well, those people in the car evidently knew him,' Caroline put in. 'And we've actually made some money. Ten whole pounds! Three cheers for Jonathan, I say, however odd he may be! Golly! If it hadn't been for Veronica's pictures, we'd have made exactly five pence – not much use for hiring a pony. Awful thought, isn't it?'

'Tell you what,' said Sebastian. 'Let's go into the cottage and scoff all that gorgeous Fizzy-Fountain stuff. It's clear that nobody want it.'

'Yes – let's!' we said in chorus.

Chapter 8

Arabesque

You've no idea what a difficult job it is hiring a pony. It's not that there aren't any animals available, but none of them seemed exactly what we needed – according to Sebastian, anyway. Sebastian took the matter into his own hands, and guaranteed to find me the ideal mount. But after we had looked at what seemed to be hundreds of ponies of all colours, ages, and sizes, I began to feel that it wasn't as easy as it had seemed when we began.

Not so Sebastian. He was still quite cheerful. Moreover he still appeared to be perfectly confident that, provided we looked long and far enough, we'd find what we were looking for sooner or later.

'Now let's see,' he said, consulting his notebook, and biting the end of his pencil thoughtfully, 'after discarding all the absolutely hopeless ones, like that half-broken gelding that behaved like a bucking-bronco-in-a-fit every time you got on his back, we're left with the following:

'(1) Mr Drummond of Ditchfield – black mare, ten years, twelve hands. An awful slug – nearly as bad as Keenliside's donkey. Shouldn't wonder if she isn't broken-winded into the bargain!

'(2) Mrs Lawes of Sandibraes – chestnut filly, rising four, eleven three. Too young, and a bit small. Anyway, a bit skittish for Veronica to begin on.

'(3) Sandy McFarlane, Four-Lane-Ends – bay filly, twelve

nands. Much too stocky. Back like the kitchen table. Give you bow legs, Veronica!'

'Oh,' I wouldn't have him – I mean her – not for anything!' I said in such a horrified voice that they all laughed. 'What others are there?'

'Only that piebald mare from the riding school,' answered Sebastian with a sigh.

'What was wrong with her?' I demanded. 'She seemed an awfully nice pony to me.'

'So she was – as long as you didn't leave the neighbourhood of the riding school,' said Sebastian with a laugh. 'But you try to ride her over in this direction. Nappy isn't the word, I can tell you! Of course we *might* cure her in time, but after all, we're *hiring* the animal, not buying it. We don't want to spend all our time curing its faults for someone else to benefit. Anyway, I don't think a nappy pony is much good for a beginner.'

'Well, if there aren't any more, what do we do?' I asked.

'Think deeply,' replied Sebastian. 'We've still got that man who lives at the inn by the bridge at Merlingford. Someone said he had a nice little pony they were sure he would let out on hire. If it turns out to be a dud, we'll just *have* to fall back on one of these. I think it's a toss-up between the riding-school one and Mr Drummond's mare. We might brighten the latter up a bit with a spot of corn. But we'll investigate the Merlingford pony first. "Never cross your bridges before you come to them" is my motto!'

'Except the Merlingford bridge!' laughed Caroline.

Our luck was in. According to Sebastian the Merlingford pony was the very thing. Keen, but not too frisky for me to learn on. Just the right size – twelve hands. His age didn't really matter, because, as Sebastian said, we weren't buying him. But as a matter of fact he was eight. He was what I called grey, but

Sebastian called him a blue-roan, and he wasn't too stocky.

'I think there's no fear of your becoming bow-legged,' Sebastian assured me.

I looked at him suspiciously.

'I believe you're making fun of me.'

'On such a grave matter as legs straying from the vertical I would not dare to joke,' Sebastian said in mock solemnity. Then he turned in his toes and walked off down the road, swaying from side to side and looking so exactly like a racing jockey that we all burst out laughing.

'He is an idiot!' giggled Caroline.

'It's no use – Sebastian can't be serious for one minute,' Fiona put in. 'Really, I don't know how Uncle Adrian stands him!'

'You stand him yourself very well,' Caroline declared. 'You only came this afternoon because Sebastian was here. You know very well you're not a bit interested in Veronica's pony, really.'

'You shut up!' ordered Fiona, turning red.

When Sebastian came back, we asked the man at the inn – his name was Tompkinson – how much he wanted for the hire of his pony. To our horror he said fifty pence a day.

'Oh, but we don't want him for just one day,' Sebastian explained. 'We want him for several months – two anyway. Perhaps we may want him for a very long time, if we can get up another Wayside Stall to pay for him. Honestly, it'd be worth your while to let us have him cheap. We'd give you cash down,' he added hastily, as the man looked at us doubtfully, and he took the two five-pound notes out of his breeches' pocket and rustled them.

Mr Tompkinson scratched his head and said all right – 'thirty-five pence a day.'

'Nothing doing,' said Sebastian. 'Still far too much.' Then he walked round the pony – we were back in the stable yard by this time – and looked at it critically. 'He's not a terribly keen animal, is he?' he added. 'Wouldn't suit anybody but a beginner. He would do for Veronica to learn on, though. We'll give you fifty pence a week.'

'Split the difference and make it a quid,' said Mr Tompkinson cheerfully, which seemed peculiar to me since he was losing such a lot of money on the deal.

'Right-ho,' answered Sebastian equally cheerfully 'A quid it is.' He laid down the two five-pound notes on the edge of the horse-trough. 'That'll do for ten weeks. Would you mind giving me a receipt.'

Mr Tompkinson scribbled on a bit of paper, torn off the back of an old envelope, words to the effect that we had paid for the hire of his pony, Prince, for ten weeks, signed it, and the deed was done.

'Prince?' echoed Caroline as we left the stable yard, Sebastian leading the pony by the bridle, which was included in the terms of the hiring, as also the saddle – we had made that clear. 'Golly! What a name! Let's change it.'

'Unlucky to change a horse's name,' pronounced Sebastian.

'A lot you care about superstition!' retorted Caroline. 'Let's call him something romantic like Nomad, or Petulengro, after the gipsy.'

'Petulengro?' Sebastian said with a grimace. 'Too long! Can't be shortened, either. Fancy yelling out: "Petty. Petty! Come here, will you!" Anyway, he's Veronica's pony. How about Veronica choosing his name?'

'Yes, of course,' Caroline said at once. 'Those were only suggestions. Go on, Veronica.'

Fiona looked scornful, but she didn't say anything. I couldn't help feeling glad it happened to be my pictures, or rather Jonathan's, that had made the money to hire the pony.

'I'll call him Arab – short for Arabesque,' I said after a moment's thought.

'Jolly good name,' Sebastian declared.

'I think it's awful,' declared Fiona. 'He's not an Arab. He's not even black. And what's an *arabesque*, anyway?'

'It's a position in dancing, ignoramus,' Sebastian told her. 'Something Veronica has learned to do that you'll never learn – not until you stop pinching the cream off the top of the trifle. You're too fat!'

'You beast! I'm not too fat. I'm not fat at all!' Fiona yelled.

As a matter of fact she wasn't, and Sebastian was only teasing, but Fiona really hadn't got much sense of humour and she was usually taken in by him. After her outburst she rode on ahead of us and sulked, while Sebastian gave me a riding lesson. He showed me how to mount, telling me not to dig my pony in the ribs while I was doing it, if I didn't want him to charge off without me. To spring up into the saddle, instead of hauling myself there by the reins.

'You must be a spring balance not a haulage contractor if you want to learn to ride properly,' he said as I mounted for the umpteenth time. 'There – I think you've got the idea now. You'd better stay up.' He patted Arab's neck reassuringly. 'He's a dashed good little pony.'

I looked at Sebastian in astonishment.

'You didn't say that to poor Mr Tompkinson.'

Sebastian grinned sheepishly.

'Oh, I forgot about that little bit of by-play! Well, I had to say *something* to make the fellow bring his price down, hadn't I? Anyway, he didn't believe me. It's all part of the game. When the horse trots in at the stable door, truth flies out at the window, as the saying goes! By horse I mean dealing in horses, of course, my innocent Cockney brat, as I called you once before if you remember! Well, shall we try trotting now?'

We tried, and Arab trotted beautifully. As for me, I bumped

up and down madly, trying hard to look as if I were enjoying it, and not to show how precarious I felt.

'G-gosh! The s-saddle's a b-bit s-slippery, isn't it?' I gasped. Then all at once something happened. I caught the rhythm of the trot, and the world became smooth again.

'Sebastian!' I yelled. 'I've got it! I can trot!'

But alas! I had rejoiced too soon. Before my yell of triumph had died away, I had lost the rise and fall, and was once more bumping up and down like a cork on a rough sea, or a pea in a bottle.

'Gosh! Riding isn't as easy at it looks,' I said ruefully when we came to a steep hill and were walking the ponies.

'No, it isn't – like most other things,' answered Sebastian. 'Playing a violin looks as easy as falling off a log until you try to do it. So does ploughing a field. And I expect your dancing isn't as easy as it looks, either, is it?'

My thoughts flashed back to Madame's studio in Baker Street, and I remember how much practice it took to learn to do even a single *pirouette* well. I thought of my very first dancing lessons and how difficult it had seemed to do a simple *plié* properly.

'Turn out from ze 'ips. From ze 'ips I said, Veronique – not on-lee from ze feets. Ah, but do not displace ze 'ips; zat one must do nevaire. Keep ze 'eels on ze floor, leetle one. Now with ze music begin! One – two – three! Turn out from ze 'ips! Stop! You are bending ze back. Ze back – he must be straight, straight! Not bent like a bow. Now once again – one – two – three!—'

'No – it isn't easy,' I agreed.

'By the way, Veronica,' Caroline said curiously – we had got to the top of the hill by this time and Fiona, having emerged from the sulks, was waiting for us – 'what is an – whatever it is that your pony's named after?'

I laughed.

'Oh, you mean an *arabesque*? It's like this...' I slipped my feet out of the stirrups and slid carefully off Arab's back. 'I'll show you.'

There in the middle of the deserted country road I demonstrated an *arabesque*, balancing on one leg and raising the other to form a line with my outstretched arm. Madame had once said that my *arabesque* had 'a good line', but now out here in the hot blue air with the young larch trees standing knee-deep in bracken, and the ring-doves cooing lazily from the depths of a little fir plantation by the side of the road, I felt that she'd have been even more pleased with my *arabesque* could she have seen it today. The beauty all around me did something to me inside. I can't describe what it was, but it made me want to turn my *arabesque* into something better than it had been before. I wanted to express in my dancing the lovely effect of the sunlight flickering through the trees in the wood, the delicate green of the larches, the grace of the foxgloves growing on the Roman Wall that marched side by side with the road just here.

'Oh! – *lovely*!' breathed Caroline. 'I didn't know your dancing was like that, Veronica.'

Sebastian said nothing, but his blue eyes met mine, full of understanding and admiration.

'I think it's perfectly silly,' came Fiona's voice, shattering my dream. 'The silliest thing I ever saw in my life – standing on one leg like a stork!' She dug her heels into her pony's flanks, and dashed away up the road as if the foul fiend was after her.

'Funny how different people like doing different things,' Sebastian said thoughtfully as he helped me to mount my pony again. 'That's what Fiona likes doing – charging about the countryside with a horse under her to do all the work. Some people' – he carefully didn't say himself, I noticed – 'like playing five-finger exercises on the piano, or scraping with a

87

I dreamt I'd been accepted for Sadler's Wells Ballet

bit of catgut on another bit of catgut, and making harrowing noises. Now Caroline—'

'I like cooking,' Caroline said promptly. 'I'm going to be a cook when I grow up. Imagine being able to cook anything you like to eat! I'd make chocolate éclairs for lunch, tea, and dinner every day.'

Sebastian laughed.

'Golly! How sick you'd be after a week! Well, as I was saying, there's Veronica – she likes standing on one leg like a stork. Funny isn't it?'

'Yes,' I said rather vaguely. 'It is strange.' My thoughts had flown back again to that Baker Street studio with its polished floors and mirrors, and the *barres* along the walls. In my imagination I could hear the music – Handel's *Water Music* that Madame's pianist always played for some of the exercises – and Madame's voice saying in her funny broken English:

'One and two and three and four and! ... Stretch ze feet, leetle one. Stretch till it hurt! Point ze toes beau-ti-fully, so! Zat is right! Once again. One and two and three and four and! ... Turn and repeat on ze uzzer side. Begin! ...'

That night I dreamt I'd been accepted for Sadler's Wells Ballet School, and that it was my very first day there. Quite clearly I saw in my dream the portico, and the plate beside the door with '45 Colet Gardens' upon it.

When I woke up my dream was still so vivid that I could hardly believe I was still here in Northumberland, and not in London hurrying off to my ballet class.

I determined to begin practising again that very day.

Part Two

The Dream Comes True

Chapter 1

A Year Later

It was the end of July – not the same July as the one when I had sat miserably in the Flying Scotsman on my way north, but exactly a year later. I wasn't sitting in a train this time, but in the Scotts' palatial car, and Fiona and Caroline and Aunt June were there too. We were haring smoothly along the white country road towards Newcastle, the reason being the school prize-giving and breaking-up. This was the usual sort of affair – a cross between a concert and a lecture, the concert provided by us, all in white dresses; the lecture by the head mistress, backed up by the celebrity who had been roped in to present the prizes. The prizes, by the way, were the sort of books no one in his right mind would read – like *Coleridge, Poetry and Prose, Bacon's Essays* or somebody's *Anthology of English Verse*. Nothing decent like the latest ballet book, or a book on horses, or even as Caroline said, a cookery book. No wonder we sat in the car feeling gloomy!

As I sat there, I thought of the past year, and all that had happened in it. I'd learned to ride for one thing, and now I was nearly as keen on ponies as my cousins were. We still had Arabesque, by the way. When the ten weeks were up and we'd taken him back to Merlingford, Mr Tompkinson had shot a look at him and said that he certainly *was* improved with all the grooming we'd given him, and that we could go on keeping him a bit longer for nothing, if we liked – in fact, until he wanted him. Well, so far he hadn't wanted him, and as Sebastian said: 'Sufficient unto the day is the evil thereof.' I'm not sure whether this is Shakespeare or the Bible, but it's a jolly good motto!

At the end of last summer holidays, the gloomy question of school arose as was to be expected. It had been settled at last by my going to the same day school in Newcastle as Fiona and Caroline. It took me at reduced fees because I was a clergyman's daughter, and an orphan at that. I was to leave at the end of this term and go to a boarding school that specialized in clergymen's children. I tried hard not to think of it. For one thing, I'd grown quite fond of the Newcastle school (despite the footling prizegivings), and for another and much greater reason – I knew that boarding school spelt death to my dreams of a dancing career. You can't train to be a ballet dancer at a clergy boarding school!

And then my dancing ... From the day when I'd done that *arabesque* in the middle of the road until now, I'd practised faithfully – mostly in the big, nursery bathroom, with the towel-rail as a *barre*. It had worked out very well, especially in the winter, as the rail was heated! I'd worn a bare patch on the linoleum underneath the rail, which puzzled Trixie quite a bit, as of course *she* didn't know about my practising; in fact no one did. I always wedged a chair under the handle of the door when I was supposed to be having my bath, because as I have explained before, there wasn't a key. I'm afraid my baths were a bit sketchy in consequence.

The centre exercises – *pirouettes*, *arabesques*, *attitudes*, and things, I did in the bathroom too, rolling back the bathmat for the job. I did the *pointe*-work there as well. The things that took a lot of space – like *glissades grands-jetés*, ordinary *grands-jetés*, *full-contretemps*, *déboullés*, *cabroilés*, *jetés portés de côté*, and suchlike I did in the morning-room when I was supposed to be practising my music. I asked Aunt June if I might use the gramophone – I think she imagined I wanted to listen to chamber music, or symphony concerts, or something of the kind; anyway she said yes, and handed over to me a pile of records that someone had given to her, and that she didn't like. When I looked through them, I found to my joy a recording of Chopin's waltzes – the ballet music from *Les Sylphides*, and two or three from Delibes' *Coppélia*, besides the whole of Tchaikovsky's *Lac des Cygnes*. I had a grand time with them! I practised the Waltz from *Les Sylphides*, that Madame had taught me, until the record was quite worn out. Now I only put it on when I was feeling especially happy, because very soon you wouldn't be able to hear it at all! Needless to say, I always locked the door during my music practice too. Caroline didn't seem to mind, but Fiona was rude about it. Fortunately she came to the conclusion that I played so badly that I didn't want anyone to hear me, and after this I was left in peace.

When I'd plucked up courage and asked Aunt June if I could have some dancing lessons, she hadn't been nearly as awkward as I'd feared. It appeared that Fiona and Caroline went to an expensive dancing school in Newcastle where they learned to dance gracefully and take part in displays, wearing wonderful dresses, so really Aunt June couldn't very well refuse me my one weekly lesson with Miss Martin. It cost me one pound a term, whereas Caroline and Fiona's lessons were five pounds a term each. I got the idea that Aunt June wasn't exactly sorry to grant me my wish about going to Miss Martin. It was obvious that both Caroline and Fiona were going to cost their parents a lot of money in the near future. Fiona was to go to Harrogate College next term, and after that to a finishing school in Switzerland; Caroline was to go to Roedean soon afterwards.

'It's really refreshing to find young people wanting anything cheap nowadays,' she had said with a shrug when we'd been discussing the matter.

'Oh, Aunt June – I can pay for my lessons myself,' I said eagerly. 'I've got the money – honestly I have.' It was true; I still had the five pounds that Mrs Crapper and the people on the other floors had given me 'to buy something to remember them by'. I have an idea that Jonathan had given most of it. Incidentally the five pounds had risen to five pounds and twenty-five pence through being in the post office.

Aunt June answered that she wouldn't hear of my paying for my own lessons. There was a reasonable amount of money for my education, so I could keep my pocket money to buy something else with. In some ways Aunt June was very decent.

I didn't argue, merely making a mental resolution to go on keeping my money in the post office so that it would get still more interest. I had an idea that I'd need it some day to buy shoes and tights with, and perhaps even a ballet dress.

Well, I had gone to my lesson with Miss Martin once a week. It was every Monday, and it wasn't till half past four, which was very convenient because we had to stay in town until a quarter to six, when Uncle John finished at his office. Then he brought us home with him in the car.

I discovered that Miss Martin had another class on Thursdays; it was a children's class, and she tried hard to persuade some of her students to stay for it, so that the kids would have people more advanced than themselves to copy, but none of them would. I volunteered for the job, and Miss Martin was so pleased that she offered to let me join in her Friday class as well, free of charge, as a reward. So now I had three lessons a week, though to be sure one of them was rather elementary. As they were all after school, in the time when we were just waiting about for Uncle John, I told Fiona and Caroline that I was going to Miss Martin's studio for a bit, and they thought I was just going there to practise. I'm afraid is sounds a bit deceitful, but I couldn't help it. I stilled my conscience by telling myself it wasn't as if I were actually doing something wrong, or hurting anybody in any way. After all, it was my precious career that was at stake, and I knew quite well that I couldn't possibly hope to become a ballet dancer on only one lesson a week.

Miss Martin said she'd had a letter about me from Madame, but she didn't tell me what was in it. When I unfolded to her my secret ambition, and asked her not on any account to give me away to Aunt June, she just smiled her little secret smile, which was one of the most attractive things about her, and said she'd do her best for me.

For my classes I still wore the old black tights and tunic I'd had in London. The tights were so much darned it was difficult to tell where the darn stopped and the tights began! The tunic was getting a bit moth-eaten, too. I was quite well off for shoes, as Stella, the girl who was at the Wells, had given me all the pairs she'd outgrown. I carefully stiffened the blocked ones when they went soft with some marvellous stuff Miss Martin told me about – shellac and methylated spirit.

But I must get back to the car. We were nearing Newcastle by this time, and in a very short while we were in the school hall listening to Miss Glover, our head mistress, telling an appreciative audience of parents and friends how well the school had done during the past year. Little bursts of clapping accentuated her remarks, for instance when she mentioned about Audrey Mason getting her scholarship to Cambridge, and Primula Smith being awarded a special travelling scholarship. I wondered if they would mention the fact when I danced the Lilac Fairy in *The Sleeping Beauty,* or took the lead in *Lac des Cygnes.* Looking at Miss Glover, I thought it unlikely, to say the least!

After the presentation of prizes and certificates, which didn't interest me much because I hadn't won any, there was the usual concert – if you could call it that. There was the head girl's recitation, all in Latin; a scene from *Peer Gynt* by the sixth form; several terribly dull duets for two pianos by music pupils; a violin solo by a girl who squeaked frightfully, and, last but not least, a French play by our form – the Fifth. I was a waiter, and all I had to say was 'Monsieur?' in an inter-rogating voice. So that didn't weigh on my mind very much, and I was able to think about the Lilac Fairy all through it. In fact I was so busy in my imagination doing my curtsy on Covent Garden stage that I very nearly forgot I was in the school hall and missed my cue!

After this, there was a cup of tea and a cake for the parents and friends, and lemonade and a biscuit for us. At five o'clock it was all over, and we were free to go home. I realized with a queer sinking feeling in my inside that the holidays had begun and that I was saying a final goodbye to the school I had grown to love.

After I had said farewell to several mistresses and girls who were my special friends, I packed all my books and shoes and other things into the car, which was waiting outside, and rushed round to Miss Martin's studio to say goodbye to her, because dancing school was finished too. When it began again in the autumn I wouldn't be there, alas!

Luckily it was only a few minutes from the school. When I got there, I found that Miss Martin had a visitor, and to my surprise it was Aunt June!

'Miss Martin asked me to call,' she explained, seeing my startled face. 'She wanted to discuss your career with me. Miss Martin thinks you dance rather well, Veronica; she wonders how you'd like to be a dancing mistress?'

'Oh, but . . .' I began in a horror-stricken voice. Then I met Miss Martin's eyes – far-seeing grey eyes they were, and there was an expression in them that I couldn't fathom. But I understood enough just to keep quiet and let Aunt June go on talking, which she did without any help from either of us.

'Miss Martin thinks you'd make an excellent dancing teacher, Veronica. Of course it's not *my* idea of a career for a girl. Still, it's not as if you were going on the stage.' Aunt June said this as if the stage was something disgraceful – not to be mentioned in polite society! 'And after all,' she went on, 'you certainly don't show much aptitude for anything else. I understand from Miss Stanley, your form mistress, that she'll be greatly surprised if you've passed your School Certificate. And judging by the reports of the other mistresses, you don't show a great deal of promise in any special subject. All except your drawing, and that I understand Miss Lishman, the art mistress, thinks "extraordinary". I'm not quite sure what she means by that word.'

I couldn't help smiling, because I knew exactly what Miss Lishman meant. I remembered my first lessons. Miss Lishman had looked rather puzzled over my drawing – I seemed to do things so much bigger than anyone else. Finally she asked me where I'd learnt, and what sort of paper I'd been used to drawing on.

'Oh, I've never learnt drawing,' I explained. 'But I used to watch Jonathan. He was an artist who lived on the floor above us and he was a great friend of Daddy's. I used to paint in oils mostly, on the backs of Jonathan's old canvases – the ones he hated. Sometimes, though, I used brown paper.'

'Brown paper?' echoed Miss Lishman in a startled voice.

'Oh, yes, done with size it's quite good for oils, and – it's marvellous for pastel drawing, you know. Then sometimes Jonathan gave me some sugar-paper—'

'I see,' said Miss Lishman doubtfully, and not a bit as if she did. 'Well, I'm afraid we haven't any of those things here. You'll have to make do with ordinary drawing paper.' She handed me a piece of cartridge paper. It was about eight inches square and looked to me like a postage stamp.

'Oh, and sometimes Jonathan and I used to draw on the walls,' I went on, thoughts crowding in upon me. 'Friezes and things. We did a perfectly marvellous one of Bacchus riding on an ostrich, and all his followers in the most ridiculous attitudes. When we got tired of the things we drew, we just painted them out and did some more on top. We kept Bacchus for ages though. Jonathan said he was the only bright spot in the gloom of a London fog! He said it cheered him up no end to look at that ostrich, and realize what funny shapes animals have—'

'That will do, Veronica,' said Miss Lishman firmly, cutting me short. 'That seems to me to be a very queer way of drawing.'

I felt like saying that to paint a still-life consisting of a large pottery jug, draped with a violet curtain, a flower vase full of nasturtiums, at least a pound of tomatoes, several oranges, not to mention a large grapefruit – well, to paint all this on a bit of paper eight inches square seemed queer to *me*. But I didn't say so because it might have sounded rude. Anyway, I didn't consider the point worth arguing about. I did the painting, and I must say it was frightfully bad. Jonathan would have had a fit if he'd seen it!

It was after this lesson that I'd heard Miss Lishman use the word 'extraordinary'. She was talking to another mistress at the time.

I dragged my thoughts back from the drawing and tried to listen to what Aunt June was saying.

'Of course it will rather alter our plans for you – educationally, I mean. As Miss Martin says, you'll have to stay on at school here in Newcastle, so that you can go in for your dancing exams with her. And of course you'll have to have extra dancing lessons . . .'

Then I understood the look in Miss Martin's eyes!

She knew as well as I did what boarding school meant, and she was determined to save me from it. The careers of dancing teacher and ballet student march side by side for quite a long time, and who knew what might happen before their ways divided?

'Oh, Miss Martin!' I gasped, when Aunt June had gone on her dignified way, telling me to follow her in a very few minutes. 'Oh, Miss Martin, you *are* a darling! I see now why you wanted to talk about me to Aunt June. I see it all!' Then I'm afraid I forgot that Miss Martin was my dancing mistress. I put my arms round her and hugged her and Miss Martin hugged me back. That's the best of dancing mistresses – they're not like the mistresses in ordinary schools. They're much more human. I certainly can't imagine anyone hugging Miss Glover, not even if they'd just passed their School Certificate with seven credits!

'But you understand of course, Veronica,' Miss Martin said when we were both calm again, 'that if, when the time comes, your aunt won't let you take up dancing – professionally, I mean – you'll have to give in and teach, you know.' Then, seeing my downcast face, she added cheerfully: 'After all, my dear, teaching dancing is a good life. I've done it for a long time and been very happy – perhaps happier than I'd have been on the stage, though I don't expect you to see it like that just now. In any case, I'm quite sure you'd rather teach dancing than, say, Latin or domestic science, wouldn't you?'

'Oh, yes – *rather*!' I agreed fervently.

'Then I think we've done the right thing,' went on Miss Martin. 'And for the present you must work hard. There's your Elementary RAD exam* – you haven't passed it yet, you

* Royal Academy of Dancing

know. Of course you're a long way beyond it now, but you'll still have to take it. And that reminds me' – she broke off, and went over to a tall cupboard where the best fancy costumes were kept – 'Mrs Grantly brought this in' – she held up a most gorgeous *tutu*. With its snowy frills of tarlatan it made me think of the corolla of a beautiful white flower. 'Marigold has outgrown it. Poor Marigold! I'm afraid she's going to be too big for ballet. Her mother thought I might find someone who would like to buy it. She wants two pounds fifty for it. That seems to me a great bargain.'

'I should just think it is!' I exclaimed. 'Why a *tutu* like that, new, would cost the earth! Can I buy it, Miss Martin? I've got loads of money of my very own. Several pounds, anyway.'

'That's what I thought,' smiled Miss Martin. 'You'll need it for your exam at Christmas.'

'Will I go to London for it?' I questioned, thinking of dear Mrs Crapper, and Jonathan, and all my other friends. '*Couldn't* I please go to London for it, Miss Martin? It's really not much farther than Edinburgh, is it?'

'Just a few miles!' teased Miss Martin. 'Well, perhaps we might manage it. If you take it in London, it will have to be in January. That might be just as well, after all; it will give you more time to work on the syllabus.'

'Oh, *thank* you!' I said with a gasp of joy. Although I had grown to love beautiful Northumberland dearly, London was still my home. Even to think of the Tube, and Trafalgar Square with its pigeons, Piccadilly Circus with Eros poised ready to take flight, made me feel quivery in my inside. 'Thank you, Miss Martin. Thank you for everything, I *will* work hard.'

I ran down the stairs from the studio and out into the street, clasping the precious frock to my breast like a baby.

'Goodness!' I said aloud. 'I hope I haven't kept Aunt June

waiting. Golly! – I'm awfully sorry!'

The person I had collided with extricated himself from the ballet dress, and began to laugh.

'Veronica! Why the hurry?'

'Sebastian!' I yelled. 'I always seem to barge into you! I thought you didn't break up until tomorrow.'

'Chap in our form got chicken-pox,' Sebastian explained. 'Awful spot of luck – with the accent on the spot! The Powers-That-Be thought it wisest to pack us all off home, as it was so near the end of term.'

'That doesn't mean that you'll be in quarantine?' I asked anxiously.

'Good Lord, no! I've had the foul D spelt F-O-W-L – *disease*!' laughed Sebastian. 'Not a snag anywhere, I assure you! In other words, everything in the garden's lovely! But what's all this?' – he pointed to the mass of white tarlatan in my arms. 'Are you taking home the laundry, or something?'

'Idiot! It's my new ballet frock,' I explained. 'Oh, Sebastian – I'm getting there! Really, I am. Aunt June says I'm to be a dancing teacher—'

Sebastian's brow puckered. 'But I thought—'

'Oh, yes – I know what you're thinking,' I burst out. 'But you're wrong. Of course I'm not *really* going to be a dancing teacher, but Aunt June thinks I am. It's the thin end of the wedge, if you see what I mean. I'll try to win Aunt June over later on, and you bet I'll do it!'

'Aunt June . . .' Sebastian said thoughtfully. 'Does that mean she's here, in town?'

'Oh, yes. She's just round the corner, at school,' I said. 'You see it's breaking-up day, and we've had a prize-giving and all that stuff. Ghastly! And by the way, she'll be waiting for me in the car. I must simply *dash*! What about you? How are you getting home? Why not come with us – there's loads of room?'

'What? With Aunt June and Cousin Fiona, not to mention

101

the obsequious Perkins?' laughed Sebastian. 'And I suppose the sumptuous Rolls? Not for this child! Couldn't stand it – altogether too overpowering! Besides, I have quite a few things I want to do in town. No, I'll come back in the homely bus. Fortunately this is Tuesday – Market Day!'

Our eyes met and we laughed. Sebastian still lost no opportunity of teasing me about my sad attempt at running away.

'D'you know,' I said, 'I've never realized it before, but if you and Fiona and Caroline are cousins, then you must be a sort of cousin of mine, too, Sebastian.'

'Sort of,' agreed Sebastian. 'But only sort of, if you know what I mean. Different side of the family. Well, I'll be getting along. See you tonight most likely – provided I don't miss the bus. So long, Cousin Veronica-sort-of, dancing-teacher elect!' He swung himself on to a passing bus, waved his school cap gaily, and in another moment his teasing face was lost to view in a maze of traffic.

I went on my way somewhat more soberly, but my heart was singing with joy at the wonderful thing that had happened to me.

Chapter 2

The Holidays Begin

We didn't see Sebastian that night after all. When seven o'clock came and he still hadn't arrived, we rang up the lodge to see what had happened. Bella McIntosh, the woman from the village, who'd looked after Sebastian and his father ever since Sebastian's mother had died five years ago, answered our ring. She told us that only a few minutes ago Sebastian himself had rung up from Newcastle, saying that he'd met his father in town, and that they were doing a show. He also said that, if we rang up, Bella was to say that he was very sorry about tonight, but he couldn't make it.

'Well!' Fiona said, putting down the receiver. 'What do you think of that? Going to a show when *we're* here waiting for him. And after telling Veronica he would see us tonight—'

'He said he *expected* he'd see us,' I put in, determined to be fair to Sebastian. 'But, after all, if his father wanted him to go to a show, well, Sebastian could hardly insist on dashing back here, just to be with us for nothing in particular, now could he?'

'Yes,' he could,' Fiona retorted. 'After he'd *promised*.'

I said no more. It was never any use arguing with Fiona. Instead, I retired to the bathroom and did an hour's practising, and after this it was time for bed.

Next morning I got up early as usual and practised before breakfast. After breakfast I locked myself into the morning-room by sheer force of habit, and practised scales and exercises conscientiously for half an hour, and did centre-work for another half. After which I felt free to join the others and share in their plans. Miss Martin said that an hour and a half's work a day was enough for anyone to do during the holidays.

I crashed round to the stables where I guessed the others would be. Fiona was rubbing Melisande down with a silk hankie, and Caroline was out in the field trying to round up Arab and Warrior – she'd already caught Gillyflower, she told me.

'Right-ho! You leave Arab to me!' I yelled back. 'I can get him easily with a lump of sugar. He always falls for it.'

'Not with me he doesn't!' grumbled Caroline. 'I've used up nearly half a pound on him. He always snatches it, and then dashes off just when you're going to grab him.'

'Watch me!' I answered, stealing up to my pony with the sugar on my outstretched palm. 'Come along, old boy!'

Sure enough, Arab allowed himself to be caught. I expect he knew that I was his mistress and Caroline only my understudy, so to speak, because the same thing always happened whenever *I* tried to catch Gillyflower for her. He just wouldn't let me get near him.

'Gosh! This is a hopeless job!' poor Caroline panted, as she stood in the middle of the field, hands on hips, watching Warrior charge round, head up, tail streaming. 'I do wish Sebastian would turn up and catch his own beastly pony!'

Just as the words left her lips, there was a shout, and Sebastian took a flying leap over the fence into the field.

'I've just been calling your pony names!' yelled Caroline. 'I've been chasing him round this field for *hours* – ten minutes, anyway. I'm through!'

OK!' laughed Sebastian. 'Gosh! He's fat, isn't he? I'll bet you lot haven't been exercising him as you promised you would while I was away at school.'

'We did try,' Caroline said apologetically. 'But he's so awful to catch for anyone except you, Sebastian, and Fiona—'

'Oh, I know all about Fiona! *She* wouldn't do a fellow a good turn if she could help it—'

'I didn't mean that—'

'Maybe not,' drawled Sebastian. 'But it's true, all the same.' Unfortunately Fiona was standing at the stable door and had heard everything. I have an idea that Sebastian meant her to hear.

'Of course dear Veronica was no end of a help,' Fiona said scoffingly. 'She rode Warrior every day for you, Sebastian!'

Sebastian stared back at her scornfully.

'You *are* a little cat!' he stated. 'You know very well that Veronica isn't up to Warrior yet. By the way, how's the riding coming on, Veronica?'

'Oh, I like it no end,' I assured him. 'But then anyone would like riding Arab – he's so good-mannered. He never takes nips at me like Melisande does when Fiona isn't looking, or bucks me off—'

'No – he's a nice animal,' agreed Sebastian. 'Well, I'll be off to catch my steed. See you later!'

We walked back into the stable, and I began to groom Arab.

'If you want Sebastian to like you, you won't make him do it by saying unkind things about Veronica,' Caroline observed.

'Who said I wanted him to like me?' flashed Fiona. 'I don't care in the least whether he likes me or not. I think he's detestable!'

'When people keep on saying other people are detestable, it makes you think they rather like them!' stated Caroline.

In less than no time, Sebastian was with us, leading Warrior by the forelock.

'I vote we go for a ride this afternoon,' he said as he rubbed him down with a dandy-brush. 'Let's go right up on to the moors. You don't know how I've been longing for a ride ever since half-term. Let's have a picnic on Corbie's Nob. We haven't been there for ages and ages – two years, I should think.'

'Oh, but Sebastian,' Fiona said, 'there's a tennis party over at the Frazers – Lingfield, you know. I've promised to go, and I said you'd go too. They'll be expecting you—'

'What? Me go to a sticky tennis party at the Frazers on the first day of the hols. Not jolly likely!' Sebastian said. 'Anyway, by rights we shouldn't have broken up until today, so they can't be expecting me.'

'I told them you'd be home by lunchtime, and the party doesn't begin until three o'clock, so there'd still have been loads of time,' argued Fiona. 'And you're my partner—'

'*Your* partner?' Sebastian retorted. 'Oh, no – think again! I'm not anyone's partner. I'm going riding—'

'But I shall be without a partner—'

'Well, that's your fault. You shouldn't go including me in your rash promises. I like to be *asked* when I'm going to do a thing.'

'But I *can't* go without a partner,' wailed Fiona. 'Oh, Sebastian – you *might* be obliging just for once.'

'I'm not obliging,' said Sebastian. 'Never was! Anyway, you don't oblige *me*. What about that pony? You never exercised him once for me.'

He went on imperturbably grooming Warrior, whilst Fiona stood in the doorway with clenched hands.

'Are you going to come?'

'No, I'm not. I've told you – I'm going riding.'

'You're perfectly beastly!' exclaimed Fiona, seeing that Sebastian was not to be moved. 'I told Caroline you were, and it's true. Since Veronica came, you—'

Sebastian's imperturbability vanished. He snatched up his riding-crop from where it lay on the window-sill.

'Just one more word in that strain . . .' he threatened.

Fiona didn't know whether he was serious, and neither did

we, but she evidently thought that discretion was the better part of valour, for she said no more, but dashed out of the stable like a whirlwind, flung herself upon Melisande's back, and was away.

'Well, I suppose that means we don't include *her* in our plans,' Caroline said as she picked up her brushes and things and put them into her bag. 'Even if she's out of the tennis, she certainly won't come with us. Sebastian you *are* naughty! You always rub Fiona up the wrong way!'

'I like that! She always rubs *me* up the wrong way. Me be her partner at tennis? The very idea! Why, I'd have to do every spot of the work and then take all the blame when we lost! I know all about Fiona and her tennis! And without as much as a "Will you?" let alone a "please".'

'Corbie's Nob? That's the peak you can see from the ponies' field, isn't it?' I put in, anxious to take Sebastian's thoughts away from Fiona. 'Can we ride all the way?'

'Every step,' Sebastian replied. 'Except for the very top. I know all the gates, and the gaps in the walls, and everything. We go across Three Tree Moor and then up on to the Nob. It's a stiffish climb, but it's worth it when you get to the top. You can see three counties and right over into Bonnie Scotland on a clear day.'

'Let's collect up the stuff for the picnic now,' suggested Caroline. 'Then we'll be able to start off straight after lunch. I saw Trixie making some girdle scones – let's beg some.'

'Girdle scones,' mused Sebastian. 'Gosh! They sound good! When you're away at school you forget there are such things.'

Chapter 3

Corbie's Nob

Fiona regarded us scornfully as we loaded ourselves with eatables and drinkables ready for our climb. She herself was arrayed in spotless tennis finery – white silk pleated shorts-frock, snowy shoes and ankle socks. Under her arm she carried a Slazenger tennis racket.

'Won't you be rather the worse for wear?' Sebastian asked innocently, buckling Warrior's girths, and pulling down his stirrup irons. 'I mean, after you've ridden all the way over to Lingfield in those togs?'

'I'm not going to ride,' Fiona told him loftily.

Sebastian gave a whistle.

'Gosh! You don't mean to say you're going to trek there – leg it – shanks' pony? Who would have thought it?'

'I'm going by car, of course,' Fiona said. 'Any objection?'

Sebastian shrugged his shoulders. The look on his expressive face told Fiona more clearly than any words exactly what he meant. 'Fancy going to play tennis in a *car*,' that look said. 'I knew it would be a sticky party!'

'Well, so long!' he said, swinging himself into the saddle. 'Ready, you two? Then let's be off. By the way, Fiona, don't forget that the super-charged tennis racket you hold beneath your arm is to do more than make everyone at the party jealous!' With which parting thrust he was away before Fiona had time to reply, we following close on his heels.

We rode out into the North Meadow where Fiona's pony was grazing – Fiona had turned her out before she went off for her tennis. As we cantered across the short grass, Melisande charged round on her own, tail streaming. Every now and then she would stop to snort. When we left the field by the gate on the far side, she looked after us longingly and whinnied, her ears pricked. We did feel mean, leaving her behind.

'It's Fiona's fault,' Caroline said. 'She oughtn't to have wanted to go to a stupid tennis party on the very first day of the hols.'

'Of course tennis is OK,' Sebastian observed. 'Don't think I despise a game of tennis – far from it. But a spot of tennis here among ourselves, where you can get a decent game, is one thing, and a sticky party at the Frazers, all dolled up, is quite another.'

After this none of us said anything for quite a bit. The going was hard, and we were fully occupied urging our ponies onwards and upwards through the shoulder-deep bracken that encircled the lower slopes of Three Tree Moor like a huge girdle. When we had got above the bracken the going was easier. Here the fell was covered with short heather and outcrops of rock with now and then stretches of sheep-nibbled turf. Leading away in all directions were the narrow, ribbon-like tracks made by the sheep.

Up and up we climbed, the air seeming to become more hot and blue every minute. And then, suddenly, we breasted the brow of the fell, and saw Three Tree Moor before us – a lonely expanse of rock-strewn turf with another steep ascent on the far side.

'Oh!' I said disappointedly, gulping down draughts of the cool mountain air that blew across the moor. 'I thought Corbie's Nob was on top of here.'

Sebastian laughed.

'That's always the way when you're making for a peak. It's always just over the top of the next slope, and then when you get there, sure as anything you find there's still another one to climb. I should say there are quite three more before we get to the Nob. Take a dekko at the jolly old Hall and surroundings because you won't be able to see them again till you get on top of the Nob.'

We dismounted and sat on the edge of the steep, heathery hillside, letting the ponies graze on a patch of turf nearby. We knew they'd be easy enough to catch when we wanted them – the climb had sobered them down considerably.

Everything was so quiet up here that you could hear the sheep nibbling, and the bees taking the honey from the heather all around us. While we'd climbed upwards, several peewits had collected and had flown round us in circles, uttering their plaintive cries. But now even these had flown away, and the silence was unbroken unless you could count umpteen larks, so high up in the blue air that they were quite invisible. Their song was so continuous that in time it became part of the silence. Occasionally a curlew, with long curving beak, flew languidly over our heads, startling the ponies by its shrill cry of alarm, so different from the lovely notes it utters when it rises from the ground into the sky.

Far below us lay Bracken Hall looking incredibly small and neat. Tiny fields lay spread out around it like pocket handkerchiefs, and in one of them a little animal we knew to be Melisande cropped at the grass. The lake glittered like a jewel with a crescent of sombre fir woods for its setting. Beyond the Hall lay the little village of Bracken with its square-towered church, and a glint of blue that Sebastian told us was the burn that flowed through it.

'Well, let's be getting on, shall we?' Sebastian said, when we had rested for a bit. 'We've still a good way to go. "Excelsior" as the highwayman said when they hung him on the gibbet.'

'Oh, Sebastian, but it wasn't ...' I began, when I saw the laughter in his blue eyes. 'Oh, I see – you were joking.'

'Lady, I never joke,' Sebastian assured me solemnly.

'May you be forgiven!' I retorted. 'You never do anything else – at least hardly ever,' I added, remembering the Sebastian I had met on that far-away railway journey.

When we got to the lower slopes of the Nob, we left the ponies at the bottom of the final ascent and started to climb on foot. The Nob was composed chiefly of black rocks that jutted out of a precipitous, shaly hillside, like raisins in a rock bun. On the top was a stone cairn.

'It marked a British Burial ground in the first place,' Sebastian panted, leaping upwards. 'Then the Borderers used it for a beacon turret to warn the other places round that the Scots were coming. Excelsior! Higher and still higher, and mind the snakes!'

'Snakes?' I gasped.

'Idiot!' panted Caroline. 'I mean *you*, Sebastian. Veronica thought you were serious.'

'Well, so I was,' answered Sebastian. 'There might be some. There are lots on the moors.'

'Only grass snakes—'

'Well, they're snakes, aren't they?'

'I suppose so, but they're quite harmless.'

'There are adders, too,' persisted Sebastian. 'I saw one the other day. A black one – they're deadly poisonous. I mean their bites are.'

'Oh, Sebastian – *where*?'

'In a bottle in the Jingling Gate Inn parlour,' Sebastian said with a grin. 'It was caught up here on the Nob fifty years ago.'

We breathed again.

Sebastian, you are a beast, frightening us like that!' Caroline exclaimed. 'My heart's going pit-a-pat.'

'I thought you wanted a thrill,' said Sebastian. 'So I provided one. Always the little gentleman, yours truly! Well, here we are. How's this for a view?'

We stood on the summit of the Nob and gasped, partly because of the exertion of our climb, but chiefly because of the beauty and wildness of the scene spread out before us. At our feet lay what looked like an uninhabited land of huge, rounded hills – the Cheviots, the Border country that lies between England and Scotland. To the north-west lay what looked like a dark, woolly carpet.

'That's the new forest the Forestry Commission has just planted,' Sebastian explained. 'It's going to be the biggest forest in England when they've finished. It's going to stretch right up to the Border. When it grows up, these hills won't look nearly so bare and desolate.'

When our eyes had got accustomed to the view, we were able to pick out villages and hamlets. We could even see a tiny puff of smoke that marked the little station of Deadwater.

'It always puzzles me why on earth they went and built a station at Deadwater, of all places,' mused Sebastian. 'There's nowhere to go to from here except the open fell. D'you see that misty, blue streak over to the east, between those two hills? That's the sea.'

'The sea?' we echoed excitedly. 'Just where will it be?'

'Oh, away up by Holy Island, I should say,' answered Sebastian. 'No, on second thoughts, it won't be as far north as that. It'll be somewhere round about Alnmouth, or Hauxley – the coast opposite Coquet Island, you know. It's hard to tell though. How about having our picnic up here?'

We all agreed that you couldn't get a better place for our meal. 'Come on, then! Walk up, walk up, ladies and gentlemen to see the lions fed!' Sebastian dislodged a big, flat stone from the side of the cairn for us to use as a table and we spread out our provisions.

'Apple cake, gingerbread, rock buns, sandwiches and, of course, Trixie's girdle scones,' I said, unwrapping the things Caroline and I had brought. 'What have you got, Sebastian?'

'Fruit cake, sausage rolls, and a jam tart,' he answered handing them over to Caroline. 'I've got lemonade, too.'

'Golly!' Caroline exclaimed as she unpacked the things 'The jam tart's got mixed up with the sausage rolls! Will i matter, do you think?'

'Oh, no – not at all,' Sebastian said airily. 'Improve them, J should say. Give 'em a unique flavour. We might try a dash of lemonade on them as well. *Sauce citronnade.* Sausages *à la* whatever-the-French-for-jam-is.'

'*Confiture,* of course,' I said.

'No "of course" in that superior manner, my child,' said Sebastian, his eyes snapping, 'or you won't get any! Well, as I was saying, sausages *à la confiture avec sauce citronnade.* Any offers?'

'No, thank you,' Caroline and I said both together. 'We prefer our sausage rolls *without* lemonade.'

'Just as you like,' said Sebastian with a wave of his hand. 'I'm always ready to pander to the common taste. You can have them *ordinaire* or whatever it is they call it. What's the matter, Veronica? You look struck all of a heap.'

'Did I? I was thinking, that's all.' I didn't volunteer to tell them what I was thinking but, as a matter of fact, I had once again noticed Sebastian's wonderful hands, and the way he used them to express himself. Most people talk with their voices; Sebastian did it with his hands. When he said 'No, you can't do that' he didn't just say it. He moved his hands, and they forbade you. I can't explain it, but that's how it was.

Meanwhile he had fished three cups out of his haversack and was pouring lemonade into them.

'Do you prefer your champagne dry, or the other thing?' he inquired.

'Dry?' I echoed. 'How on earth cane wine be *dry*?'

'Search me!' said Sebastian. 'But I assure you it can. All the best wine lists say so.'

113

'Well, what's the other thing?' I asked. 'Wet, I suppose? I think I'll have mine wet.'

'I've an idea it isn't wet,' Sebastian said. 'I've an idea it's – it's – dash it all, I can't think what it can be.'

'Well, never mind – let's all have it wet,' suggested Caroline.

And this is what we did. We held up our glasses – I mean cups – and drank toasts to all the people we knew. Most of them were perfectly idiotic toasts, but at the end, when there was only a drop of lemonade left in our glasses, the bantering look died out of Sebastian's eyes, and he said quite seriously: 'Here's to our secret – yours and mine, Veronica! May we both achieve our heart's desire.'

Of course Caroline wanted to know what the secrets were, and of course Sebastian refused to tell her.

'They wouldn't be secrets then, would they?' he teased.

'Well, I think you're terribly mean,' she grumbled. 'And anyway, you can't drink toasts to yourselves – it just isn't done.'

'Isn't it?' retorted Sebastian. 'Watch me!' So saying he clinked his glass against mine, said 'Here's to US, Veronica!' and finished the rest of the lemonade in one gulp.

After we had packed the cups and the sandwich paper back into the rucksacks, we hid the empty lemonade bottle in a crevice in the cairn, and climbed down from our rocky eyrie.

'Let's try to find some white heather while we're here, shall we?' said Sebastian. 'There used to be quite a big patch over to the right of that boggy ground. I remember getting some there once. White heather is very rare, you know,' he explained to me, 'and if you *do* find any, it's supposed to bring you good luck. That's what we both need just now, eh Veronica? A spot of real good luck.'

We looked and looked but although there were masses of bell heather in full bloom, and quite a lot of the ordinary just beginning to come out, not a trace of white did we see.

'Queer – I'll swear it was somewhere about here,' Sebastian declared as we squelched about in the boggy ground. We'd taken off our shoes for the job and I must say it was lovely to feel the cool, peaty mud oozing up between your toes. There were lots of marsh flowers growing on the bog. Sebastian explained that the little white ones, like tiny wind anemones, were called Grass of Parnassus.

'It doesn't grow in many places,' he added. 'Here and on Holy Island are the only ones I know. Pretty, isn't it?'

'Lovely,' I agreed.

'We'd better be making tracks,' he said, after we had squelched round for a long time, and come no nearer to finding anything that even faintly resembled white heather.

It was on our way back to the patch of grass where the ponies were grazing that the dreadful thing happened. We had picked our way over the boggy part, jumping from clump to clump of coarse grass so as to avoid sinking in knee-deep, and had got to where the rocks and heather began, when I felt a sudden pain shoot through my ankle. Looking down I saw something wriggle away into the heather, and disappear amongst an outcrop of rock – something long, and black, and sinister.

'Sebastian!' I yelled. 'Sebastian! Come quick! I've been bitten by something! It was a snake – I saw it!'

'Gosh!' Sebastian came rushing up, not bothering to step on the tufts of grass, but plunging through the bog all anyhow in his effort to reach me quickly. 'Golly! Are you sure?'

'Of course I'm sure!' I said, tears of fright springing to my eyes. 'You can see the mark. Look!'

I pointed down at my ankle and there, sure enough, was a small red mark like a scratch.

'Was it green – the thing that bit you, I mean?' Sebastian demanded. 'What was it like?'

'It wasn't green!' I yelled. 'It was b-black. It was a black adder—'

'Nonsense!' snapped Sebastian, but all the same I saw him go white under his tan. 'There aren't any black adders now.'

'You said you saw one—'

'Yes, in a bottle. It was caught fifty years ago. There hasn't been another one found since.'

'This might be the time,' I hiccuped. 'And it was here the last one was caught. You said so.'

Then Sebastian seemed to make up his mind. He suddenly became the serious boy I'd met in the train.

'Sit down,' he ordered curtly, 'I don't for a moment believe it was a black adder you saw, but just in case—' He took a penknife out of his pocket, and a box of matches.

'W-what are you going to do with your knife?' I asked anxiously.

'I'm going to sterilize it,' he answered, lighting a match and holding the blade in the flame. 'Now don't be scared. I won't hurt you – at least not much.'

When the blade had cooled, he took my ankle in one slim, strong hand and began to scratch the red mark with the knife until it began to bleed quite fast. Then he put his head down, and before I knew what he was about, he had placed his lips to the wound and was sucking it, spitting over his shoulder into the heather at intervals. I was so interested that I nearly forgot it was me that had been bitten!

'There now – I think that will do. If it *was* an adder, that ought to have put paid to his little game! As for black adders, I just don't believe it. All the same, we must get down quickly and find a house where we can get spirit of some sort.'

'What about the doctor?' said Caroline.

'Yes, I'd thought about him,' said Sebastian. 'But today is Wednesday, and it's his day at Depton. Goodness only knows where he'll be just now. Anyway, we must find somewhere

116

nearer than that. I know! Sandy Mactavish's cottage at the foot of the fell – Pasture Cottage, it's called. We'll make for it.'

'Why Sandy Mactavish?' Caroline asked, as he bandaged my ankle with a not-too-clean hankie he'd pulled out of his pocket.

'Red nose,' said Sebastian shortly.

'Red nose?' echoed Caroline in astonishment. 'What on earth has Sandy's nose got to do with Veronica's bite?'

'Whisky,' Sebastian said shortly. 'Best thing for snakebite. Sandy'll be sure to have some on hand – red nose. See?'

'You are clever,' Caroline said admiringly. 'I'd never have thought of that.'

The ride down to the little cottage at the foot of the fell was a nightmare. Every few minutes we kept stopping to have a look at my ankle just to reassure ourselves that it wasn't swelling. Every second or two Caroline or Sebastian kept asking me if I felt sick, or anything. When at last we arrived at the cottage and knocked on the door, I had begun to feel quite light-headed, though I know now that it wasn't snakebite, but only shock and imagination.

The door opened as if the person inside had been waiting for us on the mat, and a Scottish voice said: 'Weel?'

Sandy Mactavish was small and thin. He had red, tousled hair, small watery blue eyes, set close together, a long, thin mouth buttoned up tightly at the corners, and, of course, a red nose.

'Oh, Mr Mactavish – have you got a spot of whisky handy?' Sebastian said. Sebastian never wasted time in beating about the bush.

'Whusky?' echoed Mr Mactavish, with a startled look. 'Noo why should ye be thinking I'd hae the whusky in ma hoose?'

Sebastian's eyes strayed past Sandy Mactavish's shoulder to

117

the untidy room beyond, where, on a rough wood table, stood a dirty tumbler and a tell-tale bottle.

'Mebbie ye'll be telling me what bairns like ye'll be wanting wi' the whusky?' said Sandy, moving his shoulders so that it hid the table from our anxious eyes.

'Oh, don't worry – we don't want to *drink* it,' Sebastian assured him. 'We want to put it on Veronica's foot.' Then, seeing Sandy's outraged expression, he added: 'She's been bitten by a snake. We only want a spot – honestly. A teaspoonful will do.'

'Och aye,' said the Scotsman. 'Come awa in wi' ye, and a'll dee ma best for ye under the circumstances. Bitten by a snake ye say?'

He led the way into the dark kitchen, toddled over to a cupboard by the mantelpiece, took out a small medicine glass, and poured some liquid into it out of the bottle on the table. He held it up to the light for a second, then glanced at us.

'A teaspoonful ye said ye'd be wanting?'

'Och aye,' said Sebastian, with a glint of mischief in his eyes. 'If ye're sure ye can spare it.'

The man poured about half of the liquid back into the bottle; then he handed the glass to us.

'Then ye can hae that,' he said. 'And never let it be said that Sandy Mactavish didna dae what he could tae help a puir bit lassie in distress.'

Sebastian pushed me on to the one chair the room contained and unwound the handkerchief. Then he stood holding the medicine glass and looking down at me anxiously.

'I have an idea this will hurt like the dickens,' he said. 'Think you can stand it, Veronica?'

'I expect I can,' I said weakly.

'Well, here goes!' He poured the whisky on the wound gripping my foot tightly at the same time.

I gave a shriek.

'Ouch! It burns like anything!'

'It'll go off in a minute,' Sebastian assured me. And sure enough, after a second or two, the burning pain faded and I was able to smile.

'Puir lassie!' said a Scottish voice behind us – we'd almost forgotten Sandy in our agitation. 'Ye look awfu' white. Would ye no' like a cup o' tae, lassie?'

'Oh, *please*,' I answered gratefully. 'I would like a cup of tea most awfully.'

He went to the fireplace where a small, brown teapot stood on the hob, and poured some thick, black liquid into a cracked cup, added a drop of milk and some sugar, and brought it to me. Now that he knew his beloved whisky wasn't in danger, he was quite affable, was Sandy. I drank the stuff he brought me, and though it was anything but nice, it was hot and I felt better for it.

'Well, let's be getting on, shall we?' Sebastian suggested after he had replaced the bandage. 'Feel equal to riding, Veronica?'

'Yes – I think so,' I said feebly.

We had had to go some distance out of our way to reach Sandy's cottage, and now we found ourselves out on the moorland road that skirted the fell, running more or less east and west from Newcastle to the Border.

'We may as well go home this way, now,' said Sebastian. 'It'll be just as quick and much easier going.'

There was a wide grass verge to the road, and we could have cantered along it, but none of us felt like cantering. We walked soberly in single file, feeling anything but easy in our minds.

Suddenly there was a hoot from behind us and the sound of a car approaching.

'I wonder who it is?' Caroline said. I had learned by this time that, barring weekends, you usually knew all the cars and their occupants.

'Gosh! Of all the luck!' Sebastian yelled. 'Why, it's Dr Ridley! I know his car.'

'So it is! ... Hi! Stop! ...'

We pulled our ponies across the road and the car slid to a standstill.

'What's the matter now?' said the doctor, letting down the window and putting out his head.

Breathlessly we explained about the snakebite and immediately the doctor was all attention. In fact, before we'd finished our explanation he had switched off the car engine and was out of the car, bag in hand.

Once again the none-too-clean hankie was unwound and my foot scrutinized – this time minutely – the doctor firing off questions all the while.

Had I actually seen the snake?' Had Sebastian or Caroline seen it? What colour was it? Did my foot hurt? Did it feel stiff? How did I feel myself?

'It was black,' I said firmly. 'The snake, I mean. And no one but me saw it. No, my foot doesn't hurt – except where Sebastian cut it.'

The doctor looked round at Sebastian questioningly.

'I sterilized the blade of my pocket-knife, sir,' Sebastian explained, 'and opened the wound to make it bleed. Then I sucked it good and hard.'

'Ah!' said the doctor, nodding his head. 'Good old-fashioned remedy, what!' Then he began to sniff. 'And what's this you've been putting on it, eh? Spirit?'

'Whisky,' said Sebastian. 'We got it at old Sandy Mactavish's – Pasture Cottage.'

'Yes – you'd get it there all right!' laughed the doctor. 'Trust old Sandy to have a spot of whisky about!' Then he turned to me. 'Well, young lady – there don't seem to be any symptoms of snakebite as far as I can see, but of course that may be due to the prompt action of Sebastian here. Couldn't have done better myself under the circumstances. If there's the least swelling or pain in that foot, ring me up at once. I'm quite sure you can wash out any fears of a black adder. Most likely what you saw was a harmless grass snake.'

'But the pain?' I said. 'The scratch on my ankle?'

'Done by a sharp stone, or a bit of heather perhaps, and you imagined the rest. It's amazing what the imagination can do!' He dived back into his car, produced a roll of bandages, and did up my foot again rather more professionally. 'Well, I'll be getting along.'

'Just a jiffy!' said Sebastian, his foot on the running-board. 'You don't have to tell them at the Hall – I mean Aunt June and the rest – about all this, do you, Dr Ridley? They'd get into a flat spin—'

The doctor's eyes twinkled.

'I see how it is! You're afraid they might cut up rough and curtail your activities, eh? Well, I won't give you away, if Veronica's foot stays as it is now. You'd better ring me up tomorrow morning, all the same, just to let me know everything's all right.'

'I'll do that,' agreed Sebastian. 'I'll ring you up from our place.'

We watched the doctor's car disappear and then rode homewards ourselves, feeling much more cheerful.

'I'll bet that's what it was – just coincidence,' Sebastian declared, as the Hall chimneys came into view amongst the trees. 'The grass snake just happened to be there when you cut your foot, Veronica, so of course you thought it had bitten you – especially when we'd been talking about that black adder at the Jingling Gate.'

'It was *black*,' I insisted.

'Imagination,' retorted Sebastian, 'as Dr Ridley said.'

Well, we were never to know. The fact remained that my foot didn't swell, nor did I have any after-effects. But I still stuck to my point – that the snake I'd seen was a black snake. We were thankful that Dr Ridley was such an understanding sort of man, for we felt that if he'd given us away the grown-ups might easily have forbidden us to go out on to the moors alone. The fact that nothing had actually happened to me wouldn't weigh with them in the least. Grown-ups can be terribly unreasonable!

'By the way, Veronica,' Sebastian said, as we rode round to the stables, 'just when you gave that blood-curdling yell up there on the Nob, I found that patch of white heather. I clean forgot about it in the uproar! The patch is a lot smaller than it used to be, so perhaps that's why it took such a lot of finding. Also it isn't out yet, but it's white all right – I remembered the place when I found it again. So all's well that ends well! Here's your spot of good luck!' He took a sprig of heather out of his buttonhole – I'd been far too het up to notice it before – solemnly broke it in two, and handed the bigger piece to me.

We met Fiona in the hall. She looked as fresh and cool as if she'd never heard the word 'tennis' in her life.

'Did you have a good time?' Caroline asked.

'Oh, super!' Fiona said, regarding us distastefully. I must admit that we weren't exactly tidy! Sebastian had bits of heather in his hair; my leg was daubed with blood, and there was a distinct smell of whisky about me. Caroline's face was streaked with the tears she had shed, and she'd caught her cardigan on a gorse bush and pulled the stitches, which certainly didn't improve the look of it.

'I had a perfectly marvellous time,' went on Fiona. 'Ian Frazer was my partner, and I must say he was decently dressed – new whites and everything.' She cast a sidelong glance at Sebastian to see how he took this world-shattering announcement.

'He *would*!' Sebastian answered. 'The little tick.'

'Well, anyway, we won,' Fiona went on triumphantly. 'And

look what I got for a prize.' She proudly held out for our inspection a brooch made in the form of two crossed tennis rackets.

'Jolly nice!' I exclaimed. It really was an awfully attractive brooch. 'What did Ian get?'

'Oh, the boys' first prize was a tennis-racket press,' said Fiona. 'It was awfully lucky because Ian broke his press last week, so he was just wanting a new one.'

'So of course you won,' Sebastian said in a scornful voice. 'For obvious reasons!'

Caroline and I glanced at each other significantly. We both knew quite well what Sebastian meant. It was no secret that Ian Frazer was the world's worst cheat.

'I don't know what you mean,' declared Fiona. 'Ian's a jolly good player. I wouldn't have won if I'd played with you.'

'Not in that way you wouldn't!' Sebastian flashed. 'So isn't it a good thing I cried off?'

'Who was there?' Caroline asked quickly, seeing that things were getting strained. 'The Listers, I suppose?'

'Yes, Richard and Elizabeth were there. And David Eliot of Dewburn, and of course Patience. There were two girls called Moffit, and some cousins of theirs – Alan and Dick something or other. I forget their surname. Well, I think I'll go and change – it's nearly seven o'clock. You'd better do something to your face, Caroline,' she added. 'Trixie will have a fit if she sees you like that.' She sauntered off, and we looked after her.

'Yes, I expect she's right – I'd better have a wash,' Caroline said, after a glance in the hall mirror. 'Coming, Veronica?'

'In just a minute,' I answered. 'I must just have a look at my foot to see if it's still OK. You go on; shan't be long!'

'Why do you always rub Fiona up the wrong way?' I asked Sebastian, as I replaced the bandage, having satisfied myself that my ankle hadn't swollen. 'Why do you hate her so much?'

123

Sebastian raised his eyebrows.

'Didn't know I did hate her. Now you come to mention it, though, I suppose I do. She's so – so – what I mean to say is she's decent-looking, and she never forgets it, or lets anyone else forget it either. She goes about all day long looking at herself – oh, I don't mean in mirrors, though she does plenty of that, too. I just mean she's never thinking about anything else but herself and her stupid good looks. I'd give anything just to take that smug, self-satisfied look off her face! One day I'll do it! She infuriates me.'

'I see...' I stared at Sebastian curiously. There was no denying the fact that there was a queer streak in him. He either liked you or he didn't, and woe betide you if he didn't – there were no half-measures about Sebastian! Moreover, it seemed to me that his likes and dislikes had neither rhyme nor reason. He disliked Fiona and Aunt June and Uncle John. Well, I could understand that all right, because, after all, they were living in his ancestral home. But then he disliked Perkins, the Scotts' chauffeur, too. I wondered if it was because Perkins was hired by Uncle John, but decided it couldn't be, because Trixie was the Scotts' dependant, as well, and he liked Trixie.

He disliked the village schoolmaster, and when I asked him why, he said: 'He roars in church like the bull of Bashan. Drowns everyone with decent voices. Can't stand people who roar!'

Another of his dislikes was Andrew Pilks, the under-gardener.

'He wriggles like one of the worms he digs up,' explained Sebastian. 'He agrees with every blooming thing anyone suggests – especially Aunt June. He'll promise you anything, but in the end you'll find it's Dickson who delivers the goods. Can't stand people who wriggle!'

124

Chapter 4

We Celebrate

The holidays slipped away. We made the most of them, I can tell you. Every day we went out riding, or played tennis, or had a picnic. Sometimes we swam in the lake at home, but several times we rode to a lovely place called the Monks' Pool, near Bliss Castle, where you could dive off the rocks. Often we joined up with friends of the Scotts – the Eliots. They lived some miles away, on the other side of the river where the Monks' Pool was, and there were two of them – David, who was fifteen, and Patience, his half-sister. She was only eleven, but she was a jolly good swimmer. Sometimes they brought friends of their own, the Listers that Fiona had talked about when she'd been telling us about the tennis party, and a dark girl called Judy Milburne. We had a grand time!

Don't think I forgot about my dancing in all this. I practised faithfully every morning before breakfast, and often again before we went out. I didn't have to keep my practising secret, now that Aunt June had decided I was to be a dancing teacher, so I didn't lock the morning-room door when I worked in there.

Sometimes Caroline came and watched me, always asking me first if I minded her being there. Fiona came too – without asking – and there was a strange, scornful look on her face as she watched me doing *pliés*, *grands battements*, and *développés*. Once Sebastian came, but I think he considered it rather on the dull side – all those exercises, and no real dancing at all –

but he was too polite to say so. Or perhaps he realized that my *pliés* and *battements* were like his scales and exercises at the piano – dull, but necessary.

Well, as I say, the summer holidays passed like a flash, and one awful day we realized with a shock that it was the beginning of September, and school looming up in the all too near future. It was beginning to feel like autumn. Already the swallows were collecting on the eaves of the house and on the telegraph wires; the heather was covering the moors with a froth of purple, and the bracken was turning colour. Trixie and Aunt June were beginning to fuss about clothes – especially Fiona's, as she was going to her new school in Harrogate at the end of the month.

One marvellous thing happened to lighten the gloom. I received a slip of paper to say that, despite Miss Stanley's dismal forebodings, I had passed my School Certificate. I hadn't got my Matric with it, but I had achieved an ordinary, straightforward pass. I felt frightfully thrilled.

'We must have a real celebration,' Sebastian said when he heard the news. 'A triumphal picnic, what-ho!'

'What a fuss!' Fiona said disdainfully. 'Anyone would think Veronica had done something wonderful. Why, I passed that stupid exam last year, and I got umpteen "credits".'

'You're older than Veronica,' said Sebastian, quite ignoring the fact that there was only a month in it, and that Fiona *had* done jolly well to get her School Certificate at just under fifteen. 'And you didn't get Matric with it, anyway.'

'That was only because I didn't get a "credit" in French,' argued Fiona.

'So *you* say!' scoffed Sebastian. 'Anyhow, we're going to celebrate Veronica's triumph. You needn't come if you don't want to.'

'What sort of a celebration shall we have?' asked Caroline.

'A picnic.'

'We've had loads of picnics,' objected Fiona. 'We've had a picnic nearly every day.'

'Ah, but this is to be a different sort of picnic,' explained Sebastian. 'This is to be a picnic-by-night.'

'They would never let us,' said Caroline. 'They'd say it was dangerous. Why it should be more dangerous to have a picnic at night than during the day, I can't think -- it isn't as if there were tramps, or wild animals—'

'I wish you'd shut up and let me finish what I was saying,' put in Sebastian. 'I was going to suggest we had our picnic by moonlight down by the lake. They couldn't object to that -- not if we explained that it was a celebration. We could have a huge bonfire by the boathouse, and a swimming gala, and a concert—'

'Concert?' we echoed.

'Gramophone records,' stated Sebastian. 'That's a portable Aunt June has, isn't it?'

'Yes, but—'

'But me no buts! Surely she wouldn't object to us having the loan of it?'

'No, but—'

'Oh, all right, go on then – explain the "but",' laughed Sebastian.

'I was going to say I'm afraid most of the records are pretty well worn out,' I said apologetically. 'You see, I play them rather a lot. Still, there are *some* that are OK.'

'I've got lots,' pronounced Sebastian. 'Loads of 'em. I'll provide the records, if you get the loan of the gramophone.'

'Right-ho,' we agreed.

All that day we prepared for our celebration. We carted barrow-loads of wood, and armfuls of bracken and heather down to the lake, piled dead branches on top, until by sunset we had a goodly pile.

'It looks as if we were going to burn a witch, or do-in poor old Dido, Queen of Carthage!' laughed Sebastian. 'The funeral pyre, what-ho!'

'You do think of horrid things, Sebastian,' grumbled Caroline. 'Mind what you're doing with that gramophone! It's just where we'll fall over it in the dark. You'd better put it over here in the boathouse. We'll bring the records down tonight when we come. By the way, what about light?'

'The fire will light things up enough, but if you girls don't like undressing in the dark, you'd better bring along a couple of candles. It'll be pretty murky in this place, especially before the moon is up.'

By the way, you mustn't think that, while we were making all these preparations for a glorious blaze, we forgot about the food question. Far from it! Indeed it occupied a front place in our thoughts.

'What about sausages?' said Sebastian. 'I saw some going in as we came out this morning.'

'Going in where?'

'Into the jolly old Hall. If that green van we nearly collided with wasn't Joseph Brawn and Sons, Pork Butcher, Burneyhough, then my name's not Sebastian!'

'Gosh! I believe you're right!' exclaimed Caroline. 'What it is to go about noticing things!'

'I've noticed something else, too,' went on Sebastian. 'We didn't have those sausages for lunch today, and they certainly won't be for dinner – Aunt June is far above sausages for dinner! – and they won't be for your supper. Too indigestible, according to dear old Trixie, so—'

'So they'll still be there – in the larder!' I yelled.

'Jolly good detective work, my dear Watson!' laughed Sebastian. 'Well, how about scrounging some of them? They can't refuse when it's for a celebration.'

'By the way, Sebastian,' put in Caroline, 'how do we cook them?'

128

Sebastian considered.

'Well, there are two ways. Either in a civilized frying-pan over the fire, or skewered on sticks like savages.'

'Savages!' we yelled. Even Fiona thought that the sticks sounded more fun.

We crashed into the house and waylaid Trixie. She was very decent, and let us have quite a lot of sausages when she heard what we wanted them for – three each, to be exact. She also handed over a slab of fruit cake, and half a pound of chocolate biscuits.

'We can boil a kettle and have Kafékreme to drink,' said Caroline.

'With Fizzy-Fountain lemonade for the toasts,' added Sebastian. 'Must have toasts at a celebration!'

After we left Trixie we went down the drive to Sebastian's home to see what we could collect there. We got quite a lot of stuff. Some cheese straws that Bella had just made, half a chocolate cake, and four lamb chops.

'To be eaten cold, after we've finished the sausages,' pronounced Sebastian. 'Well, I think we're OK for food. Don't eat too much for supper, you lot! Spoil our feast.'

It was odd getting up from the supper table and, instead of going to bed as usual, trekking down to the lake laden with food and gramophone records. I'd brought some of Aunt June's, after all – the ones that weren't too bad. We met Sebastian down by the boathouse. He'd got there before us, and had spent his time poking handfuls of straw soaked with paraffin in between the branches all round the foot of the bonfire, so when we put a match to it, it broke into flames with a mighty roar and lit up the landscape all around. It looked quite like fairyland, with the reflection of the flames leaping and flickering in the water and making the trees round the edges of the lake look even more dark and mysterious than they did in the daytime. On our little beach it was as light as day, and though before we'd lit the fire we hadn't felt much like bathing, we now thought it would be great fun.

'Come on, let's get in!' yelled Sebastian. 'Did you bring the candles for the boathouse, you lot?'

I produced them and Sebastian lit them for us because we hadn't remembered to bring matches. After which the three of us retired to the boathouse and changed into our bathing costumes.

The candles made the boathouse seem quite mysterious – not a bit like its ordinary, everyday self. Even our ancient bathing costumes – the same ones that Sebastian had shown me on that never-to-be-forgotten morning so long ago – looked romantic.

'I'll have my usual stripy one,' I said. 'Rhapsody in Stripes by Molyneux.'

'What did you say?' demanded Fiona.

'Oh, nothing. It's only a joke between Sebastian and me,' I explained.

'Well, I must say it seems a terribly silly sort of joke,' declared Fiona. 'As if a famous person like Molyneux would have anything to do with an awful stripy costume like that!'

'That's the joke!' I said with a giggle, remembering the ridiculous things Sebastian had said about the other costumes.

Fiona just stared at me in disdain.

'Golly! I do wish I wasn't quite so fat!' Caroline said with a sigh. She'd put on Spotted Peril, and it certainly *was* on the small side for her. 'I wish I had a figure like you, Veronica. It's funny but I've only just noticed what a lovely figure you have. I wonder if it's all those dancing exercises you do?'

'No, of course not,' put in Fiona before I had time to answer. 'Anyway, Veronica's no slimmer than I am.'

'No,' admitted Caroline. 'But she's different, somehow. Veronica looks like – well, like a statue, if you see what I mean. You look more sort of floppy.'

'How dare you! I do not!' exclaimed Fiona in a temper. 'I'm *much* slimmer than she is.' Then she gave me a sidelong look, and added maliciously: 'I shouldn't wonder if Veronica got quite fat.'

Well, of course, I never took much notice of Fiona's remarks, but all the same a thrill of fear ran through me. Supposing – just supposing – Fiona were to be right and I did get fat. I looked down at myself anxiously, and saw in the candlelight with a feeling of relief that my thighs – the danger-spot with all dancers – were no bigger than they had been. Moreover the flesh on them, and on my calves when I felt them, was hard to the touch. Thank goodness I wasn't flabby!

'Come on, let's go!' said Caroline. 'It looks lovely out there. Sebastian's in already.'

We didn't stay in the water long, though. The bonfire made it look warm but actually it was pretty cold, and the wind, when you got out of the shelter of the boathouse, had a nip in it that told us autumn was on the way.

We dressed quickly and gathered round the fire. It had burnt down a lot while we were having our swim, but though it didn't look quite so spectacular now, it was beautifully hot, and warmed us up in no time. The kettle was singing, and the sausages were all ready skewered on the sticks, just waiting to be cooked.

'About our concert...' began Sebastian, sorting out the records. 'Let's have the heavier stuff now, shall we? Then we can put on the lighter things like Chopin's ballet music – *Les Sylphides* – when we've finished supper. What about giving an exhibition of some of *Les Sylphides*, Veronica? You know the ballet, surely?'

'Oh, yes – rather! Madame taught me the Waltz. It's the most lovely music to dance to.'

'Oh, *do* dance it for us,' pleaded Caroline.

131

'All right – I will, after supper,' I promised. 'Can't now – I'm too hungry.'

'We'll put the record over here by the milk,' Sebastian said. 'Then it won't get all mixed up with the others. What shall we have on now?'

'*Warsaw Concerto!*' I exclaimed, turning over the pile.

'Slushy!' pronounced Sebastian.

'Oh, I don't know,' I said. 'Personally I rather like it.'

'I think it's awful,' said Fiona.

'Let me see,' drawled Sebastian in his most infuriating manner, 'your taste in music, Fiona, is for what is commonly known as "Boogie-woogie", isn't it? Things like *I Gotta Have Love*. Then, after you've sung the touching words, you fill in by making queer noises like "cha-cha-cha", and "bom-bom-bom", and that's "Boogie-woogie"!'

'No, it isn't. You don't know anything about it.'

'Don't I? Well, the other day I heard a wench on the radio doing it, and I thought she was an escaped lunatic, but it turned out that she was a frightfully famous exponent of "Boogie-woogie"! so what?'

'If you don't stop talking rot and watch what you're doing, your sausages will be as black as a cinder.'

'Like 'em black as cinders,' said Sebastian, placidly inspecting his supper. 'They're not nearly black enough yet. Did anyone remember to bring the mustard?'

'*I* did!' I said triumphantly. 'The ready-bottled sort. Here it is. Gosh! No, it isn't. It's celery-salt. I must have mistaken the bottle.'

'You *would*!' pronounced Sebastian. 'You're no use for anything that hasn't something to do with dancing, Veronica! ... Kettle's boiling! Where's that Kafécreme, someone? Now *don't* say you've brought a tin of treacle or something instead!'

But all was well. Caroline found the tin of Kafécreme

nestling beside the lamb chops, and Sebastian measured it into a big jug with a tablespoon.

'Three cups each,' he said, holding the spoon poised in mid-air. 'Think that'll be enough?'

'I should say so – counting the three bottles of lemonade we've got for the toasts.'

We ate our meal to the uplifting strains of the London Symphony Orchestra playing the Rachmaninoff Concerto. It was one of Sebastian's records, and it was the one they played in the Coward film, *Brief Encounter*, that Sebastian and I had talked about that day I'd met him in the northbound train.

When we had finished the lamb chops, and the chocolate biscuits, and drunk the last drop of Kafécreme, Sebastian rinsed our mugs with lake water and refilled them with lemonade. Then he stood up.

'Ladies and gentlemen,' he announced. 'The Queen! You always toast the Queen first.'

We all rose to our feet and clinked glasses. Then Caroline said: Speech!'

'Well – er...' began Sebastian. 'On this august occasion of Veronica's passing her School Certificate, I would like to say that we all think – we think—'

'Go on! Go on!' we all yelled. 'What do we think?'

'That she's done jolly well to pass the thing at all,' went on Sebastian. 'It's a wonder to me that anyone ever passes it – considering the stupid things they ask!'

'But you've passed it yourself – ages ago,' said Caroline.

'I was meaning *ordinary* people,' stated Sebastian. 'I was never ordinary. Always the little genius, yours truly. I remember how fluently I used to prattle away in Latin when I was in my cradle. "*Nil desperandum*," I used to say. "*Veni, vidi, vici!*" "*Noblesse oblige.*"'

'But that last's French,' I objected.

133

'French or Latin – it was all the same to me,' said Sebastian loftily. 'Now what was I saying when I was so rudely interrupted? Oh, yes – I want to give you the toast of the evening – Miss Veronica Weston!'

They all stood up, but I sat still because you never stand up yourself when your health is being drunk.

'And now what about a spot of *Les Sylphides*, Veronica?' went on Sebastian. 'Can you manage to dance after all that supper?'

'I'll try!' I laughed.

Suddenly there was an exclamation from Fiona.

'Gosh! I've slipped! Somebody pushed me! Look what's happened!'

'Well, what *has* happened?' said Sebastian, not sounding very interested.

'I've sat on it!'

'Sat on what? Not the marmalade?'

'No, you idiot! On the record – the record of *Les Sylphides*.'

There was a horrified silence. We all knew that Fiona had done it on purpose, but of course we couldn't prove it.

'You shouldn't have put it over there,' she said to Sebastian. 'How could I be expected to see it in the dark? I never expected a record to be there when I sat down.'

'I thought you said someone pushed you?'

'So they did.'

'Then in that case it wouldn't matter whether you could see it or not,' said Sebastian coldly. 'Well, that's the end of our dancing exhibition, Veronica. Never mind, we'll have it later on. And that's the end of the celebration, too – for *you*, Fiona, at any rate. You get out of here, and quick's the word!'

Fiona didn't argue – she knew Sebastian better than that! She left us without a backward glance. I have an idea she thought she'd got the best of it this time, as she'd had all the fun and we were left to clear up the mess. As Sebastian said, the beach wasn't big enough to hold both him and Fiona at that particular moment!

Chapter 5

A Pair of Ballet Shoes

Next morning I did my *barre* work as usual before breakfast. After that meal I went into the morning-room to finish off the centre work. I did a little piano practice as well, remembering Miss Martin's advice not to neglect my music, as it was very important that I should have a good musical groundwork if I wanted to be a dancer.

After I had finished it was nearly eleven o'clock. I changed out of my practice shoes and went off to the schoolroom, carrying them under my arm. Incidentally one of the ribbons was showing signs of wear and tear, so I resolved to sew it on before it got too bad to mend.

The others were all in the schoolroom when I got there: Caroline playing Patience on the hearthrug; Sebastian lounging by the french window; Fiona reclining on the ancient settee in one of the consciously graceful attitudes Sebastian hated so much. Her feet were tucked underneath her.

'I've got it out this time!' exclaimed Caroline, turning over the cards at lightning speed. 'No, I haven't! That king's in the way!'

'Put him in the space; then you *may* turn up a queen to go on top. Then the jack'll go on top of that, and you're out,' said Sebastian lazily.

'Gosh, so I am! What a brainwave! — if there *is* a queen. But there isn't, so I'm not out. Oh, dear! That's the fourth try this morning. I believe these cards have a spell on them!'

'How you can spend your time doing such silly things, I

can't imagine,' came Fiona's supercilious voice from the settee. 'Really, the things some people do!' She yawned delicately. 'For instance, those *pliés*, or whatever they're called, that Veronica does. Of all the stupid, ugly things—'

'I know they're not pretty,' I burst out. 'They're not meant to be. They're to keep your muscles supple. And *développés* are to give you strength—'

'Strength!' laughed Fiona. 'Are you aiming to be a strong man, then – like they have in a circus!'

I said nothing, knowing that it was quite useless to argue with Fiona when she was in a mood like this. Not so Sebastian, though. He liked nothing better than to take Fiona down a peg.

'I've seen you do some pretty silly-looking things,' he declared. 'For the uninitiated, I mean. What price those exercises you did when you learned to ride – lying down flat on Melisande's back and then sitting up again? Pretty mirth-provoking, what! Especially when she shied!'

'They were necessary!' snapped Fiona.

'So are Veronica's exercises. And they do at least make her graceful. You might try doing a few yourself, Fiona. They might improve your figure.'

Now Fiona's figure was perfect by any ordinary standards, and Sebastian knew it, but, as I say, he never could resist teasing her.

'How dare you!' she yelled, turning red. Then she uncurled her feet from beneath her, and stretched them out. As the settee back was between her and Sebastian, and Caroline was still busy with her Patience cards, neither of them saw anything peculiar about Fiona's feet. But I did! She was wearing a pair of pink satin ballet shoes – my shoes; the shoes Madame had given me; the shoes that had danced *Giselle* on Covent Garden stage. And this wasn't all either. She'd daubed a comic face on the toe of each of them with ink and red paint.

I gave a shriek of anguish. Then the blood rose to my head and I sprang at her. I'm afraid I lost my temper completely. I shook her as hard as I could, and then as she still laughed, I boxed her ears. Then I went on shaking until someone caught me by the arms and held me fast.

'What the dickens? Look here, this is going a bit too far!' said Sebastian's voice in my ear. 'Stop it, I say, Veronica! Fiona was only teasing.'

'Was she?' I yelled. 'Then what about my shoes?'

'Your shoes?' echoed Sebastian. Then he caught sight of Fiona's handiwork, and his voice froze.

'You did that, Fiona?'

'Yes, I did,' said Fiona. 'I think I've improved them, don't you? Brightened them up quite a bit. I never saw such mouldy-looking things when I took them in hand!'

'They were Madame's shoes!' I shouted at her. 'She'd danced *Giselle* in them. You *knew* how I loved them! You knew, Fiona. I told you!' Then I covered my face with my hands and burst into tears.

'You certainly have told us!' drawled Fiona. 'I'm sick to death of hearing about the stupid things! You ought to be grateful to me for ornamenting them a bit.' Then she added with a hateful little laugh: 'Cry-baby!'

But I was past being annoyed by a mere epithet. All I could think of was the awful thing that had happened to Madame's shoes. I just sobbed and sobbed, and Fiona went on laughing. Then, through my tears, I heard Sebastian say in a furious voice:

'You take that back, Fiona – what you said about Veronica!'

'I never take back what's true,' Fiona said sweetly. Then she turned and made a dash for the door. But Sebastian was there before her, barring her way.

'You go back and apologize to Veronica,' he ordered. 'On your knees, and be quick about it!'

'I will not! Let me go, this minute!'

Sebastian didn't move. Instead he said meaningly: 'Have you ever been beaten, Fiona?'

'Of course not! How dare you!' she said furiously. 'I'm a girl. Girls don't get beaten.'

'Don't they? Well, there's one who's going to, if you don't be quick with that apology,' drawled Sebastian. Then he snatched up one of my canvas practice shoes, that I'd put on the table, and stood brandishing it threateningly. 'Now, be quick! I can't stand here all day.'

At the time we were so het up that it all seemed terribly dramatic, but afterwards, when I thought about it, I saw how funny it really was – Sebastian standing there like an avenging angel, brandishing, instead of a flaming sword, an ancient canvas ballet shoe! Well, as I expect you know, an unblocked ballet shoe is as soft as a glove and couldn't possibly hurt anybody. So it says something for Sebastian's strength of personality that Fiona came back to where I stood, went down on her knees and made her apology. With a shock I realized that she was crying, a thing I'd never seen Fiona do before. I realized, too, that Sebastian had carried out his threat, and had effectively wiped off her face the self-satisfied look he so hated. Whether Fiona's tears were tears of shame, or anger, or both, I don't know.

'And now what about the shoes?' went on Sebastian, when she rose from her knees. 'What do you propose to do about them?'

'I d-don't know,' gulped Fiona.

'Well, start thinking about it, and be quick,' ordered Sebastian, still flourishing the shoe.

'I s-suppose the d-dry-cleaners...' hiccuped Fiona. 'M-mummy sent my party shoes to Britelites when I got ice-cream on them.'

'Good idea!' pronounced Sebastian. 'Get a letter written.

I'll dictate it.' He went to a cupboard, pulled out a writing pad, ink and a pen, and placed them on the table. 'Are you ready? . . .

'Messrs Britelite and Sons, Dyers and Cleaners, Newcastle-upon-Tyne.

Dear Sir,

Would you please dry-clean the ballet shoes I am sending you. I would be greatly obliged if you would take extra special care with them as they are irreplaceable and of great sentimental value. Thanking you in advance for the special care.

Yours faithfully,

(Miss) Fiona Scott'

Obediently Fiona wrote as he directed, and, glancing at Sebastian's face, I knew why!

'Now you'll have to find a box to pack them in,' he said inexorably when she'd finished. 'And lots of tissue paper. Oh, and some of that corrugated cardboard stuff to stop them getting squashed. And, of course, you'll have to pay for them yourself – out of your pocket money.'

'Well, can I go now?' Fiona asked when he had folded up the letter and put it into an envelope.

'Go?' Sebastian echoed. Then he struck an attitude. ' "Why get you gone! who is't that hinders you?" That's Shakespeare – *Midsummer Night's Dream* – in case you don't know. In other words, scram! Scoot! Begone! And the sooner the better!' His face had once more taken on its usual teasing aspect, and I knew that, as far as Sebastian was concerned, the episode was closed.

I often think how amazed grown-ups would be if they could know the things we do and think when they imagine we're 'playing nicely together' as they call it.

When Aunt June opened the schoolroom door not long after Fiona had fled, you'd have thought she'd have felt the tension in the air – the sobs, and slaps, the shrieks of anger and cold fury. But all she said, as she looked round, was: 'Ah! There you are – having a nice game of cards!' This was because she'd just caught sight of Caroline's Patience cards still lying on the hearthrug.

'Do you want us, Mummy?' Caroline asked hastily, trying to give me time to pull myself together.

'Well, yes, darling. I've just had a letter,' said Aunt June, holding up a sheet of thick, expensive notepaper. 'Such a nice letter. It's from dear Lady Blantosh of Blantosh Castle. She's having a garden fête – or if it's wet a "Do" in the parish hall – in aid of her Destitute Babies, and she wants us to help.'

'What at? Serving tea, or selling things?' demanded Caroline.

'Neither, dear. She wants you for the concert. I thought you might play the piano.'

There was a horrified silence. Then Caroline gave a positive wail of despair.

'Oh, *Mummy*! I couldn't – really, I couldn't! I'd die of fright – honestly I would. Fiona might do it though. She likes playing things in front of people.'

'U – m,' Aunt June said doubtfully. 'Fiona isn't as good as you are, Caroline. By the way, where *is* Fiona?'

'She – er – she went out,' stammered Caroline.

'Well, you might ask her about it,' Aunt June persisted. 'I do think you might at least *try* to play something, Caroline. Nobody will mind, I'm sure, if you make a few mistakes. What on earth is the use of your father giving you expensive music lessons if you never play anything to anybody?'

Poor Caroline grew red.

'I'm sorry, Mummy,' she said miserably. 'I just can't help it.'

'Well, you'll really have to do *something*,' went on Aunt June inexorably. 'Lady Blantosh says she's counting on you.'

Suddenly Caroline gave such a whoop that poor Aunt June jumped visibly.

'*I* know! Veronica will dance. She knows lots of dances don't you, Veronica? There's that one about a Sugar Plum Fairy that you were telling us about at the celebration, and that other one – Les something or other ... Veronica knows lots of them, Mummy!'

Aunt June turned to stare at me, and I was thankful that by this time my tears had dried.

'Dance?' she repeated, as if she'd never heard of the word. 'You don't mean that atrocious tap dancing, I hope?'

'Oh *no*, Aunt June!' I exclaimed. 'Caroline means ballet. The dances she's talking about are out of ballets – the Dance of the Sugar Plum Fairy is out of the *Casse Noisette*, and the Waltz is out of *Les Sylphides*. Then I expect she's seen me practising the Odette solo out of *Swan Lake* ...'

I stopped abruptly, afraid lest Aunt June might think I was wasting my time practising the dances from the ballets, but to my surprise she only said: 'Well, that's certainly an idea, if we can't think of anything better. I'll ask Lady Blantosh what she thinks about it. She's got some famous person, Madame somebody or other – I think she's a singer – coming up from London especially to open the fête. Under the circumstances she mightn't think dancing quite – quite – well, you know what I mean – not high class enough.'

'Ballet is one of the arts,' said Sebastian's voice from the window. 'You couldn't get anything higher class than ballet.'

We all turned to stare at Sebastian. I think we'd forgotten that he was still there.

'Indeed,' Aunt June said coldly, and I knew by the sound of her voice that she didn't like Sebastian any more than he liked her. 'And what do you know about it, may I ask?'

'Oh, I know something about ballet,' Sebastian confessed casually. 'I've often been to Covent Garden with my father.'

'I see,' said Aunt June, not sounding as if she were really very interested. 'Well, as I say, I shall consult Lady Blantosh. If she wants you to dance, Veronica, I suppose she'll provide you with something suitable to wear?'

'Oh, but I've got a frock, Aunt June!' I exclaimed eagerly, thinking of the snowy *tutu* hanging in my part of Fiona's wardrobe. 'And if I need anything else, Miss Martin will lend it me – I know she will. She often lends her students costumes for shows.'

Aunt June went out, muttering things about her family and its shortcomings, and we were left to discuss the concert. I wasn't terribly excited. According to Caroline and Fiona, Lady Blantosh wasn't a very exciting person, though there was no denying the fact that she had a heart of gold. Still, I didn't feel that she would appreciate the lovely Waltz from *Les Sylphides*. All of which goes to show how Fate has things up her sleeve for you, because that self-same concert proved to be the turning-point of my life.

Chapter 6

Les Sylphides

The next morning Aunt June said that she had rung up Blantosh Castle, and Lady Blantosh wanted me to dance at her garden fête.

'She seemed quite keen about it,' said Aunt June. 'I was really most surprised. And now I suppose you'll have to see about your costume, Veronica. You think Miss Martin would lend you one?'

'I'm quite sure she would,' I answered. 'Couldn't I go into town this afternoon? Trixie told me yesterday that she had some shopping to do, so I could go with her. I shall need a gramophone record of the Waltz besides the frock.'

'I thought you had the record,' Aunt June said. 'I understood Caroline to say you'd been using it to practise with?'

'I – as a matter of fact it's pretty well worn out,' I stammered.

'I never imagined gramophone records wore out,' stated Aunt June. 'I always thought they went on for ever.'

'It's not worn out,' came Caroline's voice. 'At least it is, but it's squashed as well.'

'Whatever do you mean?'

'I mean Fiona sat on it,' said Caroline. 'She did it on purpose, too!'

'Oh, no,' said Aunt June, who always took Fiona's part. 'If Fiona sat on it, I'm sure it was an accident. But, in any case, if the record is broken, of course you must get another one, Veronica.'

'I'll pay for it myself,' I volunteered. To tell you the truth, my conscience was pricking me a little when I remembered that I had worn out Aunt June's record by dancing to it, not by listening to it to improve my music as she thought, even if Fiona *had* sat on it afterwards.

But Aunt June said no; she'd pay for it herself as the garden fête was her affair, and what about the other dances?

'You did say you could do two?' she added.

'I'd simply love to,' I answered, 'if you think the people won't be bored.'

Aunt June said that that was beside the point – everyone went to a garden fête prepared to be bored. Anyhow, Lady Blantosh had mentioned two dances – one before the interval and the other after.

'She did say that you ought to have a third ready – in case of an encore,' added Aunt June. 'But I shouldn't think that's very likely!'

'Then I'll do the *Swan Lake* solo,' I said, 'and the Waltz from *Les Sylphides*. Then if they *do* want another, I can do the Dance of the Sugar Plum Fairy – I've got the record for that.'

'Then you'll need two new ones,' said Aunt June.

'Yes, the Tchaikovsky *Swan Lake* solo and the Chopin *Les Sylphides*,' I answered. 'Goodness! I hope there *is* a recording of the *Swan Lake* solo; I've never seen one. Anyway, I'll ask at the shop.'

I left Trixie in the town doing the shopping while I went to see Miss Martin. She was most interested when she heard about the garden fête, and she lent me a lovely white *Sylphides* dress. She packed it into a cardboard box, saying that of course I should have to iron it out before I wore it. For the benefit of those who don't know, I must explain what a *Sylphides* dress is like. It has a tight-fitting bodice made of satin

145

– dull, if possible – and a long, full net skirt reaching to the middle of the calves. It has tiny cape-like sleeves, and little wings fastened on to the back of the bodice.

Miss Martin also lent me some pale pink tights, which she said I'd need if I was going to wear a classical *tutu*. They weren't real silk, because these are almost impossible to get nowadays, but they were made of very fine lisle-thread, and they were fully fashioned. I can tell you they stayed up an awful lot better than the artificial silk ones I already had! Miss Martin also happened to have a pair of pink satin blocked shoes, exactly the right size – so I bought them out of my own money.

After this, I took a bus back to the centre of the town, where the gramophone shops were. And here my good luck changed to bad. Each shop I went to had every waltz of Chopin's except the one I wanted! They hadn't a recording of the Odette solo out of *Le Lac des Cygnes* either. The salesman in the last shop I went to was most obliging. He brought out all the catalogues and we pored over them together. Finally he stood upright, shook his head, and said that he was *afraid* there wasn't a recording of that solo, of if there was, he certainly hadn't come across it.

'Well, have you the Waltz from *Les Sylphides* – Chopin?' I asked despairingly.

The man said he thought he had. If I would wait just a moment... He retired to the back of the shop, and began to run his hands over the hundreds of records that were stacked on the shelves, whilst I waited at the counter in a frenzy of impatience. Finally, he came back and said he was frightfully sorry, but that the gentleman who was in this morning must have bought the last one.

I could have wept with disappointment. I could also cheerfully have killed the gentleman who'd come in that morning and taken away my beloved Waltz!

'Can we order it for you?' asked the record man, politely. But I explained that it was no use – it wouldn't be in time, because the thing I wanted it for was on Saturday.

All the way home in the car I wondered what I should do about it; whether I should cry off the whole thing, which I knew would make Aunt June furious; or whether I should just dance the Sugar Plum Fairy and trust to luck that the record behaved itself, and didn't go on playing the same bit over and over in that maddening way records have when they're getting old. The only other alternative was to ask someone at the garden fête to play for me, but to be quite frank, I didn't think it at all likely that anyone could play Chopin's music, let alone Tchaikovsky's, at a moment's notice – even if anyone *had* the music for the Odette solo.

I was so silent that Trixie asked if I felt ill.

'No – not ill. Just worried,' I told her.

Then, just as we approached the Hall gates, I had a sudden idea . . . Sebastian! I wondered if, by any chance, he had any of the records I needed. I was amazed I hadn't thought of it before.

'Trixie!' I shrieked. 'I must get out quickly! Perkins – stop!'

Perkins obligingly stopped and I got out.

'It's all right – I'll walk up,' I said. 'You needn't wait. I'm going to see Sebastian. I've just had a brainwave.'

The casement windows of the lodge were open and, as I walked over the grass towards the little green door, the sound of music reached me. Someone was playing Grieg's *Holberg Suite*, and playing it extremely well.

I stood still and listened. I had often tried to play it myself, but had never been able to render it with such – 'authority' I think is the word. The music began on a rising crescendo of lovely, broken chords; then came the haunting melody, picked out by the left hand. After this, the loud bass part, and a new

147

air brought in by more broken chords in the treble.

Then I knew that the unseen pianist was none other than Sebastian – Sebastian whom I had never heard play, but whose secret ambition I knew was to make music his career. Yes, I knew without a doubt that it was Sebastian. It was *like* Sebastian. Nobody but he could play it in exactly that way.

The music ended on the final, crashing chords, and the trill. There was a pause. Then, before I had recovered from my daydream, another melody came floating out of the window – a dreamy melody, this time; a melody that made you think of green woods, and graceful larch boughs of glimmering water and the pale evening sky . . . the Waltz from *Les Sylphides* . . .

Before I knew what I was doing, I had kicked off my heavy shoes, thrown aside my cardigan, and was dancing. There, in my faded cotton frock, my feet bare, on the strip of velvet lawn which was my first stage, I danced the Waltz as I had never danced it before. The lacy, arching trees, the emerald turf, the pale ghost of a new moon between the larch boughs – I put them all into my dancing. It wasn't till afterwards, when I thought it over, that I realized I had danced the Waltz in its rightful setting – a woodland glade.

Then suddenly the dance was ended. The music died away, and I was brought down to earth by a voice from the window – Sebastian's voice. It said: 'Very nice, Veronica! I watched you all through. It was grand!'

An awful feeling of disappointment shot through me.

'Oh – but I thought it was *you* playing, Sebastian.'

He laughed.

'Oh, no! That was the jolly old gramophone – Eileen Joyce, in fact. I bought that record in town this morning, so I was trying it to see what it was like. Then I looked out of the window and saw you dancing.'

'It's strange,' I said, 'but when I was listening to the *Holberg*

Suite, I thought how like *you* it was, Sebastian. That's strange, isn't it?'

'The *Holberg Suite*?' repeated Sebastian. 'You heard that too? Oh, the record I was talking about – the Eileen Joyce – was that last thing, the Chopin waltz. It was *me* playing the Grieg *Holberg Suite* on the piano all right. I often play it – it appeals to me.'

I gave a sigh of relief.

'Oh, I'm so glad! I'd have been terribly disappointed if the *Holberg Suite* hadn't been you, Sebastian.'

'What made you come down here, anyway?' asked Sebastian, swinging himself over the window-sill to stand beside me on the garden path. 'Were you just passing, or what?'

'Oh, no. I've just come back from Newcastle,' I explained. 'I went in with Trixie to borrow a frock to wear at the garden fête on Saturday and to try to get a record for my dance. But they hadn't got it – a beastly man had been in this morning, and pinched the last one – so I was coming to see if *you* had it...' Then I gave a shriek of joy. 'But of course everything's all right now – you *have* got it. I can borrow yours.'

'Welcome!' said Sebastian promptly. 'If you wouldn't mind telling me which record you're talking about.'

'I mean the one I just heard, of course – the one I danced to – the Waltz from *Les Sylphides* – the one—'

'The beastly gentleman pinched,' laughed Sebastian. 'That would be me all right! I got it this morning at Windows. You can have it and welcome. As a matter of fact I was going to hand it over to you – to make up for the one Fiona squashed.'

'Oh, *thank* you, Sebastian,' I said. 'That was most awfully decent of you. Well, now there's only the *Swan Lake* Odette solo. I suppose you haven't a record of *that*?'

He shook his head.

'I doubt if there is one. I can play it, though.'

I stared at him unbelievingly.

'Not really?'

'Honest injun.'

He swung himself back into the room again, sat down at the piano, remained for a moment in thought, then played my solo – perfectly, and with that same indefinable air of authority I had noticed in the *Holberg Suite*.

'And you'll play it for me at the garden fête?' I said when he'd finished.

He made a face.

'I'll do it for you, Veronica,' he said, 'because you're in a jam. We *artistes* must stick together. Otherwise I wouldn't go near the dashed thing!'

'Oh, Sebastian – you *are* decent!' I said again. 'I'll never, never forget it. I'll be grateful always.'

'Utter not rash vows, fair lady!' said Sebastian, relapsing once more into his usual bantering self. 'You don't know what I might want you to do for me in the near future, when you're a world-famous *ballerina* and I'm a poor, struggling musician, playing at street corners to earn my daily crust!'

'I think,' I said looking back at him, 'it's much more likely that *you'll* be a world-famous conductor, and I'll be a struggling dancer, trying to eke out a living on the halls!'

'Well, here's the record,' said Sebastian, handing it over to me. 'And now, get thee hence, damsel! I have work to do!' So saying, he shut the window firmly, and in a moment or two I heard the sound of scales being played on the piano. There being nothing else for it, I went up the path towards the house, holding the precious record carefully under my arm.

Chapter 7

I Meet an Old Friend

It was wet on Saturday, so the garden fête was hastily changed into a Bring and Buy Sale, and was to be held in the parish hall instead of in the grounds of Blantosh Castle. There was one good thing about it – I'd have a proper stage to dance on, instead of just grass. Grass might have done all right for the Waltz, but it certainly would have been awkward for the other things, as I couldn't have done them *en pointe*.

Of course we *would* have a puncture! It was the little car too because something had gone wrong with the big one, and you had to get out and fix a jack under the wheel. Perkins wasn't with us, either, because Aunt June said there wasn't room for him. She was right too. By the time Fiona had spread herself out so that her frock wouldn't get crushed, and Caroline had got in front with a whole lot of cakes that Aunt June was taking over for the tea, there wasn't any too much room for me and my precious *tutu*. I'd packed the *Sylphides* dress in a suitcase along with my tights, shoes, and other things, and put them in the boot.

'I do wish you wouldn't squash me, Veronica!' Fiona said, as we drove off. 'I've never known anything take up so much room as that frock.' She shot a venomous glance at my unoffending ballet dress. 'Couldn't you have put it in the boot as well?'

'It would have got frightfully crushed,' I retorted. 'Really, the only way to carry a *tutu* is out flat like this.' I glanced

151

down with pride at the snowy ring of tarlatan, resting lightly on my knees.

'Well, it wouldn't really matter if it *was* crushed,' went on Fiona. 'A village concert like this isn't at all an important thing, you know.'

'Every time you perform is important when you're a dancer,' I told her. 'You must always do your best, no matter who your audience is.'

'But you're *not* a dancer,' insisted Fiona. 'You're only going to *teach* dancing, so I don't see that it matters.'

I blushed hotly, having totally forgotten my guilty secret. Then just at this moment, as I say, we got a puncture. In a way it was a relief, because it stopped me having to answer Fiona's awkward questions, but in another it was awful. Aunt June didn't seem to know the least thing about punctures. At first she wanted Caroline and me to walk back home – about a mile and a half – and bring Perkins to change the wheel, but, as I pointed out, by the time we'd got there and Perkins had walked back with us to the car – because he'd *have* to walk seeing that there wasn't another car – the Bring and Buy would be over.

In the end, Caroline and I did it, whilst Fiona made what she considered to be helpful suggestions, being very careful all the time not to touch anything that might dirty her hands. Fortunately I'd often seen Daddy's friend, Mr Salmon, take off a wheel, and sometimes I'd helped him, so I knew all the things you had to do and not to do – like not jacking up the car until you'd got the nuts unscrewed, and putting two chocks of wood under the back wheel to stop the car slipping off the jack, once you'd got it wound up, and so on. Still, it's one thing to watch a grown-up person do a thing, and even to help him, and quite another to do it all by yourself. However, as I say, we managed it at last; we even remembered to put the tools away.

We got back into the car, and Aunt June told Fiona to hold my frock, because my hands were anything but clean. I have an idea she was thinking more of the effect my muddy *tutu* would have on Lady Blantosh than my own feelings in the matter!

By the time we got to the parish hall and had parked the car, the Bring and Buy was well under way. We went into the building by a back entrance in order to avoid the masses of people who were surging about in the main hall. When we got to the ladies' cloakroom we had to wash, owing to the puncture, and I can tell you it took us ages to get clean because we'd managed to get an awful lot of oil on ourselves, as well as mud, and oil is about the worst thing on earth to wash off! We used the same water to save time, and bumped our heads together during the process. As the saying goes – 'More haste, less speed!' It was certainly so in our case!

At last we were clean once more, and then I began to dress in readiness for my first dance, while Fiona washed her hands in hot water in preparation for her pianoforte solo. It was to be one of Brahms' waltzes, and I must say, when I'd heard her playing it yesterday, she didn't do it awfully well. She kept the loud pedal down all the time to cover up her mistakes, and her fingering was all wrong, because she never could be bothered to practise slowly. Fiona always tackled a new piece of music at top speed, and then said she 'knew it'.

Caroline had propitiated Aunt June by agreeing to play a duet with Fiona, on condition that she played the bottom part, because no one ever listened to that.

Meanwhile I had retired behind a screen that someone had thoughtfully provided, and removed all my things – that's the worst of a ballet dress; you can't leave anything on underneath or it shows. I pulled on my tights, wriggled my jock-belt on top to keep them up – and me in! – and then, with the utmost care, I proceeded to insert myself into the *tutu*. It's made all in one

153

with the frilly trunks, so you step into it, feet first. Fortunately it had a zip fastener down the side, so I didn't have an awful lot of hooks and eyes to do up. Finally, I put on my beautiful pink satin point shoes, criss-crossing the ribbons, the outside ribbon over the inside one, and tying them in a neat little bow at the side of the ankle. I sleeked back my hair in the severely classical style, put a net over it, and fastened it down firmly at the sides and the back with hairgrips, so that it would not come down, no matter how many *pirouettes* I did. After which I made up my face – not with heavy greasepaint, for there was no artificial lighting to speak of in the parish hall, but with ordinary lipstick, eyeshadow, and powder. I'd bought them all in Newcastle yesterday. I'd also bought an eyebrow-pencil and I used it to lengthen my eyes a little at the corners. When I stepped back to see the effect in the long glass, thoughtfully provided by the same unknown person, I gasped. Was it really me – that slim dancer, clad in the traditional, classic *tutu*; that girl with the dreamy face, and large, dark eyes? Did those beautifully shaped limbs – slender, yet rounded – really belong to me? For a few seconds I stood quite still, refusing to believe it. Then, with a singing in my heart, I knew that it was true!

'Veronica!' came Caroline's voice, shattering my daydream. 'Veronica! Are you nearly ready? They're just going to begin the concert now. Lady Blantosh is taking her Madame Some-body on to the platform to make a speech. Then, after she's finished, it's Fiona's Brahms, and after that it's your dance.'

I came out from behind the screen, and there was a queer little silence that I knew was admiration. Then Caroline looked round – she'd been watching the people on the platform through a crack in the door.

'Veronica! How perfectly *gorgeous* you look!'

'Thank you,' I said, dropping a curtsy. 'It *is* a nice frock, isn't it?'

'Oh, but it isn't just the frock,' persisted Caroline. 'It's *you*, Veronica. You look like a flower, doesn't she, Fiona?'

Fiona said nothing, but I knew by her silence, and by the way she turned her back on me, that I looked nice. I'm afraid that I gloried in it!

Then, as I stood there, a startling thing happened. A voice came from the hall beyond our little dressing-room – a voice whose tones I knew well. How often had I hung upon them in those far-off days in London! I couldn't believe my ears, because the voice, speaking in broken English, was Madame's voice!

I dashed to the door in an effort to see the stage.

'Look out!' came Caroline's warning tones. 'They'll see you! It'll spoil the whole thing if they see you.'

'But don't you *understand*,' I said, shaking her off. 'It's Madame – Madame herself!'

'It's Madame Viret,' Fiona said stiffly.

'Of course I know it's Madame!' I exclaimed. 'I don't need you to tell me that. No one else – no one in all the world could speak just like that. It's Madame – my Madame! She taught me how to dance.'

Fiona stared at me.

'Oh, no – she couldn't have. She couldn't *possibly* have taught you to dance, Veronica. You're making a mistake; lots of people talk in broken English. She's a very famous person; besides, she's a singer. Mummy said so.'

'Then Aunt June's wrong,' I said flatly. 'She isn't a singer at all – she's a dancer. I mean, she *was* a dancer, and of course she's famous – I told you so, only you wouldn't believe me. She was the most famous dancer of her day, but of course you can't go on dancing for ever and ever, so now she's passing on her art to other people.'

'You needn't get so excited about it,' Fiona said loftily.

'But I *am* excited! I'm – I'm – oh, just to think of dear

Madame out there in the hall, only a few steps away, where I can see her, and speak to her—'

'Well, you certainly can't go rushing out dressed like that,' Fiona told me. 'You'll just have to wait until the performance is over.'

I sighed. Of course she was right. I certainly couldn't dash out into the middle of all those people, dressed like a swan in *Le Lac des Cygnes*! Much less could I throw my arms round Madame's neck, and cry for joy, as I dearly wanted to. As Fiona said, I should just have to wait. And wait I did, shivering a little with nerves and excitement.

Then it was time for my solo. Sebastian came to the door of the dressing-room to see if I was ready – a strange, tidy, grown-up Sebastian, with his usually ruffled black hair sleeked down flat, and long black trousers, instead of the familiar well-worn riding-breeches or khaki shorts.

'Are you coming, Veronica?'

He sat down at the grand piano and waited, whilst I walked on to the stage in the way Madame had taught me, and stood there at the back, hands crossed on my snowy *tutu*.

And then the well-known music filled the room. Sebastian played by memory, so he was able to watch me all the time. He was the most perfect accompanist, seeming to know by instinct exactly when to slow the music up just a little, and when to quicken it so that I didn't have to hold my positions too long. No wonder I danced as I had never danced before. I danced principally for Madame, to show her that I hadn't forgotten all the things she'd taught me, but I danced for Sebastian too – Sebastian playing for me so beautifully that his music made me feel as if I were floating on the melody, like a real swan on a moonlit lake.

I had forgotten all about the people in the hall, and when the dance ended and they burst into applause, I was terribly surprised and taken aback. I curtsied low as Madame had taught me – first this way, then that; then ran off into the wings (which consisted of a couple of large screens) to recover my self-possession.

The clapping went on and on. In fact it got louder, if anything.

'You'll have to do something else, Veronica,' said Sebastian's voice in my ear. 'What about the Sugar Plum Fairy? That's the right dress for it, isn't it?'

'Oh, yes,' I panted. 'Do you think I might have a minute's rest?'

'Of course,' said Sebastian. 'Tell you what – I'll go back and play them something for a couple of seconds. That'll keep them quiet!'

I leaned against the wall and relaxed, listening to Sebastian playing the *Holberg Suite*. The audience seemed to like it tremendously, for they clapped like anything when he finished, and if Aunt June hadn't appeared on the stage with the record of the Sugar Plum Fairy, and announced that her niece, Veronica Weston, would dance again, I think that Sebastian would have had to give an encore. Aunt June didn't look too pleased, I imagined. Sebastian *had* rather shown up Fiona's bad playing, but of course it wasn't his fault – he'd merely been giving me time to get my breath.

I walked out into the wings, and rose *sur les pointes*. The first notes of Tchaikovsky's music were falling on the air like drops of ice tinkling into a crystal goblet. I saw in my imagination the snowy woods round Bracken Hall on a winter's day – the fir trees standing motionless, like enchanted princesses, their frosted arms outspread. I heard in my mind the church bells sounding thin and unreal in the cold, blue air. All this I thought of as I executed the crisp, clear-cut steps of that wonderful dance of the Sugar Plum Fairy. I was a maiden of the ice; a snow queen; a frosted fairy of pink and silver,

157

I was a maiden of the ice, a snow queen

with a brittle crown of frozen dewdrops on my head. All this I tried to express in my dancing.

The clapping burst out louder than ever when I finished the dance. I had to come back on to the stage three times and curtsy, and even then it didn't stop. Some people at the back began to stamp their feet and shout *encore*, and finally I had to explain that I really couldn't dance any more just now because I hadn't got any breath left, but that I would dance again after the interval. Then I ran off into the dressing-room, and flopped into a chair, breathing hard. The Dance of the Sugar Plum Fairy isn't at all an easy dance to do, though it looks so charming and effortless.

'Oh, Veronica – you were wonderful!' Caroline said. 'I never imagined you could dance like that. I never imagined *anyone* could. I want to learn to do it. I want to learn *now*! Do you think Mummy would let me leave Miss Gilchrist and go to your Miss Martin?'

'I expect she would – if you asked her,' I laughed. 'Miss Martin's a lot cheaper!'

'Well, I'm going to ask her. And by the way,' added Caroline looking round, 'where's Fiona? It's our duet after this.'

'It's all right – I'm here,' came Fiona's voice from the window. 'You needn't get all hot and bothered.'

'But I *am* hot and bothered. I'm simply terrified!'

'Don't be silly!' snapped Fiona crossly. 'What do a few stupid people matter, anyway? They don't know a thing about music or – or dancing – or anything. They'd clap you no matter how ghastly you were – even if you played wrong notes all the time. They always do at these things!'

I glanced at Fiona curiously. I had an idea she didn't like the way the people had applauded my dance.

I had plenty of time to change, as my other dance wasn't until after the interval. I could hear poor Caroline's bass notes booming away, as she and Fiona played their duet. As I carefully hung up the *tutu* on a peg, and slipped on the long white frock Miss Martin had lent me, I heard Fiona galloping away in the treble, with the loud pedal down all the time as usual. She was playing as if she were in a rare temper, I thought.

I released my hair from the net for the *Sylphides* dance, letting it fall naturally on my shoulders, only fastening it at the sides with a couple of hairgrips, so that it shouldn't get in my way. Almost before I knew it, I was back on the stage again, dancing to Sebastian's gramophone. Sebastian himself was crouched down beside it, and I knew instinctively that he would stop it at exactly the right moment.

I can't say that I danced the Waltz as well as I had danced it that day on the grass outside Sebastian's window, but I think I did it fairly well. As Fiona said, the people were easily pleased, and they clapped as much as they had done for the other dances – indeed, I think more. When at last I escaped into the dressing-room, Fiona was looking like a veritable thundercloud.

'They like you a lot better than our duet, Veronica,' sighed Caroline. 'And no wonder! I think our duet was *awful*. I lost my place twice, and Fiona—'

'You needn't say *I* lost my place!' yelled Fiona. 'I wouldn't do anything so silly!'

'No, but you played half of it in sharps instead of flats,' said Caroline bluntly.

'I did not!'

'Yes, you did!'

And then, before there was a stand-up fight between the two of them, the dressing-room door opened, and someone came in – a small, graceful person beautifully dressed in black. She wore a tiny black hat, trimmed with white feather flowers and a veil, long white gloves, and little button-up boots of French kid.

'*Madame!*' I shrieked. Then, forgetting all about Fiona and her supercilious stare, forgetting all about the other girls in the room, forgetting everything, I threw my arms round Madame's neck, and burst into tears.

'My leetle one! *Mon petit chou*,' said Madame, patting me gently. 'So much improved! By zat I mean ze dancing and ze ap-pearance. Ze technique – he has advanced, yes. But zat will improve still more. You have had many lessons, *chérie*?'

'Oh, yes – I've had quite a lot of lessons from the Miss Martin you told me about,' I said, drying my eyes. 'But, of course, not as many as I'd have had if I'd been able to stay in London.'

'Ah, well – per'aps zat ees all for ze best. Who knows?' pronounced Madame surprisingly.

'But how could it possibly be for the best?' I asked. 'What do you mean?'

'I mean...' Madame considered the matter gravely. 'I mean eef you stay in London, you dance. Eef you are gone in Northumberland, you *think* – and you dance a leetle also. But ze *think* – he is important, yes! Your thoughts, zey are charming ones – all about ze woods, and ze 'ills, and ze flowers of zis so-beautiful Northumberland. I see eet in your dancing.'

'Then you really think I've improved, Madame?' I asked eagerly.

'*Sans doute*. You 'ave improve incomparably,' answered Madame, who loved to use long words, though she *did* accent them all wrongly. 'And your ap-pearance, *chérie*, your looks, zay are *tout à fait ravissantes*! Ze country air, and ze good food – zey 'ave assuredly transformed my leetle ugly duckling into a leetle swan – yes! Ze arms so round' – Madame put several r's into the word – 'ze shoulders – ah, *beau-ti-ful*!'

'You don't think I've got *fat*, Madame?' I said in horror, remembering Fiona's words at the celebration.

Madame laughed like a tinkle of little silver bells.

'*Oh, là! là!* Fat? But no, no, *no*! You are quite ze perfect

161

figure for ze *danseuse*. So slender – so rounded! And ze deemples, zey 'ave come, so and *so*!' She pressed her white-gloved finger gently into my cheeks. '*Oh, là! là!* And to find you here?'

'I think it's me who ought to say that!' I laughed. 'After all I *live* here now, you know. But you, Madame – to find *you* at a – a—'

'To find me at a Bring What You Buy – zat amuse you, hey? Well, it amuse me, too! But to do the obligation for my dear Lady Blantosh, I do things strange to me!' she laughed. 'Eet ees so al-ways! She command; I obey! Eet ees right, yes?'

'Sebastian says everybody does what Lady Blantosh wants!' I laughed. 'He says she's got the evil eye!'

'Ze evil eye?' echoed Madame. 'But 'ow ees eet? Ah, I ondairstand – ze squint! But no, I think eet ees ze eye full of good, even eef eet does not look quite straight.'

That was just like Madame, I thought – always to think the best of people. Incidentally it wasn't the least bit like Sebastian. He didn't like Lady Blantosh because she squinted and wore awful clothes, and nothing would make him see how good and kind she really was.

Suddenly I looked round the dressing-room. Fiona had disappeared long since – I think she didn't like Madame's flowery way of speaking, and her lavish compliments. Caroline and the other girls had gone too, and we were alone.

'Madame!' I said urgently.

'Well, my leetle one?'

'Madame – I want to dance!' I burst out. 'I *must* dance!'

'*Mais oui!* But of *course* you must dance! Of course! Of course! What else?'

'It's no use saying "of course" like that,' I went on. 'You see Aunt June doesn't realize it – or Uncle John. No one does but me – and Sebastian.'

'Sebastian?' repeated Madame.

'He's the boy who played for me.'

'Ah yes, the pianist?' said Madame. 'A very talented young man, that one! He has the touch quite exquisite! He will go far!'

'Yes, but what about me?' I said. 'What about my dancing, Madame?' I knew that soon, soon people would come and snatch Madame away, and I'd see her no more. 'What must I do?'

'You must dance, *naturellement*,' Madame said definitely, gesticulating with her small, exquisite hands. 'I will speak to ze good aunt – and ze *oncle* too, eef eet ees *nécessaire*. I weel arrange! Leave eet to me.'

'Oh, Madame – *thank* you!' I said fervently. I had implicit faith in Madame when she wore her determined look as she did now. 'I *will* leave it all to you.'

'Then *au revoir*, my leetle one! I see you soon – in London!' With a final pat on my cheek she was gone, and I was left in the dressing-room alone.

For a long time I stood quite still in the middle of the empty room, while thoughts crowded upon me. For the first time I saw Madame as she really was. In London I had merely taken her for granted as the greatest dancer of her time, but now I realized that she wasn't young any more. Her dark hair was already streaked with grey, and her figure was no longer that of the girl I had so passionately adored in the photograph on her studio wall. But I knew, also, that she would never really grow old; that she would always remain beautiful because of her charm and her vivacity; because of the grace of her every movement, her exquisite hands that spoke to you more eloquently than words, but above all because of the kindness and generosity that looked out of her large, dark eyes. Madame was one of those women about whom people say: 'Amazing how she keeps her youth! Why, let me see, she must

163

be – well, old enough to be a grandmother!'

I thought of all this as I stood there, and lots of other things besides – Jonathan, and Mrs Crapper (I hadn't thought of them for a long time – I confess it!) – and above all, the Sadler's Wells Ballet School. It seemed a lot nearer now!

Madame was as good as her word. Going home in the car Aunt June broached the subject.

'That Madame Viret – I forget the rest of her outlandish name – was quite impressed with your dancing, Veronica,' she said as we left the parish hall behind. 'She thinks you ought to take it up professionally.'

She paused, and I waited breathlessly.

'A school called Sadler's Wells I understood her to say is the best place to learn. It's in London,' went on Aunt June. 'She thinks you ought to go there. In fact she is arranging for an interview – or whatever it is they call it.'

'Audition,' I said.

'Yes – audition. She thinks that, under the circumstances, they might give you a scholarship.'

'Oh, Aunt June!'

'It isn't a boarding school,' continued Aunt June. 'We'd have to arrange for somewhere for you to stay during the term – of course you would come back here in the holidays. Perhaps that Mrs Cripps—'

'Crapper,' I corrected gently but firmly.

'Crapper, then. She seems a good-hearted sort of woman. Perhaps we could persuade her to have you as a paying guest.'

'I'm sure she'd have me,' I assured Aunt June.

'Well, yes – I think you must really go,' said Aunt June just as if it was her idea in the first place, and she were trying to persuade *me*. 'Madame Viret is a very famous person, you know. I hope you realize, Veronica, what a great honour she is doing you? You're a very lucky girl!'

I opened my mouth to say that of *course* Madame was a

famous person, and that of *course* it was an honour for her even to speak to me, let alone go to all that trouble for me. Then I closed it again, realizing that I couldn't ever make Aunt June understand what I felt. I don't believe she'd even taken it in that I'd been Madame's pupil for two whole years!

'Well, as I say, Madame Viret very kindly said she would arrange for your audition, and she will let us know when it is to take place,' Aunt June was saying. 'Of course you'll be going to London almost immediately. We shall just have to pay your school fees for the term you aren't there. A great pity!'

I felt like saying that if only Aunt June had listened to me in the first place, all this would never have happened. But I didn't. I felt that it would have sounded terribly ungrateful, and after all I *was* grateful. Aunt June had done what she considered to be her duty – had taken me in, and looked after me. She had been kind to me in her own way. I had been happy at Bracken Hall, knowing Sebastian and Caroline, learning to ride, and everything. I felt quite glad that I'd be coming back again in the holidays.

'It appears that your School Certificate won't be entirely wasted,' went on Aunt June. 'Madame Viret assured me that they like educated girls at the Sadler's Wells School. The modern idea, I suppose! Quite the contrary to what I imagined. In fact, you'll still go on with your studies – French, art, English literature, biology, history, and things like that – although, being over fifteen, you'll naturally be in the Senior School.'

She went on telling me all the things I already knew. As a matter of fact, there wasn't much I *didn't* know about the Wells!

Chapter 8

Catastrophe!

A week after Lady Blantosh's Bring and Buy Sale, Aunt June got a typewritten letter from the secretary of the Sadler's Wells School of Ballet saying that my audition was to be on the following Friday. It appeared that Madame had called to see Miss Martin in Newcastle on her way back to London, and between them they had fixed things up.

My thoughts were in a positive whirl, and by the time Thursday came, I was so excited I could neither eat nor sleep. Aunt June had booked a first-class sleeper for me from Newcastle to King's Cross, and I was to be put in special care of the sleeping-car attendant, who in his turn was to get me a porter at the other end of my journey. The porter would get me a taxi, and I was to go straight to Mrs Crapper and stay there until it was time for my audition at twelve o'clock. My ticket had already been bought and was reposing in the little drawer of my dressing-table. Perkins was to take me to the station in the car to catch the night train, which went at ten thirty-five. It was all very simple.

All very simple... How is it that it's always the simple things that turn out to be the most difficult, whereas, when you see breakers ahead, the sea is sure to turn out to be as calm as a millpond?

The Thursday morning dawned grey and misty. Aunt June was going to visit friends at Horchester, ten miles away. She took Perkins with her because of the mist, and promised she'd be back by nine o'clock at the latest so that there'd be plenty of time for Perkins to take me to the station. I was to be all ready to go, she said.

For the umpteenth time I checked over my dancing things – pink tights, black tunic, jock-belt, a pair of blocked and a pair of unblocked canvas practice shoes, a pair of my whitest socks, hairband, hairnet, not to mention plenty of hairgrips. I had washed the tights to make them fit without a wrinkle, as well as for cleanliness, and I'd ironed out the tunic, although I knew I should have to do it again at the other end. It wouldn't be exactly creaseless after it had spent the night in my suit-case! For the umpteenth time I tested the ribbons on my ballet shoes to make sure they were secure, and felt the blocks of my point shoes to see that they were hard enough. Lastly, I put into the case unimportant things like my nightie, tooth-brush and my brush and comb – just in case I forgot them in the excitement of departure.

Then, on the top of everything, I carefully placed a small parcel wrapped in tissue paper. My mascot! Madame's shoes. Yes, they'd come back from the cleaners that very morning, and they were as good as new. At least, they were quite clean, though Messrs Britelite and Sons carefully explained in a polite little note they'd enclosed in the package that *they* weren't responsible for the worn patches. No, indeed – Covent Garden was responsible for them!

Well, after all this, there was nothing to do but wait as patiently as I could for Aunt June to return.

And all the time the mist grew thicker and thicker . . .

'I say,' Caroline said, as we came in from the stables at seven o'clock to wash our hands for supper, 'this mist is awful, isn't it? That's the worst of living on the edge of the moors; it comes down from the fells. I do hope—'

She stopped, and a pang of fright shot through me.

'Do hope what?'

'I was going to say I do hope Mummy leaves the Chiswicks

167

in plenty of time. It'll take Perkins ages to get back.'

I didn't say anything. I was quite sick with fear at the awful thought of missing that train. Surely, surely Fate wouldn't be so unkind as to dash the cup from my lips before I could drink!

At eight o'clock the telephone rang. I dashed to answer it before anyone else could get there. I knew quite certainly that it was about me, and I wanted to hear the worst. When I heard Aunt June's voice at the other end of the wire, I knew that it was indeed the worst!

'Oh, it's you, Veronica,' said the voice, sounding quite cheerful, and not a bit as if my whole future were at stake, 'I'm sorry, dear, about this frightful mist. I'm afraid it's quite impossible for me to get back tonight. Perkins won't risk it — the visibility here is practically nil.'

'But, Aunt June,' I wailed. 'My audition — my audition is tomorrow morning! Have you forgotten? I must — I simply *must* catch the train to London.'

'I'm afraid it's quite impossible, dear,' said the calm voice at the other end. 'We'll arrange another interview for you. It will be quite easy, I'm sure, when we explain. You see, Perkins—'

I put down the receiver, cutting off Aunt June and her maddening voice. 'Arrange another audition for me' — you didn't arrange auditions at a famous school like Sadler's Wells just like that! You were granted an audition, and you turned up for it, by hook or by crook, whether you had a streaming cold, or a splitting headache, whether there was a bus strike and you had to walk, or a pea-soup fog, or — or anything. You let *nothing* stop you! Why — *why* couldn't Aunt June understand? As for Perkins not daring to drive in the mist — I knew quite well that it wasn't Perkins who was afraid but Aunt June . . .

'What's the matter, Veronica?' said Caroline's anxious

168

voice from behind me. 'Is anything wrong?'

'Wrong?' I repeated. 'It's finished! My career's finished!'

'You mean?—'

'Aunt June can't get back tonight because of the mist,' I said. Then I added bitterly: 'It just doesn't dawn on her that my whole career is at stake.'

'I'm sure she realizes, Veronica,' Caroline put in gently, sticking up for her mother as she sometimes did most unexpectedly. 'It really is frightful outside, you know. I don't think *anyone* could possibly drive in it.'

I dashed away to hide my tears, leaving Caroline looking after me with a worried expression on her face, and Fiona smiling her hateful, knowing smile. I knew that Fiona was pleased that all my hopes were being crushed.

'I must, I *must* do something!' I said to myself. 'What can I do? Oh, God – *please* tell me what to do!'

Then suddenly I had an idea. I expect some people would say God had nothing to do with it – that God was far too busy to bother about a little thing like my dancing, but I was sure in my own mind that my idea was Heaven-sent, and that God was telling me what to do.

I tumbled my things out of my suitcase on to the floor, dashed into the schoolroom and pulled a rucksack from the bottom of the toy cupboard, where now book and tennis rackets and suchlike were kept, dashed back with it to my bedroom and hastily began to repack my things in it. I didn't bother about my nightie and toothbrush, this time, but squeezed in the dancing things as best I could, ending with Madame's shoes. Then, like a shadow, I slipped down the back stairs and out to the stables.

I daren't switch on the electric light for fear someone saw it and began asking questions, so I had to saddle up Arab by the light of my flashlamp. It was much harder than you'd think, but I managed it at last, and led the pony out into the stable yard. I went on leading him, so as to make as little noise as possible. I don't think I need have worried, really – the mist muffled his hooves as effectively as a blanket.

When we reached the long drive, I thought the mist didn't seem to be quite so thick, the reason for which I learned later on. At last I judged it safe to mount, and I did so, my rucksack bulging to bursting-point on my back. It was quite dark, though it was only half past eight and shouldn't have been for a long time yet, but this, I supposed, was owing to the mist.

As I reached the lodge gates, I wondered what Sebastian was doing – we hadn't seen him since the morning. And then, just as I drew level with the cottage, a voice said: 'Halt! Your money or your life! This is Daredevil Dick of the roving eye and the ready hand!'

I gave a gasp.

'Oh, Sebastian! You did give me a shock! I was just thinking about you.'

'Well, in that case I oughtn't to have given you a shock, ought I?' he laughed. 'I was just coming up to the Hall to see what had happened about this mist. I imagined they'd have got you into town ages ago. And by the way, "where are you going to my pretty maid" at this time of night, if you don't mind my asking?'

My thoughts flashed back to a day, more than a year ago now – a morning in July when I'd been perched on the top of this very gate, and Sebastian's voice had asked almost the same question. I gave the same answer now. I said: 'I'm running away. I am really! I'm not joking. You see . . .'

Then out it all came. Aunt June's visit to Horchester; the mist; my audition. Of course, Sebastian knew all about that.

'So you see,' I ended, 'I've just *got* to go – mist or no mist.'

'But, Veronica, you *can't* go,' Sebastian said, his voice sounding anxious and tense. 'You couldn't possibly, you know. You'd never get there in time, anyway.'

'Of course I know I can't catch *that* train,' I argued. 'But there'll be another one – a mail train or a milk train early in the morning. There are trains to London all the time. There must be one; there *must*! My audition isn't till twelve. I might just get there. Anyway, I'm going to have a jolly good try – they say you can do anything if you really make up your mind to it.' I kicked Arab sharply, and we shot off into the mist. Fortunately the gates had been left open for Aunt June and Perkins. I felt pretty sure Sebastian wouldn't have opened them for me!

'Veronica!' came Sebastian's voice out of the mist. 'Don't be an idiot – you don't know what you're taking on – honestly you don't. The mist is nothing here to what it'll be when you get away from the trees. It's never so thick where there are trees. There are no buses, you know. This isn't a market day—'

'You said that a year ago, I remember!' I said with an excited laugh. 'Well, I shall *ride* to Newcastle if necessary. I don't care! I shall get there somehow. Goodbye!'

But I had reckoned without the mist. As Sebastian had said, the moment Arab and I left the trees it closed round us like muffling folds of cottonwool. A figure loomed up beside us and caught hold of Arab's bridle. Sebastian again! I might have known he wouldn't be so easily shaken off.

'Veronica – you've *got* to stop. I order you to stop!'

'You take your hand away from my bridle, or I'll – I'll . . .' I raised my crop threateningly, though I didn't really mean to strike him with it.

Then suddenly Sebastian let go. With a gasp of relief, and not a little of astonishment, I saw him vanish into the mist, and I was once more alone. I say 'with relief' but really it was with rather mixed feelings that I saw him go – he seemed to be my last friend in a nightmare world. But I set my teeth and determined not to give in. I *must* get there somehow, I told myself – mist or no mist. The audition – Sadler's Wells – my beloved dancing career ... Thoughts raced round in my head as I urged Arab onwards.

Strange noises came from all round me. Then I realized that they were only the sounds of the countryside – sounds you don't notice in broad daylight with the sun shining – a cow coughing, or blowing down its nose on the far side of the hedge; an owl screeching; the metallic whirr of a grouse rising in alarm out of a nearby thicket. It was terribly eerie and queer. My heart began to beat quickly and I wished that Sebastian hadn't given in like that and gone away. It would have been a comfort to have had his company, even if he *had* argued all the time.

Then, out of the mist, came a familiar sound behind me – the sound of a horse trotting.

A thrill of fright went through me. I was being pursued! I thought of all the people Sebastian might have told about me running away. His father, Uncle Adrian; then I remembered Sebastian saying that he was away. Uncle John – but he'd rung up to say he'd be staying in town for the night, as he always did if there was a mist. Trixie – she certainly couldn't ride on horseback. Pilks, Dickson. Neither could they – certainly not in a mist like this! It could only be Sebastian himself. Perhaps he thought he had more chance of stopping me when he was mounted. Well, he'd see! I drew in to the side of the road and waited for the rider to come up with me – I knew by the way he was trotting that I hadn't the ghost of a chance of escaping by speed, not being able to do more than a very slow walk myself.

'That you, Veronica?' came Sebastian's voice after a few minutes. 'I thought you couldn't have got far.'

'If you think you're going to stop me ...' I began desperately. 'If you think—'

'Stop being melodramatic, my dear cousin-sort-of,' said

Sebastian in his usual bantering tones, 'and let's get going! We'll have to step on the gas – and how! – if you mean to catch your milk train – if there *is* a milk train.'

'You don't mean that you're coming with me?' I said with a thrill of joy and hope.

'I certainly *do* mean it,' said Sebastian. 'Nothing else to be done as far as I can see – or rather I should say *feel*. More accurate! I always know when I'm beaten, and I could tell by the sound of your voice just now that nothing short of prison bars would stop you from venturing into the wild. Well, as I haven't any prison bars handy, the only thing to do is to come along with you myself and see you don't exceed the speed limit! I said to myself: "The girl's quite determined – obvious she can't go by herself. Get lost for one thing; take the wrong turning; get run over most likely. Anyway, certainly wouldn't get anywhere – not in this mist, being a Cockney brat." So I had to do the Boy Scout stunt. Can't let a fellow *artiste* down, if you see what I mean. This is my good deed for today!'

'Sebastian, you're a *brick*!' I said, trying not to burst out crying for joy and relief. 'As you say, "let's get going".'

Chapter 9

Journey Through the Mist

To be caught in a mist at night on a moorland road in Northumberland doesn't sound so dreadful, but you try it! I was quite hardened to the London fogs when you could only see a few inches in front of your nose, but in London you were at least among other people. There were lighted shops on all sides to cheer you, even if you *could* only see them dimly, as if through smoked glass. There were kindly policemen at crossings and corners, doing all they could to help you; there was noise, and bustle, and the friendly Underground where you could nearly forget about the fog outside. But here, on this lonely road, with the unseen hills wrapped in cloud all around you, the silence was intense. The only sounds that broke it were the occasional prattle of a moorland stream as it tumbled over its stony bed, or the plaintive cry of a peewit or a curlew.

The moorland road was unfenced and at first I'd been terrified for fear my pony strayed off the path on to the endless open moor that stretched away on every side. But I found that Sebastian knew exactly what to do about that – he just let Warrior have his head and Warrior kept to the road all right. He hadn't been born and bred on the Northumbrian moors for nothing! I found that Arab was just as wise. Our only worry was knowing which way to go when we came to a fork, or a crossroads. Fortunately Sebastian had brought his torch, which saved the situation. Although several times he had to climb the signposts to get near enough to flash the light on to the names we did at least know we were going in the right direction.

'It's a good thing you brought that torch, Sebastian,' I said, after one of our many stops. 'I had one too, but I left it in the stable. I never thought of bringing it with me.'

'No, I rather guessed you wouldn't,' said Sebastian with laughter in his voice. 'All you would think of bringing would be a pair of ballet shoes and some tights! Not much use for a night out in the mist!'

I blushed guiltily in the dark, when I remembered how carefully I had packed Madame's precious shoes into my rucksack, not bothering to bring a brush and comb, or even a nightie! Sebastian came perilously near the truth!

'I wonder what they thought when they found I'd gone?' I said suddenly. 'Trixie, and Caroline, and all of them. Oh, Sebastian – I quite forgot to leave a note to explain! How dreadful of me! Do you think they'll be awfully worried?'

'Oh, no – shouldn't think so,' said Sebastian. 'I expect they'll say: "Oh, well – that's the end of her", shut the door and go to bed. "No need to worry; people disappear every day."' Then I think he sensed how upset I really was at what I had done – or rather what I had *not* done, for his teasing tone changed and he said seriously: 'It's OK, Veronica! I left a letter to my father telling him what had happened. He'll get it when he comes back from the village. I think he'll agree that it was the only thing to do – sensible chap, my father! By the way—' He stopped suddenly.

'Yes – what?'

'Well, you remember when we were discussing our Matric results the other day?'

'Yes, what about it?'

'Well, you remember when Fiona said something about me *needing* to do well because of my career. She said: "You'll have to be pretty clever if you're going to be a barrister." And I said: "Yes – *if* I'm going to be a barrister."'

175

'Yes,' I said. 'I remember.'

'The fact is,' went on Sebastian, the excitement in his voice making it wobble a little, 'the fact is, Veronica, it's definitely fixed, and I'm *not* going in for Law. I had it out with my father the other day, and I'm going to make Music my career. You're the very first person to know.'

'Oh, Sebastian, I'm so glad!' I exclaimed. 'I know what it's like to want to do something most awfully and have everyone against you.'

'When all came to all,' continued Sebastian, 'Father said he'd half suspected the truth. He said that no one could remain totally oblivious of the fact that my heart was in the piano, judging by the number of hours I spend sitting at it! I *have* practised rather a lot these hols,' he added apologetically. 'In fact I've done nothing else – except ride with you lot now and then. Well, my father agreed that it was no earthly good my taking up Law as a profession if my heart was set on other things, so I'm to try for a scholarship to the Royal College of Music next year. He really was most awfully decent about it – he's an understanding chap is my father. If I get the scholarship I'm coming to London to study, so you'll be able to come to the Albert Hall with me, and I'll go to Covent Garden with you, what!'

After this there was silence between us for a long time. We were each far too deep in our own thoughts to talk. It was a good thing our thoughts were blissful, because the outlook was anything but cheerful. 'Outlook' is quite the wrong word, really, because we couldn't see anything at all now – not even the ditches at the sides of the road. If it hadn't been for the wonderful sixth sense of our ponies we'd have been blundering into them at every step. The mist seemed to get thicker and thicker, and we got colder and colder.

'This is the top of the road over Cushat's Crag, you know,' said Sebastian, breaking the long silence. 'I shouldn't be surprised if the mist isn't at its worst here. It usually is. If the mist is rolling off the hills, as it is tonight, and not rising off the low ground – well, you're right in the middle of the clouds up here. When we get over the top and go down the other side it may thin out a bit.'

'How many miles have we come?' I asked. 'We seem to have been riding for hours and hours.'

'About ten miles,' said Sebastian. Then he flashed his torch on to his wristwatch. 'It's half past eleven, so it's taken us two hours. We have another twenty miles to go to get to Newcastle. When we get on to the Military Road that runs along the Roman Wall, we might come across a garage. There's one at the crossroads – at least I *think* it's a garage, but it may only be a filling station. We might knock them up and get a taxi – at least we might if the mist lifts a bit. I'm pretty sure they wouldn't turn out in this, no matter what we offered them. We'll have to get a lift somehow, you know, and hang the expense! You won't be fit for anything tomorrow after this.'

'Oh, yes I shall,' I said, trying to stop my teeth chattering. 'B-ballet dancers are pretty t-tough.'·

'Hullo! What's this?' exclaimed Sebastian, reining in Warrior. 'Golly! A covered-in bus stop. What a find! Let's stop here and rest the ponies for a bit, shall we?'

We tethered the ponies to an iron railing that stretched away into the mist on either side of the tiny shelter, and sank down thankfully on the hard wooden seat inside. Once more Sebastian flashed on his torch, and I saw by its light that he had swung round his rucksack and was taking something out of it – a Thermos flask and a packet of sandwiches.

'I told you once before that I always carry my own canteen about with me, didn't I?' he said. 'Brainwave, what! It was a good thing Bella had just made the coffee and stood it on the stove to keep hot. I'd like to have been there when she found it gone. She wouldn't even be able to blame the cat – not with

177

hot coffee! I'm afraid I made a bad job of the sandwiches. Hadn't much time, you see, and I couldn't find anything to go in them, except cheese.'

'It tastes like caviare!' I laughed. 'I mean, just as wonderful.'

'I hope not!' Sebastian said solemnly. 'Personally I loathe caviare. Filthy stuff!'

'Oh, I love it,' I said. 'Jonathan always had it when he sold a picture and threw a party!'

'It's a good thing we don't all like the same things,' pronounced Sebastian. 'I'll have the ice-cream, and you can have the caviare.'

'Oh, but I like ice-cream, too!'

'Well, what *don't* you like?'

I thought long and deeply. Finally I said: 'Tripe.'

'Don't like it either,' laughed Sebastian. 'So what?'

'Deadlock, I'm afraid,' I said. 'I seem to be frightfully easy to please. I like simply everything. Oh, no – I've just thought of something I simply *loathe* – caraway seeds!'

'Love 'em!' declared Sebastian. 'So the situation is saved at the eleventh hour. You can have my caviare, and I'll have your caraway seeds!'

We stayed quite a long time in the shelter so as to give the ponies a good rest – and ourselves too. When at last we decided it was time to move, it was twelve o'clock.

'The witching hour!' exclaimed Sebastian as we rode off. 'Now is the time for hobgoblins, witches, earthbound spirits, and every sort of uncanny thing to be abroad!'

'Ugh!' I said. 'Don't! You make me feel creepy! The mist is uncanny enough – without your ghostly et ceteras!'

For ages and ages we rode onwards, and the silence between us grew longer as we grew more and more weary. Arab was beginning to stumble and Warrior's trot had lost its springy

178

sound. We walked the ponies quite a lot of the time.

'I wonder where we are now?' I said, with a sigh of utter weariness. 'It seems hours and hours since we left that bus stop.'

'It is,' answered Sebastian. 'Two, anyway... Gosh! D'you see what's happened? The mist is thinning. I can see that signpost clearly. We're coming to the crossroads I told you about. Now for our garage!'

But alas! The garage proved to be a mere filling station as Sebastian had feared. It was as black and dead-looking as the dodo.

'The chappie probably lives miles away,' Sebastian said. 'It's no use our trying to ferret him out, because we don't know in which direction the nearest village is. Of course we might go back and try Simonburn—'

'Oh, let's *not*,' I said. 'Simonburn is the other way to Newcastle, isn't it? I don't want to go back – I want to go *on*!'

We went on. We passed an AA box, with a telephone inside, but alas! it was no use to us as we hadn't a key.

'A friend of mine lives somewhere about here,' said Sebastian after a bit. 'Or rather his father does. His name is Dillon – Jack Dillon – and they have a farm hereabouts. Ah, I thought so! Here it is – Hunter's Copse.' He stopped in the middle of the road and flashed his torch so that I could read the name on the gate.

'Look out!' I yelled. 'There's something coming!' It was a car, judging by the two pale lights gleaming through the fog. To my surprise Sebastian flung himself off Warrior's back, and leapt into the middle of the road, waving his arms wildly and yelling at the top of his voice.

'Stop! Stop! Hi – wait a minute!'

Fortunately the driver had good eyesight and was going at a snail's pace. He stopped at once, let down the window of the

179

car and yelled back: 'What's that? You in any trouble?'

'You've said *it*!' yelled back Sebastian. 'Half a mo' and we'll tell you about it. You can help us a lot if you will. Filthy night, isn't it?'

'Filthy?' said the man in the car. 'I could find a better name for it than that! Are you two youngsters alone?'

'Yes,' said Sebastian. 'That is, we've got our ponies, of course. You see . . .' There, on that foggy and deserted road in the wilds of Northumberland, with a bit of help from me, he told our story – all about the Bring and Buy Sale, Madame, my audition at Sadler's Wells, and finally the last awful catastrophe – Aunt June and the mist. I expect it sounded a bit fantastic. Anyway, when we'd finished, the man whistled and said in an awestruck voice: 'My holy godfathers! And you two have ridden on a couple of ponies all the way from Bracken to here, and you are prepared to do another twenty miles or so to Newcastle, in order to catch a hypothetical train to London. My sainted aunt!'

'We *did* hope you would give us a lift, sir,' said Sebastian hopefully.

'A lift?' said the man. 'I should just say I could! But look here – I can get you two in the back all right but how about the animals? I doubt if they'd go in the boot! Do we tow them, or what? No doubt you have ideas! You don't seem lacking in ingenuity!'

'I have a friend who lives at this farm,' Sebastian explained, waving in the direction of the gateway on our right. 'We could leave the ponies here and I could collect them tomorrow morning. The mist'll have cleared off by then, and I could ride them back all right – I mean ride one and lead the other.'

'But, Sebastian,' I expostulated, 'won't your friend object to being knocked up at two o'clock in the morning?'

Sebastian laughed shortly.

'I should just say he would! We needn't disturb him,

though. As a matter of fact the farm is a couple of miles off the road, but I happen to know that this field is pasture' – he flashed his torch on to the short grass inside the gate to reassure me – 'and the animals will be quite OK. I'll be back to collect them before he even knows they're there!'

'Well, that's an idea, certainly,' said the man in the car. 'You two do the doings, and I'll have a smoke meantime. The night's young! I ought to have been in Newcastle before midnight, but now it's of no account when I get there. May as well be hung for a sheep as a lamb!'

He flicked open his lighter, and I saw his eyes. They reassured me, being all crinkly round the edges, as if he laughed a lot. I breathed a sigh of relief. Being town bred, I felt it was a bit risky to go making friends with strangers in the middle of a moor at two o'clock in the morning!

As I fondled Arab's warm, silky neck before setting him free, I suddenly realized that I was saying a long goodbye to my pony. If I was accepted as a pupil of the Wells School I shouldn't be coming back here until the holidays, and who knew what might happen to Arabesque? Aunt June would most probably send him back to his owner at Merlingford, and I would see him no more. A tear stole down my nose at the thought of it.

'Come on! What are you waiting for?' said Sebastian's voice at my elbow. 'We're all ready, aren't we? I'll dump the tack in this spinney – I certainly don't feel like taking it with us to Newcastle – I should have to cart it all the way back tomorrow. Just shine the light, will you?'

I held the torch whilst Sebastian climbed the railings into a little copse that lay between the field and the road on one side of the gate. He pushed the saddles and bridles under a thick tangle of blackberry bushes, and piled bracken on top of them.

'Nobody will know they're there,' he declared when he had finished. 'Only hope it doesn't rain really hard, that's all!'

We went back to the car and got inside. Never had a car felt so warm and luxurious as that old and battered Ford Eight – not even Aunt June's palatial Rolls! We sank down on the imitation leather cushions with a sigh of thankfulness, feeling that the worst of our long trek was over.

We got to Newcastle Central Station at exactly half past four, the mist having thinned considerably as we drove eastwards. We learned that there was a train to London at a quarter to six, so Sebastian led the way to the one and only buffet which was open all night, and procured two large, thick cups of steaming hot coffee and a plate of doorstep sandwiches. Ordinarily we might have turned up our noses at them, but after our ordeal we were only too thankful to get a hot drink and something to eat. When we had finished, we went to the general waiting-room. There were several people sitting or lying on the seats and quite a few slumped over the centre table, fast asleep, their heads on their arms. Sebastian found the woman who was in charge of the place, and tipped her to wake us up in time for the London train. Then we lay down on an empty bench, our heads at opposite ends like a couple of sardines. Sebastian had taken off his coat and he covered us both with it. We used our rucksacks for pillows because the bench was made of wood and was pretty hard to lie on. I must add that I removed my point shoes (and Madame's) from the rucksack before I lay on it for fear I squashed them!

'Goodnight, Veronica,' Sebastian said with a yawn. 'We managed it OK, didn't we?'

'Oh, Sebastian,' I said, half to myself. 'You *are* sweet!'

'What's that?' asked Sebastian sleepily.

'Oh, nothing,' I answered, knowing by past experience that under no circumstances must you call a boy 'sweet'! 'Goodnight!'

*

Fortunately the train started from Newcastle, so it was punctual. There were no sleepers on it, even if I had the necessary cash, which I hadn't, but Sebastian managed to hire me a rug and a pillow. How he did it I don't know, but I was full of gratitude and admiration. I couldn't help thinking of the time when I had held the view that people who lived in Northumberland were next door to savages. Sebastian knew a great deal more about travelling than I did – there was no denying the fact.

'Mind you get a taxi straight to the school,' he said as the guard began slamming carriage doors. 'And don't forget the address – 45 Colet Gardens, Baron's Court.'

'As if I should!' I laughed. 'Why, it's written on my heart!'

'So long, Veronica!' he yelled, as the train began to slide away from the platform. 'Good luck!'

'Goodbye!' I yelled back. 'And thank you for everything!'

His face swam in a mist before my eyes, and I realized that I was no longer laughing – I was crying! It wasn't only leaving Sebastian behind that made me cry, but all the other things too – Arabesque, the moors, Caroline, Bracken Hall itself. I realized, too late, that I hadn't even said a proper goodbye to them.

As the train got up speed, I lay down on the seat and tried to sleep, but the carriage wheels seemed as if they were turning in my head, and the melody they played was the *Holberg Suite*. My heart had a queer feeling – as if someone was slowly squeezing it – a feeling I hadn't had for a very long time; in fact, not since that journey north more than a year ago. How odd, I thought, that on that occasion I had been homesick for the noisy Underground and all the sounds and sights of London. Now my heart was aching for the moors and woods of Northumberland!

The *Holberg Suite* changed to the Dance of the Sugar Plum Fairy, then to *Les Sylphides*, and finally the whirring of the wheels merged into the unearthly music of Tchaikovsky's *Swan Lake*. I slept at last.

Chapter 10

Sadler's Wells at Last

The train was only a quarter of an hour late. I learned from some well-informed passengers that the fog had lifted as soon as we had left Darlington behind, and the train had made up time on the southern part of the journey. It was half past eleven when I dashed through the barrier at King's Cross and made for the taxi rank. There was a touch on my arm.

'Veronica!'

I turned in surprise; then gave a gasp of joy. There in front of me was a well-known figure, towering above the other passengers – a young man with a shock of unruly black hair, and a little black beard.

'Jonathan! Whatever are you doing here?'

'It looks as if I'm meeting *you*!' he laughed.

'But how did you—' I began.

'Look,' said Jonathan, taking my arm and hurrying me along. 'D'you mind if we leave the explanations until we're in the taxi – we'll have to get moving, you know, if we're to get to Baron's Court by twelve o'clock. And I expect you'll need a few spare minutes to get ready—' He whirled me along and into the taxi.

'Five minutes will do!' I laughed, as I sank on to the seat. 'Oh, Jonathan, it *is* good to see you! I was feeling dreadfully homesick, but now it's as though I've come home instead! But please, will you explain how you knew I was on that train. I didn't know I was going to be on it myself until half past five this morning.'

'Just a moment,' said Jonathan. 'Mrs Crapper, the dear old soul, said I was to give you this, and to be sure you drank it' – he pulled a Thermos flask out of his pocket. 'She said she was sure you wouldn't have had any breakfast. Have you?'

'Well, no – I haven't,' I confessed.

'Get on with these then,' went on Jonathan, producing a packet of sandwiches out of the other pocket. 'You've only a few minutes. Well, now for the explanation. At a most uncivilized hour in the morning – six-thirty to be exact – I was roused from my downy pillow by a long-distance telephone call. It was from a friend of yours way up north – a young man, I guessed, from the voice.'

'Sebastian!' I gasped, pausing with a sandwich halfway to my mouth. 'He isn't a young man; he's a boy, and my cousin. At least a sort of a cousin. But how did he find your number? I never told it to him – in fact I don't know it myself. At least I did, but I've forgotten it.'

'Well, I'm as much in the dark there as you are!' laughed Jonathan. 'All I can suggest is that he knew my address and badgered the exchange until they looked up my number.'

'Oh, he'd do that all right!' I exclaimed. 'Trust Sebastian!'

'Anyway, he got me all right,' went on Jonathan. 'And he told me the tale, and here I am, half asleep through being robbed of my beauty sleep, but willing! And by the way, Veronica – congratulations!'

'Keep them till afterwards!' I said, finishing off the coffee. 'They may think I'm frightful and turn me away. Gosh! Here we are. Oh, Jonathan – I feel *awful*!'

'Keep your pecker up!' said Jonathan. 'I'll be waiting for you with the taxi at the corner. Best of luck!'

At exactly twelve o'clock I walked into the studio where I'd been told my audition would take place. My hair was neatly fastened in the net, my tights pulled up, and the creases in my tunic smoothed out as much as possible. I had a queer feeling in my inside, like when you dive off the high springboard at the swimming baths for the first time, and my legs felt as if they belonged to somebody else. My hour had come – the hour I had thought of, and dreamed of for so long. I could hardly believe it.

The audition wasn't really so terrifying after all. Only a pretty fair-haired lady and a quiet gentleman with sad, dark eyes that looked as if they saw through you, and far beyond you, and yet made you feel at home just the same. I learned afterwards that usually part of the audition takes place in an ordinary class, but Madame had managed to get me one all to myself because the school hadn't yet started after the holidays.

While I was doing some *grands-jetés* the door of the studio opened and another gentleman looked in. He watched me for a moment, and then said: 'Come! You can spring higher than that! Try again!'

I was very tired, but he didn't know that, of course, and I certainly wasn't going to tell him, because that would have looked like making excuses for myself. I made up my mind to jump higher than I had ever done before – somehow he made me want to do it.

'Good!' he said approvingly. 'I knew you could! Your elevation is excellent. You've got a nice line, too.'

Then suddenly I recognized him. He was the temperamental ballet master I had watched the day I'd gatecrashed. And here he was being quite friendly! With a smile and a nod he shut the door again, and went away.

When I had done all they asked, the lady told me to take off my socks. She examined my feet most carefully, asking me all sorts of questions as to whether I had ever had any trouble with my feet, whether they ever ached, whether I had ever sprained either of my ankles, all of which I answered truthfully in the negative. Finally she murmured: 'Very nice!' told me I could put on my socks again, and go.

'Please – *please*!' I begged. 'Is it all right? Can I come? Of course I expect it's all against the rules, but couldn't you – couldn't you just tell me if I can come?'

The gentleman looked at the lady and they both smiled.

'Well,' said the gentleman, 'it *is* a little – shall we say unusual, but I think we can put you out of your misery. If you really think you'll be happy here, and don't mind hard work, well, yes – you shall come.'

'Oh, *thank* you!' I said. 'I know I shall be happy. When your dream comes true, you're bound to be happy, aren't you? And as for work – I'll – I'll work my fingers to the bone ...' I stopped suddenly, realizing that this was rather a funny way to put it when one was referring to ballet! 'I mean, I'll do the very best I can if you'll let me work here.'

'That is all that is necessary,' said the lady, writing something in a book. 'And now I expect you'll want to be going? The secretary will write to your aunt about times and so on. Term begins on Monday and you'll be in the Junior class.' Then she looked at me rather hard, and added: 'You look tired, dear. Were you very excited about your audition?'

'Yes,' I said, 'but not as excited as I would have been if it hadn't been for missing the train last night.' Then out it all came – Aunt June's visit, my flight from Bracken Hall, and my encounter with Sebastian. As I talked, I realized how unbelievable it must all sound, here in civilized London, with the Underground, and the buses, not to mention taxis at every street corner, all taking you wherever you wanted to go at a moment's notice.

'And then the car came along,' I finished, 'and that was the end of our adventure – except that Sebastian will have to collect the ponies this morning and ride them all that way back – twenty miles, at least.'

'A real friend in need – that young man!' said the quiet gentleman. Then he murmured something to the lady about

188

the grit and tenacity of these North Country children. 'And, after all, it's what we need,' he added. 'That, along with other qualities.'

'Oh, but it was Sebastian who was tenacious,' I said quickly. 'I'd never have managed it if it hadn't been for him. You don't *know* how marvellous he was!'

'I think there was grit on both sides,' declared the gentleman with a smile. 'I'm glad to see that you don't easily give up, my dear, when you make up your mind to do a thing.'

And that was the end of my audition. As I left the building, I looked back and gave a sigh of happiness:

45 COLET GARDENS – SADLER'S WELLS SCHOOL OF BALLET.

My dream had come true!

Lorna Hill

Veronica
at the Wells

Illustrated by
Kathleen Whapham

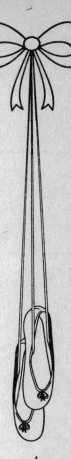

PIPER
PAN MACMILLAN
CHILDREN'S BOOKS

To Claude Newman, the real 'Gilbert Delahaye',
in sincere admiration of his whole-hearted devotion
to the art of Ballet

Contents

Chapter 1

The Great Day Arrives

WHEN I woke up that morning, with the autumn sun streaming across my bed, I had the old familiar feeling that something wonderful had happened to me. For several days now I'd had that feeling, and, as I lay there, it suddenly burst upon me what it was that had happened. I'd had my audition, and had been accepted for that most romantic of all schools – the Sadler's Wells Ballet School!

Then the wonderful top-of-the-world feeling changed to a fluttering in my inside – the sort of feeling you get when you jump into the swimming bath for the first time in the season or go on the scenic railway. It was a feeling partly of excitement, partly joy, but most of all apprehension, because today was THE DAY! Yes, this very morning, in less than two hours' time, I'd be walking up to the porticoed building that said 45 Colet Gardens on a brass plate by the side of the door, and from that moment I'd be a member of the most famous dancing school in the world. No wonder I felt excited!

I jumped out of bed and ran over to a chair whereon stood a small attaché-case, opened it, and peeped inside. Yes, everything was there – the new, grey silk tunic (oh, the awful job I'd had to get it made in time!), pink tights, belt, and matching hairband, blocked and unblocked shoes. I'd even remembered to put in hairgrips and a hairnet. I couldn't help giggling when I thought of the things you usually take to a new school with you – things like fountain pens and india-rubbers! On top of everything was a note from the secretary, telling me how to get to Colet Gardens. I'd put it in because it was sweet of her to think of it, but really there was no need for it – the locality of the school was written on my heart!

9

I washed and dressed quicker than I had ever done in my life before, and flew to the door.

'Mrs Crapper! Mrs Crapper!' I yelled down the stairs. 'Is my breakfast ready, Mrs Crapper? I've got to be there before ten o'clock, you know!'

Mrs Crapper, who kept the apartment house where I lived and who had looked after me since Daddy died, came to the foot of the stairs and stood looking up at me, her hands on her hips.

'Lawks, Miss Veronica! Why, it's barely half past seven! But I knew as how you'd be up with the lark this mornin', and your kipper's in the pan. I've just turned it over this very minute, and it'll be done in a trice.'

'Don't bring my breakfast up here, Mrs Crapper,' I shouted back. 'I'll come down there and have it with you – honestly, I'd rather.'

I thought how shocked Aunt June would be. Aunt June had made all arrangements for Mrs Crapper to look after me. I was to have my own bedroom and share a sitting-room with another ballet student, and we were to have our meals brought up to us in state. Instead, we usually had them in Mrs Crapper's basement kitchen, where we could make toast at her open fire – much more homely!

I finished my toilet, made my bed, shut my case, and then put on my outdoor things so that I shouldn't have to come back to my room again after I'd finished my breakfast. At the door I paused and looked back. I suppose it was really a shabby room, but I'd always been happy there. So, although the floor was covered with cheap canvas of a hideous green-and-yellow shade, the bedstead a cheap iron one, and the wallpaper faded to an indiscriminate rust colour, yet I loved the room because I loved Mrs Crapper, and she'd put all her most precious possessions in it for me. The painted dressing-table with all its little drawers for your hairpins and buttons, the thing that Mrs Crapper called an 'overmantel' and which consisted of a lot of little brackets with bits of looking-glass

10

above them, yes, even the very curtains, were the identical furnishings which Mrs Crapper had bought when she was married. And as that had been over thirty years ago you really couldn't blame them for looking a bit the worse for wear! Mrs Crapper assured me that they'd been lovely when they were new, and I quite believed her. On the brackets of the over-mantel stood a proud array of coronation mugs, collected by Mrs Crapper from various members of her family, together with several souvenirs of her honeymoon – a jug with 'A Present From Margate' on it; a teapot with a spout made in the form of a mermaid, and which wouldn't pour out because I'd tried it with water out of my toothmug; and a much-gilded flower vase with 'Margate Remembers You' in flowing letters on its bulging middle.

As I dashed down the three flights of stairs to the basement I passed the closed bedroom door of my fellow ballet student, Stella Mason. How I wished she'd been there to take me to school on my first morning! But she was on tour with the Opera Ballet and wouldn't be back till tonight, so it was no use wishing.

I ate my kipper dutifully when Mrs Crapper put it in front of me, but, really, when I'd finished I couldn't have told you what I'd eaten. My thoughts were far away from Mrs Crapper's basement kitchen. They had flown ahead of me, and were already at Colet Gardens.

'Lawks, Miss Veronica!' exclaimed Mrs Crapper when I got up from the table. 'You'll never be able to dance on what you've eaten for your breakfast. Only a kipper, neat, as you might say! No bread and butter at all, and not even your usual toast and marmalade. All this bally's gone to your head; it has that!'

She insisted upon making me up a huge packet of sand-wiches to sustain me in the middle of the morning. In vain I tried to explain to her about the canteen at the Wells, and the milk so thoughtfully provided by the Government for students under eighteen, but it was no good. She didn't give *that*, she

11

said with a snap of her fingers, for them canteens. As like as not they'd have nothing but lemonade and biscuits! I took the sandwiches because I wouldn't hurt Mrs Crapper's feelings for the world, but since both my case and my handbag were full to bursting, I had to unwrap them when I got safely outside the kitchen and do them up again in two smaller packets. I crammed one in each pocket of my coat, where they stuck out on either side and made me look like an old-fashioned shepherdess with panniers!

I suppose to the ordinary person the journey by Underground to Baron's Court, which is the nearest station to Colet Gardens, is a long and dreary one. But to me it was like the journey to Fairyland. Every rattle of the train, every lurch and every bump, brought me nearer to my heart's desire. A little man in a bowler hat apologized politely as the train swung round a corner, and flung him against my shoulder.

I murmured: 'It's quite all right. It wasn't your fault really,' when all the time I wanted to say: 'Do you know who I am? I'm Veronica Weston, and I'm just about to become a pupil of the Sadler's Wells Ballet School. I'm going to be famous like Margot Fonteyn and Moira Shearer!'

I wanted to turn *fouettés* down the middle of the carriage. I wanted to pose *en arabesque* in the entry every time the train stopped at a station. I thought how surprised they'd be if I did! Then I caught sight of my reflection in the window opposite. Alas! They would never believe me! In my navy-blue reefer coat and beret, chosen for me by Aunt June as suitable wearing apparel for a person only just fifteen, I looked much more like a schoolgirl than a glamorous ballet dancer. In fact – I have to admit it – my small pale face looked a great deal younger than fifteen.

It was exactly nine-twenty by the clock of St Paul's School when I reached the door of 45 Colet Gardens – the fateful door! Girls, and quite a lot of boys too, were pouring through a door that led into what looked like nothing so much as a greenhouse. I stayed for quite a long time outside, trying to screw up my courage to follow them. When at last I did so I found myself in a big, light room rather like a conservatory. There were little green tables dotted about, with green chairs to match. The chairs were of the modern, tubular type, and they looked as if they'd collapse if you sat down on them, but I found out that they were very strong really. They had to be, because they weren't exactly gently treated! Two girls, one fair, the other dark, were standing by a radiator looking at a notice-board that hung on the wall above.

'Golly! Myrna's got an understudy for a Court Lady in *Lac*. What an honour – I *don't* think!' said the dark girl. 'Theo and Linda are Pages. Delia's got one of the Nymphs in *Sleeping Prin*, and Mary's an understudy. Oh, and she's one of the Pages as well. You know – the ones with the ghastly violins in the First Act. I'm on the other list – one of the Black Lackeys in *The Gods Go A-Begging*, down at the Wells. Oh, well, it'll be a change from Covent Garden, anyway! Nothing for you, Pauline ... *Well?*' This last exclamation was due to the fact of my having plucked her by the sleeve.

'Please, would you mind telling me where the dressing-rooms are?' I asked.

The girl stared at me witheringly. Then she jerked her head nonchalantly towards a passageway and said:

'Through there. Down the passage, on your right. Don't knock.' Then she turned her back on me.

I followed her directions, and approached a closed door from behind which I could hear the confused hum of voices. When I opened it I found, to my amazement, that it was full of boys and young men. A burst of laughter from the Winter Garden told me without more explanation that I had been made a fool of.

I retreated hastily, my cheeks burning. Then, as I stood, not knowing which way to go, I felt a touch on my arm.

'Here – come this way, if you please.'

13

I turned and found myself facing a dark boy wearing a pair of very old flannel slacks and a grey pullover. He wasn't good-looking in the ordinary sense of the word, but he had kind, brown eyes and he looked friendly.

'I – I'm most awfully sorry,' I stammered. 'I mean, barging in among you all like that. You see, I didn't know—'

'Do not apologize,' said the boy, and then I noticed that he spoke with a foreign accent. 'It was obviously a mistake. We all knew it, of course. The girls' dressing-room is over there.' He indicated a short flight of stone stairs with a door at the bottom. 'If you need any more help, ask me, please. The name is Toni.'

'Thank you so much,' I answered. 'I'll be all right now, I expect.'

The door of the girls' dressing-room was ajar, and above the general chatter of voices I could hear snatches of conversation.

'It's a fine thing when I have to be understudy to Delia McFarlane! Why, she's the world's worst!' ... 'Don't worry, darling; nothing will happen to Delia; she's the world's healthiest, besides being the worst.' ... 'No, I haven't seen your tights, Lily. I expect they're in the lost prop, as usual. I can't think why you *will* keep on leaving them on the floor. Hey! Has anyone seen Lily's tights? Colour pink once upon a time; now a delicate grey – something like Mrs Wopping's floorcloth.' ... 'Whoever gave you your name, Lily, was playing a joke. Anything less like a lily than you in your tights no one ever saw!' ... 'Sorry, I can't lend you mine. Oh, yes, I know I haven't a class till three o'clock, but these are the only decent pair I possess, and you'd split them.' ... '*Belinda!* Why don't you get properly dressed? It looks awful dancing *Les Sylphides* in your undies!'

At this point I entered. The voices ceased as if they'd been cut off at the main like the water, and thirty to forty pairs of eyes were turned on me curiously.

'I – I was told to come in here,' I said tentatively.

'Oh, new, I suppose?' said a fair girl standing near the door.

14

She had a small, round face, and her lint-fair hair was tightly plaited and pinned on top of her head. It gave her an odd look, as if she was going to have a bath. 'Well, we've all got to be new some time, haven't we? Cheer up, and don't look so scared! You'll soon drop into things.'

'You will find a peg over on the other side,' put in another girl. She was dark-skinned and spoke with a slight foreign accent. I found out in due course that her name was Taiis (pronounced Ty-eece) Sircar, and that she had been the cause of great embarrassment to poor Miss Smailes who taught in the Junior School where Taiis had been training until a year ago. Miss Smailes had been explaining to the class that they ought not to behave like a herd of unruly school-children.

'You ought to make believe that you are all little princesses,' said Miss Smailes, 'and carry yourselves accordingly.'

She hadn't realized until some time afterwards that Taiis, one of the worst offenders, *was* in fact a princess in her own country! Incidentally, she was one of the gentlest girls I met while I was at the Wells, and the least regal in the ordinary sense of the word.

'Thank you,' I said gratefully, glad that they were not all as unfriendly as the girl I had addressed in the Winter Garden when I'd first come in. As a matter of fact I'd had a spot of beginner's luck in reverse on that occasion. Marcia Rutherford was quite the nastiest girl at the Wells; in fact, she was the only really objectionable one I met while I was there.

The girl who'd been dancing twirled her imaginary skirts.

'Bet you I dare dance round the Winter Garden!' she announced to the room in general.

There was a gasp of horror.

'What? Like that? *Belinda!* Why, you might meet Gilbert Delahaye, or Serge, or – or even the *Director!*'

'What odds! Cheer the old boy up a bit!'

The girl with the plaits, whose name appeared to be Sara, planted herself firmly in front of the door.

15

'Oh, no you don't, Belinda!' she pronounced. 'You know what they said in your report.'

'SHE MUST LEARN TO BEHAVE WITH DECORUM!' chanted a dozen voices.

'The Director's frightfully keen on Decorum,' went on Sara. 'It'll be written on his heart when he dies! I do hope you're decorous, New Girl.'

'I hope so!' I laughed.

'I can't *think* why they took you into this ballet school, Belinda,' pursued Sara. 'It's so strict here – tradition, and all that, don't you know. Such and such a thing was never done in the Russian Imperial Ballet School – *never*! And so it can't be done here. It's really terribly straitlaced, and you're so – so – well, sometimes you're not very decent, you know.'

'I really don't know what you're all so shocked about,' declared Belinda. 'Personally, I think I look rather nice.'

I stared at her thoughtfully. 'Rather nice?' It didn't describe her in the very least. She was completely beautiful from the crown of her red-gold head to her slender white feet. And yet there was something – something you couldn't quite put your finger on – that spoilt her. I'd discussed it with Sara one day when I'd been at the Wells for some time.

'I think it's because her thoughts aren't nice ones,' I said. 'Madame says that if your thoughts aren't nice, it shows in your dancing, just as it does in music or painting.'

'Madame who?' questioned Sara.

'Madame Viret – where I used to learn dancing,' I explained. 'She has a studio in Baker Street.'

'Oh, yes – I've heard of the Wakulski-Viret School, of course,' said Sara. 'Everyone has. Madame Viret's a wonderful teacher, isn't she?'

'Absolutely wonderful,' I answered. 'Well, Madame says that if you're like – well, like Belinda is, you'll get three-quarters of the way to the top – perhaps even to solo parts – but you'll never get *right* there, because your mind will stop you, no matter how brilliantly you dance.'

'She's right,' said Sara, after a minute's thought. 'I never thought of it like that, but it's perfectly true.'

But to get back to the dressing-room. Belinda had now sobered up a bit, and was shrugging herself into her grey silk tunic.

'I suppose you haven't come here with a scholarship?' she asked, smoothing it down over her lovely slender figure, and addressing me.

'Well, yes – as a matter of fact I have,' I admitted.

'Oh!—' The whole dressing-room was suddenly alive with attention. 'A whole one, or only a bit of one?'

'A whole one, I suppose,' I answered, 'At least, I don't have to pay any fees, but of course there are my lodgings, and everything.'

'I get more out of them than that,' put in Belinda, doing high kicks to the danger of all around her. 'They pay all my fees, *and* give me something towards my keep as well. They even pay for my lunches. They know they jolly well have to, or I wouldn't be here. My dad is out of work, and likely to be. He's like me, is Dad – bone lazy! Mum does part-time in a shoe factory, but she's got veins in her legs with standing, and she may go sick any day. Well, what Mum gets is all the cash we have coming into our house, and there are ten of us.' She began to recite the names and ages of her family, ticking them off on her slim, white fingers: 'Doug, Maisie, Walt, Mabel, Ernie, Ruth, Willie. Then there's Alfie – he's ten, and he's got TB. He's in a Home, so that's got rid of *him* for a bit, thank goodness! Oh, and there's Gertie – I nearly forgot about Gertie. Let me see, she must be six; or is it seven? I can't remember. Anyway, she can't walk, poor kid – infantile paralysis. Well, I think that's the lot. Personally I consider I deserve a scholarship! They threatened to stop it at the end of last term, after that row Derek and I got into, but I knew they wouldn't. I'm far too good a dancer.' She began turning *pirouettes* – trebles, and even fours, and they were so wonderful that I couldn't help gasping. 'I parked myself outside the staff-room door,' she went on, 'when I knew they were having a pow-wow, and I pretended to be talking to a friend, and I said in a loud voice, so that they simply couldn't *help* hearing, "OK," I said, "if they stop my schol, I'm going straight to the Windmill. *They'll* have me like a shot." ... I knew my schol wouldn't be stopped, and it hasn't. They like a bit of temperament in this place, anyway,' she added, stopping in the middle of a *pirouette* and throwing back her hair. 'How's this for *entrechat-six?*' She jumped into the air and seemed to stay there for ages, while her slender feet twinkled. 'Good enough even for Gilbert, eh?' She gave her tights a last hitch and danced away.

'Hey!' yelled Sara after her flying figure. 'You've forgotten your hair!'

'Oh, I'll come back later on to do it up,' shouted Belinda. 'Only practising, now. Thanks, though!'

'She's quite a decent sort,' remarked Sara when she'd gone. 'Really, you can't help liking her. If only she wasn't so – so—'

'We know what you mean, darling!' laughed a girl called Margaret. 'It's a bit difficult to describe, I'll admit. For myself, I certainly shouldn't call Belinda Stout a "decent sort". Fascinating and scintillating is more like it! She's got oceans of personality, and lashings of sparkle, but not one ounce of ordinary common or garden decency. But she'll be in the Company before any of us staid people. You'll see!'

'Yes – if she doesn't go just a bit *too* far,' said Sara. 'As I said before, it's a wonder to me why they keep her in this school. In my opinion it's touch and go with Belinda.'

'Oh, I think she's safe enough,' argued Margaret. 'They can't afford to turn out anyone who can dance like Belinda.'

'You never can tell,' put in Marcia, giving me a sidelong look which showed that she disliked me just as much as I disliked her. 'A scholarship means nothing. Remember Patsy, that pale-faced girl who came here with a schol, flags flying and the band playing? Everyone thought she'd be in the Company, and into solo parts in a twink. And in less than a year she was turned out. She went into another company – I forget which.' She yawned loudly.

'The European,' supplied Sara, who seemed to be a positive well of information. 'And there was a reason for her being turned out, you know. Her thighs got too big, and of course for a company like the Sadler's Wells Ballet your figure's got to be perfect as well as your dancing. Incidentally, I read about her in some magazine or other, and she seems to be doing quite well. I'm glad – she was quite a decent sort.'

Marcia shrugged her shoulders.

'You and your decent sorts! She had no pep. Not a bit of good for the Ballet.'

'Oh, I don't know,' argued Sara. 'What about Beryl Grey? You couldn't call *her* exactly peppy, and she's ever so nice. Why, she even kissed me the night I gave her that bunch of willowherb I gathered off the wasteland near Cadby Hall. *Some* people would have been frightfully sniffy, but *she* wasn't. She knew that I hadn't any money to buy her real flowers. By the way, I've still got the bit of cottonwool I rubbed the greasepaint off with where she kissed me. I'm saving it for an heirloom to hand on to my grandchildren!'

'By the way,' put in the dark-skinned Taiis half-apologetically to me, 'you do not need to put on your tights and tunic just yet, you know. The Continuation classes come before our dancing.'

'Yes – English and French, and all that rot,' said Marcia. 'Waste of time, I call it!'

'Must be well educated to be a good dancer,' said Sara briskly. 'The Director says so, and so does Madame, and I expect they're quite right, even if it does seem a bit hard to us to have to stodge French verbs when we might be dancing.'

'But Belinda—' I said, thinking of the Titian-haired girl dancing off in her tights and tunic.

'Oh, Belinda cuts most of the Continuation classes,' said Sara with a shrug. 'But *you* mustn't do it. Come on!'

Chapter 2

Gilbert

MY first morning passed like a dream. Before I knew it, the English lesson was over and there was an interval for milk and biscuits. After this we had French, and then a longer interval before afternoon school, when most of the dancing classes were held. I had lunch at school, and I may say that it was an excellent meal.

'Too good!' laughed Sara, who was sitting next to me. 'According to Gilbert, that is! Gilbert, by the way, is Mr Gilbert Delahaye who takes most of our classes. He's English, in spite of his name and the way he behaves.'

'What do you mean – "the way he behaves"?' I asked curiously.

Sara laughed.

'He's what you might call temperamental. He shouts, and bangs his stick on the floor and on the *barre*, and sometimes you imagine he's going to attack *you*, but of course he never does; he's a lamb really, and most awfully popular with everybody. The Senior class is wild with jealousy because we have Gilbert. Well, as I say, he positively *raves* about the lunches.'

Wickedly Sara propped her elbows on the table and mimicked Gilbert in his fury:

'What on earth have you girls been eating? Suet pudding again! Well, I must say, you certainly dance like it! Really, it's absurd to expect a ballet dancer to execute *entrechats-six* on four helpings of suet pudding! Now, come along! There must be *some* of you who have not feasted on suet pudding! ...'

After Sara's vivid description, I stared curiously at Mr Gilbert Delahaye – by the way, he pronounced it 'Dellerhaye'

20

– when I entered the Baylis Hall for my first class with him. At first sight he had public school and 'varsity written all over him. He might have been a rowing blue, or a county cricketer, or indeed any sort of athlete. He certainly wasn't the least bit like the traditional dancing master – not in appearance, anyway. But appearances are sometimes deceptive, and it was so in Gilbert's case. He'd been a famous dancer, and he had all the well-known characteristics hidden under that old-school-tie exterior. Artistic temperament, flow of sarcasm, generosity of nature. All dancers aren't generous, but most really great ones are. Gilbert Delahaye was known to have helped many a struggling student by giving him free coaching and encouraging him generally.

Well, as I say, Gilbert would enter the room, mount the platform, polished of manner, calm of eye. In less than ten minutes, however, he would have shed his restraint, together with most or all of his pullovers – he often wore several – and would be striding up and down the room, banging his stick and delivering a continuous stream of sarcastic remarks. In fact, he would behave in such a temperamental way that it was indeed hard to believe that he really *was* English. I came to the conclusion, when I had been at the Wells for a short time, that most of it was a pose to make us work, and, if so, it certainly succeeded. We adored him – the boys especially – and slackness in his classes was unknown. Incidentally, he worked harder than anybody, and at the end of the day he would have put so much into his teaching that he was quite exhausted himself.

At the end of this first class, after we had made our curtsies, he mopped his damp forehead with a silk handkerchief that he kept expressly for the purpose, and motioned me to stay behind the rest.

'You're new, aren't you?' he said. 'Ah, yes – I remember now – I barged into your audition, didn't I? I knew I'd seen you somewhere before. Where were you trained – Wakulski-Viret, I suppose?'

21

'Yes,' I answered in astonishment. 'However did you know?'

He laughed.

'Oh, by certain characteristics – little movements of the head and hands that Madame Viret passes on to her students. Oh, don't look so dismayed – they're not *bad* characteristics! On the contrary, they're good ones. Madame Viret is a wonderful teacher – one of the best in the world.'

I nodded.

'Yes – it's marvellous just to watch her move,' I said. 'I began learning from her when I was ten, and I've never been anywhere else, except for last year when I went to live with my cousins in Northumberland. While I was there I went to a dancing school in Newcastle – a Miss Martin was the head of it. She was wonderful, too.'

To my surprise Gilbert seemed to know all about Miss Martin.

'Ah, yes,' he said. 'Another excellent teacher. Well, with all that behind you, you've certainly got something to live up to! You've got a nice "line", you know. By the way – your name?'

I told him my name, and he dismissed me with a smile. As I went out of the Baylis Hall I nearly had a head-on collision with Marcia Rutherford. It was quite obvious that she'd been listening outside the door, and I wondered how much she'd heard. By the expression on her face, as she looked at me, I knew that she'd caught Gilbert's last remark, and with a sinking feeling in my heart I knew also that Marcia Rutherford was my enemy.

As I went home by the Underground that night after school, my thoughts were very different to those I had had when I'd travelled in the opposite direction that morning. No longer did I ache to turn *pirouettes* down the centre of the compartment, or to pose *en arabesque* in the entry. For one thing, I was much too tired, and for another I had had a good deal of the self-conceit knocked out of me during my first few classes at the Wells. I wasn't so sure, now, that my *pirouettes* were so very good, after all – not after seeing Belinda's! I didn't feel that my *arabesque* was as perfect as I had always believed it to be. I lived again in my mind the classes I had attended that first day at the Wells – the Ballet, Character, and Elementary Mime – and to be quite frank, I hadn't received the attention I'd expected. Apart from Gilbert, who'd been kind and asked me where I'd been trained, no one else had taken the least notice of me. I don't believe that Serge Lopokoff, the Russian dancing master, who'd taken the Character class, had even *seen* me, as I manfully struggled with new steps in the back row, let alone been dazzled by my brilliance. If it hadn't been for Toni Rossini, who'd came forward and offered to be my partner and had helped me all he could, I'd have been hopelessly out of my depth. Yes, Serge Lopokoff hadn't been very helpful. Still, I liked the gentle little man with his exquisite hands and his mild blue eyes that had a far-away expression in them, as if his thoughts had strayed back again to the Leningrad school where he was trained.

As the train rumbled along I couldn't help smiling to myself and thinking how utterly unlike a temperamental Russian dancing master Serge Lopokoff was.

I hadn't fared any better at the Mime class either. Everyone knew more than I did, for I hadn't learnt any Classical Mime at Madame Viret's or at Miss Martin's. It took me all my time to manage the gestures 'I' and 'you' correctly. I consoled myself with the thought that, if you could go by what you read, Margot Fonteyn hadn't been noticed at first either – not outwardly, anyway. 'Perhaps,' I said to myself, 'they're watching me all the time, although they don't show it. Anyhow, they'll jolly well *have* to before long, because I mean to work and work, even if I have to do it in the backest of back rows!'

The train got fuller and fuller, and I stood up to let an old lady, who carried two enormous brown-paper parcels, have my seat. After all, if I *had* been on my feet all day, so probably had she, and she was quite three times my age. Two outsize businessmen hung on straps on either side of me and talked racing over my head. I felt in danger of being squashed any minute! I looked at my wristwatch and saw that it was half past five already. Mrs Crapper would have finished her tea long ago, but I hoped that Jonathan would have waited for me, so that we could have it together in Mrs Crapper's kitchen.

I don't think I've told you about Jonathan, have I? He was an artist and he lived on the top floor of Mrs Crapper's apartment house. The top floor was really one large attic, with two smaller ones opening off it. Jonathan used the smaller attics for his bedroom and kitchen. The big attic was his studio, and Jonathan said that, now he'd had the big skylight put in the roof, it suited him down to the ground – if you can say that about an attic!

Jonathan was enormous – over six feet tall, and broad in proportion. He had curly black hair, brilliant dark eyes, and a little black beard. He was really quite young – about twenty-six – although he looked older because of the beard. In spite of being so big and strong, you couldn't have met a gentler person than Jonathan. Not even the kitten that used to climb in from the next-door attic and rub itself against his legs, nor the little grey mouse busily picking up stray crumbs from his floor; not even the spider that had the temerity to spin a web over the top corner of his easel had anything to fear from Jonathan.

'They have as much right to live on the earth as I have,' he'd say, as he put a bluebottle carefully out of the window. 'Why should I believe that the sun only shines for me?'

'You wait till your meat gets fly-blown, Mr Jonathan,' put in Mrs Crapper, sensible as ever. 'Then you'll think different. You will that!'

'I don't eat meat,' Jonathan answered with a flash of his white teeth. 'Surely you know that by now, Martha! I'm a vegetarian.'

'Yes, I *do* know it, Mr Jonathan,' said Mrs Crapper

severely. 'And it ain't right, that's what I says, that a great strapping fellow like you should be living on lettuces and tomatoes and suchlike bits of things. It ain't nat'ral. You'll be fading away before long, I shouldn't wonder!'

Jonathan said no more. I think that Mrs Crapper's logic, or rather the lack of it, was beyond him!

Besides Jonathan, several other people lived in Mrs Crapper's apartment house. There was a middle-aged woman who was secretary to a corset manufacturer. Her name was Broadbent, and she was very straightlaced – perhaps her job had got the better of her! I'm pretty sure she didn't really approve of the rest of us. The 'rest' comprised a girl named Miriam Samuels. She was dark, pretty, and very vivacious. She was a dancing student at a stage school, and she'd shared a room with Stella Mason, the ballet student I told you about before, until a few weeks ago when a talent scout had spotted her. Now she was at the Windmill Theatre, and doing well. She'd left Mrs Crapper's so as to be nearer her job.

The deep rumbling voices of the two large businessmen kept breaking in upon my thoughts. They had stopped talking about horses and were now discussing somebody's preference shares, and why they were a good thing, and why George had parted with somebody else's ordinaries, and that a slump was bound to come; didn't George think so? I couldn't help thinking what funny things men are interested in!

At last the welcome words 'Chalk Farm' slid past the window, and I fought my way out. I got a bus the rest of the way, but of course I had to wait for it, so it was well after six o'clock by the time I found myself walking down the long row of houses called – ironically enough! – Heather Hill, where Mrs Crapper's apartment house was. Unluckily, No 242 was at the opposite end of the road to the bus stop! It seemed years and years since I had left it this morning, and really it was almost impossible to believe that the sun, which had shone down on me out of the cold eastern sky this morning, was only just now setting in a flurry of pink cloud behind the laburnum tree in the garden opposite. I felt that at least a week of sunrises and sunsets had passed since I had set out on my great adventure.

I ran down the basement stairs to Mrs Crapper's kitchen, but the room was empty, although there was a beautiful coal fire roaring in the grate. My heart gave a throb of disappointment. But, of course, both Mrs Crapper and Jonathan would have finished tea long ago. Why, it was nearly time for supper!

I left the cosy kitchen with a sigh of regret, and toiled slowly up the three long flights of stairs to my own room. I noticed, just as I had done when I'd come back from Northumberland, the strong smell of carbolic soap, wet wood, and boiled cabbage that hung over the house – especially the bottom half. I must say that, when you got to Jonathan's top floor, the smell was drowned by the more pungent one of oil paint and turpentine!

When I reached my own room I switched on the light and looked round. My tea was on the table, and there was a note beside it which said: 'Mind you make a reel good tea ave gon round to the shop for tin of beans and pkt soap powder back in a jiffy martha crapper.' Other than this, everything was exactly as I had left it when I'd dashed out this morning – even to a pair of tights on the table with the darning needle sticking in them. It was quite evident that Stella hadn't got back from her tour yet.

Chapter 3

Stella

I TOOK off my outdoor things, made myself some cocoa on the gas-ring, and sat down to my belated tea. I had just finished, and was wondering what to do until suppertime – mend my tights or darn a new pair of practice shoes – when my eye caught sight of an orange envelope propped against the tea-caddy. I expect that Mrs Crapper, being tea-minded, had put it there thinking I couldn't possibly miss it. She hadn't thought about cocoa!

The telegram was from Aunt June, and I've often wondered since what on earth the post-office authorities must have thought about it. It said:

CAN REMEMBER ONLY WHOOPING-COUGH. PLEASE WIRE OTHER DISEASES. AUNT JUNE.

Of course! I'd sent the health certificate and other forms from the school on to poor Aunt June, quite forgetting that she couldn't possibly know what infectious diseases I'd had, since I'd only lived with her for about a year. Evidently I'd told her about the whooping-cough at some time or other, and that was how she knew about it.

The wire was prepaid, so I hastily scribbled on the reply form:

SCARLET FEVER. MUMPS. CHICKEN-POX TWICE. MEASLES NOT SURE. LOVE VERONICA.

I had just finished, and was putting on my hat and coat again to go out to the post office, when there was a footstep on the stairs – a footstep that certainly didn't belong to Mrs Crapper who clamped, or Jonathan who bounded.

'Stella!' I yelled.

'Yes, it's me,' said Stella's well-known voice. 'Hullo, Veronica! Gosh! It's wonderful to see you again. You haven't altered much either – except that you aren't so pale, and you aren't skinny any more.'

'*You've* altered lots,' I said. 'Why, you're quite grown up!'

'I'm eighteen,' laughed Stella. 'I don't feel a bit like it sometimes. Golly! How time flies!'

I looked at Stella as she took off her coat and hat, and thought how pretty she'd grown. She had soft, fair hair that waved naturally; it was shoulder-length, as every ballet dancer's hair must be, and it was turned under in a simple page-boy style. Her face was heart shaped, and she had a lovely creamy complexion that needed no powder or cream to make it look like the petal of a flower. Then I noticed that she was looking tired. Her soft, generous mouth drooped a little at the corners, and there were violet shadows under her eyes.

'Stella, you've been slimming?' I said severely. Although Stella was three years older than I was, I always 'mothered' her. There was something about Stella that made you want to take care of her. 'Have you been going without your meals?'

'No, I haven't – honestly,' said Stella. 'I've had jolly good breakfasts, and – and suppers. I have, really, Veronica. I expect I look tired because I've been travelling all night.'

'What about your lunches?' I persisted. 'Have you been skipping them?'

'Just a few,' Stella admitted guiltily. 'But not because I'm slimming, though I *am* getting horribly fat, but because lunches are so expensive. Seventy-five pence a lunch – it mounts up.'

'But I always thought you got paid the earth in the Opera Ballet – more than in the real ballet!' I exclaimed.

'Oh, the pay is quite good,' said Stella. 'But you see, since Granny was ill I've been sending home as much as I possibly could for her to get someone to help her in the house and to do her washing for her, and so on. She's getting old, you know; she's over eighty. By the way, there aren't any letters for me, are there? I haven't heard from Granny all this week.'

'There are no letters for you,' I answered. Then I was about to explain about Aunt June and her funny wire, when Stella saw the orange envelope lying on the table.

'Oh, Veronica,' she said in a strange far-off voice. 'The telegram? Is it for me? ... Granny ...'

'Oh, no!' I laughed. 'It's from Aunt June, and guess what she says? She wants to know – why, what's the matter, Stella?'

Stella's little heart-shaped face seemed to have grown even smaller and whiter. She swayed a little as she stood.

'Oh, Veronica – I – I feel so funny,' she whispered.

Then, to my horror, she crumpled up at my feet in a dead faint.

'Jonathan!' I shrieked, rushing to the door. 'Mrs Crapper – Jonathan! Come quickly! – Oh, Jonathan!'

They both came running – Mrs Crapper had evidently got back from her shopping – but Jonathan was there first. He came tumbling down his attic stairs like a thunderbolt.

'What is it, Veronica? What's the matter?' Then he saw Stella lying at my feet, and his face went white.

'Oh, Jonathan!' I sobbed. 'Is she dead? Do you think she's dead?'

Jonathan looked up – he'd gone down on his knees beside Stella, and was chafing her hands.

'Dead? Good Lord, no! She's just fainted, that's all. Get a spot of brandy, Martha, there's a good soul. There's some in the cupboard in my bedroom.' He lifted Stella up as if she were a baby – and indeed she was, compared to him – and propped her in a chair by the window which he'd already opened. 'She's coming round. Put the kettle on, Veronica, and

29

get her a cup of something hot to drink. I suspect she's been living on tea and buns. She feels like it!'

After she'd sipped the brandy that Mrs Crapper brought, Stella revived very quickly. She drank the tea that I made, and Jonathan fed her like a baby with strips of toast dipped in the hot liquid.

'No dancing for you tomorrow,' he pronounced, when the colour had come back into her cheeks. 'Bed for you, my child, and no nonsense. I'll bring you your meals myself.'

'Oh, but I couldn't do that,' protested Stella. 'I'm supposed to be in class as usual tomorrow morning.'

'If you don't do as you're told,' threatened Jonathan, 'I shall ring up that confounded school and tell them you fainted—'

'Oh, *no*, Jonathan!' cried Stella, 'No, *please*! They'll say—'

'They'll say that this dancing business is too much for you,' said Jonathan. 'And they won't be far wrong either.' He looked down at her anxiously. 'What do you want to go on doing it for?'

'Why, Jonathan, it's my *life*!' cried Stella. 'It's the only life for me. I'd die if I didn't dance! Anyway, why all the fuss? Veronica's doing it.'

'Veronica's tough,' pronounced Jonathan. 'If she likes to be mug enough to dedicate her whole life to a stupid thing like ballet, well, it's her own affair.'

'It's *my* own affair too,' argued Stella.

'No, it isn't – not when you frighten the life out of – of people by fainting away like that. It's not your own affair at all. You're not strong enough to do it. Veronica's a chirpy Cockney. You're – you're just a North-Country primrose.'

'I always thought that North-Country people were tough as tough,' I put in. 'The Director said so at my audition. And anyway, *I'm* partly North Country. My mother was Aunt June's sister, and she came from Northumberland.'

'I give it up!' said Jonathan. 'I always regarded you as one hundred per cent Cockney, Veronica. Let's not argue about it, anyhow. Let's roast chestnuts. I got a bag this morning. Here they are.' He delved beneath his overall into one of his capacious pockets and brought forth a brown-paper bag. 'Now we'll see who's going to be rich. This one is Stella's; this one Veronica's, and the little one is mine.' He placed them carefully in front of the gas-fire. 'Now for the pops! The first one to go off is going to be rich; the second is going to be loved; the third is going to be the successful one – in the eyes of the world, that is!'

We waited for a long time, but nothing happened. Then we forgot about them and began to talk. Jonathan was just telling us about his latest picture – the one of Covent Garden Market – when there was a loud explosion.

'It's yours, Jonathan!' I yelled. 'You're going to be rich. Golly! It's Stella's too – a dead heat! How funny! So you're *both* going to be rich, and you're both going to be loved as well. And it looks as if I'm going to have all the success.'

'Of *course* it's true,' pronounced Jonathan. 'I've always found chestnuts to be most reliable. Naturally, Stella will be loved. No one could possibly help loving Stella.'

Yes, that was certainly true, I thought. Stella was very gentle and sweet. She hadn't an unkind or an ungenerous thought in her head, and she was as pretty as she was good.

'What about me?' I demanded, pretending to be annoyed. 'Isn't there a bit of love left over for me?'

'Not a spot!' said Jonathan, striking an attitude. Incidentally, he looked magnificent, standing there drawn up to his full height. 'You, Veronica, cast aside the flower of love for the tinsel blossom of fame. What more do you want?'

'I think I'd like a little bit of love as well, please – if you don't mind,' I said meekly.

'Don't be greedy, Veronica! You can't have both,' said Jonathan flatly. 'Not in the world of ballet, anyway. It's either love or fame; you've only to see that well-known film – what's its name? – to learn that. If you flirt with both, you come to a messy end!' He spoke so seriously that I stared at him. But he was looking down at Stella with the strangest expression in his dark eyes, and really it was just as if he was addressing *her*, and not me at all, so I said no more.

After a while Jonathan went away to 'see to something', as he put it, and I helped Stella to get to bed. It wasn't long before we heard his well-known step on the stairs. There was a knock on the door, and when I opened it there he was, almost hidden behind an enormous bunch of chrysanthemums and goodness knows what else besides.

'A geranium in a pot!' cried Stella. 'How lovely! I've always wanted one, but I never seemed to have enough money left over to buy one. Oh, Jonathan – you shouldn't – you *shouldn't* have got me all these things. Why, you'll be absolutely broke!'

'Not a bit of it!' laughed Jonathan, tumbling bags of sweets pell-mell down on the counterpane. 'Didn't I tell you? I sold that little sketch of "Winter in the Cheviots" yesterday. Got quite a bit for it, too. What's the matter, Veronica? You look struck all of a heap.'

'I was just thinking of something,' I admitted. 'You know, while I was living with my cousins in Northumberland we had a Wayside Stall. I don't think I ever told you about it, did I, Jonathan?'

Jonathan shook his curly head.

'No. Out with it!'

'It's just that talking of paintings reminded me that we – Sebastian, Caroline, and I – put some of *my* choicest paintings on it. You remember the ones I used to do on the backs of your old canvases?'

He nodded.

'Do I not! You used to make me take my efforts off the frames and tack them on again the other way round!'

'Poor Jonathan! Well, as I say, I put them on our Wayside Stall to brighten it up a bit, and some highbrow people turned up and bought them. You see, they saw *your* things on the backs.'

Jonathan gave a great snort.

'Jumping Jehoshaphat! You don't mean to tell me, Veronica, that you sold that rubbish of mine to a lot of art dealers?'

'Not art dealers, Jonathan,' I corrected gently. 'They were a woman called Yvonne, and her brother. He had a little black beard – like yours.'

Jonathan groaned.

'Veronica! What have you done? That would be Yvonne and Claude Millhaven. They own most of the big art shops in these fashionable holiday resorts – like Cheltenham, Harrogate, Scarborough, and so forth. The Art Room, The Treasure Shop – you know the sort of thing! And you've sold them my – *my* canvases. I'm willing to bet that frightful daub, "Sunset on Skye", was one of them—' He groaned again.

'I'm afraid it was,' I admitted. 'I'm most awfully sorry, Jonathan.'

'Oh, well – I suppose it can't be helped,' said Jonathan philosophically.

'It was in aid of a very good cause,' I volunteered. 'The money was to hire me a pony to ride.'

'In that case,' said Jonathan grandly, 'you shall be forgiven. The affair shall be forgotten. Say no more!'

After this little incident we were all very happy. I sat on the end of Stella's bed, and Jonathan sat astride the one chair the room contained, and we all ate sweets and nuts and told funny stories. At about nine o'clock Jonathan said he'd have to go because he had a lot of work to do. I knew he meant housework; he always did it at night because of the light. I mean, he wanted the daylight for his painting, so he did his chores in the evening.

I said goodnight to Stella myself soon afterwards and went to my own room, for I was dead tired after my day's work. As I reached the door there was a roar from above my head, and, looking up, I beheld Jonathan's unruly black head looking over the banister rail. His teeth fairly shone in the dusk.

'Hey, Veronica! You might tell Stella that if I catch her up and about tomorrow there'll be trouble! I'll be down with her breakfast about nine.'

'I'll tell her,' I shouted back.

While I was undressing that night I thought about Jonathan and what a puzzle he was. He didn't seem to be really poor. In fact, whenever any money was needed for anything, he'd always come forward. When Daddy had died, and I'd had to leave Mrs Crapper's house, they'd all made a collection for me as a goodbye present. I knew, from what Mrs Crapper said, that it was Jonathan who'd given the lion's share. Yet surely no one but a really poor person would live in Mrs Crapper's dingy apartment house. I'd once asked Jonathan why he went on living there, now that he was quite a well-known artist. He'd lit his old black pipe and puffed away at it very slowly for a long time before he answered.

'Well, Veronica,' he'd said at length. 'Perhaps it's because I want to look after you all – Mrs Crapper, dear soul, and you, Veronica, and Miriam before she went to the Windmill and got rich, and – and Stella. But, of course, you don't understand – you're too young.'

'Oh, no I'm not,' I assured him. 'I understand perfectly. I've often felt like that myself about dear Mrs Crapper – especially now that her eyes aren't what they were.'

'That's right; you've hit it!' said Jonathan, his eyes crinkling at the corners. 'So now you know why I stay on.'

But there were other things that puzzled me about Jonathan. He didn't seem to have any 'people' belonging to him, or if he had he never mentioned them. Yet he'd obviously been what Uncle John would call 'well brought up'. For instance, he'd always open the door for you, and let you go through first, and he'd stand up when you did. Also, I noticed that, although he worked with his old black pipe continually between his strong white teeth, he'd always stuff it into his pocket when he talked to us, or when he came and sat in Mrs Crapper's kitchen. Although his overalls were stained with paint and clay, his linen was spotless. He 'did' for himself, and although his

34

studio was littered with canvases, frames, palettes, brushes, and all the artist's paraphernalia, yet his bedroom and the little kitchen where he cooked his meals were spotlessly clean and tidy.

Yes, there was no doubt about it – Jonathan was a puzzle.

Chapter 4

We Celebrate

I DIDN'T see a great deal of Stella, apart from going to school with her in the mornings and sharing the same dressing-room. She was in the Senior class, of course; so all her lessons were at different times to mine, and, besides that, she'd got several parts in the Theatre Ballet, which is what is known to students as the Second Company. We didn't often have lunch together either, because she'd be rehearsing down at Sadler's Wells; and most evenings she had performances, so I didn't even see her then.

One day, towards the middle of term, just as I had arrived home and was taking off my coat, I heard her voice on the stairs.

'Veronica! – Jonathan! – I've the most wonderful news! The most marvellous thing has happened!'

I dashed out on to the landing, and Jonathan appeared as if by magic. Strangely enough, he always happened to be there when Stella came home. Even Mrs Crapper came up from below, wiping her hands on her apron.

'What is it, Stella?'

'I'm in!' said Stella, laughing and crying both at once. 'Yes, it's true! I'm actually in the Company – the Second Company, of course.'

'Oh, Stella! How glorious!' I burst out. 'When did you get to know?'

'This afternoon – at the three o'clock class. Miss Jackson, the ballet mistress down at Sadler's Wells, you know, came in and chose several of us. Belinda's one; but, of course, everyone knew *she'd* be chosen; Mary and Jocelyn and me. We start on Monday. Oh, isn't it glorious?'

36

'Glorious,' said Jonathan flatly.

'What's the matter?' said Stella, a pucker between her brows. 'Aren't you pleased?'

'Of course I'm pleased – if it's what you want,' Jonathan answered.

'Of *course* it's what I want.' Stella exclaimed. 'It's – why, it's my dream come true.'

'Well, now you'll have loads of money,' I said. 'You can have three-course lunches every day. You won't have to worry now; you're safe – permanently in the Company.'

A cloud passed over Stella's happy face and she gave a little sigh.

'There's nothing permanent in life,' she said soberly. 'Not in ballet, anyway. I might break my leg, or get fat, or anything. And that goes for the three-course lunches, too. I must think of my figure. My thighs are getting terribly big.'

'Let's not be gloomy now!' I exclaimed. 'Let's cast dull care aside and celebrate! Let's have fun! What show would you like to see most, Stella?'

Stella considered.

'I know it sounds funny and like a busman's holiday,' she said at length, 'but I'm simply longing to go to Covent Garden tomorrow night. It's Irma Foster in *Les Patineurs*, and they *say* it's her last performance. Ivan Stcherbakof is guest artist, and everyone says he's the most wonderful male dancer in the world. I might be able to get a free ticket from school. What about you, Veronica?'

I shook my head sadly.

'I had one last night for *Lac*, so I can't expect another this week. Anyway, Jonathan couldn't get one, so that's no use. How about going in the gallery slips? They're not too ruinous!'

'I've got an idea worth two of that,' Jonathan said quietly. 'How about doing it in style and going in a box?'

'A b-box?' Stella and I laughed both together in such awestruck voices that Jonathan laughed aloud.

'Are you joking, Jonathan?' I added. 'Why, a box at Covent Garden costs pounds and pounds!'

'Look – this is *my* treat,' Jonathan said firmly, 'so we won't discuss costs, if you don't mind. Didn't I tell you I sold a picture not so long ago?'

'Yes, but—'

'Don't argue, just leave it to me. We'll have a box for four and we'll take old Martha along with us, eh?'

'Oh, yes, that'll be lovely!' exclaimed Stella. 'I don't believe Mrs Crapper has ever been to what she calls "the bally". By the way, where *is* Mrs Crapper? She was here just a minute ago.'

'She went back to her kitchen when she heard your news, Stella,' said Jonathan. 'I don't think Martha realized how world-shattering it was! And, by the way,' he went on, 'we're going to see this performance as *ordinary theatre-goers*. Coffee in the first interval, ices in the second, and no going backstage.'

'All right,' Stella agreed. 'It'll be terribly strange, though.'

We didn't wear evening dress for our celebration. For one thing, I hadn't got a long frock yet, and for another we knew that Mrs Crapper would want to wear what she called 'me ciré lace'. This had been her wedding dress, but had been dyed black, being more useful that colour. Since Mrs Crapper's wedding day had been over thirty years ago, the dress wasn't exactly what you might call the latest fashion. It was knee-length and had long flowing sleeves and a beige jabot that cascaded down the front like a waterfall. The waistline came somewhere about the knees. I can't imagine what the creation would have looked like on anybody else, but it certainly suited Mrs Crapper as no other dress would have done. On top of the ciré lace she wore 'me fur coat', which was a mat-like garment smelling of mothballs, and on top of the lot went a pudding-basin hat with a bunch of glass grapes at one side which rattled when she moved. When she was dressed in her best,

Mrs Crapper adopted a slightly aloof manner to go with her finery, except when excitement overcame her, and she forgot!

When we had settled ourselves in our box we scanned the programme eagerly to see who were dancing the principal roles.

'*Les Patineurs*,' read out Stella. 'The classical *pas-de-deux*, Foster and Linsk; *pas-seul*, Ivan Stcherbakof; that's the Exhibition Skater in blue,' she added for Jonathan's benefit. '*Spectre de la Rose*, with Stcherbakof and Beryl Grey. *The Rake's Progress*, with Gordon Hamilton as 'The Rake', and – let me see, oh, yes, Linsk as the Dancing Master. I love the Dancing Master, don't you?'

'I've never seen the ballet,' I confessed.

It was lovely watching the ballet from the front and being looked after. Jonathan produced a box of chocolates from his overcoat pocket, and we ordered ices and coffee as he had promised. As for Mrs Crapper – she sat with her eyes glued to the stage, watching the skating couples. Every few minutes she'd say in an awestruck voice: 'Ee, but it's lovely! All them folk skating to the manner born!' When the solitary Skater in Blue appeared, she was spellbound.

'There now! You wouldn't believe it, would you? My! but he's a grand skater, and no mistake! Good enough for an exhibition, I shouldn't wonder. He oughta be in them Ice Folies, he should that! I'm told they're wonderful, and very well paid.'

It wasn't a bit of good trying to explain to Mrs Crapper that Ivan Stcherbakof was a *dancer*, and not a skater at all; that he was world famous, and that he wouldn't be in the least bit flattered by being told he ought to be in the Ice Folies, however marvellous or well paid they might be.

'Gosh! Isn't he wonderful?' whispered Stella as we watched him breathlessly. 'He's even better than they say. He's electrified the whole house!' Indeed, there wasn't a sound from that great audience – not a cough or the rustle of a programme – so thrilled was it by the brilliant personality of the young Russian dancer.

Ivan Stcherbakof: the Exhibition Skater in Blue

'They say he has the best elevation since Nijinsky,' whispered Stella. 'I can quite believe it, can't you? When he jumps, it's just like a bird flying!'

The young man in blue was followed by a skating couple in white – the classical *pas-de-deux*.

'Irma Foster,' said Stella. 'You haven't seen her before, have you, Veronica? She doesn't often appear now. She's thirty-eight, you know, and that's old for a dancer.'

Irma Foster was very beautiful. If she lacked brilliance on account of her age, she certainly made up for it with other things. Her dancing was aristocratic in the extreme, and her line was so pure she made you think of fields of virgin snow and frosted fir branches; of a calm frozen lake with the moonlight shining down upon it out of the northern sky.

Then the lovely slow music of the classical *pas-de-deux* changed to the urgent, compelling melody for the girls in brown and blue, and then two others in maroon and white. The latter had evidently not learned to skate very well, for they kept slipping! At last some young men arrived on the scene to help them, and gallantly pulled them across the frozen pool. The ballet now worked up to an exciting finish, the whole Company whirling round the stage in various figures. At last they all skated away, leaving the Exhibition Skater turning his endless *fouettés* on the icy pool. The light faded, the snow began to fall, but still he turned effortlessly. As the curtain fell he was still spinning, and you felt that he would go on spinning for ever.

'Wonderful ballet!' Stella said with a sigh of happiness. 'I can't count the number of times I've seen it, but I like it better each time.'

'I saw it once, ages ago,' I said, 'but it wasn't nearly as good as it was tonight. That young man – Ivan Stcherbakof – is a marvellous dancer, and Irma Foster is lovely too.'

The lights went on and the coffee arrived, brought by a pert usherette who stared at Jonathan in open admiration. Mrs Crapper produced a pair of ancient opera-glasses out of her

41

handbag, and we amused ourselves by getting close-ups of the people in the auditorium.

'Look!' said Stella. 'You see that little girl in the fifth row of the stalls – the one with the bright red-gold hair and the brown velvet dress with the lace collar? That's Mariella Foster, Irma Foster's only daughter. They say she's training to be a dancer herself. I wonder if she'll be any good at it?'

'Shouldn't think so,' put in Jonathan. 'The talent has probably culminated in the mother, and the kid will be something altogether different, I expect – like a doctor or a mathematician.'

'Do you see the man she's with? That's Oscar Deveraux, her father. He's a famous critic, but in spite of that he's always known as "Irma Foster's husband", poor little man!'

'Why is the kid's name Foster, when her father's name is Deveraux?' I asked.

'Well, Irma Foster made her name long before she met Oscar Deveraux,' explained Stella. 'So she still dances under her maiden name, though really she's Mrs Oscar Deveraux. The kid's known by her mother's name too – for dancing purposes. I expect she's hoping for a bit of reflected glory! ... Well, it's *Spectre de la Rose* next. I wonder what Stcherbakof will be like as the Spirit of the Rose? It's a question not only of technique, but "feeling", if you know what I mean.'

'Perhaps he'll be even better than he was in *Les Patineurs*,' I answered. 'I wonder if he'll give us some idea of what Nijinsky was like. I wonder—'

But the packed auditorium was destined never to see the brilliant Russian's interpretation of the famous role. We had just given back our empty coffee cups to the attendant, and were watching the members of the orchestra filing back into their pit, when suddenly Stella gripped my arm.

'Look!' she whispered. 'Something's happened! There's going to be an announcement. That's the stage manager, and he's going to speak.'

There was a short roll of drums, and the noise in the

auditorium died down as if by magic. It was so quiet that you could hear the clink of cups and glasses, and the hum of voices from the crush-bar. Then these sounds died away, too, as the news spread that an announcement was being made.

'Lords, ladies, and gentlemen,' said the manager. 'I very much regret to have to tell you that Monsieur Ivan Stcherbakof has had a slight accident. His place in *Le Spectre de la Rose* will be taken by Mr Josef Linsk.'

There was an audible sigh from the audience. One or two people in the gallery, who were Linsk fans, clapped feebly, but were drowned by the disapproving 'sh' of their neighbours of better taste. The feeling of the house was undoubtedly that of disappointment. Of course, Linsk was a brilliant dancer, but he was a member of the Company; they could see him any time. Moreover, they had come especially to see the world-famous Russian, and, after his brilliant exhibition in *Les Patineurs*, they were unable to hide their disappointment at not seeing him dance again. Yes, Ivan Stcherbakof had indeed captured the hearts and fired the imagination of the large audience.

'I can't believe it!' said Stella, when the manager had disappeared behind the curtain. 'I simply *can't* believe it! Why, only a minute ago he was turning those *fouettés* in the middle of the stage. What can have happened?'

'He must have tripped over something,' I said. 'Or fallen down some stairs.'

'Or perhaps bumped into someone,' Jonathan put in. 'I was once at a performance of *Coppélia* in which there was a proper chapter of accidents. Moira Shearer had a collision with Veronica Vale, and poor Veronica put her kneecap out, and had to sit on the stage with it out until the curtain went down. Things like that are always happening to ballet dancers.'

We both stared at Jonathan.

'I didn't know you knew anything about ballet, Jonathan,' said Stella. 'I always thought you despised it.'

'On the contrary – I love it,' Jonathan said. 'I've yet to meet an artist who doesn't.'

'Well, I never knew that!' Stella said in amazement.

Jonathan smiled down at her.

'I don't think you really know an awful lot about me, Stella,' he said.

'Whatever do you mean?' Stella said indignantly. 'Why, I've known you ever since I was a kid.'

'Perhaps that's why,' Jonathan said enigmatically.

'I wish you'd stop talking in riddles,' Stella said crossly. 'If I don't know everything there is to know about you, I should like to know who does?'

'Sh!' said Jonathan warningly. 'The curtain's going up!'

The rest of the performance was a sad come-down after the beginning. Nothing is so sensitive to atmosphere as a theatre audience, and we all felt that something awful had happened, and that the dancers were merely living up to the old adage: 'The show must go on.' They were dancing with their feet, all right, but their hearts weren't in it.

As we came out into the frosty night Stella plucked Jonathan by the sleeve.

'I simply must fly round to the stage door and see what's happened,' she said. 'I shan't be long. Wait for me here.'

In a very few minutes she was back again.

'Oh, it's awful!' she said, with a sob in her voice. 'Someone had left a tube of greasepaint lying on the stairs going up to the dressing-rooms, and he slipped on it, and fell right down to the bottom. All those awful stone stairs! He's hurt his knee, and they think it's pretty bad – you can tell by the way they talk. They've taken him to the hospital straight away for an X-ray. Oh, Jonathan – Veronica – isn't it awful! Poor, poor man!'

As we walked home under the frosty sky I thought of the young Russian dancer, struck down at the height of his fame, and in my imagination I still saw him turning his effortless *fouettés* on the frozen pool, with the snowflakes falling all around him like tears.

Chapter 5

A Pair of Tights

THE news was all over the school when I got there next morning. Tongues wagged a hundred to the dozen.

'Ivan Stcherbakof ... yes, on the stone staircase going up to the dressing-rooms ... never dance again, they say ... oh, you never can tell; remember Bettini? Everyone said ... slipped on a tube of greasepaint. Golly! How awful for the person who dropped it! Imagine going down in history as the owner of the greasepaint Stcherbakof slipped on! ... Marcia was there when they carried him out on the stretcher; she says he looked like Death. Tell us what he looked like, Marcia ... Did you hear the house groan when they gave it out? Gosh! Josef would be mad! Not used to playing second-fiddle ... conceited? I should just say so! ... What? You don't think he is? But of course you *wouldn't* – I forgot you had a crush on Josef ... Hullo, Veronica! Heard the news?'

'Yes, I was in the theatre when it happened – in the audience,' I answered. 'Do you think it's serious?'

'Oh, yes – fatal, I should say,' Belinda said cheerfully, pulling up her tights. 'He's probably broken his back.'

'Oh, *no*!' I said with a gasp of horror. 'It's only his knee. They said so, didn't they, Stella?'

Stella nodded. She'd come with me as usual. As she didn't start in the Company until Monday, she had to attend classes until then.

'Yes, Mr Rogers said it was a slight accident when he gave it out.'

Belinda shrugged her shoulders.

'Oh, you can't go by *that*,' she declared. 'They always make light of an accident that happens to anyone famous. It's like

45

royalty – if they gave it out on the radio that the Queen has got a slight cold, you can bet your life she's pretty bad. By the way, I expect you've all heard I'm to go into the Company on Monday. Anyone like a pair of old tights?' She threw the tights into the middle of the floor, whereupon they became the centre of what looked like a rugger scrum.

'He who fights gets tights!' she yelled, dancing about on her toes like a referee at a boxing match. 'Odds on Lily! She's got a hard head!'

Lily did indeed emerge victorious, if dishevelled, the tights clutched firmly under one arm.

'I shall have to change my name,' went on Belinda. 'It's essential now I'm really in the Company.'

'Your name?' echoed Lily, her mind obviously still on the tights.

'Yes, my daydreamer. My *name*. N-A-M-E. Can't go on the stage as Belinda Stout, now can I? Think of it in the repertoire of *The Sleeping Beauty*: "Fonteyn and Soames, with Stout as the Lilac Fairy! ... The classic role of the Queen of the Wilis in the romantic ballet, *Giselle*, was danced most gracefully by Stout . . ."'

'You don't dance the Queen of the Wilis *gracefully*,' I put in firmly. 'You dance it coldly and inhumanly.'

'You *would* think of that, Veronica Weston,' said Belinda, not sounding too pleased at being corrected. 'Anyway, you don't dance it *stoutly*. I shall change my name to Beaucaire. Belinda Beaucaire,' she repeated dreamily. 'Goes well, doesn't it?'

'But you aren't French,' objected Sara.

'No more is Margot Fonteyn – or de Valois herself, for that matter. Yes, I'm quite determined – I shall be Belinda Beaucaire.'

She began to turn *déboulées* across the dressing-room, almost colliding with someone coming in at the door.

'Hullo, June! What's up?' she exclaimed, finishing off the

*déboulée*s with a treble *pirouette*. 'You look struck all of a heap!'

'Do I?' laughed June. 'That's always the effect Madame has upon me!'

It was our turn to look struck all of a heap, as Belinda put it.

'Madame? ... Madame...' The name had the effect of an electric shock upon the lazy dressing-room.

'Yes – Madame the Director, herself. I suppose you *have* heard of her?' said June sarcastically. As if anyone hadn't! 'Well, she's on her way here. I heard old Willan talking to her on the telephone – the office door was open, so it wasn't like eavesdropping. She's coming to take the Junior class – Madame, I mean.'

The effect of this speech was a series of sounds ranging from excited squeals to yelps and groans.

'Gosh, how awful! My tights ...' This was Lily.

'Madame! How wonderful!' This Belinda. 'How I wish I was still of the Juniors for just this one morning! Wouldn't I enjoy myself!'

'Madame herself!' I murmured. At last I'd really see her – be taught by her. To be taught by Madame – wonderful, legendary Madame – seemed to me to be the height of bliss. At the back of my mind I could hear a babel of voices. The dressing-room had got over the shock and was becoming really excited.

'Do you think this hairband will dry in time if I put it on the radiator?' ... 'You'd better unplait your hair, Sara – she likes it done on top in a scarf. Oh, I know yours stays up as if it was glued, but remember the fuss there was when Jacqueline's came down last time!' ... 'Has anybody got a darning needle and a bit of cotton? These tights.' ... 'Here you are, darling! I know the thread's green, but it'll be better than nothing.' ... 'Thanks awfully, Mary. Now if I only had a bit of elastic for my trunks.' ... 'Anyone got a spot of elastic for Delia's trunks? *I* know! I'll give you the bit off my hat. It'll be tight, but you can put up with it for just this morning. What it is to have brains!' ... 'Golly! Look at Veronica! She's in a brown study! Wake up, Veronica! You'd better buck up and change or you'll be late.'

The words reached my subconscious mind. I gave myself a shake and looked round for my case. It lay open on the bench near the window.

'Gosh! Yes – I must change like a flash! My tights—' I rummaged in my case for them, but they weren't there.

'Have any of you seen my tights?' I yelled in a panic.

'This seems to be a general refrain!' drawled Marcia Rutherford. 'Don't say you've lost *your* tights, too, Veronica Weston? I thought you never lost *anything*.'

I hardly heard her. I was searching frantically in every nook and cranny of the dressing-room – under the benches, on the table littered with other people's belongings, behind the radiators, everywhere.

'You've probably left them at home,' Sara said, joining in the search. 'I'm always doing things like that. Last week it was my hairpins, and I had to fasten my hair up with nails and string! Think back – when did you have them last?'

'This morning,' I answered, crawling round on my hands and knees. 'I *know* I put them in my case because I had to carry my sandwiches separately; they wouldn't go in as well.'

'Sure it wasn't yesterday?' put in June.

'No, it wasn't; it was today,' I said firmly.

'Have you tried the lost-property office?' said Taiis helpfully.

'Gosh, no!' I dashed away to the little office, opening off the entrance hall, where all the things we lost, or were found lying about on the floor, were impounded. But there were no pink tights with 'Veronica Weston' on them. In fact, there were no tights at all, or I might have persuaded Elizabeth, the assistant secretary, to let me borrow them for just this one class.

When I got back to the dressing-room I found it empty. The Juniors had gone off to the Baylis Hall to be ready for

Madame; the Seniors to their Character class with Serge.

I sat down on a bench by the door, my heart filled with despair. What was I to do? Go into class without tights? Unthinkable! I'd be sent out in disgrace on the spot. Nobody – nobody ever attended a ballet class without tights – let alone Madame's class.

A tear stole down my nose. I'd waited so long for this chance – the chance to shine in Madame's eyes – and now, it seemed, it was going to be denied me. I wasn't even going to *see* Madame, let alone be taught by her. As I sat there, my thoughts flew to the Baylis Hall where the others were all enjoying this honour. I heard in my imagination the tinkle of the piano, Madame's voice crisply giving orders, addressing Gilbert, singling me out ... 'What is the name of the dark child in the back row, Mr Delahaye? Yes, the second from the end? I like her. She has a good "line". Very promising ... Come farther forward, dear ...'

The telephone ringing in the Director's office broke in upon my daydream. Oh, well – crying about it didn't help. I'd better wash my face, and forget about it.

I went over to the mirror and looked at myself critically. Yes, I certainly was in a bit of a mess. My dark eyes had smudges round them where I'd rubbed them, my hair was untidy, my nose red. I walked round the dressing-room, collecting up my belongings. Although I was usually fairly tidy, I'd been in such a frantic state about the disappearance of my tights that I'd scattered my things all over the place. My towel was on the floor, and my soap had skidded across the table and shot underneath one of the radiators. As I poked it out I nearly upset a bowl of dirty water deposited on the floor by Mrs Wopping, the charwoman, when she'd been cleaning the windows. Mrs Wopping was anything but a tidy soul, and the school was strewn with her wash-leathers, dusters, floorcloths, and all the other insignia of her calling. Whenever Mrs Wopping was mildly reproved by the authorities for her untidy ways, she replied with dignity: 'I does me work in me own way, and if it ain't satisfactory, there's a remedy.' She never went so far as to give the remedy a name, but spent the rest of the day muttering ominously: 'take it or leave it ... warning ... notice given ... folk as oughta mind their own business.' Then the whole affair would blow over, and for a few days tidiness would reign. But before very long, back would come the dusters and the floorcloths, and all would be as before. In disgust I poked at the dirty cloth that raised its head in Mrs Wopping's inky water like an inquiring seal, or a volcanic island in the midst of the ocean. Then I bent closer. Somehow it didn't look like a floorcloth. It looked familiar – like – like – yes, it *was*! It was my tights!

I fished the filthy object out of the water and wrung it out. Yes, there was no doubt about it. My tears began to flow afresh. It was so awful to realize that my tights had been there all the time, right under my very nose, and it wasn't much of a consolation to know that they wouldn't have been the least use to me if I *had* found them. For a long time I stood there, wondering how the dreadful thing had happened. I was still puzzling my brain when the door opened and Sara dashed in.

'It's all right, Veronica!' she panted. 'You needn't cry. I dashed down to tell you – said I wanted to change into my point shoes – Madame didn't turn up after all.'

'What? *What* did you say?'

'No – she rang up and said that someone had come to see her just as she was setting out to come here – someone most awfully important, so she couldn't come after all. The Director sent up a message. Didn't you hear the phone? Oh, but of course you wouldn't know it had anything to do with Madame. And anyway, I don't expect you even *heard* it – you'd be thinking of us in the Baylis Hall being taught by Madame, I shouldn't wonder. You're an awful dreamer, you know, Veronica!'

'I know I am,' I laughed. 'And you're quite right. I've been sitting here having the most wonderful class with Madame –

even if it *was* all in my imagination. I expect when I *do* have a class with her, it won't be a bit like that!'

'No – I expect it won't,' agreed Sara. 'By the way, what are you holding that dirty old thing for? I suppose it's old Wopping's floorcloth?'

'You suppose wrong!' I answered. 'This dirty old thing' – I held aloft the dripping black object – 'this is my tights.'

Sara stopped in the middle of tying on her point shoes, and her eyes flew wide.

'Your *tights*? But how on earth did they get in there?'

'That's exactly what I was asking myself when you came in,' I answered. 'I simply can't *think*. I'm pretty sure old Wopping—'

'It's not old Wopping's doing,' declared Sara, cutting me short. 'She would never do a thing like that. Of course, I can't *prove* anything, but I've a shrewd idea I know who it was.'

'You mean?'

'I mean Marcia,' said Sara. 'You see, I've just remembered something. Last term we had a class with Miss Jackson from the Theatre Ballet – an important class. Well, Delia's tights disappeared. We couldn't find them *anywhere*. Just at the last moment, when everyone had gone into class and poor Delia was in despair, who should walk in but Marcia and offer to lend her a spare pair. Delia put them on, and they happened to be fishnet ones, which aren't allowed – goodness knows why, but they aren't. Well, Delia didn't know about the rule because she was new, and she got sent out of the room in disgrace.'

'How awful!' I said in horror. 'I seem to have got off lightly. I'd have died if I'd been poor Delia and got sent out of class.'

'Well, if I don't stop gossiping, *I* shall be sent out of Gilbert's class!' Sara laughed. 'I'm supposed to be putting on my point shoes, and I've been down here a quarter of an hour already. So long, Veronica! See you after class!'

51

With this she was gone, and I was alone once more. But this time I didn't care. I hadn't missed anything after all. I was so relieved that I turned *déboulées* all down the dressing-room, finishing with a treble *pirouette* as much like Belinda's as possible. My class with Madame was yet to come!

Chapter 6

The Swimming Baths

AFTER the affair of the tights, I kept as far away from Marcia Rutherford as I could, but sometimes it was impossible. The weather was warm for November – at least, it seemed warm to me in comparison with Northumberland, where I had lived all last year. Most of the others thought it was chilly, though, and when I suggested going to the swimming baths before afternoon school, they shivered.

'The swimming baths?' echoed Sara. 'Ugh! Not for me! I'm not one of your Spartan people! I couldn't go, in any case, because I have an Advanced Mime class from two to three. What on earth do you want to go swimming in November for, Veronica? It's not civilized!'

'When I lived with my cousins, Fiona and Caroline, we used to go swimming in the lake in the grounds,' I explained. 'And once Sebastian broke the ice on it. Sebastian was Fiona and Caroline's cousin, and he was an awfully good swimmer. Well, when I passed by the baths today, I saw a placard of a swimming gala, and that made me think of the lake at Bracken Hall, and that made me want to go swimming. I feel I simply *must* go swimming today, or bust!'

'Well, don't bust!' laughed Sara. 'Too messy! I expect June will go with you. She's another of the Spartan kind.'

But June wasn't keen either.

'Matter of fact,' she said apologetically, 'I've got a bit of a sore throat. Mother would take a fit if I went swimming. Marcia and Kay usually go on Fridays, though. Are you going to the baths today, Kay?'

Kay said she was, and Marcia too. I wasn't a bit keen on their company – especially Marcia's – but I could hardly say so, because Kay really wasn't a bad sort of girl. Her only crime was that she was a friend of Marcia's.

'Oh, all right – I may see you there,' I said, rather unenthusiastically.

'By the way, Veronica,' put in Sara. 'You won't be late for afternoon class, will you? It's the audition for the Youth Festival, remember.'

'The Youth Festival?' I repeated, coming back into the dressing-room. 'I've never heard of it.'

'Oh, I forgot,' said Sara. 'You'd gone home yesterday when Miss Willan came into the dressing-room and told us about it. It's not terribly important, but it would be a first part for you.'

I stared at her, aghast. Not terribly important! My very first part!

'Tell me all about it,' I urged, putting my towel and bathing costume down on the centre table. 'It sounds thrilling!'

'Well, it's to be in Finsbury Park,' explained Sara, 'and we're to do the ballet part – demonstrate the different kinds of dancing, and so on. Miss Jackson, from the Theatre Ballet, is coming to class this afternoon to choose people for it. She's in charge of the dancing part of the Youth Festival.'

'I'll be there,' I assured her. 'Trust me not to be late for an audition! Gosh! What a good thing you told me about it, Sara!'

'Well, you'd have been there in any case,' laughed Sara. 'You're never late for any of the classes, Veronica – not even Eurhythmics!'

It was lovely at the swimming baths. The water felt beautifully warm – a lot warmer than it does in the summertime when the air outside is hot. I wondered why more people didn't go swimming in the winter.

Marcia and Kay had cubicles next to mine, but fortunately neither of them could swim well, so, once I was in the water, I didn't see much of them. I spent most of my time in the deep end, diving off the high springboard.

As I swam leisurely towards the steps to have yet another dive, Marcia came running towards me along the edge.

'Oh, Veronica,' she shouted. 'I'm going out now. Would you mind if I did my hair in your cubicle? The mirror in mine is cracked right across.'

'All right,' I yelled back – the baths were anything but a quiet place. 'You can have five minutes – no more. I'm coming out then – mustn't be late for class.'

When I hauled myself, dripping, on to the edge of the bath at the end of the five minutes, and pattered back to my cubicle, Marcia had already gone, leaving stray hairs all over the little corner shelf, and a cloud of heavily scented face powder on my mirror. I wiped it off with my hankie, and scanned my hair anxiously. Oh, well, I thought, if it *was* rather wet, it would be all the tidier for the audition.

As I dressed I nibbled one of Mrs Crapper's sandwiches that she'd given me that morning to eat with my mid-morning milk. Then, when I'd pulled on my frock, I glanced at my wristwatch, where it lay on the shelf beside my kirbygrips, just to make sure I'd got plenty of time.

It wasn't as late as I'd thought – only half-past two. As my class wasn't till three-thirty, I had loads of time.

'What about a coffee at the snack bar round the corner,' suggested Marcia, joining me on the steps outside.

'Oh, I don't think I'd better,' I said doubtfully. 'There's my class, you see—'

'Well, of course don't let me influence you,' said Marcia, 'but I'd say you really *ought* to have something hot before your class. If you go dancing with nothing to eat after your swim, you may collapse or something during the audition – you never know!'

'Oh, I wouldn't do that!' I laughed. 'Anyway, I've already had one of Martha's sandwiches – and they're not dainty, afternoon-tea sort of sandwiches, I can tell you!'

'OK. Don't say I didn't warn you,' declared Marcia.

Suddenly I turned back and walked along with her.

'Perhaps you're right,' I said. 'I think I will have a coffee after all. By the way, where's Kay?'

'Oh, she had to dash off – she'd got some shopping to do for her mother. Proper slave driver is Kay's mother! It's all right, Veronica – you've loads of time,' she added, seeing my eyes on my watch. 'It's only just twenty-five to three.'

Hastily I swallowed a cup of hot coffee and ate a bun. After this I stood up firmly.

'I really must go now, Marcia. I've simply got to find a shop that sells hairnets. If I'd only known this morning that there was an audition today I'd have got it then.'

'Gosh! What a fuss about a stupid little audition!' sneered Marcia. 'Anyone would think it was to get into the Company!'

'Well, it may seem unimportant to you,' I retorted, 'you've had lots of small parts, and you're dancing with the Second Company now – but it's very important to me. Goodbye, Marcia.'

'S'long, Veronica,' said Marcia, adding sarcastically: 'I do hope you're not late for the audition.'

I tried several shops before I found one that sold hairnets – not the fine ones you use during the daytime, but the strong coarse ones. It had to be dark, too, so that it wouldn't look like a sleeping-cap. I got it at last, however, and dashed into the Underground.

I looked at my wrist-watch again. Just after three. It was only ten minutes in the Underground to Baron's Court, so I really had plenty of time. All the same, I began to wish I hadn't had the coffee after all. I wasn't going to have as much time to get ready as I liked – not for such an important thing as an audition! Thank goodness, I thought, the Underground wasn't like a bus – at least you couldn't be held up by a traffic-block!

As I dashed out of Baron's Court station and hurried round the square to Colet Gardens, I glanced up at the clock of St Paul's School. I just couldn't believe my eyes – it said ten minutes to *four*!

'No,' I said aloud. 'It can't be! It's impossible! Why, it was only just after three when I left the coffee bar.'

I looked down at my wristwatch and held it to my ear. Yes, it was wound up all right, and it said a quarter past three. Clearly something must be wrong with St Paul's clock.

But, with a sinking heart, I knew that it wasn't St Paul's clock that was wrong – it was my watch. I remembered Marcia doing her hair in my cubicle, putting her comb on my shelf, cheek by jowl with my watch, and I knew what had happened as clearly as if I had seen it. She had altered the hands of my watch and put it half an hour slow. But, of course, I couldn't *prove* it. It was all what you might call circumstantial evidence. With a lump in my throat, I heard the tinkle of the piano in the Baylis Hall, and knew that in there was the great Miss Jackson, choosing out all the lucky people who were to be in the Youth Festival. And I – I was left out.

I sat down on a bench in the dressing-room, and wept. If I had only known what Fate had in store for me up her sleeve, I'd have laughed and shouted for glee. Yes, I'd have chuckled to think that Marcia Rutherford, of all people, had done me a good turn instead of a bad one. If it hadn't been for Marcia Rutherford, I'd have been in the Youth Festival, and then—

But all this was in the far-distant future. I must keep to the present, and, as I said before, I was very miserable on that November afternoon as I sat alone in the deserted dressing-room.

Chapter 7

A Visit to the Zoo

MARCIA seemed determined to act the role of my bad angel. One morning, near the end of term, she turned to me and announced in a triumphant tone of voice:

'Oh, by the way, Veronica, you'll have to be getting another partner for Character. Toni's been taken into the Company – the Second Company down at the Wells, I mean, of course.'

I said nothing, but my heart was full of dismay. Toni had been my mainstay in the Character class. No one knew what a help he'd been to me; I would miss him terribly. Still, I was glad he was getting his chance.

Meanwhile, the whole dressing-room was agog.

'Toni Rossini?' echoed June in astonishment. 'Why, he hasn't been in the school for more than a couple of terms. Of course he's good – there's no denying it. Still—'

'He worked with George Lejeune for ages,' Belinda put in. 'He was fully trained before ever he came to the Wells. Besides, he's an up-and-coming choreographer – no end of an asset to a company these days. Remember that ballet he made up for the RAD Production Club – *The Sailor's Wife*? Well, they're going to do it down at Sadler's Wells.'

'Golly! Are they really,' Sara said in an awestruck voice. 'He *must* be marvellous. Good old Toni! I always said he'd get on.'

'He'll probably fizzle out.' Marcia said with a shrug. 'Those brilliant sort generally do.' She flashed a look of hatred at the unconscious Belinda, who was now using the edge of the dressing-room table for *pas-de-deux* practice. 'It's fatal to be too good at the beginning.'

'*You* ought to be OK, then, Marcia,' Delia put in rather

nastily, I have to admit; but, then, I consider that Marcia had asked for it.

'Are you ready, Veronica?' said Taiis from the door. 'It is five minutes to three.'

'Just coming,' I answered, buttoning the straps of my Character shoes. 'Don't wait for me.'

I can't say that I enjoyed the Character class as much as usual that day. All the time I executed the gay, peasant steps, I was thinking to myself: 'This is the last time I shall dance with Toni. The last time ... the very last time.'

At the end of the class we said goodbye solemnly.

'The very best of luck, Toni,' I said. 'And – and thank you for being so decent to me.'

I turned away so that he shouldn't see there were tears in my eyes. But it was too late – he had already seen.

'Why, Veronique!' he exclaimed. 'What, then, is the matter? You are crying?'

'It's n-nothing,' I gulped. 'It's only that I may n-never see you again.'

Toni laughed.

'Not see me again? But, of course, you will see me again – of course, of course! Why not?'

'I may n-never get into the Company,' I said with a catch in my breath. 'S-sometimes when I see B-Belinda turning *pirouettes* so wonderfully, I feel I shall never, never be able to do them like that.'

'Belinda?' repeated Toni. 'Ah, she is the girl with the hair of red. She is good – that is true. She is brilliant – yes. But you are good, too, Veronique. You will, perhaps, be better than this Belinda one day, when you acquire the technique. You have more of the soul in your training.'

'It's sweet of you to say so, Toni,' I said through my tears. 'And now – goodbye again, Toni.'

'One moment, Veronique,' Toni said, putting a hand on my arm. 'Why should we not have a, what you call him – a little

59

celebration? Why should we not go somewhere – anywhere you wish – and drink to my good fortune and to your future, in the squash of a lemon?'

I burst out laughing at his funny English.

'Oh, that would be *lovely*!' I exclaimed. 'There's practically nothing I like quite so much as the squash of a lemon!'

'Where, then, shall we drink it?' urged Toni. 'Where most would you like to go, Veronique?'

'The Zoo,' I said promptly. 'I've got a pet monkey in the Zoo. I call him Jacko, and I want to say goodbye to him.'

'Goodbye?' echoed Toni, with raised eyebrows. 'You go away?'

'Oh, don't be alarmed!' I laughed. 'I'm not going away for good or anything – only for the holidays. Exactly a week tomorrow I shall be on my way to Northumberland.'

'Ah, your home, he is in the north of England, then?' said Toni.

'Well, you see, I've sort of got two homes,' I told him. 'Before Daddy died, we lived in London. But afterwards, I went to live with my cousins in Northumberland. I didn't like it much at first – it was all so different, but now – well, sometimes I get most frightfully homesick for the moors and the fir wood and Arabesque, my pony. I think it's partly because my mother was North Country.'

'Yes, I expect that is so,' Toni answered gravely. 'I am happy that you have somewhere joyful to go in the holidays. And now – about this celebration of ours. Will the morning of Sunday be convenient for you?'

'Oh, but you can't go to the Zoo on Sunday morning!' I objected.

'Oh, yes, you can – if you have got a member's card,' Toni assured me. 'Both my father and I have one.'

'Your father?' I said. 'I didn't know you had a father. At least, I mean, I didn't know he was in London.'

'Oh, yes,' said Toni. 'He is at the Italian Embassy. He is

very fond of animals, my father, and so we go most of the mornings of Sunday and look at the wonderful creatures in the Zoo. We like the snakes especially.'

'Snakes? Ugh!' I said with a shudder. 'I think snakes are ghastly!'

'Ghastly, but fascinating,' said Toni with a smile. 'Well, our celebration, he is then settled. It is to be the Zoo on the morning of Sunday. Where shall we meet?'

'Oh, I'll be at the main gates at eleven o'clock,' I answered, 'if you're quite sure you want to go with me.'

'Quite sure, Veronique,' Toni assured me gravely.

It was a lovely day on Sunday, not a bit like November, and even the thought that I was losing my helpful dancing partner couldn't depress me. The Zoo was beautifully quiet and select, and we were able to feed the animals without crowds of people breathing down our necks. Even the panda came out and looked at us sleepily, as if he knew we were distinguished Sunday members!

We made our way slowly to the cages where those queer-looking members of the monkey tribe, the mandrills, are kept. My little monkey, Jacko, was in a cage alongside, and we fed him with nuts and liquorice all-sorts, which he loves. In the next cage was a most evil-looking baboon, all-over multi-coloured stripes and spots that made him appear as if he'd got some awful disease. I think he must have got out of bed on the wrong side that morning, for he wasn't at all friendly. Whenever we tried to give him something to eat he sprang at us, rattling the bars and shaking the whole cage in his fury. So we left him and spent most of our time feeding Jacko.

Someone had given Jacko an ancient bus conductor's peaked cap, and he was having the time of his life with it, putting it on at the most absurd and rakish angles and causing roars of laughter among the onlookers by lifting it politely whenever an especially well-dressed lady paused in front of his cage. I expect he'd noticed visitors doing this and had stored the idea away in his clever little brain, to trot out on some future occasion. He certainly liked to be the centre of attraction, did Jacko, and very soon he was in his element with quite a crowd in front of his cage.

It was after we'd been there some time that I noticed two particularly unprepossessing schoolboys lounging among the spectators. One of them, whose name appeared to be Hamish, had bright red hair, blue eyes, and a wide, thick-lipped mouth. He looked about fifteen, but might have been older because, between his thick lips, dangled a cigarette. He puffed away at it for a time, staring at Jacko with his little blue eyes; then, to my horror, he quietly passed the lighted cigarette through the bars to the little monkey, and stood back in the crowd. None of the onlookers seemed to realize what had happened except me, and I expect that was because I always regarded Jacko as my own little monkey.

I stood in front of the cage in an agony of indecision, hoping that Jacko would drop the cigarette on the floor when he saw it was lit. But he didn't; instead he put it straight into his mouth.

After this there was pandemonium. Poor Jacko spat out the cigarette, and fled gibbering to the roof of the cage, where he clung, huddled against the wall, whimpering and moaning, and blinking down at us piteously with his sad brown eyes. Real tears ran down his wrinkled cheeks, and all the time he stroked his face with his little paws, as if trying to take away the pain. You could almost see him telling the people all about the wicked boy who had played him such a mean trick.

I turned round to look for the boy, rage in my heart. Yes, there he was, hovering at the back of the crowd, with a hateful grin on his silly face.

'That's the boy who did it!' I yelled to the astonished people, and I pointed to the red-haired Hamish. 'That's the boy – the one with the beastly red hair! He gave Jacko, my darling monkey, a lighted cigarette. How dare he! How dare he!'

I sprang at Hamish, the crowd parting, like the Red Sea did before the Israelites, to let me through.

Vaguely I heard Toni's voice behind me.

'One moment, Veronique – allow me, please—'

But I was past taking any notice of Toni, or anyone else. Hamish was rapidly making his escape, and I wasn't going to allow that – not if I knew it!

We crashed down the paths, the boy dodging this way and that, with me close on his heels. People turned round to stare at us – I think they imagined we were playing Hide and Seek, or Tag, and by their disapproving expressions I could see that they were going to complain about us to the management – playing such rowdy games on a Sunday morning of all days! But I didn't care. I was determined to bring my enemy to justice.

We crashed past an enclosure full of long-necked birds which fled in terror at our approach. Then up we dashed into the galleries above the Bear Pit, and down again, Hamish drawing ahead a little but not very much.

Suddenly the Snake House loomed up in front of me. I shot round the corner of it and barged right into a gentleman, who was standing talking to a very elegantly dressed lady, and nearly knocked him flat.

'S-sorry!' I gasped as we rocked to and fro in each other's embrace. 'Can't – stop! Must – catch – that – boy!'

Behind me came Toni's urgent voice.

'Veronique – I beg you! Veronique – *please*!' He put on a spurt and caught my arm. 'Please – I ask you to stop!'

I shook him off.

'Let me go, Toni! That beastly boy will get away!'

And then, right ahead, was the pond where the pelicans are kept, and I saw with delight that Hamish was making straight for it.

'Right-ho!' thought I grimly as I ran. 'Here's where you go for a swim, Hamish, my lad!' I urged my legs to run just a bit faster and, being the legs of a trained ballet dancer, they obeyed me. I caught up with Hamish just as he drew level with the pond, and gave him a push. Pelicans flew in all directions, uttering the funniest noises and flapping their ridiculous beaks. As for Hamish, he'd gone flat, and was now sitting up in one foot of water, wondering what had happened to him. Water dripped from his red hair and ran out of his large ears. It even oozed out of his mouth. He looked for all the world like a very disreputable dolphin or a statue for Father Neptune!

From near at hand came the angry voice of a keeper, and in another moment my arm was seized.

'Hi, miss! What d'you think you're doing, eh? How dare you push the young gentleman in that there pond! Now don't you go denying it, or saying it was an accident, for I saw you do it.'

'I'm not denying it!' I yelled indignantly. 'And he's not a young gentleman. He's a cruel, horrible little boy! He gave my monkey a lighted cigarette, and he's crying – Jacko, I mean. It's Hamish who ought to be made to cry. He *deserves* a ducking!'

The keeper looked nonplussed. Then, fortunately for me, Toni came dashing up and began to explain.

'It is true,' said Toni. 'The boy did give the monkey a cigarette which was lighted. The little creature was cruelly hurt. You must certainly give the boy in charge, Keeper. My friend here' – he indicated me – 'my friend has a strong sense of justice. She was determined to see that he did not escape. I think she was, as you say in English, a little of the sport!'

'Ah, now that's altogether different, sir,' said the keeper, letting me go and looking respectfully at Toni, who, I must say, had a way with him when it came to dealing with officials. 'If the lad 'as been ill-treating anythink in this 'ere Zoo, now that's altogether different. It is that! Wot 'ave you got to say for yourself, me lad?' he added, turning to Hamish, who, I must say, looked the picture of guilt.

'How was I to know the silly creature would go putting it into its silly mouth?' muttered Hamish truculently. 'I thought it would just play with it.'

'You ain't got no business to go thinking at all,' declared the keeper severely. 'You oughta stop outside this 'ere Zoo, you ought, if you can't 'elp ill-treating the hanimals in it. It's somethink that oughta be put a stop to, and I thank you, sir' – he nodded to Toni – 'for puttin' me on to it.'

'Oh – er – that is quite all right,' murmured Toni, and as he said it I could see him working out the keeper's last words in his mind, wondering how you would analyse the sentence and making a mental note about the queerness of the English language! 'I had better take Miss Weston along to the ladies' cloakroom, had I not? She looks rather the worse for the wear, do you not think? Come, Veronique—' He took my arm firmly, and tried to lead me away.

'Wait a moment, Toni,' I said doggedly. 'What about Hamish?'

'You just leave 'im to me, miss,' said the keeper with a grin. 'I'll take care of 'im, and enjoy doing it! Come along, me lad!' He beckoned to the dripping Hamish, who had by this time issued forth from the pond and was standing in a rapidly growing pool on the path. 'Come along, you!'

I was thrilled to think that, all through me, Hamish had descended from being a 'young gentleman' to a mere 'lad' – in the keeper's eyes, anyway!

'You know, Veronique,' said Toni as we made our way to the nearest cloakroom, 'I wish most particularly for you to stop just now. I wish very much to introduce you to those people.'

'What?' I said. 'Oh, you mean that gentleman I barged into just now? Well, I'm most awfully sorry if he was a friend of yours, Toni, but really he shouldn't have stood right in my way. I simply couldn't *help* barging into him, now could I?'

'It was unfortunate,' said Toni gravely, but with a hint of laughter in his voice, 'because it will most certainly go down in your biography, Veronique. I see it in the eye of my friend, Oscar Deveraux.'

For a moment the name didn't mean anything. Then it dawned upon me.

'You don't – you can't mean *the* Oscar Deveraux?'

'Exactly,' answered Toni with a smile. '*The* Oscar Deveraux, as you put it. The author and ballet critic. This is what he will say of you when you become famous: "I remember Veronique Weston when she was a young girl. I met her in the Zoological Gardens – or rather it would be more accurate to say that I have her barge into me! I see her push an unfortunate youth into the pond of the pelican – not by accident, mind you, but by the design!"'

'Do stop being silly!' I giggled, 'and tell me who the lady was. I mean the lady who was with Oscar Deveraux.'

'Oh, that was his wife, Irma Foster, the ballerina,' Toni said casually. 'As I say, I wish to introduce you, Veronique, only you will not stop.'

'Oh, *Toni!*' I wailed. 'Where are they? Let's go and find them! Come quickly!'

'It is already too late,' said Toni with a smile. 'They are gone since a long time. And I think it is well that they are. Your appearance, my dear Veronique, is not prepossessing! I think if Oscar Deveraux were to see you now, your appearance, too, would go down in your biography!'

'Perhaps you're right,' I admitted. 'I expect I do look a bit of a wreck!'

After I had made myself presentable we went to the café beside the Snake House, and drank each other's health in lemon squash. The waitress brought us a plate of cakes and another of chocolate biscuits, and I'm afraid we ate the lot, only keeping one of the latter for Jacko. Outside the café, there was an ice-cream man, and Toni bought me a cornet.

We went home by way of the mandrills' cages, and poor Jacko was still crouched at the back of his cage, refusing to come out. He wouldn't even come out to take half a banana from a little girl who had several in a bag. When he saw me, though, he came at once; and when I offered him the end of my cornet he took it. I noticed that he smelt it very carefully before putting it into his mouth. Jacko had learnt something from the affair of the cigarette – and that was not to trust human beings!

Chapter 8

End of Term

THE last week of term flew by, and, almost before I knew it, it was Wednesday – only three days before the holidays began. The people who were to be in the Finsbury Park Youth Festival were all very excited. It was awful, having them dashing into the dressing-room, talking a hundred to the dozen about Miss Jackson of the Theatre Ballet, what she'd said and done, and to know that you were going to take no part in it.

'We're going to do *Les Sylphides*,' Sara said, as we got ready for class that afternoon. 'Sandra Vane is to do the Waltz, and Jessica Todd and John Godolphin the *pas-de-deux*. That's for the classical ballet. Then we're to do the Czardas from *Coppélia*, to show them what a national dance is like, and Carmen is doing one of her wriggly, Spanish dances with castanets and a swirling skirt. Lulu is doing Danse Arabe from *Le Casse Noisette*, and we finish with the Dance of the Little Swans from *Lac*. The Swans are June, Lily, Delia, and me. Then, at the end of the ballet part of the programme, we're to give a short demonstration of classical technique ... Oh, Veronica, what a shame you're not going to be in it! It's going to be such *fun*!'

'Oh, well,' I said with a sigh, 'I'll be able to go home for the hols, anyway, which I shouldn't be able to do if I were in the Youth Festival. I shall think of all of you working away at rehearsals while I'm riding on the moors. I had a letter from my cousin this morning.'

'Gosh! Have you got a pony all of your own?' asked June. 'You lucky thing!'

I shook my head.

'No, he doesn't really belong to me,' I admitted. 'But you

see, my cousins have both got ponies, and Sebastian – he's a boy cousin of theirs – well, he rides too, so I just had to have a mount. We tried a donkey first, but that wasn't awfully successful, because he wouldn't go unless Sebastian walked behind him with a stick and whacked him! In the end we had a Wayside Stall to make some money to hire a pony for me. The man we hired him from said that we could hang on to him until he wanted him. So far he hasn't wanted him,' I added.

'What's his name?' Sara demanded.

'Arabesque,' I said.

'What a lovely name for a pony!' exclaimed Taiis. 'It is one that I have never heard before. But, of course, you would call him something like that, Veronica – something to do with the dance, I mean. You are so one way of the mind! Always the dancing it is with you!'

As I sat in the train that night I took out Caroline's letter and read it through again. She wrote as follows:

Bracken Hall,
Bracken,
Northumberland.

Dear Veronica,

It seems ages since you went away, although I know it isn't so long really. I'm sorry I haven't written more, but you know how it is – school takes up so much time. It'll be glorious when the holidays are here, and there's time to do all the really important things, like grooming Gillyflower, and riding on the moors with Sebastian. Sebastian came home from school for half-term, and we rode right up to Corbie's Nob just to celebrate the occasion. Sebastian stood right on the very top of the cairn and said – you know his dramatic way; you never can tell whether he's serious or not! – 'Shades of Veronica! 'Twas here she set her foot upon the treacherous snake. Oh, hapless day! Oh, thrice-happy snake to be trodden upon by the foot of a world-famous ballet-dancer-to-be!'

Fiona is frightfully grown up, now that she's gone to her Harrogate school. She's got a long party frock, and I suppose she does look rather beautiful in it. She's had her hair permed, too – much to Sebastian's disgust – and she uses lipstick, though she says it isn't allowed at school – only in the Sixth Form for evenings. She went to the Hunt Dance at half-term, and who do you guess took her? Sebastian has broken up early, and he's looking over my shoulder as I write this letter. He says just think of the rottenest little trick you know, and you'll be right! I expect by now you've guessed. It was that awful Ian Frazer!

Sebastian has gone away at last and left me in peace, so I can tell you some news about *him*! He's going to leave school next term, and he's working like mad at his music. He spends simply *all* his time playing either the piano or the violin, and I have a frightful job persuading him to come out for an occasional ride! He's started a music club in New-castle, and he says he's written a symphony. It's called the *Woodland Symphony*, and he's going to conduct it himself at a concert during the hols. I expect it will be while you're here. I think it won't be long before he tries for his scholar-ship to the Royal College of Music.

Would you believe it, but Mummy has got quite keen about ballet. I think she imagines it's fashionable! Anyway, she goes about telling people about 'my niece at Sadler's Wells'! Really, to hear her talk, you'd think you were a *prima ballerina* already! I heard her telling Mrs Musgrave the other day at a Woman's Institute meeting that her niece, Veronica's, dancing wasn't the ordinary kind that you see in musical comedies and pantomimes, but a *much* more diffi-cult and superior kind! Mrs Musgrave looked most im-pressed, and I heard her say: 'Really, Mrs Scott? You *must* be proud of her!' Then Mummy smiled smugly, and said: 'Yes, I am a little proud, Mrs Musgrave. You see, it was

really through *me* that Veronica was discovered. You remember dear Lady Blantosh's concert? Well ...' Then
Mummy went on telling Mrs Musgrave all about you dancing at the matinée and Madame Viret turning up, and your
audition at Sadler's Wells, and by the time she'd finished,
you'd really have supposed that *Mummy* had invited
Madame to the matinée especially to discover you! You
know Mummy when once she gets into her stride!

I couldn't help laughing out loud as I read this bit. Yes, I
did know Aunt June and her infuriating way of taking all the
credit to herself. All the same, she was kind, as the next part of
the letter showed.

Mummy is enclosing a cheque for your train fare next
weekend. She says will you be sure to book a first-class
sleeper because she doesn't like the idea of you travelling
third, as you did when you came to stay with us first.
Sebastian says he's going to groom and exercise Arabesque for you, so that he'll be in the pink of condition by the
time you get here on Saturday night.
Much love from Caroline.

P.S. Mummy says she'll send Perkins with the car to meet
you on Saturday. And, by the way, Lady Blantosh is having
another concert on Boxing Day, and she wants you to dance
at it.

I laughed when I read the bit about the first-class sleeper. I
believe Aunt June thought that no one except thieves and
robbers travelled third class!

As I came out from the Underground at Chalk Farm I met
Stella, and we walked to the bus together. I saw quite a lot of
Stella nowadays. She didn't seem to have a great deal to do,
and when I asked her the reason, she smiled ruefully.
'I never seem to get much beyond understudying people,'

she answered. 'In fact, the only real part I've had since I joined the Company has been one of the Black Lackeys in *The Gods Go A-Begging*, and *then* I got into an awful row because I lost my wig.'

'Lost your wig?' I echoed, fully alive to the seriousness of the admission. It's an awful crime to lose or destroy stage property. 'How on earth did you do that, Stella? I thought you were frightfully careful about your things.'

'So I am,' agreed Stella, a puzzled frown creasing her forehead. 'I simply can't think how it happened. I'm positive I put it away all right after I'd had it at the last performance, and how it came to be perched on the swan's head – you know, the mechanical swan they have in *Lac des Cygnes*? – well, how it came to be there in the wings at all, I just can't imagine.'

I couldn't help laughing. It must have looked so queer to see that dignified old swan wearing a curly black wig! But poor Stella was far from being amused.

'It's all very well for you to laugh, Veronica, but it was the night Madame was there, and she was *furious*. When Marcia yelled out: "Oh, *there's* Stella's wig – the one she lost," and Madame turned round and saw it, I thought I'd be dismissed on the spot!'

'Marcia?' I said thoughtfully. 'Now I wonder . . .'

'What's the matter?' asked Stella.

I didn't answer for a moment. I was thinking back in my mind to that day when Madame was supposed to have taken the class, and I'd found my tights in Mrs Wopping's bowl of dirty water. Also Sara's story about Delia's fishnet ones.

'Look here, Stella,' I said urgently, 'you must watch your step with Marcia Rutherford. She's the sort of girl who would stop at nothing to put a spoke in the wheel of a rival – nothing!'

'You think she put my wig there on purpose?' said Stella in amazement.

'I don't *think*; I know she did,' I pronounced. 'Well, you just watch out, Stella, or you'll find yourself stepping out of your parts, and Marcia Rutherford stepping into them! Take my word for it!'

Stella didn't answer because just at that moment our bus came, and we had to keep our place in the long queue that had formed while we were waiting.

'It's the end of term on Friday,' I said when we had taken our seats. 'I'm going to Northumberland to stay with my cousins.'

Stella gave a funny little sigh.

'Northumberland – it makes me think of hills and moors, with no sound except the sheep cropping the grass, and fir woods with the bracken knee-deep – lovely!' she said dreamily.

'What? In November!' I laughed.

'When I think of Northumberland, I always think of bracken and heather, and the curlews calling,' said Stella. 'Sometimes I wonder—'

I never knew what she wondered, for just at that moment the conductor came for our tickets.

'Talking of holidays,' I went on after he had gone, 'Jonathan thought we ought to have a sort of breaking-up dinner party. Actually, we don't break up till Friday, but, as I'm going north by the night train, we thought it might be a bit of a rush if we had it then, so we're having it on Thursday. That's tomorrow. You see, somebody in the country sent Jonathan a brace of pheasants, and, as he says, they're no earthly use to him as he's a vegetarian. He can't even make a still-life of them because they're all plucked and trussed up! So he's given them to Mrs Crapper for our party. And Mrs Crapper made two Christmas puddings, and now she says she'll only need one, with me away, so we're having the second one for our party. Isn't it perfectly sweet of her?'

'Yes – she is a dear soul,' agreed Stella. 'Really, I don't know what any of us would do without her.'

'Or Jonathan either,' I put in firmly. 'They're *his* pheasants, you know.'

'Or Jonathan either,' laughed Stella. 'Well, I've a party of my own on Thursday night. Some ballet club or other are giving it, and they've asked the whole Company as guests. Well, a lot of them say they can't be bothered to go, but I think it'll be frightfully disappointing for the ballet club, so I've said I'll turn up. Oh, it's all right – it's not till nine o'clock,' she added, seeing my downcast face, 'so I'll be able to come to the dinner party first. There'll be loads of time.'

'You're sure?' I said anxiously. 'Jonathan will be fearfully disappointed if you don't turn up, Stella.'

'I'll come,' promised Stella. 'At seven o'clock I'll be there.'

Chapter 9

Mrs Crapper Has a Dinner Party

OUR dinner party was a great success. We had it in Mrs Crapper's sitting-room (she called it simply 'the room'), and we sat at the round centre table which was covered by an enormous damask tablecloth, especially brought out for the occasion. It had been Mrs Crapper's mother's best tablecloth when *she* was married. In the middle of the white expanse was a square of looking-glass meant to look like a lake, and on the lake floated a white china swan that Mrs Crapper had won at a hoopla stall in Margate. The swan was filled with ivy leaves that Jonathan had gathered (under Mrs Crapper's orders) from the wall of the yard at the back of the house, and there were trails of ivy at various places all over the table 'to give a artistic effect', as Mrs Crapper put it!

Besides the pheasants and the Christmas pudding, Mrs Crapper had brought out a bottle of home-made ginger wine which we drank in wineglasses all of different sizes and patterns because Mrs Crapper had won them at a hoopla stall, too. It occurred to me that Mrs Crapper had Margate to thank for quite a lot of her household furnishings! We had white sauce with the plum pudding, with brandy in it out of the medicine chest.

After we'd finished, Jonathan asked permission to light his old black pipe, and we roasted chestnuts over the fire, ate almonds and raisins, told funny stories, and tried to make-believe that it was really Christmas. Stella didn't smoke, because it's not good for your breathing, and neither did I, as I was too young, and anyway the same reason applied to me, even if I hadn't been.

At eight o'clock Stella went upstairs to get ready for her

party. She wore a black taffeta picture frock that she'd made herself. It was ankle-length, and it had a lace yoke and cuffs, and huge bouffant sleeves. With her fair hair brushed back into a shining 'page-boy', and her little pointed chin, she looked exactly like a painting by an Old Master. Jonathan took her to the bus. He said he never *could* believe that Stella was capable of looking after herself.

When he came back, Jonathan said we'd have a symphony concert in Mrs Crapper's kitchen while we washed up the dinner dishes, and away he dashed up the four flights of stairs to his own floor to get his portable gramophone.

'I'll carry down the records!' I yelled, following on behind rather more slowly. 'Let's put on the whole of *Lac des Cygnes*, and that lovely thing by Prokofieff – *Peter and the Wolf*. Oh, and let's have—'

I stopped suddenly. Jonathan had swung wide the door of his studio, and there, facing me, was a large picture. It stood on an easel, and I had seen it many times. But whereas before it had always been covered by a piece of old black velvet, now it was triumphantly displayed. It was a picture of a ballet dancer. She was seated, backstage, on a piece of scenery, tying her shoe which had come loose, her head was bent down, and her fair hair was falling all over her neck and shoulders in soft abandon.

A shadowy figure in the background, evidently her partner, was surveying her sardonically.

Suddenly, something in the turn of the neck, the way the soft hair grew, seemed familiar to me.

'Why – why, it's *Stella*!' I cried in astonishment. 'When did you paint it, Jonathan? I didn't know Stella had ever sat for you.'

'Oh, yes,' smiled Jonathan. 'Stella has sat for me many times. She sat for this while you were away, living with your cousins. I haven't shown it to you because it wasn't finished, and I wanted it to be a surprise. Do you like it, Veronica?'

'Like it?' I echoed. ' "Like" is quite the wrong word. I think it's *wonderful*, Jonathan.'

Jonathan made me a mock bow.

'Thank you, Veronica.'

I stared at the picture, fascinated. The subject might be ordinary enough, but the execution was anything but commonplace. The girl's flesh was a beautiful creamy colour and seemed so real that you felt it would be warm to the touch. There was a luminous quality about the dress and the hair, that shone out of the shadowy background with an almost unearthly radiance. The youth and softness of the dancer contrasted vividly with the sardonic expression of her partner, and the sordidness of her stage surroundings.

'Have you sold it, Jonathan?' I asked. 'What are you going to do with it?'

'I'm going to keep it for myself,' Jonathan told me. 'But first it's going to be in the Spring Exhibition of Young British Painters at the Monmouth Gallery.'

'Golly!' I breathed. 'The Monmouth Gallery! You *are* getting famous, Jonathan!'

'Oh, I expect they had a job to find suitable canvases,' Jonathan said modestly. 'And, by the way, I have another picture here that's going to be in the same exhibition.' He drew forward a small canvas that had been standing with its face to the wall. 'Remember this?'

The picture facing me was of a small, pale-faced little girl, sitting on the extreme edge of a chair. One foot was wearing a darned sock, and the other a very old and battered canvas ballet shoe. There was a frown of concentration on the child's face as she painstakingly darned the shoe in her hand.

'Why, it's *me*!' I said. 'It's that picture you did of me, Jonathan, ages ago. Gosh! What a plain child I used to be!'

'Plain, but interesting,' said Jonathan with a smile. '*I* thought so, anyway. In the exhibition it will be called: "Study of a Dancer", because it isn't the fashion to give pictures names. Privately, though, I call it: "A Dancer Takes a Holiday!"'

'Yes, it's perfectly true,' I said, smiling at the irony of the title. 'An awful lot of our so-called free time *is* spent in darning shoes, washing tights, ironing tunics, and so forth.'

'And yet you still like doing it?' said Jonathan, pulling out the gramophone from the bottom of the cupboard and dumping a pile of records in my arms. 'You still think a ballet dancer's life worth living?'

'Of course I do,' I answered. 'It's a *wonderful* life – at least, it is when things go well.'

Jonathan switched off the light of his attic studio and shut the door behind him.

'U-um,' he said dubiously. 'It seems to me to be no sort of life at all for a girl. What about when you fall in love and want to get married?'

'I shan't ever fall in love,' I pronounced. 'I shall be "wedded to my art".'

'So you say – at sixteen. Or is it fifteen?' said Jonathan, dumping down the gramophone on Mrs Crapper's kitchen table, all among the dirty dinner dishes. 'But when you're *really* old – say, twenty-six, like me – you may think differently. What do *you* say, Martha?'

Mrs Crapper wiped her hands carefully on the overall that she wore on special occasions in place of a common or garden apron. Then she clamped into the sitting-room, took up a photograph in a green plush frame that stood on what she called 'me occasional table', came back with it, and stood for a moment gazing at it lovingly. The photograph showed a weak-chinned little man with a drooping walrus moustache and watery eyes. This was he whom Mrs Crapper called her 'better half'. Personally, I thought the term slightly misleading, since Mr Crapper had undoubtedly gone to the dogs – literally, as well as the other way! After gambling away every penny of his wife's hard-earned savings, he had finally taken himself off, in the company of a flashily dressed female who carried a crocodile handbag nearly as big as herself and wore an imitation diamond ring that was a close rival to the Koh-i-noor.

'Well,' said Mrs Crapper with a gusty sigh, 'I always say, when I thinks of poor Crapper, it's better to 'ave loved and lorst than never to 'ave loved at all. That's wot I says.'

'You're right there, Martha,' said Jonathan, winding up the gramophone and putting on the first record of *Swan Lake*. 'Dead right. There's only one thing to beat your theory, Martha, and that's to have loved and *not* lost.' He picked up a tea-towel and began to dry the dishes that Mrs Crapper had put on a tin tray to drain, while I followed suit.

'Ah,' said Mrs Crapper, with another look at the photograph, 'but it's only when you've lorst, Mr Jonathan, that you realizes the pearl of great price that was giv' you till death you do part. Only,' she added with yet another sigh, 'it weren't death, but dogs, that parted Crapper and me.'

So saying, Mrs Crapper wiped the soapsuds off her work-worn hands and replaced the erring Mr Crapper on the 'occasional' table in the sitting-room, and with this last gesture she put her romantic past behind her.

'And now,' she said in her ordinary voice, 'how about a nice box of liquorice all-sorts to cheer us up?'

At about ten o'clock I said I thought I'd go to bed, because I was tired and wanted a good night's sleep before my long journey north.

Jonathan said he'd sit up with Mrs Crapper and listen to the wireless, if she didn't mind; then he'd hear Stella come in.

'She won't be late,' I assured him. 'She's got a dress rehearsal tomorrow, and the opening performance of the new ballet they're doing down at the Wells. That's something you can't do if you're a ballet dancer – stay out late at parties!'

Chapter 10

Stella Disappears

CLASSES were just as usual next day. Character finished at five, and soon after that I was racing homewards. The holidays had begun! I had oceans of time, really, as I had packed my things yesterday, and my sleeper was booked.

I arrived at the door of 242 Heather Hill exactly as the postman got there with the evening post. There was a sale catalogue for Mrs Crapper, a registered parcel for Jonathan, and, to my astonishment, a letter addressed to me in Stella's big, open handwriting. I opened it as I walked upstairs, after leaving Mrs Crapper's catalogue on her table, wondering what on earth Stella could have to write to me about, when she'd promised to come to the station to see me off before her performance. When I had read the first few lines I wondered no longer.

My darling Veronica [said the pencilled scrawl], I don't know what you'll think when you know what I've done – or rather what I'm going to do. Actually it's another hour before I shall do it, and that's why I'm writing you such a long letter.

For ages I've been feeling terribly depressed. When I got into the Company I thought things might be better, but very soon I knew that it wasn't any use. You see, I can't push myself forward like some people can; it just doesn't seem nice to get to the front that way. But there's no denying the fact – a bit of push gets you there quicker than any amount of hard work, and if you can manage to put in a bit of the latter, and push as well, then you'll have the world at your feet in no time!

As I told you a bit ago, Belinda and Marcia are getting all the parts that ought by rights to be mine. Of course, Belinda *is* wonderful, but Marcia – well, she's not even in the Company yet, and I know quite well that I can dance lots better than she can, but she manages to convince the Powers-That-Be that she's the best, and I expect the audience thinks so too. There's an awful lot in showmanship, as Gilbert is so fond of telling us! Anyway, there you are; they get the parts, and I understudy them!

After you'd gone this morning, just before I had to set off for rehearsal, a letter came from Granny. Of course, I knew she'd been ill, but the writing was all thin and shaky; she must have been an awful lot worse than she said to have written like that. Oh, Veronica – why have people got to grow old and die – people one loves? It's so cruel! You see, I haven't got anyone else to care what becomes of me – only Granny, and she's over eighty.

Suddenly, as I was passing King's Cross Station, I knew what I was going to do. I wasn't going to that rehearsal; I wasn't going to a rehearsal ever any more; I was going to walk on to the northbound train, and go back to Granny to look after her for as long as she lived. And that's why I'm sitting here in the waiting-room, writing this letter.

Goodbye, darling Veronica, from your

unhappy Stella.

PS. I can't help thinking how queer it is that it should be *me*, of all people, who should walk out on the Sadler's Wells Ballet. I don't suppose anyone – I mean anyone in the mere *corps-de-ballet* – has ever done it before, but I know quite well in my heart that my contract won't be renewed, so I've only got in my thrust first.

PPS. I'm very sorry not to be able to wait and travel with you, Veronica, but you see I happen to know that you've got a first-class ticket, and the exchequer just won't

81

run to it. Besides, if I wait, I may be a coward and change my mind.

Tell Jonathan he was quite right – I *am* a failure.

Of course, as soon as I had read the letter I flew up the stairs to Jonathan's studio.

'Jonathan!' I yelled. 'Jonathan! Stella's gone! She's gone home. Oh, not for a holiday – she's gone for good!'

Jonathan didn't seem to be nearly so amazed and put about by my shattering news as you'd have thought. He wiped his paintbrush carefully on a bit of rag, and said: 'Gone home, has she? About time she did!'

'But Jonathan—' I expostulated. 'You don't understand. She's gone *altogether*; she's left the ballet; she can never go back – not after walking out on them like this. Don't you understand, Jonathan? Oh, Jonathan – what are we to do?'

Jonathan stood up and stretched himself leisurely. Then he rummaged in his pockets for his ancient pipe.

'Look,' he said, when he'd found it and lit up. 'Honestly, Veronica, thinking it over calmly, do *you* think Stella is a fit person to spend her life fighting for a front place on the stage? Do you honestly think she'd make a go of it, or that she'd be happy even if she did?'

I met Jonathan's dark eyes, and I saw that the anxious look I had so often seen in them had disappeared. There was nothing in them now but relief.

'Y-es,' I said slowly, 'I see what you mean, Jonathan, and perhaps you're right. Stella is a bit – well, sort of gentle and retiring for a stage career. You've got to be tough as tough, and not let yourself get discouraged, whatever happens.' I thought of the awful things that had happened to me this term, and I sighed.

'Why the sigh?' questioned Jonathan.

'Sometimes it's dreadfully hard *not* to get discouraged,' I answered. Then I threw up my chin and added: 'But I'll manage it somehow. I refuse to let a girl like Marcia Rutherford get me down! I'm going to dance, and no one – no one is going to stop me! Certainly not Marcia Rutherford!'

'That's the spirit!' said Jonathan approvingly. 'It's people like you, Veronica, who ought to go on the stage – not North Country primroses like Stella.'

We were both silent for a long time. Presently there was a scraping sound at the window. Jonathan got up and opened the casement, whereupon a small but very important kitten of a bright yellow colour bounced in and began to rub itself against Jonathan's corduroy trousers in an ecstacy of affection. Really, it was almost impossible to believe that such resounding purrs could come from so small an animal.

'Good evening, Picasso!' Jonathan said solemnly, tickling the little creature under its chin. 'Just in time for a spot of condensed milk. I was about to open a tin for Veronica's coffee.'

The kitten belonged to the people next door, and its real name was Marmalade, but since it spent nine-tenths of its life in Jonathan's studio, he'd given it the rather more artistic name of Picasso, not out of any disrespect to the artist, as he carefully explained, but just because its fur reminded him of Picasso's passion for primary colours!

We sat drinking the coffee Jonathan had made, and we were both so deep in our own thoughts that neither of us spoke for a long time. Picasso meanwhile proceeded to make short work of the condensed milk that Jonathan had poured into a saucer for him.

'But what are we going to do about Stella?' I said after a bit. 'We can't just say "that's that!" and never see her again, can we?'

'Rather not!' agreed Jonathan cheerfully. 'I have no intention of not seeing Stella again. Not the least intention in the world, I assure you. In fact, I'm coming along with you this very night, Veronica, to follow Stella to her home in far-off Northumberland.'

'Northumberland?' I echoed in astonishment. 'You don't mean to say that Stella lives in Northumberland?'

'Oh, yes,' said Jonathan. 'At least her granny does. She lives in a little village at the foot of the Cheviot Hills. Didn't you know?'

I shook my head.

'Of course, I knew her home was somewhere up north, because you kept on calling her "a North Country primrose", but I always thought of places like Manchester, or Leeds. But if she lives in the heart of the Cheviots, as you say, where on earth did she learn to dance?'

'Ah, you see, she didn't live there then,' explained Jonathan. 'She used to live with her mother, not so very far from Darlington, and that's where she learned to dance, I suppose. Then, when her mother died, Stella came to London. In the holidays she went home to her granny at Broomyhough.'

'You seem to know an awful lot about Stella,' I said thoughtfully.

Jonathan puffed away at his pipe, while Picasso, having finished the milk, sprang upon his shoulder and playfully bit his ear.

'I've known Stella for a long time,' he said at length. 'When she came here first she was only a kid of fourteen, and I was just twenty-two and still a student at the Slade. By the way, I'm North Country myself, you know.'

I stared at Jonathan in amazement. I had always thought of him being born within sound of Bow Bells.

'You, Jonathan?'

'Oh, yes,' smiled Jonathan. 'My people come from a village called Ravenskirk, near the Scottish border.'

'*Now* I know why your voice always sounded strange to me!' I exclaimed. 'Strange, yet sort of familiar. It was the faint burr that all North Country people have, and never seem to lose, no matter how long they stay away from home. But you never said you lived in Northumberland,' I added reproachfully. 'Not even last year, when you knew I was going to live there.'

'I forgot all about it,' Jonathan declared. 'Matter of fact, I never go home, so it didn't signify.'

'You are funny, Jonathan,' I said. 'What is your home like, anyway? Is it a big house?'

'Oh, so-so,' he answered.

'Yes, but is it *big*?' I persisted. 'Or is it a teeny-weeny cottage?'

'Just a house,' Jonathan said noncommittally, and I knew by past experience that he didn't intend to say any more. 'By the way, it's seven o'clock. Hadn't we better trek down to Martha, and break the news to her that one of her birds has flown, and that the other two are sitting on the telegraph wires preparing to migrate! She might take pity on us, and give us some real supper to speed us on our journey! I shall have to ring up King's Cross, too, and see if they can give me a sleeper.'

'Oh, by the way, Jonathan,' I said uncomfortably, 'you know my Uncle John and Aunt June are disgustingly well off?'

Jonathan nodded.

'I'd gathered that fact.'

'Well, Aunt June sent me the money for my ticket,' I went on. 'A first-class sleeper. It – it was *frightfully* expensive.'

'Thanks for the tactful warning, Veronica,' Jonathan said with a grin. 'All the same, I think I'll travel first class too, and act the knight-errant. After all, I don't do *much* travelling.'

'Perhaps I could change over to third class—' I began, but Jonathan stopped me with a wave of his hand.

'Not at all, my dear Veronica. We'll *both* travel first class on this historic occasion. After all, it will give me an opportunity of studying the habits of the idle rich! Useful for a struggling artist! I might be able to turn out a satirical masterpiece in the vein of Hogarth, and call it: "Night Life on the Flying Scotsman"!'

'You may not get the sleeper,' I said with a giggle. 'You may have to go third with the thieves and vagabonds!'

Chapter 11

Journey to Northumberland

BUT Jonathan was lucky. Someone had cancelled a sleeper booking at the last minute, so at exactly eleven forty-five we made our way up the long platform at King's Cross Station to the first-class sleeping car, and boarded the northbound train. The sleeping-car attendant took our luggage and ushered us along the corridor to our respective compartments and left us with the assurance that he'd bring us tea at seven forty-five in the morning.

'Gosh, Jonathan!' I said, stopping short on the threshold of my compartment, 'I never imagined a first-class sleeper was like this! Why, it's a real little bedroom with a proper bed, and a washbasin with hot and cold water!'

'We live and learn!' said Jonathan, with a flash of his white teeth. 'Well, goodnight, Veronica! See you at crack of dawn in Newcastle. By the way, I suppose they're sending someone to meet you?'

'Oh, yes – Perkins!' I said with a grimace. 'Aunt June said I was to wait for him in the tea-room. He's the Scotts' chauffeur. Do you get out at Newcastle too, Jonathan?'

'Yes, that's as far as this train goes,' he answered. 'I get another one later in the day to Rothbury; then a bus to Alwynton, and from there I expect I walk!'

'It sounds lovely,' I said.

I must have been very tired, for I slept soundly, not even waking at Grantham or York. When I opened my eyes it was very early in the morning, and the train was slowly sliding through a station. I pulled back the blind a little, and saw the towers and spires of Durham Castle and Cathedral, shining in the frosty moonlight like a fairy city. A puff of cold North Country air came in through the window which was open a little at the top.

I gave a shiver, half of cold and half of excitement. Then I snuggled under my eiderdown again, because, although we were only twenty minutes' journey from Newcastle, I knew that we didn't have to leave the train for ages yet.

I remembered the last time I had seen Durham. It had been in broad daylight, over eighteen months ago, and I had been sitting in the corridor of this very train, talking to Sebastian. I'd thought, then, how cold and alien it looked; now, I was greeting it as an old friend, which just shows how your ideas can change in a short time.

The next time I woke it was after seven o'clock, and we were in Newcastle. By the time I had washed and dressed, it was half past seven, and the attendant was at the door with my tea and a biscuit. Jonathan came down the corridor, cup in hand, and we had our tea together, sitting on my bed.

'How long shall you be staying at – I forget the name of the village where you said Stella lives?' I asked him.

'Broomyhough,' answered Jonathan. 'I shall only stay a couple of days, I expect.'

'It seems a long journey for just a couple of days,' I said. 'Couldn't you stay a bit longer, now you're here, Jonathan?'

'I might – who knows?' Jonathan answered slowly, breaking his biscuit into four and putting them all into his mouth at one go. 'It all depends upon how Stella receives me.'

'Oh, Stella will receive you with open arms,' I assured him. 'She's awfully fond of you, Jonathan.'

'That's what I'm going to find out,' Jonathan declared. 'I want to know just how much Stella thinks of me. If she can't bear the sight of me, I shall come back by the night train tomorrow; if she thinks I'm not *quite* a blot on the landscape, I shall stay for as long as she and her granny will put up with me.'

'You'll be here for an awful long time, then, I'm thinking!'
I laughed.

At exactly eight o'clock I went along to the tea-room as arranged. Jonathan came too, and hovering behind was our porter, carrying my small suitcase and the large, square hatbox of plywood that Jonathan had made to hold my ballet dress. The latter wasn't heavy, but it was awkward to carry, so Jonathan had insisted upon the porter. Standing just within the door of the tea-room were two well-known figures.

'Sebastian, and Caroline!' I shrieked. 'How lovely of you both to come and meet me!'

'Well, we thought the impeccable Perkins might afford rather a chilly welcome!' said Sebastian solemnly. 'It wasn't that we were at all anxious to see *you*, Veronica.'

'Don't take any notice of him!' laughed Caroline. 'He's just as batty as ever! The truth is, it was great fun getting up in the middle of the night! Gosh, Veronica – it's wonderful to see you again! You look quite different – lots more grown up, and – and prettier.'

'I feel just the same,' I laughed.

'Did you have a good journey?' went on Caroline. 'I think it must be great fun to travel by sleeper.'

'Oh, it was frightfully comfortable,' I declared. 'It was just like travelling in your own bedroom. And, of course, I had Jonathan with me – oh, by the way, where *is* Jonathan? He was here just a moment ago.' I looked round the tea-room, but Jonathan had vanished.

'Bloke with a beard?' queried Sebastian. 'When he saw Caroline and me, he decided he didn't like the look of us, and hopped it.'

'Don't be ridiculous!' I said, taking him seriously. 'Of course, Jonathan would like both of you. Oh, how annoying! I did so want you to meet.'

'Well, it's no use wishing,' said Sebastian. 'He's gone, and that's that. Funny, but I always imagined your Jonathan as a middle-aged sort of chap. Why, he seemed quite young!'

'Jonathan is twenty-six,' I said.

'He's not exactly my idea of an artist,' went on Sebastian, 'except for the beard. I always imagined artists to be rangy sort of chaps – thin, and knock-kneed, with a hungry expression.'

I couldn't help laughing. It wasn't a bit like Jonathan!

'Well, come on; let's be going,' said Caroline. 'We left Perkins outside in the car, and he'll be getting impatient. We've brought some sandwiches and a flask of coffee, and we can have them on the way home; it'll be better than this place.' She cast a disparaging glance at the marble-topped counter with its piles of doorstep sandwiches, and thick, chipped cups of greasy coffee.

We had a picnic breakfast in the car, and I must say that for once I really appreciated the smoothly running, palatial Rolls, with its pull-out table and picnic cups and saucers.

'I'll bet this is the first time these things have ever been used,' Sebastian remarked, filling up my cup with hot coffee. 'Aunt June doesn't approve of picnics; she thinks they're beneath her – morally, as well as in actual fact!'

'Well, most grown-ups prefer meals on tables,' Caroline said loyally.

'Most, but not all,' declared Sebastian. 'My father is as keen on picnics as anyone.'

'D'you mind if I put my head out of the roof?' I asked, when he had finished the coffee and the sandwiches. 'Oh, look – there's that funny bit of Roman Wall at Heddon! Gosh! Doesn't it smell wonderful!'

'What – the Roman Wall?' said Sebastian. 'Shouldn't have thought the smell would have lasted all this time! Anyway, those Roman johnnies were very clean, if you can go by what you read. They did nothing but bath, day and night!'

'I didn't mean the Wall, you idiot! I meant everything generally.'

'Just smell to me,' drawled Sebastian. 'On the chilly side, too.'

'That's just what's so marvellous about it,' I declared. 'When you've been breathing air full of petrol fumes, and dust, and other people, you can't imagine how *fresh* this smells. It's full of trees, and moors, and snow just round the corner.'

'You've said it!' agreed Sebastian. 'There's a cap of snow on Corbie's Nob.'

We turned right at the bottom of Brunton Bank, and sped along the Bellingham road. The odd thing about Bracken was that you could reach it by two different roads – either the Newcastle–Otterburn one, or the Bellingham one that we were now on.

The scenery got wilder, and the air keener. I was glad to let Sebastian shut the sliding-roof, and to snuggle down under the rugs. After all, it wasn't yet nine o'clock in the morning, and as Caroline said, the world wasn't aired – not the world of the Northumberland moors, anyway!

'I'm getting soft!' I said with a shiver. 'A ballet school is such a warm place, you know. Gilbert positively *raves* if anyone so much as opens a window! One day they had the painters in doing something to the Baylis Hall, and the men left the windows open to dry the paint. Gilbert slammed them shut and roared: "Do you men realize that these girls are *dancers*? That they must not be exposed to sudden draughts of cold air? That they may strain their muscles by exercising in a cold room? In other words," yelled Gilbert, "these windows must be kept *shut*!"

'The poor men went out, their tails between their legs, and I heard them murmuring things about "those poor girls, and that brute of a dancing master"!'

'Gosh! He does sound a bit of a dragon!' Caroline exclaimed.

'He's not a dragon at all – he's a perfect lamb,' I told her indignantly. 'It's just his way. He's temperamental; most *artistes* are.'

'And you feel you're getting on?' Sebastian asked. 'With your dancing, I mean?'

I considered for a few moments. Then I said slowly:

'I seem to have had a run of awful bad luck this term. First of all I missed the audition for the Youth Festival because my watch was slow. Then the very day I got into the *pas-de-deux* class Serge suddenly decided he wouldn't have any Juniors in it, so I'm *still* not in. Then Toni and I went to the Zoo and I barged into a Mr Deveraux and nearly knocked him flat.'

'Who's Mr Deveraux?' demanded Caroline.

'Oh, he's a *frightfully* important person,' I explained. 'He's a ballet critic, and Toni says he'll be sure to put it all down in my biography. Not that I shall ever be famous enough to have a biography,' I added. 'Still, it was awful—'

'Who is this Toni?' drawled Sebastian. 'I'm not sure I like the sound of him.'

'Oh, yes, you would,' I said emphatically. 'Everyone likes Toni – he's frightfully popular.'

'You haven't told us who the fellow is yet,' said Sebastian. 'Or how it was you were traipsing round the Zoo with him.'

'I wasn't traipsing!' I laughed. 'As a matter of fact it was Sunday morning, and we had members' tickets, so I was walking very sedately. At least I was until Hamish gave Jacko the cigarette—'

'Hold on a bit!' begged Sebastian. 'You seem to have been in the centre of a positive crowd of male admirers! Toni – Hamish – Jacko—'

I burst out laughing.

'Admirers! You *are* funny, Sebastian! Why, Jacko is my little monkey in the Zoo – I'm sure I've told you all about Jacko. And Hamish – gosh, you should just have seen Hamish after I pushed him in the pelicans' pond! Why, he—'

Then I told them all about the fight with Hamish, and the triumphant ending it had had. Caroline laughed so much that Perkins turned half round in the driving seat to see what all the row was about.

'The keeper called him "my lad" when I'd finished with

him,' I said triumphantly. 'So it all goes to show what you can do if you really set your mind to it.'

'You *still* haven't told us who this Toni fellow is,' grumbled Sebastian.

'Toni is my dancing partner,' I said. 'At least, he *was* my partner, but now he's been taken into the Company, and I don't expect I shall ever see him again. That's why we were at the Zoo that Sunday morning; we were having a goodbye party. Toni's not only a dancer – he's a choreographer. That's a person who makes up dances,' I added, in case they didn't know.

'Of course we know that,' declared Sebastian.

'Well, *I* didn't,' admitted Caroline. 'I thought it was a person who trimmed your toenails and cut off your corns!'

'That's a chiropodist, ignoramus,' said Sebastian. 'Well, you do seem to have had a cheerful term, Veronica – I *don't* think.'

'Oh, but I've enjoyed every minute of it,' I declared. 'All the things that went wrong were my own stupid fault. At least, I suppose they were. Anyway, I shall take jolly good care nothing like that happens to me next term. Everyone has bad luck sometimes. Stella – she's the girl who shares my sitting-room at Mrs Crapper's – well, Stella had a spot of bad luck, too. Her wig—' I stopped suddenly. With a shock I remembered the awful thing that had happened to Stella, and I shivered.

'What's the matter, Veronica?' queried Sebastian. 'You shivered! Has someone walked over your grave?'

I laughed. 'No – I was only just thinking.'

'Penny for them!' persisted Sebastian. 'They must have been queer thoughts by the peculiar expression on your face! Come on, Veronica; let's hear what they were.'

'No,' I said slowly, shaking my head. 'They were thoughts best kept to myself.'

'There's Daddy!' exclaimed Caroline, as a car passed us with a hoot. 'He said he'd probably meet us about here.

Go on, Veronica – you were telling us about your dancing school.'

'There's nothing more to tell,' I said, 'except that I seem to be just as far off the Lilac Fairy as ever – in fact, sometimes I feel further off. By the way,' I added, as we turned off the main road, 'how far is a place called Broomyhough from here?'

'You mean the Strong's place, north of Alwynton?' said Sebastian. 'Oh, not very far as the crow flies. About fifteen miles, I should say.'

'Yes, but I'm not a crow!' I laughed. 'How far is it the other way – I mean by the road?'

'Miles and miles,' put in Caroline. 'You see, there just isn't a road across from Bracken. It's open moorland, so you've got to go all the way back to Bellingham, and then get a bus along the Jedburgh road. Do you want to go there, Veronica?'

I nodded.

'Yes, you see . . .' Then I told them all about Stella and the awful thing that had happened about her stage career.

'And now that Jonathan has told me exactly where she lives, I feel I'd like to go and see her while I'm here,' I ended.

'Well, why not ride there?' suggested Sebastian. 'Better still – why not let's all ride there tomorrow? After all, what better could we do than go out riding, if it's a decent day?'

'Oh, that would be *lovely*!' I said, with a sigh of happiness at the thought. 'You don't know how I've ached for a gallop on Arabesque ever since I knew I was coming back here these holidays. You don't think it'll be too far, do you?'

'Not a bit of it,' declared Sebastian. 'We'll start at crack of dawn and take it in easy stages. Trixie will give us lunch and tea, and we can make a whole day of it.'

As we turned in at the gates leading to Bracken Hall I thought of that night, last autumn, when I had run away in the mist. How different everything had looked then!

'Gosh!' I exclaimed, 'the last time I saw these gates was when they loomed up out of the mist like – like—'

'The gallows,' supplied Sebastian cheerfully.

'I never even thought of such a horrible thing,' I declared. 'But now you come to mention it, Sebastian, they *did* look a bit sinister, especially with you standing in the middle of the road yelling: "Have at you! Your money or your life!" or whatever it was you did yell.'

I let down the window of the car so that I could see everything more clearly. Yes, it was all the same – the little cottage at the bottom of the drive where Sebastian lived, with its diamond-paned windows, and low, overhanging eaves where the swallows built their nests in the summertime; the lake with its ruffled grey waters, seen clearly now through the leafless trees; finally, the long, low house with the Northumbrian moors rising in steep folds at its back.

We went into the hall, and Perkins followed with my luggage. Someone was coming from the kitchen quarters – someone carrying a tray with a glass of orange juice on it.

'Trixie!' I shrieked. 'It's me! Veronica! I'm back! I'm home again!'

I flung my arms round her neck, and the orange juice – Fiona's orange juice – nearly went west. Sebastian saved it by taking it out of Trixie's hands and depositing it on a table nearby. Trixie had been my cousins' old nurse, and now she was Aunt June's housekeeper. 'Oh, Trixie – it's lovely to be back! Not that it isn't lovely in London, too, but it's so gorgeous to see you all again. Oh, hullo, Fiona!'

Fiona, my elder cousin, returned my greeting coldly. She had never really liked me, and I knew in my heart that she never would. Sebastian said that Fiona loved nobody but herself, and I couldn't help feeling that he was right.

'Is that Veronica?' said a voice from the top of the stairs – Aunt June's voice. 'Well, Veronica! And how are you? Just as pale as ever, I see, and not a bit fatter!' I felt this to be a compliment, though I knew that Aunt June didn't mean it as such.

'We've waited for breakfast,' Aunt June went on, kissing me. 'So just put your things in the cloakroom for now, dear, and come along.'

She led the way into the morning-room, and we followed. We had a real North Country breakfast – porridge with moist brown sugar and cream on it; home-fed bacon and new-laid eggs, and after that, toast and honey. We had coffee, made with milk, to drink. No wonder both Fiona and Caroline had lovely complexions, I thought! I couldn't help thinking of my own breakfast at Mrs Crapper's – baked beans on toast, or kippers more often than not, and weak tea.

Chapter 12

Bracken Hall Again

AFTER breakfast we went straight round to the stables. Sebastian had been as good as his word and had brought in Arabesque and groomed him. For the last week he'd been up at six o'clock every morning, Caroline told me, exercising him. I was full of gratitude to Sebastian when I looked at my beloved pony, so sleek and shining.

'He knows me, too,' I said, rubbing his nose. 'I expect he wondered what had happened to me when I left him at that farm in the mist and never came back to him. Wouldn't it be lovely if we could tell what horses think?'

'Oh, I don't expect they think at all,' put in Fiona loftily. 'Horses are terribly stupid animals; they haven't any brains really – they're just creatures of habit.'

'Oh, I don't agree with you there,' Sebastian said, and then Fiona and he were off on one of their arguments. Fiona and Sebastian were always arguing, and if ever Sebastian could say anything that he knew would annoy Fiona, he did so. There wasn't much love lost between Sebastian and his cousin! I put it down partly to the fact that Fiona was living in the house that belonged to Sebastian, by rights – Sebastian's father being the eldest son – and partly that Sebastian and Fiona were so unlike by nature. Fiona hadn't the ghost of a sense of humour, whereas Sebastian was never serious – not outwardly, anyway.

'I'll come out riding with you this morning,' he agreed, when we suggested going up on to the moors. 'But this afternoon, I've got to go to Newcastle by bus. I've a rehearsal.'

'By the way, how is the music going, Sebastian?' I asked, as we saddled up.

'Oh, it's OK,' he answered. 'If all goes well, I'll be with you in London in the summer.'

'And the orchestral concert you're giving?' I questioned. 'Where is it to be held and when?'

'It's to be in the Blackett Hall, Newcastle,' answered Sebastian proudly. 'On the Saturday after Christmas. I specially arranged it to be while you're here.' Then he struck an attitude and added in his most dramatic manner: 'All the world of music was gathered together in the Blackett Hall, Newcastle-upon-Tyne, to hear the young composer, Sebastian Scott, conduct his own *Woodland Symphony*. This is the first time this major work has been performed in this country. The first movement shows the influence of the composer's countryside upon his work – one can hear the northern wind blowing through his music. The second is a complete contrast in its exquisitely gay and delicate broken chords and *arpeggios*, the personification of larch trees in spring; whilst the last movement works up, in a rising crescendo, to a terrific climax of crashing chords, making one think of the stormy winter wind as it shrills and trumpets through the bare branches of the northern forests. Gradually the storm subsides, the snow begins to fall softly, and a winter moon sails out over the tree-tops . . .'

'Gosh Sebastian – it sounds wonderful!' I exclaimed. 'I can hardly wait until next week! I like the idea of the trees in all their moods.'

'I hope the critics will do likewise,' said Sebastian solemnly, making me a little mock bow.

I stared at him thoughtfully. He hadn't changed a bit since last September – not outwardly, anyway. He had never been what you might call good-looking, but he had an interesting face with a high-bridged, sensitive nose, deeply set blue eyes, so dark that they looked almost black, and a crooked mouth. His black hair was cropped very short, and it fairly shone and bristled with life. Yes, that was what struck you about Sebastian – he was so very much alive. From the crown of his black head to the soles of his restless feet, tapping out an imaginary tune on the stable floor, he was full of energy. Looking at his tense young face, I knew that this concert in a tiny unknown hall somewhere in one of the poorest parts of Newcastle, meant just as much to Sebastian as it would to me if I were going to dance the Lilac Fairy on Covent Garden stage.

'Will there be many there – critics, I mean?' Caroline was asking.

'Well, I'm hoping that Billy Wilson of the *Northumbrian News* will turn up,' answered Sebastian. 'He sort of promised me he would.'

'Billy Wilson?' repeated Fiona. She had turned her back on us, and was standing looking out of the stable door, but now she turned round. 'You mean that awful little man who runs the ghastly women's page in *Northumbrian News* – "Aunt Emily's Whispers", or something?'

'"Aunt Emily's Whiskers"?' I echoed in astonishment.

'*Whispers*, girl; *whispers!*' corrected Sebastian solemnly, while Caroline burst into a gale of laughter. 'And let me tell you, Fiona, that just because a fellow has to earn his daily bread by catering for a lot of neurotic women, isn't to say he doesn't know anything about music. Matter of fact, Billy Wilson is dead keen on it; he's thinking seriously of joining my Scott Musical Society.'

'Oh, I see,' said Fiona sweetly, leading Melisande, her pony, out of the stable and springing into the saddle. 'Perhaps that explains why he'll be at the concert.'

Before Sebastian had time to make a suitable retort she was away over the field and out of earshot.

We had a glorious ride on the moors that stretched away on every side round Bracken Hall. Fiona joined us on our way back. She seemed as if she didn't really want to be with us, yet didn't want us to go off on our own. Perhaps she was afraid of missing something. The keen air made us so hungry that we couldn't wait for lunch, so we all trooped into the kitchen, and ate home-made scones covered with yellow country butter.

'And here's your milk, Miss Veronica,' said Trixie, putting a glass of it down on the table. 'Your Aunt June's orders! She says you're paler than ever, and indeed you are. It's all those late nights, I shouldn't wonder, and parties and that!'

In vain I tried to explain to Trixie that I didn't have any late nights; that life at the Sadler's Wells Ballet School was almost monastic in its simplicity – in other words, we did nothing but work, work, work, until at night we were too tired to do anything but go to bed. She only looked at me unbelievingly.

'Well, I *am* surprised, Miss Veronica. I always thought the stage was as gay as gay. I've no doubt you squeeze in a few parties somehow.'

'No, Trixie – really I don't,' I assured her. 'You see, I'm not actually on the stage yet, and even if I were—' I stopped trying to explain to Trixie that a ballet dancer – even a famous one – has to keep on exercising all the time; has to lead such a highly specialized and artificial life that she has no time for the sort of pleasures ordinary people enjoy.

'Oh, look!' I cried, changing the subject, as a beautiful blue Persian cat strolled into the kitchen. 'There's Cleopatra! Oh, she's forgotten me, the old hag!'

Both Sebastian and Caroline began to laugh.

'*That's* not Cleo,' Caroline said. 'That's Ptolemy, Cleo's kitten. You remember – she had four of them just before you went back to London. Well, we got homes for three of them, but we just couldn't bear to part with Ptolemy; he's so beautifully dignified!'

I stared at Ptolemy in amazement. It seemed quite impossible to believe that the tiny kitten I'd played with last autumn could have grown into this beautiful cat in so short a time.

We stayed in the kitchen for a long while. I always think that the kitchen is the nicest room in the house – especially if it's a big country house. The kitchen at Bracken Hall was lovely; it had a red tiled floor, and an oak dresser with masses of deep blue willow-pattern china upon it. There was a long table, scrubbed to gleaming whiteness with silver sand, and a deep window-seat with red-and-white gingham cushions on it. Fiona didn't stay long, though. I think she imagined that sitting in the kitchen lowered her dignity! She said she'd go and 'tidy for lunch'.

'And I suppose we ought at least to wash our hands,' Caroline said with a sigh.

We trekked into the little cloakroom in the hall, and washed. I stole into the lounge, because I hadn't been in there yet. It was just the same as I remembered it. There was a huge oval posey bowl full of scarlet geraniums on the table between the long french windows, and another of yellow jasmine on the top of the grand piano. Opposite the jasmine was a photograph of Fiona in a silver frame, a photograph I hadn't seen before. She was wearing the new party frock that Caroline had told me about in her letter, and the photographer had got the light shining through her hair so that it looked like a halo. There was a smile hovering round her lips, and I was just thinking how beautiful she was when a voice behind me said:

'Self admiration society, what! Fiona thinking how devastating Fiona is!'

'Oh, Sebastian! What a fright you gave me!' I exclaimed. 'Why will you steal behind people like that?'

'Sorry!' he apologized. Then he seated himself at the piano, after first turning the photograph so that its back was towards him, and began to play a gay, Hungarian tune. Of course, I couldn't resist it, and when Caroline and Fiona came in to see what was happening, they beheld me, skirts swirling, heels clicking, dancing the Czardas.

'That would be a lovely thing to do for Lady Blantosh's concert,' said Caroline. 'The people would adore it!'

'I haven't got a dress,' I objected. 'I've only my classical *tutu* with me, and I couldn't possibly dance a Czardas in *that*!'

'I've got a Hungarian skirt that I wore at a fancy-dress party,' Caroline said. 'And Fiona's got a lovely peasant blouse that Aunt Judith sent her from Czechoslovakia. It's got wide, embroidered sleeves.'

'It's not clean,' declared Fiona promptly. 'The last time I wore it I got jam on it.'

'Lie not, fair lady!' said Sebastian softly.

'How dare you! I'm not lying!'

'Aren't you? Well, let's go and find that blouse right now, and when you show me the jam on it, I'll believe you're telling the truth.'

'I shall do no such thing!' flashed Fiona. 'I don't allow boys to go messing about with my clothes. Anyway, it's gone to the laundry.'

'Oh, never mind,' put in Caroline. 'I've got a blouse you can wear, Veronica. It hasn't got embroidered sleeves, but it's a peasant blouse all right.'

'And I'll play for you,' Sebastian volunteered. 'That is, I will if you want me to.'

'Of *course* I want you to,' I said. 'I don't think there's a record of that thing, anyway. So if you don't play for me I can't dance.'

I said the words jokingly, never dreaming that before long they'd be anything but a joke.

Chapter 13

Northumbrian Interlude

THE holidays simply flew. The next day was Sunday, and I'm afraid that none of us went to church – at least, none of us except Fiona. As Sebastian said, we went to church most Sundays, so we could be excused for taking just one day off.

'It'll be a relief,' he added, 'not to have to listen to old Robson singing flat!'

As I have said, when we told Fiona of our proposed ride over to Broomyhough, she said she was going to church.

Sebastian made a face.

'Oh, yes, of course!' he remarked. 'I forgot you'd want to wear your new hat.'

'I want to do no such thing!' declared Fiona hotly. 'I don't go to church just to wear a new hat.'

'Don't you?' said Sebastian, goading her. 'It's a queer thing, Fiona, but whenever you go to church you happen to be wearing something new you want to show off. I've noticed it most particularly.'

'You've got a horrible mind,' stated Fiona.

'Granted,' Sebastian retorted imperturbably. 'Horrible, but discerning. By the way, that little tick, Ian Frazer, will be home for the holidays this weekend, and I shouldn't wonder if he wasn't at church too. I suppose that couldn't be the reason why you're so keen on going?'

Sebastian had at last achieved his goal. Fiona blushed hotly.

'You are a beast!' she flashed. 'And there's one thing about Ian – he wouldn't go about on Sunday dressed like you are, in a sweater all over leather patches, and a pair of riding-breeches that look as if Perkins has been cleaning the car with them!'

'I'm going riding, my good girl!' retorted Sebastian, tapping his riding-boot with his crop. 'I don't go riding in a white tie and tails! I don't go riding just to show off my clothes – like some people do!'

Sebastian had got in the last word, as so often happened. It was a well-known fact that Fiona only rode when she could look nice.

We sat in the lounge while Trixie put up our sandwiches, and we talked a hundred to the dozen. We discussed the exact locality of Broomyhough, Caroline's domestic-science career, and, last but not least, Sebastian's concert. Eventually Trixie arrived with an enormous mountain of food, all done up in separate packages so that we could share them out between us, and so divide the load ... We stowed away the packages in our rucksacks, wound woolly scarves round our necks because there was a cold wind blowing from the north-east, and after this we were ready for our adventure.

'Come on, you lot! Let's be off!' yelled Sebastian, picking up his string gloves from the table. 'I hope you enjoy the vicar's sermon, Fiona, and that there aren't too many things – or people – to distract your attention! And, by the way, it looks like rain or snow; you'd better take an umbrella to protect the new hat.'

'*I haven't got a new hat!*' Fiona yelled, and really I couldn't help feeling sorry for her – Sebastian was too bad with his teasing.

I loved that ride across the moors. Except for an occasional shepherd and his dog at an outlying farm, we didn't meet a soul, unless you could count curlews and rabbits and an occasional family of partridges solemnly taking a walk in the heather. Once we saw an old dog-fox standing motionless on a heathery crag, sniffing the wind. As we approached, he loped off and disappeared into the bracken like a shadow.

We crossed the main Newcastle–Jedburgh road, northwest of Otterburn, and then set off again across the open moorland, Sebastian leading us by ways known only to himself. We skirted dangerous patches of bog, crossed deep ravines that cut great gashes in the hills, trotted along sheep-tracks.

We stopped at eleven o'clock to have lunch and to rest the ponies, and I can tell you we made short work of the food Trixie had given us! Slices of ham-and-egg pie, sandwiches, slabs of fruit cake – all vanished as if we had never had a square meal in our lives!

'We simply must save something for later on,' Sebastian said firmly. 'Look here – let's keep the granny-loaf, and the rice cake, and some of the biscuits.'

'What about something to drink?' asked Caroline. 'We've finished off every spot of coffee.'

'We can try to get some tea or milk at a farm. I know the people at Corbyrigg; they'll give us something to drink like a shot, if we call there. They'll probably come up trumps and trot out a few eatables as well – when they see how little we've got left.'

'Oh, Sebastian!' I expostulated. 'How can you! Why, we've got *masses* left.'

'You wait till you've ridden to Broomyhough and back,' quoth Sebastian. 'You won't call it masses then!'

I must admit, here and now, that he was quite right. It's funny how, when you've just finished a meal, you think you can never be hungry again, but in an hour or two's time you feel you can eat a house!

It was one o'clock when we crossed the River Coquet above Alwynton, and then we had only a few more miles to go, and we'd be at our destination. The country was getting very wild and beautiful. The Coquet left off being a river and became a mountain stream, with waterfalls, and shallows, and a stony bank. To the north brooded Cheviot, her round brow capped with snow. The air was so cold that when you took a gulp of it, it was like drinking iced lemonade!

We dismounted to rest the ponies, and sat down with our backs against a drystone wall which sheltered us from the wind. Caroline produced a packet of clear gums, and we sat chewing them for quite a long time without speaking.

'Here's somebody on horseback,' said Sebastian suddenly. 'Let's ask him exactly where Broomyhough is, and the quickest way to get there. My knowledge of the country gives out hereabouts.'

The newcomer was mounted on what Sebastian called a heavy hunter. At first we thought he was a farmer, but when he got near enough to hail we saw that, although he wore breeches and a deerstalker, he had on a round collar.

'Parson,' whispered Sebastian. 'Golly! He looks a tough customer!'

The clergyman was a middle-aged man with two-coloured hair, and a fair skin that had been tanned to a ruddy brown by the winter winds. He had very blue eyes that looked like a sailor's do – as if he were used to looking long distances. He seemed very much at home on his big horse.

'Hullo!' yelled Sebastian. 'Please, could you tell us how to get to Broomyhough?'

The stranger reined in his mount, and sat smiling down at us. His splendid white teeth shone in his bronzed face.

'Broomyhough? Just a mile or so to the west. If you keep to the right of the crags' – he motioned to an outcrop of black rocks in the distance – 'and ride straight on, you'll see it in front of you. You'll want to be at the farm, I suppose?'

'No,' said Sebastian. 'We want a Mrs Mason. She lives at one of the cottages.'

'Granny Mason, who lives with young Adam Herdman?' said the parson. 'Oh, Granny's in great fettle, as they say round here! I saw her as I passed that way not half an hour ago; she's got her granddaughter home from London.'

'Yes, we know,' I put in eagerly. 'Stella's a great friend of mine.'

'Nice girl, Stella Mason,' volunteered the parson. 'Nice fellow she's got engaged to, as well.'

I gasped.

'Engaged? Stella engaged?' I stammered at length. 'You mean – engaged to be married?'

'Why, yes,' laughed the parson. 'This very day – to someone she knew in London – an artist chap.'

'*Jonathan!*' I shrieked. 'Gosh! How wonderful! I never *thought* of Jonathan!'

'They came to me this morning, early, to put the banns in,' went on the parson. 'Good-looking pair.' Then he sighed. 'I fear it'll be a blow to young Adam Herdman; always had an eye for Stella, had Adam.'

'Adam Herdman?' I questioned.

'Adam is shepherd to Mr Strong of Broomyhough,' explained the stranger. 'That's the big farm,' he added for our benefit, although we knew it already. Then he went on, almost to himself. 'Of course, you can understand Stella's point of view. A full-blown baronet is a different proposition altogether to a poor hill shepherd, and you can't blame her. All the same, it will be a blow to Adam.'

But my thoughts weren't for Adam Herdman, whoever he might be. They were all for the astonishing news about Jonathan – Jonathan, engaged to Stella; Jonathan, the poor artist, living in Mrs Crapper's dingy apartment house; Jonathan, whom our new friend was calling a full-blown baronet. It just didn't seem sense!

'*What* did you say he was?' I demanded when I had got my breath. 'You didn't really say he was a – a *baronet*, did you?'

'Exactly,' laughed the clergyman. 'That's what I said. Didn't you know? His father was Sir William Craymore, and then Mr Jonathan quarrelled with the old man, and went off to London to paint. He used the name of Rosenbaum because it belonged to a great friend of his who had been killed. Well, just a year ago, the old man died, and young Mr Jonathan came into the title.'

'Then Jonathan is really Sir Jonathan Craymore?' I said,

feeling more and more astonished. 'And, in that case, Stella will be Lady Craymore.'

The parson nodded his head.

'That's right. The family seat is at Ravenskirk, on the Border.' He jerked his head northwards. 'It's a fine old hall.'

'I wonder if they'll live there?' I said thoughtfully. 'Somehow, I just can't imagine Stella as Lady of the Manor, and president of the Women's Institute, and all that – she's much too shy. And I simply can't think of Jonathan as Squire either. Why, he'd hate hunting and shooting and all the rest of it. Jonathan wouldn't kill a fly!'

'I expect they won't live there,' smiled our new acquaintance. 'Or at least, not all the time. I understand an agent is looking after the place.'

'And this Adam Herdman you were talking about?' I questioned. 'Does he live with Stella's granny? How funny Stella never mentioned him.'

'I expect she was shy,' said the parson, 'seeing she knew how Adam thought about her. Old Granny Mason has lived in that cottage for close on sixty years. She went to it as a bride when she married Andrew Mason, who was shepherd to the Strongs. She was only twenty then. Andrew died a while ago in the Great Storm. Both Adam's brothers died with him. They were lost in the hills in a blizzard, looking for sheep. More than five hundred sheep perished on the moors here.'

'Poor things – were they buried?' I asked.

'Some of them. Ordinarily, of course, sheep can lie buried for quite a long time and emerge hale and hearty, but this particular storm was just one long succession of blizzards, and, at the end, the sheep were so exhausted they just lay down and died. Those that didn't actually die in the snow, died afterwards when they gave birth to their lambs. It was a bad business altogether.'

'It must have been awful,' I said, looking round at the huge, rounded hills, and endless expanse of wild moorland. 'I can just imagine this place deep in snow. Looking for sheep would be like looking for needles in a haystack!'

'Well, Mr— I'm afraid we don't know your name,' put in Sebastian, getting up and tightening Warrior's girths. 'We shall have to be moving off, or we shan't be home before dark. We've enjoyed the "crack".'

The parson smiled.

'I've enjoyed it myself,' he answered. 'My name's Robson, by the way.'

'Goodbye, Mr Robson!' we chorused. Then we swung ourselves on to our ponies' backs, and rode off towards the crags, and he rode away in the opposite direction.

When we had rounded the corner of the rocks, we could see below us the big farmsteading of Broomyhough, and the one or two small cottages clustered round it like chickens round a hen. The friendly sounds of a dog barking and a cow lowing in a byre reached our ears, and, far up on a hillside above the farm, we could see the figure of a man with a sheepdog at his heels. His tiny figure served to accentuate the spaciousness of the rolling landscape.

The farm was situated on the north bank of the Coquet, so that it stood with its broad front facing south. A small plantation of stunted fir trees sheltered the house from the north winds. To the east, where the stream curved, we could see that the valley narrowed to a mere gash in the hills, and a glint of silver betrayed the presence of a waterfall.

'It will be glorious in the summer,' I said, half to myself. In my imagination I saw the bare, brown hills standing deep in bracken and purple heather, the larks singing in the blue air, the curlews wheeling.

'Come on – what are you stopping for?' said Sebastian impatiently, urging Warrior into a canter. 'We haven't any time to waste, you know, if we're to be home by dark. We shall have to ride back an awful lot quicker than we came, I can tell you!'

We had just crossed the stream by a tiny stone bridge and were trying to decide which cottage was the one we were looking for, when a young man appeared round the corner of the wall surrounding the farm. He had a stout stick in one hand and carried a bucket of water in the other.

'Good morning,' he said politely. 'It is a nice day for a ride.' He spoke in a slow, hesitating voice that sounded as if he wasn't used to talking to many people. Incidentally, I noticed that he was a handsome stripling of about twenty, tall and sunburnt, with hair bleached almost white, and a lean, tanned face. His eyes were very blue, and had the same far-away expression in them that we had noticed in the clergyman's. Altogether, he reminded me of a picture of 'The Boy David' in one of Caroline's Bible story-books.

'Look here,' said Sebastian, reining in Warrior. 'You don't happen by any chance to be Adam Herdman, do you?'

'That is my name,' answered the young shepherd with a smile. 'You will be wanting Mr Strong of Broomyhough, maybe?' He nodded over his shoulder at the big farm behind its wall.

'Oh, no,' said Sebastian. 'It's you we want. At least, it's the cottage where you live. We've come to see Mrs Mason. Veronica, here, is a great friend of her granddaughter, Stella.'

A cloud passed over the young man's face. He bent down and flicked a bit of wool from off his riding-breeches.

'This is where Mrs Mason lives,' he told us, indicating the cottage, 'but you will not find Stella here. She has become hand-fasted this day to a London gentleman, and they are gone to Ravenskirk, where he lives.'

'Oh, I see,' I said with a sigh of disappointment. 'Well, we'll just call and see her granny, now we're here. We've come from Bracken,' I added.

'Bracken? That is a very long way in the wintertime,' said the young man gravely. 'You must have something to eat – it will be late before you get home. There is a stable where you can put your horses. If you will please go in, I shall be back shortly. You can tie up your ponies here.' He indicated some hooks on the wall by the side of the door. 'I will see to them for you.'

He pushed open the door a little wider for us, set down the brimming bucket on the stone slab outside, and disappeared in the direction of the farm. He was certainly one of the most courteous and softly spoken young men we had ever met.

'I say,' said Sebastian, knocking on the door with the butt end of his riding-crop, 'we can't just walk in, can we? She might be having a bath, or anything!'

But there was no answer to his knock, and finally we stepped inside the door and looked around us. We were in a small kitchen in which everything that could possibly shine, shone. Even the patterned canvas on the floor reflected the simple furniture, so that the effect was rather like that of a lake, with the 'clipping' mats floating in it like islands. There was a bright fire in the hearth, with a steel fender in front of it, and a glittering array of fire-irons at either side. The knob of the oven door and the hinges shone and winked, and on the tiny dresser, brass plates and jugs gave back the light of the one small window. On the cottage piano, which had a front of pleated green silk and two brass candlesticks on either side of the music-rest, stood an array of photographs. They were all of Stella – Stella as a little girl, playing with a puppy; Stella obviously going to school for the first time, her books under her arm, and her smile no less bright for the fact that two of her front teeth were missing! There were several pictures of Stella in her ballet dress, and very strange it looked in this wild and primitive place to see her posed *en pointe* in her classic *tutu* and severely dressed hair.

There were several pictures on the walls of the room.

' "The Stag At Bay",' I read out, glancing at the one nearest me. 'Ugh! I'd hate always to have to be looking at that! But perhaps you get used to it, and don't notice it.'

There was another picture called 'The Trysting Place', which showed a girl in a very short-waisted dress, that made her look at least seven feet tall, leaning against a tree in a very dejected attitude.

'Fellow hasn't turned up, obviously!' said Sebastian, looking over my shoulder.

For about five minutes we stood in that kitchen, wondering what to do, and where Stella's granny could have got to. Then there was the sound of a door opening somewhere at the back of the cottage, and a little old lady came into the room. She was very frail, and very, very old, but she had Stella's blue eyes, and Stella's shy smile. In her hands she was carrying two brown eggs which she placed carefully on the white-scrubbed table. Then she looked at us inquiringly.

When we had explained who we were, and what we had come for, Stella's grandmother took us to her heart. Nothing was too much trouble for the friends of her darling. She filled the kettle in a trice, and set it on the reddest part of the fire; then she covered the table with a snowy cloth, and blue-and-white willow-patterned china, and in a very short time we were sitting down to a real farmhouse tea of buttered scones and jam, a large home-made fruit cake, thick yellow cream, and cups of hot, strong tea.

Not until we had finished our meal did Stella's grandmother broach the subject which filled all our minds.

'You said you had met Adam?' she questioned. 'Did he tell you about the young man who came here for Stella?'

'Oh, yes,' I said. 'But we knew before that. Mr Robson – a clergyman we met on the road – told us all about it.'

Old Granny Mason looked from one to another of us anxiously.

'Tell me about him,' she said nervously. 'Is he a good young man, like Adam here? I've always heard that artists are such a strange sort of people – not like ordinary folk.'

'Yes,' I said thoughtfully. 'Yes, you're right – Jonathan isn't a bit ordinary. For one thing, he's so simple in his ways. He's so tall and broad, but, although he's immensely strong, he's ever so gentle. He's only twenty-six, you know, but you'd think he was lots older. He'll look after Stella like a mother, and that's what Stella needs. They'll be so happy – why, Mrs Mason, what's the matter?' – for Stella's grandmother had put her head down on the edge of the table, much to Sebastian's discomfort, and was crying.

'It's all right, dearies,' she sobbed. 'I'm just relieved, that's all. You've taken a load off my mind. I was so afraid – you see, him being a baronet, and my little Stella—'

'We had no idea he was a baronet ourselves until this afternoon,' I volunteered. 'He never told us.'

'He never told anybody,' said Mrs Mason. 'Not even Stella. When old Sir William died, over a year ago, and Mr Jonathan became *Sir* Jonathan, he said he never thought to mention it.'

'Well!' I exclaimed. 'How exactly like Jonathan! And isn't it queer to think of Stella being Lady Rosenbaum – I mean, Lady Craymore, of course. I just *can't* get it into my head that Jonathan is Jonathan Craymore and not Rosenbaum. It will be funny to hear Stella called Lady Craymore!'

'It will indeed!' said Granny Mason with a sigh. And whether it was a sigh of pleasure, relief, or just plain awe, I don't know!

We had pushed back our chairs and were preparing to go, when young Adam Herdman came in.

'Yes – it is time that you go home,' he said. 'Do not think that we want to be rid of you, but it is a long way to Bracken, and it is blowing up for snow. Already the storm has begun in the valley.' He nodded towards the east. 'Broomyhough has just come back from Bellingham, and he says it is inches deep down there already. Mistress Strong was anxious when she heard about you. She asked me to ask you if you will not stay the night over.'

'Good Lord, no!' exclaimed Sebastian. 'We must get back – I've got a rehearsal of my Music Society tomorrow.'

'It's most awfully kind of Mrs Strong, all the same,' I said. 'Please thank her for us, won't you, Mr—'

112

'Just Adam,' said the young man with a smile. 'Well, if you will not stay, you must be going quickly. It is not good for you to be caught in a snowstorm on these hills. It is all very well for me – I was born and bred here—'

'So was I,' Sebastian broke in indignantly. 'I should like to see the snowstorm that would get the better of me!'

'I was thinking, really, of the young ladies,' said the young shepherd, looking down at us.

'Well, Caroline's Northumbrian born and bred, too,' answered Sebastian. 'But perhaps you're right about Veronica. Veronica's a Londoner; she's nesh—'

'I like that!' I exclaimed. 'I'm not nesh at all – whatever it means. I'm pretty sure it's something horrid! And I'm not a Londoner. My mother was Northumbrian, so I'm half and half.'

'You *seem* like a Londoner,' insisted Sebastian. 'At least, you do since you've come back. But let's not argue about it. Adam's right, and we should be getting away. It's blowing up for snow and no mistake!'

It was a quarter past two when we left the cottage at Broomyhough and started on our long ride home.

'Your Stella seems to be a bit of a lad!' remarked Sebastian, as we left the cottage behind and set off across the open moor.

'What do you mean?' I demanded indignantly.

'Well, it seems to me she's got two strings to her bow – this Jonathan chap, and young Adam Herdman. He's obviously three sheets in the wind, or however you describe people in love.'

'Stella can't help that,' I declared. 'It's not her fault if men fall in love with her. I think it's beastly of you, Sebastian, to call her names. Why, everyone loves Stella; you would yourself if you knew her.'

'Not me!' declared Sebastian. 'I'm in love already.'

'Yes – with yourself!' I retorted.

'What a noise you two make,' put in Caroline. 'If it wasn't for you, there wouldn't be another sound.'

We reined in our ponies and listened, and it was quite true. There was perfect and unbroken silence. There wasn't even the chirp of a bird, or the bleat of a sheep. There was something unearthly about it – as if the world were under a spell.

'London is like a dream,' I said as we went on again. 'When you think of all those people at this very moment fighting for buses and trains, being carried up and down in escalators and lifts; all those cars grinding along in endless procession – well, it just seems like another world. Yet, when I'm in London, Northumberland seems like a dream. It's queer, isn't it?'

As we rode onwards, we looked back over our shoulders, but we could no longer see Cheviot. A fine veil had fallen between us and the mountain.

'It's snowing up there,' said Sebastian with a note of anxiety in his voice. 'Come on, you lot! We must ride like Jehu!'

Chapter 14

Caught in the Snow

BUT though we rode like Jehu, or like the very wind itself, the storm gained upon us. Perhaps it was because we were riding eastwards, and the storm seemed to be blowing up from that quarter. Very soon the ground was several inches thick with fine snow, and the tufts of heather and coarse grass began to look like fat white cushions. Drifts of snow crept up the dry-stone walls and along the dykes, completely changing the face of the landscape.

It was then that I understood how truly Sebastian had spoken when he'd told Adam Herdman he was Northumbrian born and bred. He led us unerringly across the white wastes towards the Coquet, crossing the stream at the exact spot where we had crossed it that morning, and then onwards over the darkening moorland towards the distant Otterburn–Jedburgh road.

'I don't know how on earth you find your way,' I said in admiration after we had ridden for a long time without speaking. 'It all looks exactly the same to me!'

'Oh, I can tell where I am by the burns,' said Sebastian. 'They stay the same for ages, even in the snow. I know the look of most of them. Then there are the rocks. That outcrop over there, for instance – I know we must keep well to the south of that.'

'What would happen if we didn't?' I asked him.

'Bog,' answered Sebastian concisely. 'Not that it would matter just now, because it'll be frozen over, but it would be out of our course, and we don't want to be any longer getting home than we can help.'

'N-no, we d-don't,' I said with a shiver. Already my feet

were numb, and my face felt as if it were covered with a mask of ice.

'Here – catch!' yelled Sebastian. 'I said you were nesh!' He unwound his woollen scarf from round his neck and tossed it over to me. 'Now don't argue – put it on!'

I put it on meekly, glad of its extra warmth.

We rode on doggedly, Caroline on one side of me, Sebastian on the other. Icicles hung from the ponies' eyelashes, and a great dome of snow hid Arabesque's well-known dish-face from me. Hour after hour we rode, only stopping for a few minutes to eat the rest of our food, and give the ponies a breather. Although I had spent a winter with my cousin before I had gone back to London, it had been an abnormally mild one, and we had had very little snow. Now I learned for the first time what a real blizzard on the Northumbrian moors is like. The fine snow blew up round us in hissing, misty clouds, stinging our faces as if it were made of particles of steel, or sharp glass. The high parts of the moor had blown clear, but the hollows were filled with great drifts, and we had to pick our way round them. They were like lakes of snow, growing deeper every moment. All around us was a desolate waste of snow, with not a village or a habitation of any sort within sight. There wasn't even a sheep-stell. Nothing but snow beneath us, and curling skies above us, as far as the eye could see. It was savage and awe-inspiring, and if it hadn't been for Sebastian and Caroline riding steadily along beside me, seemingly quite unmoved by any feeling of terror, I'd have been scared to death. Long afterwards Sebastian told me that he hadn't been quite as unmoved as he had seemed during that long ride. He'd begun to wonder whether we would ever be able to find our way home, not because of the snow, but because of the early winter twilight which was closing down upon us with terrifying swiftness. To be caught on a lonely Northumbrian moor at night in a blizzard would be almost certain death. Fortunately, I didn't know this. I had implicit faith in Sebastian. I knew he would lead us home safely.

'I thought you said there was a farm hereabouts by the name of Corbyrigg?' said Caroline, breaking the long silence. 'You talked about getting some tea there on our way back.'

'We seem to have missed it somehow,' answered Sebastian. 'I think we've come a bit far north.'

We had crossed the Otterburn–Jedburgh road long ago, and were now on the last long stretch of moor that led to home. It was getting dark and our ponies were beginning to stumble.

Suddenly Sebastian gave a great shout.

'Gosh, Caroline! Do you see what this is? This means we're OK.'

Before us rose an old stone building, something like a house, only it didn't seem to have any windows in the bottom part of it. It had a heavy iron-studded door and a flight of worn, stone steps leading to the top floor.

'It's the old peel-house above Garside!' said Caroline with a gasp of relief. 'Thank goodness! We aren't far from home now. Golly! I was beginning to think we were well and truly lost.'

'So was I,' admitted Sebastian. 'But I knew we *ought* to come to this place sooner or later, if we were where I thought we were.'

'What about staying here for the night?' suggested Caroline. 'It's quite a cosy place up top.'

But Sebastian shook his head.

'No,' he said. 'They'll dig us out at the Hall in a day or two, but up here we'd probably be snowed up for weeks, and there's my concert on Saturday – besides the rehearsals.'

I couldn't help reflecting that I wasn't the only person to have a one-way mind. Sebastian ran me very close.

We skirted the old building and rode off to the right, passing by a mountain tarn on our way. Its waters were dark and infinitely lonely, and I couldn't help giving a shudder as I looked at it. On a hot summer's day, with the larks overhead, and the bees in the heather on its banks, its grey waters ruffled by waterfowl, it would be a pleasant enough place, no doubt, but just now, seen through a veil of snow, it looked a spot of the utmost desolation. An uncanny, haunted place! I wasn't sorry to turn my back on it, I can tell you!

We were riding now almost due south, and before long we struck a country road. I say 'road', but really it looked more like a railway cutting! The snow had blown into drifts that were as high as your head on the one side and tailed off into rivulets on the other. The strips of black road, seen in between, had the effect of railway sleepers. The snowy rivulets lying across our path were so regular that I began to feel sleepy, and as though I were mesmerized. My head drooped forward, and several times I found myself slipping over Arabesque's neck. Then, as though in a dream, I heard Sebastian say:

'Ah! This is what I've been looking for! The telephone kiosk on the Bracken road. We'll ring up and let them know we're OK.'

'Veronica's nearly asleep,' I heard Caroline answer.

'Wake her up, then!' came Sebastian's voice. 'For goodness' sake keep her awake while I phone.'

I heard him dismount, go into the box, shovelling away a drift of snow first with his foot, and begin to talk. I heard him say something about our whereabouts, and then: 'Ask Perkins to get out the shooting-brake – it can get through this stuff – and come and meet us. Oh, not for Caroline and me – we're OK. It's Veronica – she's just about all in! She's not like us; she's town bred!'

I was too tired even to be angry at his words. I slipped from Arabesque's back and lay down on the ground beside the telephone kiosk with a sigh of thankfulness. It was really quite cosy in the snow – soft – cosy—

Rudely I was pulled to my feet.

'Get up, Veronica! Get up, I say! ... Caroline, I *told* you not to let her go to sleep – oh, yes, you could!— Get up this very minute, Veronica! Don't you know it's dangerous to go to sleep in the snow.'

'Let me alone!' I begged. 'Really, I'm quite comfy here.'

Then the most astonishing thing happened. Sebastian raised his hand, and struck me a resounding slap on the cheek. It wasn't a light, playful blow either; it was a hard one, and it hurt. I was so surprised that my eyes flew wide open, and I leapt to my feet.

'How dare you!' I yelled in a fury. 'How dare you!'

Sebastian's blue eyes snapped fire.

'That's better! Now will you do as you're told, and come on? Up you get, and don't you go falling asleep again, or I shall do it even harder!'

On we rode, and after what seemed hours, though Sebastian said afterwards it was only about twenty minutes, we heard the welcome sound of a motor vehicle churning through the snow, its chains clinking and grinding. A few more seconds and the shooting-brake loomed out of the darkness, its headlights turning the snowy landscape into fairyland.

'Get Veronica inside,' Sebastian said to Perkins, who was driving the brake. 'You'd better go as well, Caroline, to look after her. I'll come on behind, and Arab and Gilly will follow if we unbridle them.'

Then came the question of turning the shooting-brake in the road. We decided that it was impossible, so Perkins reversed it to the cross-roads past which he'd come a few minutes before.

And so we arrived at Bracken Hall. The whole house turned out to welcome us – even Fiona. Trixie stood in the hall, surrounded by a perfect forest of hot-water bottles, warm blankets, and cups of steaming coffee. Really, it made us feel as if we were Arctic explorers who had been thought lost, but who had reached haven at last!

'Oh, Veronica,' said Sebastian, when I had recovered a bit and was trekking off for a hot bath, 'you know, when I hit you out there it was sheer necessity, don't you? I just *had* to do something drastic to wake you up, or you'd have been as dead as a door-nail before very long. You do understand, don't you?'

'Of course I do,' I assured him. 'It certainly *did* wake me up! As a matter of fact – I've been thinking – I believe you saved my life, Sebastian.'

'Oh, rot!' said Sebastian with a grin.

Chapter 15

A Northumbrian Christmas

APART from a little stiffness, I didn't suffer any ill-effects from my adventure, and as for Sebastian and Caroline, they seemed to take it all as a matter of course.

'Snowed up!' said Sebastian cheerfully when we met at breakfast next morning – he had stayed at Bracken Hall for the night – 'I thought we would be! Christmas Eve is the day after tomorrow, so it looks as if we'll be cut off from civilization for the Festive Season. Oh, well, it doesn't really matter. I shall only miss one rehearsal, and the turkey's in the larder! Fortunately, it arrived yesterday, before the snow started.'

'By the way,' put in Caroline, 'Mrs Strong of Broomyhough rang up last night, after we'd gone to bed, to find out if we'd arrived home safely. Wasn't it decent of her?'

'Jolly decent,' agreed Sebastian. 'These outlying people are miles ahead of the others when it comes to natural good manners. I've often noticed.'

After breakfast we climbed up into the attics to view the landscape. It was a lovely sight. The snow had stopped falling, and the sky was a beautiful duck-egg blue. All round the Hall the hills rose in glittering white tiers, while nearer at hand the fir trees stood like sentinels, each branch covered with its snowy burden. During the night the wind had blown the fine snow into fantastic shapes. Each bush had its spiral, each stone a shell of snow curving over its back, while snow hung in glistening scallops round the roof and over every window. There was an arbour of snow over the front porch. Just as we stared at it, fascinated, Perkins came round the corner of the house and demolished it with a long-handled shovel.

'He *would* go and do that!' exclaimed Sebastian, who had

no love for Perkins. 'Trust Perkins to spoil the artistic effect!'

'Oh, I expect Aunt June told him to do it,' I said.

From our lofty position we could see curls of smoke rising from farms and hamlets all over the snowy landscape, and it was queer to think that we were entirely cut off from them.

'Look!' exclaimed Sebastian, who had found a pair of binoculars and was gazing through them. 'You see those black specks – over there, by the village? They're the road-gang. They've started to cut us out already. Ahoy there!'

A faint shout answered his hail.

'Let me have the glasses,' I begged.

He passed them over to me, and immediately the specks changed into a little group of men, in their shirt-sleeves, shovelling the snow into great blocks and tossing them on to the sides of the road.

'Glasses, please!' said Caroline after a few minutes. 'It's maddening to have somebody looking through field-glasses, and exclaiming about things, and not being able to see them for yourself.'

'Sorry,' I laughed, and passed them over. 'How long will it take them to get to us, Sebastian?'

'Oh, they ought to be here by the day after tomorrow,' he answered. 'We should be cut out by Christmas Eve, provided there isn't another fall.'

But that night the wind rose, and it began to snow again, so that the track dug by the roadmen was blown in, and they had to start all over again.

'Never mind,' said Sebastian. 'We're entirely self-supporting here. We've food for months in the house – except meat, and we can always kill off the hens and chickens if we're starving – not to mention the pig! By the way, you lot, we must have a Christmas tree. How about getting one out of the wood? We could chop it down ourselves, and bring it back on a sledge.'

'Oh, yes – let's!' we said in chorus. 'That would be fun!'

We spent the rest of the day digging a track for ourselves

122

towards the nearest fir plantation. I couldn't help wondering what the people at Sadler's Wells would have thought if they'd seen me cutting out huge blocks of snow and heaving them over my shoulder! At intervals I took a scared look at my arms to see if the muscles were bulging, but no – all seemed to be well! I felt sure that everyone would approve of the pink colour that was creeping into my pale cheeks.

Perkins and the gardeners spent their time cutting a path out to the field, so that Aunt June could feed her hens, and another one round to the garage for Uncle John to get to his car. This seemed to me to be rather optimistic, because, even if Uncle John had been able to get his car out, he wouldn't have been able to go anywhere in it. However, I suppose he wanted to be ready to emerge the very moment the men got through from the village. As a matter of fact, as things turned out, I was to thank Uncle John for his forethought before many days were passed.

In the late afternoon we set off, armed with axe, sledge, and ropes, along the track we had made to bring home our Christmas tree. Sebastian cut it down and we all helped to drag it on to the sledge. When I say 'all', I don't include Fiona. She didn't like messing about in the snow, or cutting down trees. She stayed behind and helped Aunt June and Trixie with the flowers that Pilks had brought in from the hothouses.

We deposited the Christmas tree in the hall, ready to be set up in a huge plant-pot, and went back to the garden for holly. We found, to our disgust, that the birds had eaten most of the berries, but Sebastian found one small tree that still had a lot on, so we piled our sledge high with branches of it.

'Mistletoe!' said Sebastian when we'd finished. 'There's some growing on that old apple tree in the kitchen garden. Come on you people!'

We trekked round to the kitchen garden, ploughing through the snow in our Wellington boots, and there, sure enough, Sebastian was right. The gnarled branches of the apple tree were covered with the pale-green leaves and waxen berries of the beautiful parasite. We picked a huge bunch and placed it carefully on top of the holly. Then we dragged the sledge round to the front door and unloaded our booty in the porch, so that we could carry it straight into the hall where the Christmas tree was to be placed and where most of our decorating was to be done.

'Make way for Santa Claus!' yelled Sebastian, striding into the hall, his arms full of greenery. He threw it down on the floor and then held aloft the bunch of mistletoe.

'Let me see,' he exclaimed, striking an attitude. 'What is this stuff for? Ah, yes – methinks I remember!'

Before I knew what he was about, he had held it over my head and kissed me under it.

'That's to make up for the horrid way I treated you yesterday, when we were out in the storm!' he declared.

'How did you treat her in a horrid way?' demanded Fiona curiously. She'd been standing in the shadows, arranging geraniums in a low rose bowl, and now she came forward. 'What do you mean?'

'Oh, I slapped her face, that's all,' said Sebastian offhandedly. He was never averse to shocking Fiona if he got the chance. 'Had to. Otherwise she'd have been like the maiden in Wordsworth's poem – Lucy somebody or other – who was lost in the snow. Dead as a haddock! I just had to wake her up.'

'So you slapped Veronica's face – how gentlemanly!' said Fiona sarcastically.

'As I say – it had to be done,' countered Sebastian. 'Better to be ungentlemanly than to have Veronica's death laid at my door! Never was particularly gentlemanly, as you may have noticed. Anyway, she's forgiven me – haven't you, Veronica?'

I couldn't help laughing. Fiona was so serious, and Sebastian so wicked, standing there deliberately baiting her.

'Of course I have,' I answered.

'Oh, well – if you don't *mind* being slapped,' said Fiona with a shrug. 'I shouldn't care for it myself, though.'

'No, you'd rather be as dead as a haddock!' said Sebastian. 'Queer tastes some people have, I must say!' He began to arrange the holly round the picture frames, singing at the same time:

> *'There was a young lady of Craddock*
> *Who'd rather be dead as a haddock.*
> > *But alas, and alack!*
> > *On her cheek a big smack*
> *Saved the life of our lady of Craddock!'*

Fiona turned a little pink – she hated to be laughed at. Then she said curiously:

'I suppose you only kiss your friends under the mistletoe, Sebastian – not your cousins?'

'Cousins?' echoed Sebastian, pausing with a piece of mistletoe in his hand. 'Oh, you mean *you*? Rather not! No fun kissing cousins!'

'I suppose that goes for me, too?' put in Caroline.

'You? You're just a kid,' said Sebastian, turning and laughing down at her. 'No fun kissing babies!'

Of course, Caroline fell upon him in her wrath, whereupon he dropped the mistletoe, and fled up the shallow oak staircase and stood mocking us in the gallery above.

'Look out! You're scattering mistletoe berries all over the place!' yelled Caroline. 'Somebody will be slipping—'

She broke off suddenly. Her words had come true almost before they were out of her mouth. Trixie had come into the hall from the kitchen and had skidded on a rolling berry. She shot across the polished floor at the bottom of the stairs and collapsed against a suit of armour. I'm afraid we all began to laugh. Apart from the crash and clatter the armour made, Trixie's outraged expression was really funny.

'Trixie! Trixie!' came Sebastian's mocking voice from the gallery. 'I'm surprised – really I am – to find *you* of all people clasping Sir Humphrey O'Rourke, my illustrious ancestor, round the middle! Really, Trixie! And from what I've heard, Sir Humphrey was more than a bit of a lad!'

'For shame, Master Sebastian!' said poor Trixie, extricating herself from the chilly embrace of the suit of armour that was reputed to have belonged to the old knight. 'It's your berries I've slipped on, and well you know it! Why you must drop everything down on the floor, I can't think. Such a lot of trouble untidy people make!' She went to the kitchen again, muttering about Sebastian and his untidiness; though, as a matter of fact, we all knew she adored him really.

Chapter 16

Christmas Day

WE all went to midnight mass on Christmas Eve, having persuaded Aunt June that it was really a good idea because it meant we wouldn't have to get up early to go to holy communion the next morning.

'Matter of fact, I've simply *got* to do some practising tomorrow morning. My concert is on Saturday – only two days off,' said Sebastian as we picked our way round the drifts by the aid of his flashlight.

'Yes, and Lady Blantosh's thing is on Friday – Boxing Day,' I said. 'I must practise as well. Why, I haven't decided yet what dances I'm going to do.'

'It's a good thing Lady Blantosh's concert is in the village hall here, and not at Blantosh,' remarked Caroline. 'Blantosh Castle is right up on the edge of the moors. I don't expect they'll be dug out there for ages. Poor old Lady Blantosh will have to walk down.'

'Do her good,' declared Sebastian, who had no love for Lady Blantosh, kind though she was. 'She's getting far too fat!'

By this time we had reached the church, and an unexpected and lovely sight greeted us as we walked up the little path to the porch. There happened to be a tall fir tree growing just outside the church door, and someone had had a brainwave and had hung its branches with fairylights, Canadian-fashion. When the wind blew, all the little coloured lights dipped and swung, and the effect was marvellous.

As I looked at the dancing tree, I thought of Hans Andersen's Karen, dancing up to the church door in her red shoes, only to be turned back by the Angel of God with his stern face

*I thought of Hans Andersen's Karen, dancing up to the
church door in her red shoes*

and shining, white wings. Poor Karen, condemned to dance over highway and byway, in summer's heat and winter's cold – condemned to dance for ever, just because she was light-hearted! It seemed a severe punishment!

'Come on, Veronica!' said Fiona's voice from in front of me. 'What on earth are you standing there for?'

'Oh, she's imagining things!' said Sebastian mockingly. 'Veronica often does, you know! What was it this time, Veronica – Giselle and her Wilis?'

I said nothing, but followed them into the church, past the carved coffin-lids that stood on end like sentinels just inside the porch, past the tomb where the Crusader, who was one of Sebastian's ancestors, lay, his dog at his feet, past the carved griffin whose outspread wings supported the Bible, and into the Scotts' family pew.

The church was decorated with holly and evergreens, and the altar was a mass of pink geraniums.

'Mummy did it this afternoon,' whispered Caroline, as we filed into our seats. 'Doesn't it look lovely?'

'Gorgeous,' I whispered back. 'I think the real candles in the candelabra are lovely, too. They give such a soft light – much nicer than electric ones.'

Walking back from the church in the snow at half past twelve at night was exciting. We made our way across the fields because the road was still blocked. Sometimes we came to huge drifts, and had to go a long way round, so it took us ages to get home. Or perhaps it was really because it was all so beautiful and unearthly, walking over the snow in the brilliant moonlight, that we didn't hurry!

When we reached the frozen lake, I lingered for a moment on its banks, and imagined myself dancing on it as Irma Foster had danced in *Les Patineurs*. The fronds of dead bracken, glittering under the frosty moon, reminded me of her white dress. I could almost hear the gentle, rippling music of the harp-strings, plucked by an unseen hand.

'Oh – lovely! Lovely!' I said half aloud.

'*Veronica!* Do hurry up!' came Fiona's impatient voice. 'Mummy will wonder where on earth we are!'

Sebastian came with us as far as the gate into the garden proper, and then went back to his cottage, whilst we trekked round to the kitchen and made coffee. After this, Caroline gave a great yawn and said that she was going to bed.

'Goodnight, everyone, and a Merry Christmas!'

'Merry Christmas!' Fiona and I said in reply. 'Just coming ourselves.'

Fiona and Caroline went to matins on Christmas morning, but I stayed at home and practised for Lady Blantosh's concert the next day. Sebastian joined us for lunch, and when that was over, he announced that he was going to spend the afternoon helping to dig out the road, together with a lot of other volunteers.

'Jolly self-sacrificing of me, I consider,' he stated, 'because it doesn't matter two hoots to me when the bally road is cut out. It's OK from the crossroads, and I can get a bus into Newcastle from there, so my rehearsal tomorrow afternoon is safe. Still, always the little gentleman, yours truly.'

'I thought you said yesterday—' began Fiona, but Sebastian cut her short with a lordly gesture.

'Quote me not dead yesterdays, woman!' he said. 'I live in the present. See you at tea, you lot! So long!'

With this he was gone, and we were left to our own devices. We spent most of the afternoon tying up the presents we had got for each other, and also the masses of small gifts that Aunt June had bought for the village children, who were coming to a party after dinner that night.

We tied the small gifts on the tree and arranged our own presents round the bottom because we were going to give them out earlier in the evening. When we had finished, it looked terribly exciting. We crawled round the tree on hands and knees, prodding and poking the intriguing parcels.

'I'll bet this one is a riding-crop,' said Caroline. 'Mummy

knew I'd broken mine at that gymkhana at Mintlaw last October.'

'And this will be a box of liquorice all-sorts,' I said. 'It's for me, and it's Trixie's writing. She knows how fond I am of them. But, of course, it *may* be a box of soap!'

'This one's got a gorgeous smell!' exclaimed Caroline. 'You can smell it right through the wrapping-paper! It's for you, Fiona; so it'll be that bath essence you wanted.'

'I wish you wouldn't keep on guessing!' grumbled Fiona. 'It spoils all the fun.'

Caroline got up with a sigh.

'Perhaps you're right,' she admitted. 'But it's an awful temptation. Oh, well – let's arrange the Christmas cards.'

'Mummy's and mine are in the lounge; we did them ages ago,' Fiona said loftily. 'You and Veronica had better put yours on the mantelshelf in here.'

Caroline had masses of lovely cards. Most of them had horses on them. Mine were chiefly ballet dancers, which was just as it should be. One was the exception, though. It was a private card from Lady Blantosh, and it was a view of Blantosh Castle, taken from the rose garden. Miss Martin, the principal of my Newcastle dancing school, had sent me a lovely card of Margot Fonteyn in *Swan Lake*, and I had a ballet calendar from Madame Viret. Sara, Stella, and several of my Northumbrian schoolfriends had remembered me, so I felt that I hadn't done too badly, all things considered. Jonathan and Mrs Crapper had both sent me exciting-looking parcels, but I had firmly put them round the Christmas tree with the others, to be opened later on.

'Let's go down to the bottom of the drive and see how the road-diggers are getting on,' I suggested, when we had got all the cards arranged to our liking. 'It's a lovely day overhead, as Trixie would say. The sun's as hot as midsummer!'

We found the road-gang within shouting distance of the gates. Sebastian was there, in shirt-sleeves, and working like a navvy. He was receiving a great deal of goodnatured chaff because he was wearing a large pair of leather gloves to protect his hands. But teasing made no difference to Sebastian. He stuck to his gloves! I stared at him thoughtfully over the intervening wall of snow, and decided that no one could be blamed for not taking him or his ambition seriously. He went through life joking about everything, and it was rarely anyone saw the serious vein underlying his teasing manner. Few people – except perhaps his father and I – ever saw the serious side of Sebastian, or knew how terribly determined he was. I knew, though, that he would let nothing stand in the way of his ambition. He was a strange mixture, was Sebastian!

'View hullo!' he yelled half an hour later as the last block of snow was heaved on to the shoulder-high walls at the side of the road. 'We're out!'

The road-gang, composed of Uncle Adrian, Sebastian's father, the village schoolmaster, the doctor, and several people from houses nearby, leant on their shovels and mopped their heated brows. Bella MacIntosh, who looked after Sebastian and Uncle Adrian, brought a steaming pot of coffee, and handed it out through the window, together with a bevy of mugs. We drank our coffee, standing in the snowy road, and Sebastian perched himself astride a huge block of snow and made hissing noises through his teeth.

'Well, now for a real tea!' he announced, dismounting at length, and passing his cup through the window to the grinning Bella. 'That stuff has just whetted my appetite! I hope you've got something substantial, Bella? Ham and eggs, for choice!'

'You think of nothing but eating,' Fiona said scornfully.

'You ought to try doing a spot of work for a change,' retorted Sebastian. 'Improve your appetite! So long, folks! See you at dinner!'

So saying, he swung himself over the window-sill of the cottage and disappeared from our view. A moment later we heard the chords of the *Sonata Pathétique* coming out of the window and knew that we had seen the last of Sebastian for some time.

Usually Caroline and I had supper in the schoolroom, but of course tonight, being Christmas night, we had dinner with the grown-ups. We had it very early, because of the party to follow. Uncle Adrian was there, and the doctor and his wife, and, of course, Sebastian.

We all wore our prettiest dresses. Fiona had on the new long frock that she was wearing in the photograph. It was honey-coloured taffeta, and it exactly matched her hair. Caroline and I hadn't real evening frocks yet, so we just wore our best party dresses. Caroline's was her school prizegiving one, so of course it was white. Mine was a flowered summer dress that Aunt June had had made for me last year. Sebastian gave us all a shock by turning up in a real, grown-up dinner jacket. He told me on the quiet that he had got it especially for his concert on Saturday.

'The conductor must wear evening togs,' he declared.

'You look so grown up, I hardly dare talk to you!' I told him.

We had the usual Christmassy sort of things for dinner: turkey, plum pudding, and all the et ceteras. I told everyone that it was my second Christmas dinner, and of course they wanted to know how that could be, so I explained about Jonathan's pheasants, and Mrs Crapper's two puddings, and our festive dinner-table with its swan on a glass lake. Dr Ridley laughed and said it carried him back to his childhood. The housekeeper they'd had when his mother died had had a 'centrepiece' just like that!

While the grown-ups were having their coffee, we dashed into the hall to light the candles on the tree, so that it would burst upon them in a blaze of glory. We left the curtains undrawn, so that the lights were reflected in the long windows, and it looked exactly as if there were two trees, one at each end of the room.

When every candle was alight, and burning brightly, we dashed back to the dining-room and commanded the grown-ups to come quickly, because we didn't want the candles to burn quite away – we wanted to light them again later on for the village children, who were due at eight o'clock.

'And now for the presents,' Caroline said, when we'd extinguished the candles and switched on the lights. 'You give them out, Veronica, as you're kind of a visitor.'

'Yes – you, Veronica!' said everyone in chorus.

So I acted as Master of Presents, if you can call it that. I won't bother with a list of all the things everyone got, but will just tell you what my own presents were. Aunt June and Uncle John had given me a lovely twinset of Shetland wool, with a Fair Isle pattern on the jumper; Sebastian a photograph of Arabesque in a frame, so that I could put it in a place of honour on the mantelpiece at Heather Hill; Caroline a box of sweets that she'd made herself; Fiona a jar of bath salts that I happened to know someone had given her last Christmas but which weren't the kind she liked; lastly, Trixie's present *was* the box of liquorice all-sorts that we had felt when we'd been poking the parcels, and Mrs Crapper's was a jumper that she'd made herself. She'd got the pattern a bit mixed in places, but I knew that this was owing to her eyes not being what they were, and I loved it just as much as if it had been perfect. Oh, and I nearly forgot Jonathan and Stella. They'd sent me a joint present, and it was a pair of opera-glasses in a brocaded case. Jonathan had also put in a book, *Ivan Stcherbakof – by his Mother*, because he thought I hadn't read it.

'Hey, Veronica!' yelled Sebastian when I'd unwrapped the parcel. 'You can't start reading that now! There are loads of other things to give out!' He snatched the book out of my hands and put it under a cushion, which he then sat on. 'On with the dance! I mean the presents!'

As I looked at my beautiful gifts, my heart grew warm with gratitude to them all. I thought sadly of the inexpensive presents I'd had to give them, and hoped they wouldn't mind them being cheap. I knew that Sebastian and Caroline wouldn't, but I wasn't sure about Fiona!

The children arrived promptly at eight, and Uncle Adrian appeared, dressed as Santa Claus, to give out the presents on the tree. Then we all played games, sang songs, and ate ice-cream that Aunt June had made in the fridge. After this, they all clamoured for me to dance. It appeared that a lot of the kids had been at Lady Blantosh's concert when I'd danced before, and they all wanted to see me again.

'Go on, Veronica!' begged Sebastian. 'I'll play for you if you like. What do you want? Something out of *The Sleeping Beauty*?'

'I can dance the Fairy of the Crystal Fountain,' I answered.

'OK. I can play that without the music,' said Sebastian.

He disappeared into the lounge and, without switching on the light, began to play. I dashed upstairs and put on my *tutu* and, in a few minutes I was back in the hall, no longer a schoolgirl in a much-washed party dress, but a real fairy. The village children thought so, anyway, if you could judge by their open mouths and wide eyes!

Uncle Adrian and Uncle John had rolled back the rugs, and the floor stretched before me, gleaming softly, inviting. The centre lights were turned off, leaving only the rose-shaded reading-lamps at each side of the fireplace.

Suddenly the hall, with its Christmas tree and its waiting people, seemed to fade away. I was in a beautiful garden. Tall cypress trees stood like sentinels, throwing their black shadows over the velvet lawns; the moon sailed free in a cloudless sky; in the shadowy depths of a magnolia tree a nightingale sang. In the middle of the garden was a marble statue – the dreaming figure of a girl. Rising and falling above her head rose a slender jet of water, glistening silver in the moonlight, and shining upon her white shoulders in pearly drops, to fall with musical splash into the marble basin at her feet.

And I was the fairy of this crystal fountain. I felt the glittering dewdrops caught in my hair, in the crisp folds of my dress. I felt the moonlight caress my upturned face like a lover. The music of the fountain spoke to my feet, and what could I do but listen to its call, and dance? So I rose *sur les pointes*, my arms *en attitude*.

I danced, and Sebastian accompanied me faultlessly as he always did. Although in my thoughts I was far away from the hall, yet I knew he was there at the piano. I'd have guessed instantly if someone else had taken his place. There was no one – no one at all who could accompany me like Sebastian!

At the end of my dance there was a burst of clapping. Sebastian said nothing, but his eyes told me what he really felt.

'Well, that's the first time I've seen you dance, young lady,' Uncle Adrian said, as I stood by the fire recovering my breath. 'And I can tell you that I shall look forward to seeing you again. It was a great pleasure to watch you – you were very beautiful. I had no idea you could dance like that.'

'Thank you,' I said with a smile. 'It's most awfully nice of you to say so.'

After the village children had gone home, I stole back to the deserted hall where the Christmas tree stood. One or two of its candles were still alight, and the log fire burned low in the grate. I went over to the uncurtained windows and looked out at the snowy garden and the white hills beyond.

'Beautiful, isn't it?' said a voice close behind me.

I jumped.

'Oh, Sebastian! What a fright you gave me! Do take care – you'll crush my *tutu*!'

He drew back a little.

'Sorry! I forgot you still had that stupid thing on. You don't think about anything but your dancing, do you Veronica? You don't think anything is as important as your dancing?'

'No, of course not,' I said in surprise. 'What a funny thing to say! No, of course, nothing is as important to me as my dancing. Neither is anything as important to you as your music. Is it, Sebastian?'

He didn't answer, but stood looking out at the snowy hills.

'As I was saying when you barged in about your silly *tutu* – it's beautiful out there, isn't it? You'll come back here to Northumberland, you know, Veronica.'

'How can I?' I laughed. 'My work is in London.'

'Oh, I didn't mean next week, or even next year. I meant – just *some day*. How long can a dancer go on dancing?'

'Till they're about thirty,' I answered. 'Sometimes longer. It all depends upon how hard they're worked.'

'Well, when you're in the sear and yellow – about thirty – you'll come back,' laughed Sebastian. 'You'll come back here to Northumberland. You'll find you have to – your mother was Northumbrian. Once a Northumbrian, always a Northumbrian! Perhaps you'll marry a North Countryman and have children. Then they'll be North Country, born and bred – instead of only born, like you!'

'You are funny, Sebastian,' I said. 'What about you? *You're* Northumbrian, and yet you're dying to get to London, aren't you? You've always said so.'

'It's a case of needs must with me,' Sebastian assured me. 'I've got to go to London – and other places besides – for my training. But when I want to compose – when I really want to think things out – I'll come back here, you bet! One day, when I'm famous, and when I've made a lot of money, I shall be able to live here in my own home.' He cast a glance over his shoulder at the darkening hall with the pictures of his ancestors gleaming on its walls in the light of the dying fire; the oak staircase, its steps worn by the feet of his forebears. 'Some day I'll come back—'

It was then I realized for the first time that, although Sebastian joked about living in the gardener's cottage at the bottom of his own drive, and pretended he loved it, he didn't really. All the time he was feeling that Aunt June and Uncle John

137

were interlopers and ought not to be living in the Hall. Of course, it wasn't their fault; in fact, they were doing Sebastian a good turn by keeping Bracken Hall in the Scott family, but that didn't alter the fact. They were living in his ancestral home.

'I believe you'll do as you say,' I said, looking at his tense face in the flickering firelight. 'I believe you'll do all you say.'

Chapter 17

The Telegram

THE next morning, soon after breakfast, the local dressmaker came up from the village to alter some of Caroline's and Fiona's school clothes, and I was left all on my own. I wandered down to the lake, realizing suddenly that I hadn't been there since I'd come back for the holidays – unless you could count the time we'd passed it on our way back from church on Christmas Eve. There was no one in sight except the distant figure of old Billy, the postman, trudging up the newly opened road from the village with the letters. I waved to him, and then went on my way down the little track through the fir plantation that Sebastian, Caroline, and I had dug. At the far side of the plantation, I left the track and set off towards the lake, picking my way round the drifts.

As I peeped into the boathouse and saw the same old bathing costumes draped stiffly round the sides of the little rowing-boat – I think most of them were frozen! – I had the same dream-like feeling about London as I had had out on the moor the night we'd been lost in the snow. It seemed quite impossible that at this very moment, while I was standing in this silent place, thousands of people were scurrying on the Underground, jostling shoulders with thousands of other people.

I stared across the frozen lake to the island where Sebastian and I had gathered wild strawberries on my first morning at Bracken Hall – the morning I had run away and he'd made me come back. It seemed only yesterday, and yet what an awful lot of things had happened in between.

Suddenly there was the sound of low whistling.

'Hullo, Veronica!' said Sebastian's voice. 'Having a last look round?'

139

'Oh, not a last look,' I answered. 'I've still got more than a week's holiday left, you know. I was just seeing if Spotted Peril and Rhapsody in Stripes were still there. By the way how did you know I was here?'

'Saw you from the bathroom window,' said Sebastian. 'You were asking about the latest creations in swimwear? Well, Spotted Peril is still in the land of the living, but I'm afraid Rhapsody has gone the way of all flesh – in other words, it's dropped to pieces, so I cleaned my bike with it. Everything decays – even bathing costumes.'

'You are horrible!' I laughed. 'You always were. I'm sorry about Rhapsody in Stripes – it was like an old friend.'

'Even old friends have a habit of changing,' remarked Sebastian, playing Ducks and Drakes with a pebble on the frozen surface of the lake.

'What do you mean?'

'Well, you're different, you know, Veronica. You're here, and yet you're not here.'

'I don't know what you mean.'

'One foot in Bracken, the other in London,' Sebastian stated enigmatically. '"Poised on tiptoe for a flight," as the poet johnny said. I forget which one, but it doesn't matter.' Then, with that uncanny insight that he so often showed, he added: 'I feel that every time you look at the lake, or the trees, or even the hills, you're thinking of some ballet or other.'

'I suppose *you* don't ever imagine things?' I retorted. 'Things to do with your music, I mean. I suppose *you* weren't thinking of this wood by the lake when you wrote your *Woodland Symphony*, Sebastian?'

He laughed.

'You've got me there, Veronica! I suppose I *was* thinking of all this' – he waved an arm, embracing the whole landscape of lake and woods beyond. 'Yes, you're right. I *was* thinking of it – among other things. But it doesn't alter what I said at first. You're different, Veronica.'

'As a matter of fact,' I said slowly, 'you're different, too,

Sebastian. You're much more grown up, and I don't think I like you as well.'

'We all have to grow up,' said Sebastian nonchalantly. 'I'm seventeen, you know – all but a fortnight. And as to whether you like me as well – it's all the same to me.'

'Oh, Sebastian, don't be offended,' I begged. 'I was only joking. You're always joking yourself, and you don't expect people to take you seriously, so why take *me* seriously?'

'Sometimes,' said Sebastian, 'there's a lot of truth in a joke. I felt there was quite a bit in that one. Come on – let's walk over to the island. The ice will bear us; I tried it the other night when I came back from church.'

We walked over to the island, and sat for a bit in the old duck-punt, moored among the reeds. It was all so white and frozen that it was almost impossible to believe that in just a few months' time the swans would again be busy making their nest among the rushes.

'A quarter past eleven!' said Sebastian, as the silvery chime of the stable clock reached us on the frosty air. 'You'll be late for your milk, Veronica! Trixie will be in a flap – feeding you up is a sort of religion with her! It's really funny, because no matter how much milk you drink, I don't believe you get one inch fatter!'

'I hope not!' I said with such a horror-stricken note in my voice that Sebastian burst out laughing.

Just as we reached the terraced walk in front of the house we were met by Caroline. She seemed to be in a state of great excitement.

'Oh, Veronica!' she panted. 'I've been looking for you simply everywhere. There's a telegram for you. It came through by phone, and Trixie tried to take it down, but she said she couldn't make head or tail of it – it was about the Bible!'

'The Bible!' I laughed. 'Oh, no – it couldn't have been.'

'Well, Trixie said it was, and she told the exchange she'd

141

fetch you, and then we couldn't find you, so the exchange said they'd ring up again in ten minutes. Do come quickly!'

'Right-ho!' I said. 'I expect it's nothing the least bit important. I can't understand about the Bible, though. I expect Trixie's got it wrong – she's a bit deaf, you know, though she won't admit it.'

'You get along, then,' said Sebastian. 'I'm going round to the stables to see Warrior. Oh, by the way, Veronica. I've written out that music the way you said you wanted it – the Czardas, you know. We can try it over some time. So long!'

He strode away stablewards, and Caroline and I dashed into the house. Just as we got to the hall, the phone rang again. I took up the receiver, and a bored voice at the other end said: 'Is that Bracken 394? A telegram for you. Are you ready? ... "To Weston, Bracken Hall, Northumberland. Return rehearsal *Job* Saturday 2 o'clock Covent Garden. Important. Willan." ... Shall I repeat that?'

'Yes, please!' I begged, my head spinning. 'What was that you said about *Job*? Are you *sure* you said *Job*?'

'J-O-B,' said the voice at the other end, sounding more bored every minute. 'J for Jack, O for Oliver, B for Benjamin.'

'Thank you,' I said feebly. 'No, you needn't send it on by post. Goodbye.'

I put down the receiver and stood lost in thought. What on earth could it mean? ....*Job*? ... I knew there was a ballet by that name, but what had it got to do with me? Surely, surely I couldn't have got a part in it? And yet it was certainly from the school – the signature, Willan, told me that. I simply couldn't believe it. I began to wonder if I'd heard the telephone operator rightly, and to wish that I'd had the telegram sent on to me, after all. But no – it would have been too late, anyway – the wire said a rehearsal at two o'clock on Saturday. That was tomorrow. I'd have to go back by sleeper tonight ... Thoughts raced round in my head ...

'What's the matter, Veronica?' Caroline's voice, sounding

142

anxious, woke me out of my daydream. 'Has anything happened?'

'Yes – no – I don't know,' I stammered. 'Really, I don't know what to think.'

'I wonder if this will help,' Caroline said, holding out a letter. 'Billie brought it a bit ago. It's for you, and it's from London.'

'It's from Sara,' I said, tearing open the letter. 'I don't suppose it has anything to do with the wire.'

But it had!

Dear Veronica, [wrote Sara]. Something frightfully thrilling has happened. We had a rehearsal of the Youth Festival thing on Christmas Eve at School, and right in the middle of it, who should walk in but Madame! Yes, Madame herself – silver-fox furs and all! She stopped the rehearsal, and began to talk to Miss Willan. Well, it seems that one of the Sons of the Morning in Madame's ballet, *Job*, has sprained her ankle, and all the understudies have been used up already because of the epidemic of flu, so Madame came along to get someone from the school. It's not a part just anyone can do. For one thing, they have to have a boyish figure and look young, and for another they have to be musical. You see, the time of Vaughan Williams' music is most awfully tricky. Madame knew a Wells student would manage it OK, though, because we've all been trained in Eurhythmics. Imagine her shock when she found out that practically everyone, except the people who had parts already in the Theatre Ballet, and Taiis, who's dark-skinned, was in the Finsbury Park thing that's on exactly when *Job* is! I don't think she was too pleased, though of course it was no one's fault.

Well, when she was safely away, I plucked up my courage and went up to Miss Willan – oh, I know it was awful cheek, because naturally I wasn't supposed to be listening, but things were desperate. Well, I went up to her and said:

'Oh, Miss Willan – Veronica isn't in the Youth Festival.'
And she said: 'You mean Veronica Weston? And why isn't
she in it?' Then I explained about your watch being slow,
and you missing the audition, and she said, half to herself:
'Veronica is quite good at Eurhythmics, isn't she?' And I
said: 'She's by far the best in the class, Miss Willan, and
she's ever so small; I mean, she'd make a marvellous boy for
a Son of the Morning.' Well, after this she rushed out, and I
guessed she was going to catch Madame before she left the
school. After a bit she came back and asked for your
address, and said she was going to send you a wire. So,
though it isn't definitely fixed yet, I think you'll get the part
all right. It'll be wonderful for you, because, being
Madame's own ballet, naturally she's especially interested
in it; she even comes to some of the rehearsals. Oh,
Veronica – I'm so *thrilled*, because I know how much you
want to be in something!

Lots of love, Sara.

PS. I heard Willan talking to Serge and asking him
whether he thought you'd be right for the Farandole in *The
Sleeping Beauty*, because Jocelyn, the girl who's sprained
her ankle, was in that too. He said he expected you would,
so you'll most likely get that part too. Guess who your
partner will be? Toni Rossini! Cheerio! Sara.

When I had finished the letter I read it all through again;
then I gave a yell.

'Caroline! Trixie! Aunt June! Everybody! I've got it!
I've got it at last! I'm actually in something! Oh, Caroline –
I'm so happy!'

Then I remembered that Sebastian wasn't there, and, above
all, I wanted Sebastian to hear my wonderful news.

'I must just dash down to the stables,' I shrieked, 'and tell
Sebastian.' I seized Caroline round the waist, and waltzed her
round. Then I dashed away, leaving her staring after me in

utter bewilderment, for of course she didn't know what I'd got, or what I was in. It might be a prize for a sweepstake, for all she knew!

'Sebastian!' I yelled, as soon as I came within shouting distance of the stables. 'Sebastian! Where are you?'

Sebastian had just finished mucking-out the stable. He had tied Warrior up to a ring in the wall outside the door, and now he emerged, dandy-brush in hand, to see what the row was about.

'Well, why the shrieks and yells?'

'Oh, Sebastian!' I said, half laughing, half crying. 'My phone call – guess what it was about!'

'Search me! Haven't an earthly.'

'It was to tell me to go back to London tonight. I've got a part in *Job*, and another in *The Sleeping Beauty*. At least, I'm almost sure I have, and the rehearsal's tomorrow at two, so I shall have to get a sleeper and go back tonight. And my partner in the Farandole – he's Toni Rossini. You remember – the boy I told you about – my dancing partner. It will be marvellous to dance with him again, and besides, he's a real choreographer. He's had several ballets produced, and I shall actually be dancing with him on Covent Garden stage! Oh, Sebastian, isn't it wonderful?'

'Wonderful,' said Sebastian flatly.

Something in his voice pulled me up with a jerk.

'What's the matter? Why do you say "wonderful" like that? – as if you weren't a bit pleased. *Aren't* you pleased?'

'Take it as said,' answered Sebastian, turning to his pony, and making a great play with the dandy-brush.

Then, with a funny feeling in my inside, I remembered.

'Oh, Sebastian, I'm so sorry – I – I'm afraid I forgot – I completely forgot all about your concert.'

'Oh, don't let that worry you,' said Sebastian frigidly.

'I'm frightfully sorry,' I said, some of my happiness evaporating. 'But even if I *had* remembered, I couldn't have done anything about it, could I?'

'No, of course not,' agreed Sebastian.

'You don't think – surely you couldn't think I ought not to go back tonight?' I said incredulously. Then, as he didn't answer, I burst out: 'You know quite well I've *got* to go back. It's my career. You'd go back if it were *your* career, wouldn't you, Sebastian?'

'Of course. I'm a man.'

'What difference does that make?'

'Quite a lot,' Sebastian said, turning his back on me, and grooming Warrior with great deliberation. 'Men are forced to have careers. Women don't have to; they just barge into them. It's just silly for a woman to give up everything – friends, beauty sleep, peace of mind – even marriage – for a stupid thing like ballet.'

'It's not stupid!' I yelled, almost crying. 'It's my *life*!'

'Then it ought not to be,' declared Sebastian.

I stared at him aghast.

'You never used to think like this before.'

'Well, I do now. Goodbye, Veronica.'

'What do you mean – saying "goodbye, Veronica" like that? What about tonight? You're playing for me tonight at Lady Blantosh's concert, don't forget.'

'Oh, no I'm not,' stated Sebastian. 'If you decide to go back to London tonight, then *I* decide here and now not to make a mug of myself and play your stupid dances for you.'

'But you *promised* to play them,' I wailed. 'It's all arranged that you should play them. I can't do them if you don't play for me.'

'That's just too bad,' drawled Sebastian. 'Why should I play it for you when you calmly walk out on my concert? You walk out on me – OK. I walk out on you. Where's the difference?'

'You know it's different altogether,' I argued desperately. 'If I don't turn up at that rehearsal tomorrow, I shall lose the part altogether. It might be the turning-point of my whole career. As for your concert – it doesn't matter a scrap whether

I'm there or not. It's *you* that matters for your concert, Sebastian. Oh, can't you see that?'

'How do you know it doesn't matter?' he answered. 'How do you know I'm not playing for you, Veronica? How do you know I haven't written my *Woodland Symphony* especially for you – inspired by your grace, your funny remote face, the lovely way you move—'

I just stared at him, puzzled.

'I don't know what you mean.'

'Are you still going back tonight?'

'You know I must,' I answered.

'Very well . . .'

He left Warrior and went back into the stable. When he returned, he carried a small roll of music in his hand.

'Then, we won't need this.' He unrolled the sheets and tore them across and across. The pieces fluttered to the ground and lay between us.

'Oh, Sebastian! What have you done?'

'You remember that day, out on the moors, I told you I was in love with somebody,' Sebastian said, turning away from me. 'Well, it wasn't a joke – it was true. I was in love with you – you, Veronica. When I said goodbye to you tomorrow night, I was going to kiss you. I thought you were the nicest girl I'd ever met.'

I was so surprised that for a moment I said nothing at all. Then I burst out: 'How dare you say that! I wouldn't have let you kiss me.'

'You wouldn't have had any choice,' declared Sebastian, with a toss of his black head. 'I wasn't going to ask you first. When I decide to do a thing, I do it – I don't ask first. But don't worry,' he added. 'I shan't do it now. I don't even want to shake hands with you – let alone kiss you.'

'You're only a kid,' I retorted. 'We're both kids.'

'I'm almost seventeen,' he answered. 'Only a year younger than your friend, Stella, who's going to be married. But you're right – you *are* a kid, Veronica – a stupid, selfish little kid.

147

Some day perhaps you'll know better. Goodbye, Veronica.'

He unhitched Warrior from the ring, vaulted upon his back, and was away across the stable yard, and out into the field before I had time to reply. I watched him gallop across the snowy meadow, and round the straw stacks at the far side – he never once looked back.

I turned again to the empty stable. On the ground lay the bits of white paper with Sebastian's painstakingly written music upon them. I knew he'd sat up late after the party last night to do it, and I felt awful. But there was no question in my own mind as to what I must do. When you're a ballet dancer you put all else behind you – even friends and sweethearts, if you have a sweetheart. Your art must come first. I felt that Sebastian ought to understand that; after all, he was an *artiste* himself. But then, Sebastian had never been reasonable; had never acted or thought in a logical way; he was a law unto himself.

I carefully picked up some of the pieces of paper and put them in my pocket, though why I did it I don't know, for of course they weren't the least use to me, all torn like that. After this I went into the loosebox next door, where Arabesque was stabled, put my head down on his warm neck and began to cry; and, whether my tears were tears of sorrow, anger or frustration, I don't know. Perhaps a bit of all three. After a while I dried my eyes and went back to the house.

Caroline looked at my red eyes in amazement.

'Why, what on earth's the matter, Veronica? I thought you were so happy—'

'So I was,' I said, with a sniff of self-pity, 'and so I am still – in one part of me. But I'm terribly miserable in the other part. You see, Sebastian is furious with me. I f-forgot all about his c-concert, and now he won't p-play for me.' I began to cry again.

Caroline didn't know what to say. Unfortunately, I hadn't noticed that Fiona was standing by the window.

'Well, now perhaps you know what Sebastian is really like,'

she said with a hateful sneering note in her voice. 'You've been a long time finding out, I must say. I always *told* you how unreliable and selfish he was.'

'He's not unreliable and selfish!' I yelled at her. 'He's – he's – oh, I don't know what he is. It's me who's selfish; I know I am, but I can't help it – I've got to go.'

I seized the telephone and rang up Newcastle Central Station. They put me through to the reservation bureau, and a girl answered my inquiry. No, they hadn't got a first-class sleeper for tonight, but they could give me a third-class.

'All right – I'll have that,' I said. After all, what did it matter if I travelled first class or third? What did it matter if I got a sleeper at all? I shouldn't sleep a wink, anyway.

Chapter 18

Journey Back to London

I WAS right! I didn't sleep much that night. My berth was a top one, and when the train slid away from the platform, and had gathered up speed, I climbed wearily up into my bunk. The other three people in the compartment were evidently friends, for they talked, and laughed, and exchanged sweets and biscuits. I gathered from their conversation that they'd come up from the south to a friend's wedding, and were now on their way home. The girl on the upper berth opposite stared at me curiously. I think I must have looked very woebegone, for she said kindly:

'Leaving home for the first time, eh? Keep your pecker up, kid! Have a chocolate cream?'

At any ordinary time I'd have accepted the offer gratefully – chocolate creams being favourites of mine. But tonight the very sound of them made me feel sick.

'No, thank you,' I said. Then, as she repeated her offer more pressingly, I added: 'Really, I couldn't. Thanks awfully, all the same.'

'OK,' she said cheerfully. 'Have it your own way. But take my word for it, you'll get used to it, kid. Leaving your ma for the first time is awful, but it'll pass off. Can't live at home, tied to Mammy's apron-strings all your life, you know. Got to go out into the wide world some day. What's your job, kid?'

'I – I'm a dancer,' I stammered.

'A dancer? What sort? Tap, and the splits I suppose?'

'No – I'm a ballet dancer,' I answered.

'Ah – ballet? Been in the panto, eh? Good show at the Empire this year. My sister lives down at Byker, and she took all the kids in the Christmas hols. Where are you going to dance now?'

'C-Covent G-Garden,' I gulped.

If I had wished to cause a sensation, I certainly did so. The two other girls came right out of their bunks, and all three stared at me as if I were a rare orchid in a botanical garden.

'You don't say!' said the girl opposite me. 'What's your name, dearie? Moira Shearer?'

I suppose there was some excuse for their not believing me. Anything less like the popular idea of a glamorous ballet dancer than me, with my red eyes and woebegone expression, you couldn't have found. But I didn't feel it was worth the bother of trying to convince them, so I lay down under my rug and tried to go to sleep.

I was very tired after the concert and all the excitements of the day but, try as I would, I couldn't sleep. Perhaps I was *too* tired; or perhaps I was too miserable. Anyhow, my thoughts kept going round and round in my head, and I kept living over again the events of the last few hours -- the awful rush I'd had finding gramophone records that I could dance to as a substitute for Sebastian's playing; unpacking the peasant costume that I now wouldn't need; doing my packing for to-night, because I was going straight from the village hall to the station.

I saw again the crowded room, and heard Lady Blantosh's kind voice announcing that: 'Now little Veronica Weston will dance for us. Veronica, as I expect you all know, is a pupil at a very famous dancing school called Sadler's Wells. I'm sure you are all simply longing to see her dance. I know *I* am!'

I danced very badly. All the time, instead of losing myself in the lovely music, I was seeing Sebastian's face when he'd said: 'Oh, don't let it worry you!' Fortunately, the people at the concert weren't the sort of people to notice that I had lost my *ballon;* that my *pointes* wobbled; that my dancing was strained and unhappy. They clapped me just as loudly as if I had been Margot Fonteyn herself, and for that I was grateful.

151

As I huddled under the railway company's prickly rug, I lived again the long drive to the station along roads piled high with snow on either side. Sometimes Perkins had to get out of the brake and dig, and I got out and helped him. Then he'd tell me to 'get back into the car, and keep warm'. Once, when we'd cleared away an especially big drift, and Perkins had stood leaning on his shovel in the glare of the headlights, I felt a flood of gratitude towards him sweep over me.

'Oh, Perkins – it is perfectly *sweet* of you to do this for me,' I said. 'Really, it's just wonderful the way people keep on doing things for me.'

'Well, miss,' said Perkins, wiping his face with a red and white spotted hankie and getting back into the driving seat, 'I sees it this way. When you comes to Bracken, you offers to get out of the car and open the gates for me. That was the very first thing you does. Remember? "*I'll* do it, Perkins!" you says. "Don't you bother, Perkins," you says. Well, I says to myself that very day – if I can do anything for that youngster, you bet I will! And I'm not one to forget my promises. So that's how it is. There's some people,' added Perkins, 'as gets things done for 'em all their lives, and some 'as don't. You're one of the first class, Miss Veronica.'

Desperately I tried to think of the exciting thing that had happened to me – my part in *Job*, and the Farendole that I was going to dance with Toni, but all I could think of was Sebastian's voice saying: 'I thought you were the nicest girl I'd ever met ... I don't even want to shake hands with you now, let alone kiss you ... You're just a selfish kid; perhaps some day you'll know better ... Goodbye, Veronica...'

'Goodbye,' the whirring of the wheels echoed sadly. 'Goodbye ... goodbye ... Veronica...'

Chapter 19

Dress Rehearsal of *Job*

IT was fortunate, perhaps, that I had so much to do during the next few weeks that I had no time to think. Only at nights, when Mrs Crapper and I listened-in to the wireless, did my thoughts stray back to Northumberland. Sometimes the cry of a curlew, given as a 'signature' to a country programme, or the sounds of sheep bleating, or the clip-clop of a horse's hooves on the hard road, would bring back to me memories of Bracken Hall, and I would rush out of the room or turn off the radio. I expect Mrs Crapper wondered what was the matter with me, but she never asked any questions. In some ways she was the soul of diplomacy, was Mrs Crapper!

I went to the rehearsal of *Job* on the Saturday afternoon of my return, and got the part of the Son of the Morning who had dropped out. Madame was there herself, and I could feel her watching me to see if I would pass muster. It was a terrifying feeling, because Madame has eyes that not only look *at* you, but *through* you, as well, in a most disconcerting way. Still, I did feel, when I was told that I had got the part, that I must have shown up quite well. Automatically I got the part in the Farandole out of *The Sleeping Beauty*, too. Toni was very helpful, as usual, and, with his assistance, I managed not to disgrace myself.

The weeks sped away and, before I knew it, the day of the dress rehearsal of *Job* dawned. I'd had a letter from Stella and Jonathan in which they said that they weren't coming back to London before the wedding, which was to be in one week's time, and they wanted me to go north for it and be bridesmaid. I wrote back and explained that I couldn't because of *Job*, and really I was quite glad to have the excuse. I didn't feel like

153

going back to Northumberland again just yet! So as it turned out, Mrs Crapper was the only person to wish me luck upon the eventful day. Miss Broadbent, the lady who was secretary to the corset manufacturer, wished me good morning on the stairs, but I'm pretty sure it wasn't anything to do with my rehearsal, but merely a 'conventional greeting', as they say.

I looked round me with shining eyes as I followed the others up the endless flight of stone stairs to our dressing-room. Although by now I had been in a real dressing-room several times, yet I was still thrilled by everything – even the notice on the door: CHORUS LADIES! For the sake of those people who have never been inside a theatrical dressing-room, I will tell you what ours was like. It was a long room, and all round the walls were narrow tables with mirrors behind them. Down the middle of the room were more tables and mirrors. There were two of us to each mirror, and I shared mine with Dorothea. We wrote our names on opposite corners of our mirror with greasepaint. Above the mirrors were shelves where you could put your clothes, make-up, and personal belongings. Some of the girls stuck photographs round the sides of their mirrors – pictures of their families, sometimes, but more often of their favourite ballet or film star. All the costumes were kept on stands and carefully looked after by dressers, and woe betide you if you threw one of them on the floor!

It took me a long time to get ready for *Job*. Not that the Son of the Morning costume was at all complicated. It consisted of a silk tunic, curled wig, and a pair of huge silver wings which were the bane of our lives. I dare say they looked wonderful from the audience, but to us, who had to wear them, they were awful. They were made of silvered wire, and after you'd worn them for about five minutes they felt as if they weighed at least a ton! Although they were padded, they still hurt your shoulders. As for dancing in them – well, now I understand why our part wasn't considered a 'dancing part'. It would have been quite impossible to dance in those wings!

Well, so far so good. As I say, the costume was quite easy to get on, even if it wasn't exactly comfortable. The trouble was that our legs were bare, so we had to cover ourselves with wet-white as far up as the thighs. Our arms and shoulders had to be done, too; so really, as someone said, there wasn't much of us that *wasn't* whitewashed! The wet-white was frightfully messy to put on, and it was even more messy to take off, as I found to my cost after the dress rehearsal. Also, my wig happened to be several sizes too small for me and, besides giving me a headache, I had a fight to the death every time I put it on! But as there wasn't a bigger one to spare, and I was an outsider, naturally I had to be the one to 'make do'.

Job, I must explain, is a rather unusual production – not a bit like the general idea of a ballet. There is no *pointe*-work in it; indeed, most of the characters dance with bare feet or wearing sandals. The ballet is all in two parts – earthly and spiritual. The earthly part, which depicts Job with his children, and his struggles in the world, is danced on the front portion of the stage; the spiritual part at the back, on a flight of shining steps. At first, when I was just learning the part, I couldn't see how you could possibly dance on a flight of steps, no matter how broad they were, but I soon found out that you didn't really dance at all; you just moved about rhythmically, and you've no idea how difficult it is to move gracefully on a staircase in time to Vaughan Williams' music, which, though it's very beautiful, isn't a bit usual.

Another thing I found very weird, when I first began to dance on the real stage, was the arrangement of drop-curtains in conjunction with the lighting. It seemed strange to me to be standing in position on the heavenly staircase, along with crowds of other people, with only a flimsy gauze curtain between us and the audience, and yet know that all those people in the darkened auditorium couldn't see us, though we could see them quite plainly. For ages I felt like yelling: 'Look out! The audience can see you!' when the almost invisible curtain had slid silently between us and the house, and Satan did an *entrechat* behind it. I found it unnerving in *The Sleeping Beauty*,

155

too, when Margot Fonteyn stood laughing behind the spider-web drop-curtain in the Vision Scene, seemingly in full view of the audience.

As I said before, Toni Rossini had been a great help to me during all these weeks of rehearsal. I expect it was a case of 'a fellow feeling makes us wondrous kind', because Toni was really in the Theatre Ballet, and he'd only been lent to the First Company for the season, so he was an outsider like me. He'd got quite an important part in *Job*, as well as the small part in the Farandole in *The Sleeping Beauty*.

'Will you go back to the Theatre Ballet as soon as this is over?' I asked him as we waited in the wings on that day of the dress rehearsal.

He nodded.

'Oh, yes; I write a new ballet for the Company.'

'Gosh! How exciting! What is it called?' I demanded.

'I call it *The Depths of the Sea*,' he answered. 'It is about a mermaid. I think of a particular person when I write it.'

'I know! Belinda?' I exclaimed.

He nodded again.

'Some day,' he said unexpectedly, 'I write a ballet for you, Veronique. You will be a very beautiful dancer. I can see it. You have an exquisite "line".'

I was so surprised that I blushed hotly. Finally, I stammered:

'Thanks, awfully, Toni; it's good of you to say so, and I hope you're right and that I do dance beautifully, but so far I don't feel I've got on much. I don't think anybody but you – and perhaps Gilbert – thinks much of my dancing.'

Toni was silent for a bit; then he said, in his stilted, too-perfect English:

'You mistake, Veronique. They think you good.'

'I imagined they did once,' I said with a sigh. 'But now – I don't know. Do you realize I'm still down in the Junior class with all the new girls.'

'You must have patience,' said Toni gravely. 'Sometimes

they keep a promising dancer back to acquire yet stronger technique before she attempt the more advanced work. I have seen it happen more than once. Perhaps it is so with you.'

I sighed again.

'Well, if they do that, why don't they *tell* you?' I burst out at length. 'Then you'd work like fury, instead of getting depressed and browned-off.'

Toni shrugged his shoulders expressively.

'I do not know. Perhaps they think that to tell you would make you swollen of the head, as you say in English. So they say nothing. You must think for yourself. If you are good — you know it. If you are not,' he shrugged again, 'you know it also.'

'That's all very well,' I said, 'but sometimes it's hard to go on believing in oneself.'

'Look — I tell you something,' Toni said, as if making a sudden resolution. 'Quite by accident this afternoon I hear *Madame la Directrice* and the *Maître-de-ballet* talk together. They stand on one side of a piece of stage scenery, I upon the other; I hear them talk before I know who it is who speak. Madame she say: "*That* one with the pale face and the big dark eyes" — that was you, Veronique — "that one," she say, "is the one to watch. I have a feeling that she will be a very great dancer, but of course — who knows?" Then she shrugged in her French way, though she is not French, but Irish!'

'Did she really say that?' I gasped, with a thrill of joy. 'Did she really? I just can't believe it! I expect it was someone else she meant, and not me at all; but thanks for telling me, all the same, Toni.'

'It was a pleasure,' said Toni, with a little bow.

As we stood there, in the wings, side by side, I stared at him curiously. It wasn't rude, because his eyes were on the dancers on the stage, and I'm quite sure he'd forgotten all about me. Toni had what you might call a gentle face, with the round forehead and large eyes of the poet and the dreamer. His mouth had a tender curve, uplifted at the corners, as if all the time his thoughts were beautiful ones. There was none of the fire and driving force of Stcherbakof or Sebastian in Toni Rossini. None of the ruthlessness, and – yes, I must admit it, though I'd denied it indignantly to Fiona – the selfishness that predominated in the characters of those other two *artistes*. In a way, Toni was more like Jonathan, although nobody could have been less like Jonathan in outward appearance. Jonathan could have put Toni in his waistcoat pocket!

I felt, as I looked at Toni, that although he was a competent and graceful dancer and had been well trained, it was not as a dancer that he would make his name. He would be remembered, not by his own dancing, but by the lovely combinations of steps and figures he composed for other people; by his sense of beauty that showed in the 'line' of his creations; in the way he grouped his dancers against the backcloth; by the way his ballets lived with the music, so that you couldn't separate the one from the other. In other words, it was as a choreographer, and not as a dancer, that Toni Rossini would be remembered.

And I was standing in the shadowy wings of Covent Garden Theatre, side by side with this as yet unknown young man – a young man who would fling the torch of his creative genius on to the dry bones of ballet and set them ablaze, just as Massine had done, and Robert Helpmann. It was a thrilling feeling!

Suddenly my dreams were shattered. There were shouts on the stage; figures came crowding into the wings.

'It is time for you to go,' said Toni's soft voice in my ear. 'See, the curtain has fallen; you must be ready for your scene.'

Chapter 20

The End of the Season

I GOT a repertoire for the ballet season at Covent Garden and saw that *Job* was to run for two months, together with *The Sleeping Beauty*. Usually *Job* was on twice each week, while *The Sleeping Beauty* was performed five times – counting Saturday matinée. Occasionally there was a week when other ballets predominated, and I would only dance once in *Job* and a couple of times in *The Sleeping Beauty*, but as a general rule it was the *Job* and *Sleeping Beauty* season. I got one pound a performance for *Job*, and two pounds for *The Sleeping Beauty*, because the Farandole, although a much easier part than one of the Sons of the Morning, was a 'dancing part'. All my first week's pay went on make-up, and after that I spent most of my earnings on meals, because I found that it was quite impossible to get back to Heather Hill between performances and rehearsals – not to mention school! There were times, I can tell you, when I wished that Mrs Crapper's apartment house was a little nearer Covent Garden!

The weeks simply flew by, and, before I knew it, we were at the end of the season. I wrote to Caroline, apologizing for not having written before.

Dear Caroline [I said in my letter]. I expect you'll be thinking awful things about me for not having told you about my exciting experience on Covent Garden stage. To my shame I realize that I've only written to you once since I came back to London after the holidays. My only excuse is the usual one – work! Really, I haven't had a minute to call my own since I got back that Saturday morning. You see, the school makes no allowance for you when you get small parts in the ballets. I mean, you aren't excused any classes on that account – only if they happen to be at the exact time of the rehearsals. So I've been at school from nine-thirty every morning, which means leaving here soon after eight o'clock, and I haven't got back most nights till after eleven! The few nights when I haven't been on, I've just crawled home, too tired to do anything but swallow my supper, and fall into bed. All the same, it's been grand, and I wouldn't have missed it for anything. The Youth Festival people have been green with envy at me going off to Covent Garden every night.

Well, last night was the last performance of the season. And what fun it was! It ended with Margot Fonteyn as Princess Aurora in *The Sleeping Beauty*; Violetta Elvin – she used to be Prokhorova, you know, before she got married – as the Lilac Fairy, and Michael Soames as the Prince. They all danced wonderfully, and of course Margot excelled herself – she always does at a time like that! At the end of the performance she got so many flowers you couldn't see her for them. Someone passed a bottle of milk up for the White Cat, and indeed everyone was so happy, and in such good tempers, that you felt you were dancing on air, and not on a stage at all! Madame was in the staff box, and she was smiling like anything, and being so gracious to everybody. At the end of Farandole – that's the thing I dance with Toni Rossini – Toni put his arm round my waist, lifted me off my feet, and carried me right across the stage and out into the wings. Yes, in full view of the audience! But, of course, *they'd* think it was all part of the dance, and even if they hadn't, nobody would have cared! That was the sort of night it was!

And now it's all over. The Company are having ten days' holiday before they go on tour on the Continent. As for me, it's real hard work from now on. I simply must show Miss Willan and Gilbert that I'm made of the stuff they thought I was made of when they accepted me for the school. I don't

160

expect to get any more parts until the late summer when the First Company is back again, except perhaps an odd one down at Sadler's Wells.

Oh, Caroline – I *do* hope I've been all right in the small parts I've had!

Lots of love, Veronica.

PS. I bought a seat for dear Mrs Crapper in the grand tier out of my weekly earnings, and she saw *Job*. I think she'd have liked *The Sleeping Beauty* better, as it's more usual, but I simply couldn't get a ticket for it – it's so popular, and I hadn't time to queue for one. Anyway, she said: 'It seemed funny to me, Miss Veronica, all them people out of the Bible, as real as real, and that poor old man' – she meant Job – 'a settin' there, as patient as patient, and nothin' but bad things rainin' down upon him like the doodlebugs on London! I liked that bit fine when Satan rolled headlong down the steps. Thrilling, that was! Poor young man! I wonder what he does for his bruises? Someone ought to tell him about that wonderful embrocation me Aunt Emily used on me Uncle Henry before he died. I liked your wings fine, Miss Veronica – not that I could see which one you was, me eyes not being as good as they were, and all of you so alike, but they looked nice, like that picture on the front of me prayer-book.'

PPS. If I ever get as far as dancing a principal role at Covent Garden in the dim, dim future – and I can tell you it doesn't seem very likely at present – but if I ever do, I'll book seats for you all. At least, all of you except Sebastian, and I don't suppose he'd want to come. What fun it would be, wouldn't it?

V

PPPS. I remember you once said that my letters were all postscripts, so I may as well live up to my reputation, and add yet another one. It's about Jonathan and Stella. They were married last month, and it was supposed to be a very quiet wedding, with *no* fuss, and absolutely no one knowing about it. But of course the papers ferreted it out – they *would*! Jonathan's estates grew in size with each account, and poor Stella became more and more lowly, until finally it appeared in the *Daily Courier* like this:

King Copetua and the Beggar-maid

Whirlwind romance between knight and obscure ballet dancer culminated last Friday in the marriage, at a tiny village church at the foot of the Cheviot Hills, of Jonathan Rosenbaum, the world-famous artist and sculptor, and Stella Mason, beautiful eighteen-year-old dancer, recently of the Sadler's Wells Ballet Company. The uninitiated may not be aware that the name Rosenbaum cloaks the identity of no less a personage than Sir Jonathan Craymore, the knightly owner of vast estates at Ravenskirk on the Scottish Border.

When I showed the account to Mrs Crapper, she was most impressed.

'Well I never!' she exclaimed. 'To think of our Mr Jonathan owning all that land! It just goes to show!'

What it went to show I really don't know, nor I'm sure did Mrs Crapper!

The bride [went on the awful journalist] is the granddaughter of Mary Mason and the late Joshua Mason of the tiny hamlet of Broomyhough at the foot of the Cheviots in Northumberland. Mrs Mason – 'Granny', as she is known locally – seated at her rustic table in her primitive kitchen, with the barnyard fowls wandering in and out around her feet, and an uncouth shepherd lad lounging on the deal settle by the fire, told me that her

162

granddaughter had met her young husband only a few days before the ceremony. She confessed that her granddaughter felt a certain amount of awe at the prospect of becoming Lady Craymore.

I must tell you, Caroline, that when I'd finished the article, I couldn't help feeling glad that Jonathan was safely away in Cornwall on his honeymoon. I'm quite sure he'd have been simply *furious*. Jonathan hates anything like that. However, I suppose journalists have to earn their livings like everybody else. This really *is* the end of my letter and its postscripts!

Love again, Veronica.

Chapter 21

A Class with Madame

AFTER the ballet season at Covent Garden had ended, nothing much happened to break the monotony of school life. There were small excitements, of course. For instance, Belinda's name began to appear in the picture papers and dancing magazines...

This promising seventeen-year-old dancer, Belinda Beaucaire, as the Mermaid in the new ballet, *The Depths of the Sea*, especially created for her by Toni Rossini, the rising young choreographer. This ballet, by the way, was inspired by the famous picture by Burne-Jones, and is a perfect vehicle for this ballerina's Titian-haired, green-eyed beauty ... The classic beauty of the red-haired Belinda Beaucaire ... ballet dancer's meteoric rise to fame ... Belinda Beaucaire's sparkle and charm ... if Belinda Beaucaire can acquire the necessary discipline ... Belinda Beaucaire danced the role with charm, but a slight hardness marred an otherwise interesting performance...

Pictures of Belinda began to appear in the *Dancing News*, the *Ballet Weekly*, and other periodicals. Belinda in *arabesque*; in *attitude*. Belinda as the Sugar Plum Fairy, the little jewelled crown setting off to perfection her classic features. Belinda, one hand caught in the misty folds of her *Sylphides* dress; Belinda as one of the Little Swans in *Swan Lake*. One weekly picture paper even had Belinda on the cover, all in technicolour, in a jade *tutu*, flaming red hair, and green eyes!

We sighed enviously as the papers went the round of the dressing-room.

'Gosh! Mustn't it be wonderful to be Belinda! ... Think of having a ballet made up especially for you! ... Mustn't Belinda be happy!'

Yes, as we pored over the magazines littering the dressing-room table, and gazed at the pictures, we all imagined ourselves as Belinda, the newly risen star, the darling of thousands of adoring balletomanes.

Another person who provided a small sensation was Marcia Rutherford. One foggy morning, towards the middle of the term, when we were changing for our first class, the door opened and Marcia sauntered in. Since it was five minutes to the hour, and she was still in her outdoor clothes, everyone stared at her in astonishment.

'You 'ad bettaire be queek, Marcia Rutterford!' counselled Denise Lebrun, who was a French girl and new this term. Incidentally, she had more assurance than all the rest of us put together! 'Zees ees ze class of Gilbert, and you know what 'e ees like eef one ees late. *En tout cas* on-ly 'alf of ze class ees 'ere because of ze fog, so Gilbert weel be *en colère*, yes!'

Marcia didn't make the slightest movement to take off her grass-green coat with its many gilt buttons, or her flamboyant hat.

'Gilbert!' she said, with a snap of her fingers. 'What do I care about Gilbert Delahaye, or what he thinks?'

'He can be frightfully nasty if he likes,' I said. 'I advise you to buck up, Marcia.'

'Oh, really! You do, do you?' drawled Marcia. 'Well, let me tell you, all of you, that I'm through with being bullied, and ordered about, and treated like dirt by your Gilbert Delahayes, and your Willans, and your other rubbish. I've got a job.'

'What sort of a job?' we gasped. 'A dancing job?'

'Sure!' drawled Marcia, moving a bit of chewing gum from one cheek to the other. 'A real dancing job. I've been taken on

165

in the new American show *Dance for Poppa*. I start tomorrow at twenty quid a week. Not bad, eh?'

'Oh, but that's not *real* dancing,' I commented. 'It's just musical-comedy stuff, with high heels and no clothes!'

'Real enough for me!' declared Marcia. 'Much I care, anyway! It's the dough I'm after. That's what I came to this mouldy hole for, if you want to know.' She cast a disparaging glance round the dressing-room. 'I put up with it just so's I could get a good job elsewhere.'

'Well, I think it's awful,' said Lily. 'It's just selling your art.'

'Much I care!' said Marcia again. 'Well, I'll leave you poor mugs to the mercy of your wrathful Gilbert. It's two minutes past the hour. Oh, boy! Two minutes. Won't he be mad! So long, folks!'

She took the chewing gum out of her cheek, and stuck it on the pictured face of Margot Fonteyn that someone had pinned up on the wall beside the door, and with that last act of revolt she was gone.

For a moment we were silent with shocked amazement. Then Denise burst into excited speech.

'I care not now eef Gilbert ees *en colère*! I care not eef he go oop in ze smoke!' she exclaimed. 'We 'ave rid ourselves of Marcia Rutterford. I care not now *what* 'appens!'

But even the irrepressible Denise didn't know just what *was* going to happen!

As Denise had forecast, Gilbert was in a filthy temper. He cast a jaundiced eye over the depleted lines of his class, and then began to lecture those of his students who had managed to turn up.

A little fog, declared Gilbert, should stop no serious-minded students from being punctual. On the contrary, went on Gilbert, it ought to make them all the more determined to be on time. Modern girls – and men too, pronounced Gilbert – have no idea about battling with the elements. A drop of rain, a spot of mist, a puff of wind, and everyone begins talking a

166

lot of nonsense about floods, hurricanes, and goodness knows what! Imagine anyone, went on Gilbert, casting a glance at the murky darkness outside, imagine anyone not daring to venture out because of a slight mist: ... 'Turn on those lights!' snapped Gilbert. 'We will begin!'

We began, and had got as far as '*pliés* on the other side', when the door opened.

'Come in,' said Gilbert in a resigned voice. 'Pray don't apologize. I *like* a little interruption. Don't mind me; come right in ... *Battements tendus*, please. *Begin!*'

Three minutes later the door opened again.

'Ah!' said Gilbert. 'Some more brave spirits? Congratulations, Monica and Kathleen! So good of you to come! I do hope you were not inconvenienced by the fog ... As I said before, *battements tendus*, please. *Ready!*'

The class went on in this vein, Gilbert growing more furious underneath, and more sarcastic on top every second. We all wondered when the lava would crack, and the volcano erupt. It happened about twenty minutes after the class had begun. A small meek girl named Kalchine, whom Gilbert disliked for no reason at all except perhaps, that she *was* meek, pushed open the door softly; then, in her fright at Gilbert's dark frown, she shut it behind her with a nervous bang.

'Please, Mr Delahaye—' she began.

Gilbert cut her short with a lordly gesture.

'If one more person comes in late,' he threatened, 'just *one* more person, and says "please, Mr Delahaye, the fog..."' – here Gilbert raised his voice to a squeak and imitated what he intended to be the female intonation – 'I shall ...'

As he said the words, the door behind him opened yet again.

'*Get out!*' roared Gilbert in a frenzy, banging his stick on the floor so hard that the ferrule broke off and shot across the room. 'Get out! Stay out! Go *away*! This fog is just an excuse for you all to be late! If your heart was in your work, you would be on time. I will not have it! Get out of my class!'

Then something in our horror-stricken faces made him swing round to see who or what had made us all freeze in our places like that game you play at school called 'Statues'. At the door, resplendent in silver-fox furs and a charming smile, stood Madame herself – Madame, the director of the Company. Behind her, like twin attendants on royalty stood Miss Willan and Miss Smails.

Fortunately, Madame had a sense of humour. Also I think she was very fond of Gilbert, and understood his odd ways.

'I stand corrected, Mr Delahaye,' she said sweetly. 'I make no excuses; I am very sorry I am late for class.'

Gilbert rose to the occasion.

'*Madame!*' he said, with what might be called reverence. Then he came forward with outstretched hand, motioning one of the girls to bring forward a chair, and another to relieve Madame of her fur cape and gloves. It happened to be me, and I placed them carefully over the back of a second chair.

Madame hadn't taken a class since I'd been at the Wells, so I was all excitement. I remembered the day when I'd sat in the empty dressing-room and dreamed about it, and now, it seemed, my dream was to come true at last. It was a frightening yet thrilling thought!

Often enough Gilbert had given us lectures on what to do, and what not to do, if ever Madame took class.

'You must not be nervous,' said Gilbert. 'Everyone is afraid of Madame, and that is all wrong. It is true that her eyes look through you in a strange, piercing way, but that is only because she is searching for talent – always searching for talent. If you are all tense and strained, she will be furious. You must relax!'

It was all very well for Gilbert to talk about relaxing, but now, as we arranged ourselves once more along the *barres,* I thought that he ought to take his own advice to heart! He was sitting on the platform, obviously in an agony of nerves. Every time any one of us did anything he knew Madame wouldn't like, the expression on his always expressive face was almost funny in its intensity.

Madame was a wonderful teacher – clear and decisive. When she told you to do anything out of the ordinary, she always explained the reason for it, and her reasons were always sound and well thought out. Of course, she had her fads – what great teacher has not? – but they were what you might call sensible fads. In short, after I had got over my awe of her, I can truthfully say that I enjoyed every minute of her class.

There were no more interruptions; no more latecomers, though the class was still nothing like complete. I have a shrewd idea that Miss Willan had posted a scout to intercept any more latecomers. It was unthinkable that anyone should break in upon Madame's class. As well break in upon an audience with the Queen!

To my surprise, I got quite a lot of attention. Several times Madame stopped beside me, and placed my arm or leg, or told me not to strain my shoulders. In the centre-work I was in the front row. Of course, this wasn't really such a very great honour, because most of the rest were new girls and weren't as advanced as I was.

At the end of the class, after we'd been dismissed and had made our curtsies, Madame went up to Gilbert and said in a voice we could all hear: 'Who is that child with the pale face and the big dark eyes? Yes, the one in the front row? I noticed her before; she was one of the Sons of the Morning in *Job*, wasn't she?'

A sound went rustling round the class. You couldn't really call it a gasp, because no one would have dared to gasp in Madame's class, but it was a definite sound for all that – a sound of positive awe.

'Veronica Weston,' said Gilbert in a clear voice, and I knew by the way he said it that he was glad Madame had noticed me.

'She's quite promising, Mr Delahaye,' said Madame graciously. 'Really, a very interesting class altogether. I congratulate you!'

I walked home that night in a seventh heaven of delight. Now, I knew quite definitely that what Toni had told me that day in the wings was really true, and that I *was* good.

When I got home there was a parcel for me from Caroline, and inside was a letter.

Dear Veronica, [it said]. Thank you for your letter. Mummy and I didn't know what to get you for your birthday. Finally we thought that perhaps you'd like a scarf and gloves to match the Fair Isle twinset Mummy gave you at Christmas. So here it is! Oh, I know your birthday isn't till Monday, but I thought I'd send your present in good time, because it's horrible not to get remembered on your birthday. Trixie is sending her gift tomorrow, so you're *bound* to get something on the right day. Daddy says he's sending you a cheque and you can buy what you like with it.

Everything is much the same here. I don't believe I ever told you about Sebastian's concert – the one you missed. It went off very well, and there was someone there – a Doctor Humphrey Messenger – who's a frightfully important person in the musical world. He seems to think that Sebastian is really good, and he's arranged for him to have an audition, or whatever you call it, for a scholarship to the Royal College of Music, on Monday the 30th April. That's your birthday; isn't it funny!

Will you be coming north during the summer hols, or will you be in a show?

Lots of love,

CAROLINE

I sighed as I put down the letter. Somehow I knew that I wouldn't be seeing Northumberland that summer, or indeed for many summers to come.

170

Chapter 22

My Sixteenth Birthday

SARA, by the way, had just got a temporary job on television, so she'd left Sadler's Wells School. She got well paid for her work, so she was very cheerful. In fact, there was only one fly in Sara's ointment, and that was her mother. Sara's mother was what is called 'possessive'. She couldn't and wouldn't believe that Sara was really sixteen and could look after herself. When Sara had been at school, Mrs Linklater had known the times of all the classes, and woe betide poor Sara if she was five minutes late home from one of them! She daren't even drop into the ABC or Forte's for a cup of tea. When Sara had a dress rehearsal, or a performance at the theatre, Mrs Linklater sat in the dressing-room with her knitting, which was never anything exciting like Fair Isle, but something strictly utilitarian, like vests or dishcloths. As somebody said – it was just like the comic song: 'And mother came, too!' It was really amazing that Mrs Linklater stopped short at the dressing-room, or the wings, and didn't venture right out on to the stage, knitting and all! Someone else said sarcastically that Sara's name on the programme ought, by rights, to read: 'Sara Linklater – and mother.'

Well, we all have our crosses to bear, and even I, in my moment of triumph, still had that nagging ache, dulled now, it's true, but still there for all that – that ache that the name of Sebastian, or Northumberland, or even the mention of a symphony concert, brought to my heart. I felt that never, never would Sebastian forgive me for what I had done. He would always bear me a grudge because of that concert of his.

As I left the Underground on the Monday morning, the

morning of my sixteenth birthday, and walked past St Paul's School along Colet Gardens, I thought of Sebastian – Sebastian playing for me for *my* first concert; Sebastian sucking the wound when I'd been bitten by an adder, or thought I had; Sebastian riding with me through the fog to catch the London train, the night before my audition. And now Sebastian was coming up to London for *his* audition this very day. How I wished I could have said 'good luck' to him, as he'd said it to me that night so long ago on the platform of Newcastle Central Station! But it was no use wishing...

My thoughts were still far away in Northumberland when I walked across the Winter Garden and opened the dressing-room door. There was a sudden hush when I walked in, as if they'd all been talking about me.

'What's the matter?' I said absently. 'Has anything happened?'

'You've been sacked – turfed out,' said Monica, leaving the glass, and perching herself on the edge of the table.

The room swam before my eyes. Then I heard the voice of Denise exclaiming in rapid French; felt her arm round me.

'*Mon Dieu! Mon Dieu! Que faire? Ells se trouve mal!* She ees going to faint! Monique, *tu es véritablement imbécile! La pauvre petite – elle prend au serieux!*'

'Veronica – it's all right,' came the voice of Monica, serious now and frightened. 'You aren't sacked really – it was only a joke. *Please* don't faint. You're turned out of the Junior class. That's all I meant. You're in the Senior. Madame's orders! *Please, please* don't faint!'

'It's all right,' I said weakly. 'I don't know what made me do that. I'm OK now.'

'You know you are a foolish one,' said Denise, smoothing back my hair. 'Eef you are turned out – sacked as they say – we in ze dressing-room would not be the first to know eet. Of a surety not!'

'No, of course not,' I said with a wry smile. 'Only here, in this school, you never know. You're always wondering, fearing,

172

and in a way *expecting* to be turned out, and when you said – by the way, Monica, what exactly *did* you say?'

'I said you'd been sacked!' laughed Monica. 'And so you have – sacked from the Junior class. And you're in the *pas-de-deux* class, *and* the Advanced Mime, *and* the Theatre class.'

'Oh, no! I can't believe it,' I said with shining eyes.

'It's gospel,' put in June. 'I heard Miss Willan telling Gilbert about it, and Gilbert said: "I'm darned glad! That kid has worked well. She's got guts. She deserves to get on, and besides – there's *something about her*!" And when he said that, Willan nodded and said: "I agree there's something about her. I shouldn't be surprised if—" Then they saw me; I wasn't really listening either. I just happened to be going down the corridor while they were talking. But anyway, they shut up after that.'

'Well, I'll miss having you in the front row to follow,' said Delia. 'It saved me a lot of trouble, and besides, I *liked* watching you, Veronica. I don't know how it is, but you're such a nice person to watch.'

'Thank you,' I said gratefully. Really I had quite a lot of friends in the Junior class. I felt almost sorry to be leaving it; though, of course, it would be glorious to be with the Seniors.

'I must find out what time my new classes are,' I said, getting up from the bench where Denise had pushed me. 'Of course, they'll all be different.'

'Are you sure you're OK?' Monica asked anxiously. 'You still look pale.'

'I'm always pale,' I laughed. 'Didn't you hear Madame call me "that pale child"! But I feel quite all right now; in fact, I feel grand.' I executed an *entrechat-six* just to convince them.

'Well, you've a class at three today – Serge,' June said – June always knew everything. 'And then there's RAD with Gilbert after that, and then you've a class with Willan five-fifteen to six, I think. So you've just a quarter of an hour for tea.'

'Then there's my performance down at Sadler's Wells at

In the pas de deux *class*

seven-thirty, and that means the theatre at six-thirty. Oh, dear! I had hoped to get home for tea,' I sighed. 'You see, it's my birthday.'

A chorus of voices wished me many happy returns of the day.

'Are you really sixteen, Veronica?' said June. 'Gosh! I can't believe it. You look such a kid. Well, I'm afraid your birthday tea will have to go west – like lots of other things when you decide to throw in your lot with the ballet.'

'Yes, but it's not as easy as all that,' I explained. 'I've asked Sara Linklater to tea, and she's on television now.'

'Well, ring her up,' suggested Monica.

'Yes, but *where*?'

'At the television place, of course. Why not?'

'I suppose I could do that,' I said rather doubtfully. 'I hope they won't mind.'

'What if they do?' said June with a shrug. 'They can't eat you!'

'No – but what about Sara?'

'Oh, well – they'll think all the more of her for having friends to ring her up,' declared June irrepressibly. 'That's my experience, anyway. People always think more of you if you cause them a lot of bother. It's human nature!'

'Um,' I said, still doubtfully. 'I suppose I shall have to do it, anyway.'

After morning school I dashed out to a kiosk and rang up the television studios, and got into touch with Sara. Like most things that you dread, it proved to be frightfully easy.

'Hullo!' came Sara's cheerful voice at the other end of the wire. 'Many happy returns of the day, Veronica!'

'Thanks awfully!' I answered. 'Look here, Sara, it's about my birthday I rang you up. I'm most awfully sorry, but I can't get back to tea today, after all. You see' – then I couldn't resist it – 'I've been turned out!'

There was a horrified silence at the other end. Then Sara burst out:

'Veronica – you *haven't*?'

'Yes I have!' I laughed. 'I've been turned out of the Junior class. Now I'm in the Senior, and the *pas-de-deux* class and everything else. Oh, Sara, I'm so happy! You just don't know how I feel.'

'Oh, yes I do,' said Sara at the other end, 'because I'm feeling that way myself. I've just been taken on to the permanent staff here. I'll tell you about it when we *do* meet. Let's have a special celebration, shall we? A double celebration!'

'Yes, let's,' I said. 'Oh, but what about your mother, Sara?—'

'Oh, I forgot to tell you with all the excitement,' came Sara's voice at the other end of the wire. 'Aunt Elizabeth's been taken ill and Mummy's had to go to her. Poor Mummy! She didn't know what to do. There was Aunt Elizabeth up in Birmingham, and me here in London, but in the end Auntie won. You see, when people are ill, Mummy just adores looking after them; she simply couldn't resist it!'

'Then let's go to the pictures next Saturday,' I said. 'I've nothing on – have you?'

'Not a thing.'

'Then let's go to the Marble Arch Pavilion. Uncle John sent me a cheque for my birthday. We'll have supper at Lyons afterwards.'

'I've got lots of money,' said Sara. 'This is a joint celebration. I pay half.'

'All right – if you like,' I agreed. 'Saturday, then, seven o'clock outside the Marble Arch Pavilion. Goodbye, Sara!'

'Goodbye!' said Sara at the other end. 'And you don't know how thrilled I am by your news, Veronica. I always knew you were frightfully good.'

I hung up the receiver, and dashed back to school. That night at eleven o'clock I let myself into 242 Heather Hill with my latch-key, and as I crawled wearily up the many stairs to my room I remembered suddenly that it was my birthday!

Epilogue: Enchanted Princess

THE terms passed. I began to get more and more small parts in the ballets. I went on tour with the Opera Ballet, and then on tour with the Theatre Ballet, or Second Company. Finally, the day I'd lived for all my life arrived, and I was really a member of the Company.

Time went on. I didn't rise to fame overnight, for no ballerina does, especially in the Sadler's Wells Company, where such a high standard of artistry is demanded. For a long time I worked away apparently unnoticed in the *corps-de-ballet*. I say 'apparently', because I learned afterwards that Madame (not my dear Madame Viret, but the Director of the Company) had been watching me closely all the time. At last I got a solo part. My photograph began to appear in the picture papers ... 'This promising young dancer, Veronica Weston ... Veronica Weston's classical line in the *pas-de-trois* from *Les Sylphides* ... a new ballet, *The Ice Maiden*, written especially for Veronica Weston by Toni Rossini whose choreography is attracting favourable notice from the critics ... Veronica Weston's charm and lyricism...'

It was like Belinda all over again!

And Belinda? What of Belinda? She had shot ahead of me at first. She was the Serving-maid in *The Gods Go A-Begging*, while I was merely one of the Black Lackeys. She was Columbine in *Le Carnival*; I was Papillon. Finally, she was taken into the First Company at Covent Garden, and I took over her roles in the Second.

Then came the never-to-be-forgotten day when Madame singled me out and talked to me, and shortly afterwards I was taken into the First Company myself. Naturally, I watched

Belinda closely; she was my rival. She had been given roles, and she had danced them with charm and brilliance. But, as Madame Viret had prophesied long ago, something was stopping her further progress, and that something was her mind.

You see, as Madame Viret had said, you put something of yourself into every role you dance, and Belinda put her own coarse mind into her interpretations. Her 'line' and her classic beauty had drawn the attention of the undiscerning in the first place, but the critics knew that Belinda would never really 'arrive'. Photographs of her appeared less and less frequently in the papers; Press notices were confined to 'This role was danced brilliantly but rather hardly by Belinda Beaucaire ... A rather vulgar interpretation was given by Belinda Beaucaire.'

Yes, that was the trouble. When Belinda danced Columbine, the lady was not only a flirt, but a vulgar flirt. She overmimed Swanilda in the ballet *Coppelia*, and made her seem vulgar too. Her dancing in *The Miracle of the Gorbals* was wonderful in the first part of the ballet, but she entirely missed the Madonna-like simplicity of the reformed girl in the last scenes. When she danced the role of the Betrayed Girl in *The Rake's Progress*, she made her seem like a waitress in a teashop, as one critic said. She began to get less and less of these parts, and very soon I began to get them myself.

All this time I had never once seen Sebastian. I knew he had come to London shortly after the Christmas holiday when I had left Bracken Hall so suddenly, because Caroline had told me so in her letters. He had got his scholarship to the Royal College of Music; had won prizes; had gone abroad to study. The music critics had already begun to sit up and take notice of Sebastian Scott. Caroline enclosed some of the Press notices in her letters: 'Clever young North Country composer conducts own symphony ... *The Lindisfarne Symphony*, by rising young musician ... brilliant score ... greatly influenced by his native moors, and rocky coastline ... atmosphere of windswept headlands, and wild, tossing seas ...'

Another review, in the *Musical Echo*, said: 'There is something very reminiscent of Tchaikovsky's ballet music in this young composer's work. I am not inferring – indeed far from it – that Mr Scott's music is in any way an imitation of the great Russian composer's, but merely draw attention to its strong balletic character – in this particular concerto, at any rate.'

There were Press photographs too. Sebastian in evening dress, baton in hand, conducting his own symphony. He looked older, of course, but his eyes still had their whimsical expression, his mouth its same arrogant twist. Many times I had gone to the Albert Hall in the hope of catching sight of him. Sometimes I had seen a close-cropped black head and thought it was Sebastian, but there had always been masses of people in the way, and I had never been able to get close enough to make sure.

Then came the wonderful day when I had sent the wire to Caroline as I had promised:

Odette-Odile in new production *Lac des Cygnes*. Will book seats for you all as arranged.

I managed to get five seats in the grand tier. They were for Aunt June, Uncle John, Fiona, and Caroline. The extra one was for Ian Frazer who was now Fiona's fiancé. They were to be married in the summer. I wrote and asked Caroline about Uncle Adrian, and she told me that he was in London, so he could get a seat for himself if he really wanted to see me dance. As for Sebastian – I pushed the thought of Sebastian firmly away from me. It was no use asking myself if *he* wanted to see me dance.

The great day arrived. There was a congratulatory telegram from Jonathan and Stella, who were living in Cornwall, and yet one more letter from Caroline, asking me to join them at their hotel after the performance, so that we could all have dinner together after the show.

In the morning I went round to the studio in Baker Street.

179

Most mornings now I went there to practise, and I felt that today of all days I must have my dear Madame Viret's encouragement.

'I feel terribly nervous,' I admitted when I had finished my work. 'I'm trembling even now. What on earth shall I be like when the time draws near?'

Madame spread her exquisite hands and shrugged her expressive shoulders.

'*Oh, là! là!* You weel be nervous, yes. Assuredly; what *artiste* ees not. You weel tremble in ze wings. You weel be white as a *pierce-neige* – a leetle snowdrop. But on ze stage – pouff! Ze audience – he ees not! You dance for yourself alone, and for your Prince in zis so beau-ti-ful ballet. You are lost in ze music – ze enchantment. Nevaire – nevaire 'ave you dance so well! I know eet 'ere.' Characteristically Madame laid her small white hands on her heart. 'Go, *ma mie*! I shall be there to watch. *Au revoir!*'

She kissed me on both cheeks, and I left the studio feeling a great deal calmer than I had done when I'd run up the stairs, reassured by Madame's faith in me.

At exactly half past twelve I crossed the road to the theatre, passed under the colonnade, and went round to the stage door. As usual, there was a little crowd of people waiting to see the principal dancers go in – those who were going to dance the leading roles – The Swan Queen, Prince Siegfried and the rest. With a shock I realized that today Odette, the Swan Queen, was going to be *me*. They were waiting for me!

'Well,' I thought, 'thank goodness they don't know me yet, even if they have seen me on the stage.'

But I rejoiced too soon! A small girl of about twelve, obviously from a dancing school, since she was whiling away the time by executing *entrechats* on the pavement, gave an excited shriek:

'*Mummy!* Look who it is! It's Miss Weston. You remember – Veronica Weston? We saw her in *The Ice Maiden* at

Sadler's Wells. And she was one of the Little Swans in *Swan Lake*, and we saw her in—'

At once the crowd surged respectfully towards me.

'Miss Weston – *would* you? ... Miss Weston, if you wouldn't mind ... Would it be an awful bother if? ... We simply *adored* your performance in *The Ice Maiden* ...' Autograph books popped out; much-read copies of popular books on ballet appeared from nowhere. Someone produced a linen teacloth with the autographs of famous ballet dancers embroidered all over it. Would I please sign here – no, just *here*. Yes, under Robert Helpmann.

'Gosh! Aren't you *tiny*!' exclaimed a large schoolgirl, with an envious sigh. 'And you're four years older than I am – yes. I read all about you in the *Dancing News*. You were eighteen last May.' She sighed again. 'No wonder you look like a fairy when you dance! What are you dancing this afternoon, Miss Weston?'

'I'm Odette-Odile in *Swan Lake*,' I answered.

There was a positive hush of awe.

'Odette? Golly! How wonderful! What a perfectly marvellous role to dance! What does it feel like to be dancing the Odette-Odile role on Covent Garden stage, Miss Weston? Breathtaking, I expect?'

'I – don't know,' I faltered. 'You see, this afternoon is the very first time I've danced it, as a matter of fact.'

'Oh, *Mummy*!' said the small schoolchild, hopping up and down on one leg in an ecstasy of longing. 'Oh, Mummy, I *wish* we hadn't gone last night. Oh, I know it was Moira Shearer, and of course she's lovely, but I'd rather see Miss Weston – really, I would. You see, I feel we sort of know her now, Mummy—'

'It's no use, Jacinthe,' her mother said firmly. 'You know we weren't able to get seats for this afternoon, and in any case we couldn't possibly afford to go to the ballet twice running. Now don't be naughty, Jacinthe!'

'Look,' I put in quickly, seeing the child's downcast face,

181

'I'll send you a signed photograph of me in my Odette dress. I had one taken at rehearsal yesterday. How will that do, Jacinthe?'

The tears that were gathering in the child's eyes turned to smiles, and several people behind me murmured approving things.

'Why, she's just like a schoolgirl herself, so pale and young-looking, and not a *bit* stuck up!'

'Thank you!' I laughed. 'And now, if you'll excuse me, I really must go. It takes such ages to get ready.'

The crowd parted respectfully for me, and I slipped in through the stage door.

'Best of luck, miss!' George, the doorkeeper, yelled after me as I sped up the stairs to my dressing-room. 'You'll do well, I'm sure.'

'Thank you, George!' I yelled back.

When I opened the dressing-room door I saw at once that there was something unusual lying on my make-up table. It was a bunch of red roses, and on the card fastened to the stems of the flowers was the one word: 'Sebastian.'

Just that! No word of apology or good luck. I gave a wry smile. How like Sebastian! He hadn't a big, generous nature like Jonathan. He was brilliant, and witty, and arrogant. Above all, he was proud. No, he would certainly never utter one word of apology to me or to anyone else – I was quite sure of that. Still, he *had* sent me red roses, and my heart glowed. We were friends again, and he had meant me to know it.

But there was no time now for dreaming. Quickly, because I was already ten minutes late, I pulled on an old pair of practice tights, together with a pair of blocked shoes, and dashed down to the stage – Covent Garden stage, a ghostly place in the half-light; a place shadowy with the memories of all the great ones who had danced there. I could almost see their faces looking at me out of the wings, hear the rustle of their dresses, the tap of their shoes ...

After I had warmed up I dashed back to my dressing-room, and began to dress. Swiftly I shed my workaday clothes, and with them my ordinary, workaday personality. I became an enchanted princess, a princess with no voice with which to plead her love, but only her large, dark, speaking eyes, her graceful arms, her dancing feet. The mirrored dressing-room threw back my image a dozen times as, with the help of my dresser, I bent this way and that, pulling up tights, fine as gossamer, settling my snowy *tutu*, putting last touches to my make-up. Behind Sebastian's roses my mirrored face looked back at me – eyes long-lashed and slanting; sleek, black hair framed in white swan feathers; slender shoulders rising from heart-shaped, satin bodice.

Now it was time for me to go down to the stage. With a last look round the quiet dressing-room, I shut the door behind me, never dreaming that I was leaving it for the last time as an unknown ballerina. Yes, that dressing-room was destined to look very different when I saw it again!

As I waited quietly in the wings, trembling slightly with nervousness, I knew that somewhere out there in the darkened auditorium Sebastian was waiting – waiting for me to appear. Long afterwards I learned that he'd seen me many times in my other roles; that night after night he'd sat in the gallery down at Sadler's Wells and watched me dance the Sugar Plum Fairy, the Odette solo, the solo from *Les Sylphides* – all the dances he'd seen me do in those far-off days in Northumberland. But I didn't know this now. All I knew now was that Sebastian had sent me red roses, that Sebastian had forgiven me.

And then came the haunting melody of Tchaikovsky's music. With a *pas de chat* I leaped gracefully into my position on the stage, ready for the famous mime scene with my partner, Prince Siegfried.

I have only a vague idea of what happened next. The lovely story unfolded itself, as with beautiful mimic gestures I told my Prince of my enchantment, besought him with my eyes to

The lovely story unfolded itself

rescue me. He swore to protect me, to shield me from evil. But alas! my Prince was deceived and became betrothed by mistake to the Magician's wicked daughter, Odile. I danced the difficult role of Odile as I had always known I should – flashing, brilliant, and cruel, keeping Prince Siegfried enthralled, never allowing his eyes to stray towards the window where his real, enchanted Princess stood, silhouetted, wringing her hands in despair. I heard the gasp of admiration from the watchers in the wings when I turned the thirty-two *fouettés*, making them look as easy as if I were running across the room.

As for the audience – I had completely forgotten it was there, until the thunderous applause broke forth and the curtain fell at the end of the last act, only to rise again while I curtsied this way and that, together with the rest of the Company. Then the other dancers disappeared, and Prince Siegfried and I were left to take a curtain alone.

But even this would not satisfy the audience. Curtain after curtain I took, whilst flowers were handed out of the wings and piled at my feet. The stage manager came to my side and made his bow, and then, miracle of miracles, suddenly Madame herself was there, holding my hand. In full view of the audience she kissed me on both cheeks.

The audience rose to its feet, and if it hadn't been an audience composed of ballet enthusiasts I'm sure it would have cheered! Then the noise ceased as if by magic. Madame was going to speak. Quietly, in her beautifully modulated voice, Madame introduced me as the youngest and newest *prima ballerina*, a worthy follower of Margot Fonteyn, Shearer, and the rest of that glittering company of Wells *artistes*.

'Here is Veronica,' said Madame, drawing me forward. 'Your own *ballerina*, whom you, yourselves, have acclaimed for her brilliant dancing this afternoon – Veronica, unheralded by the Press, totally unadvertised, until this afternoon, almost unknown. But I, and others connected with the Sadler's Wells Company, have watched Veronica's progress, and we all know how much she deserves her success.'

The thunderous applause broke out again. The audience would have me speak!

I stood hesitating, but before I could open my mouth, Prince Siegfried, who was my old friend Toni Rossini, was at my side. Quietly he addressed the waiting people.

'Dancers do not speak,' he told them, 'any more than flowers do. Veronica is very tired; she asks me to ask you if she may please go home.'

The curtain fell for the last time. People surged out of the wings to be the first to congratulate me. Never, it seemed, had there been such an enthusiastic audience at a matinée.

'Ah, Veronique – *mon petit chou,*' said a warm voice in my ear. 'Veronique, my leetle one – she 'as arrive'! I knew eet! Nevaire 'ave I seen such dancing!' It was dear Madame Viret – she who had helped me from the very beginning of my dancing career. Disheartened, tired, often sick at heart, I had gone to Madame's studio in Baker Street, and always I had left her refreshed and strengthened. Yes, I owed much of my success to dear Madame Viret.

'It was all due to you, Madame,' I said, tears in my eyes. 'I couldn't have done it without you; indeed I couldn't.'

Madame snapped her fingers.

'*Ah, ça!* Zat waz nozing zat I did – just one leetle finger in ze pie, as you say! I see you soon, my Veronique, yes?'

'Tomorrow, Madame,' I answered with raised voice, for already masses of people were crowding in upon me, and Madame's tiny figure was fast disappearing in the press.

'Felicitations, Veronique!' said Toni, pressing my hand. 'Today you were indeed beautiful. You have made my dream of you come true.'

'It's awfully nice of you to say so,' I answered. 'And thank you, Toni, for partnering me so wonderfully. I don't believe you ever thought of yourself at all!'

'Indeed, no, Veronique – no one could think of anyone else when you were there,' said Toni gallantly.

As I had foreseen long ago, Toni would never be remembered for his dancing. Yet the strange thing was that when he danced as my partner, people said that he was like another person – that his dancing reached heights that no one believed him capable of attaining.

When at last I escaped to my dressing-room, I found that it was full of people, too. They weren't stage people this time, but people from the outside world – girls who claimed to have known me before Daddy died, neighbours whom I didn't even remember. Suddenly I seemed to have an enormous number of friends!

They had brought up my flowers from the stage, and my once-bare dressing-room looked a cross between an expensive florist's and a conservatory. Sebastian's roses had been removed from my make-up table, and their place was now taken by a gilded basket of queer, bilious-looking green flowers with black markings that made them look as if they were in the last stages of decay.

'Orchids!' someone murmured with a grimace, adding with a glance at the card: 'From Oscar Deveraux – Irma Foster's husband. You know – the famous critic, my dear. Trust him to be there at the début of a new star! You've really arrived, Miss Weston, when Oscar Deveraux sends you flowers. He never makes a mistake.'

'No, he waits until everyone else is perfectly sure and have committed themselves; then dear Oscar jumps the queue!' said someone else nastily. 'You're right – no mistakes for Oscar!'

Quietly I removed the orchids and replaced Sebastian's roses on my table. If only – if only Sebastian were there himself. What would I give if all these strange people would only go away, and I could have my old friend, Sebastian, in their place.

'Please—' I begged. 'I'm most awfully tired. Would you mind if I changed now.'

After a long time the room emptied, the women taking a last

envious glance at my *tutu*, the men murmuring polite fare-wells. I was alone at last. All that remained of my triumph was the heavy scent of the flowers banked round the room and the haunting perfume left behind by my women admirers. Yes, and the thought of all the tomorrows – the glorious, unclouded tomorrows, when I would dance *Giselle, The Sleeping Beauty*, and all the other classic roles a dancer must make her own before she earns the title of *Prima Ballerina*.

Only one small cloud remained – Sebastian. I wanted to hear him say he'd forgiven me.

When my dresser had gone away, carrying my Swan Queen dress carefully on her arm, I removed the last of my make-up, and slipped into my outdoor things. In a very few minutes I stood ready to go. The mirrors reflected me as they had done when I had stood before them in all my stage finery. Now, my real self looked back at me – small, pale, childlike, only my narrow feet with their highly arched insteps showing that I was not the schoolgirl I seemed. The traces of make-up that had eluded me made my eyes seem even larger and darker than usual. They looked sad, I thought. I smiled suddenly, and dropped a curtsy to my reflection in the glass. Stupid to be sad just because a stiff-necked boy like Sebastian refused to be one of my crowd of admirers!

When I reached the stage door, I could see that there were a lot of people outside it, but not until the doorkeeper smiled down at me did it occur to me what they were waiting for.

'Hearty congrats, miss!' said George warmly. 'You deserve it, I'm sure. Big crowd outside, miss. Sure you'll be all right?'

My eyes widened.

'You mean?—'

'Waitin' for you, miss,' grinned George. ''Undreds of 'em! Autograph books galore! Take you hours to sign all that lot! Take my advice, miss, and slip out through the theatre. I'll get you a taxi in a trice, miss.'

I hesitated. Outside the stage door I could hear the news-boys shouting the evening papers:

'Late special! Late special! Scenes at Covent Garding! Unknown bally dancer leaps to fame! Late special!'

'Well – do you think I ought, George? Taxis are terribly expensive. You see – I've got a good way to go—'

George grinned again.

'Judging by the row in that there theatre this afternoon, miss, there ain't no more call for you to go counting your pennies! What address shall I say, miss?'

I gave him Mrs Crapper's address, for I intended to go home and change before dinner, and I could see him raising his eyebrows at it mentally.

'Righty-ho, miss! Hey – wait a minute, though! Know a young gent of the name of Scott, miss?'

My heart leaped, and a thrill of joy ran through me.

'Sebastian!' I cried. 'I should just think I do! Oh, yes – I know Sebastian Scott all right!'

'Well, he's waitin' art there in that crowd,' said George, nodding over his shoulder towards the stage door. 'Been inquiring for you, he has. I'll send him round to the main door, if you like, miss. Mebbe he's got a car of his own waitin'. He looked that sort of a young gent!'

In the dim vestibule I met Sebastian again for the first time since we'd quarrelled, all that long time ago. He was just the same – only a little graver and older.

'Veronica!' he said, and came forward with outstretched hands. 'Veronica, you were wonderful!'

Then he tipped up my face towards him.

'I once told you you were the nicest girl I'd ever met,' he went on softly. 'Well, I've met lots of girls since then, but I still think you're the nicest. I was going to kiss you goodbye that other time – remember? Well, I'm going to do it now, only it's not goodbye, Veronica!'

Sharon Creech
Walk Two Moons £2.99

'Just over a year ago, my father plucked me up like a weed and took me and all our belongings (no, that is not true – he did not bring the chestnut tree nor the willow nor the maple nor the hayloft nor the swimming hole nor any of those things which belong to me) and we drove three-hundred miles straight north and stopped in front of a house in Euclid, Ohio.'

There, Salamanca Hiddle begins to unravel the mystery that surrounds her world – a world from which her mother has suddenly, and without warning, disappeared. No one can tell Sal the full story – not her new friend Phoebe, the girl with the powerful imagination, nor Margaret, the lady with the wild red hair, nor her own sorrowful father. Only her crazy grandparents, with a bitter sweet story of their own to tell, finally lead Sal to the truth.

Sal's madcap journey is one full of humour as well as sorrow, captivating the imagination as its mystery unfolds . . .

Celia Rees
Every Step You Take £3.50

'The headlines told him they had found her. He had better be careful now – not do anything to attract attention. He was not safe here. He would only be safe in the place that was home.'

But home has changed – it's full of strangers on an Outdoor Pursuit weekend.

Chris O'Neill isn't even sure why she came to this miles-from-anywhere place. Still it's only for a couple of days – not enough time for anything to happen . . .

A sinister nightmare where danger lurks just one step behind . . .

'An exciting blend of emotion and drama – not for the fainthearted!'
THE SCHOOL LIBRARIAN

Patricia Windsor
The Dream Killer £3.99

'You're dead, Nancy.' Rose winced at the harsh truth in the words.

Nancy made a face. 'I *know* that,' she said, dismissing it. 'But could you come with me a minute?'

Rose wanted to scream, but found herself floating toward the door on the tidal wave that was Nancy's dress. Nancy's clutching hand was cold and dry. Rose could feel the bones inside.

Nancy Emerson disappeared the Wednesday before Thanksgiving. From that day on, Rose Potter's life was not the same. She had dreams. In the first dream Nancy appeared and brought Rose to a pine-filled forest. Two days later, Nancy's body was found.

Rose tries to put the murder out of her mind, but the dead never sleep. And when Rose closes her eyes at night, Nancy's there waiting . . .